Praise for *Roadie*

My real life experiences over the past 23 years pale in comparison to the tales contained in *Roadie*. Howard Massey lets us become the fly on the road case and observe the insanity of touring and the music business in general, with a hilarious and wry point of view. Definitely an all-access pass!
—CJ Vanston, Spinal Tap musical director

Truth may be stranger than fiction, but fiction allows us to glimpse deeper truths that reality often obscures. That's the case with Howard Massey's riveting debut novel, *Roadie*. Massey is intimately familiar with the inner world of rock & roll—not just behind the music, but beneath the glamour and beyond the carefully sculpted images. Much of it is not pretty, but it's endlessly fascinating and, quite literally, filled with mystery in this tale of rises, falls, survival, and against all odds, friendship.
—Anthony DeCurtis, Contributing Editor, *Rolling Stone*

Howard Massey has got the music business cold, and *Roadie* is as searing—and informed—an indictment of major label greed as I've ever read. With sympathetic characters, a plot that kept me engrossed to the final line, and a heartfelt love for rock and roll, *Roadie* delivers the goods."
—Lewis Shiner, author of *NY Times* best seller *Glimpses*

"Brought back the good, bad, and ugly of my life on the road."
—Butch Dener, former tour manager with The Band

ROADIE

A Novel

by Howard Massey

coral press

A Coral Press original novel

Copyright © Howard Massey 2016

All rights reserved under International and Pan-American copyright conventions.
Published in the United States by Coral Press.
All characters are fictional and bear no relation to anyone living.

ISBN-13: 978-1-935512-35-6
Library of Congress Control Number: 2015955984
Printed in the U.S.A.
1 3 5 7 9 10 8 6 4 2
First Edition

Cover Design: Beth Bugler
Front and back cover cases courtesy of the Calzone Case Company
Cover photography: Robert Dunn
Author photo: Mr. Bonzai/David Goggin

More about Coral Press books at:
www.coralpress.com

The music business is a cruel and shallow money trench, a long plastic hallway where thieves and pimps run free, and good men die like dogs. There's also a negative side.
—*Quote most often attributed to Gonzo journalist Hunter S. Thompson*

1

How odd. I appear to be dying.

No, seriously, I think this is the real deal. I can't seem to stay awake, my gut is cramping something awful, and I've just noticed that my fingernails are starting to turn a nasty shade of blue. Junkie blue. Okay, deep breath, deep breath.

Shit, wheezing. Means fluid is building. Maybe I should just go back to sleep. Any minute now, I expect I'll be passing out one last time. Then I'll drown in this damn bathtub, dead, gone, and forgotten.

I just wish I could bring myself to care.

What the hell is wrong with me? Where's that goddamn survival instinct you hear so much about?

I wonder if this is what it was like for Jim Morrison. I wonder if he gave a shit at the end. Maybe somewhere he's getting ready to welcome another wayward soul to the party. "Look at the poor bastard," I can hear him ranting, half-empty bottle of Chianti in his hand. "What a loser! Ended up in a bathtub in some shithole, just like me."

A bathtub in a Paris shithole, just like Jim. No, Paris was yesterday. Let's see, where am I now? Come on, focus. Week six, isn't it? After Paris, after Paris … oh yeah, Amsterdam. Amsterdam. Is that where I am? Hah, cool little rhyme—I'm gonna have to remember that. Might even be able to write a song around it.

Yeah, right; some chance of that happening. Hell, I'll probably be lying on a slab in some Dutch morgue by daybreak. Not that I've been able to write any music worth a damn in more than twenty years, not since those fucking lawyers ruined my life with that fucking piece of paper. A piece of paper that not only took my pride and my money, but every last shred of what used to be me. My pact with the devil, that's what it was, the moment I gave up my dream and became a roadie instead.

Cody the Roadie, that's me.

Need that mic stand put back up after you knocked it down in a drunken rage? Cody's your man. Need a towel to clean up the puke your meth-head drummer's been spewing between songs? No problem-o.

There's no broken guitar amp I can't fix in seconds, no hysterical chick I can't wrestle off the stage before she gets the singer in a bear hug, no hotel night manager about to call the cops I can't bribe with free tickets or merch, or, as a last resort, cold hard cash from the float. Procurer of groupies, procurer of dope, procurer of all things rock'n'roll. Cody the Roadie: have black T-shirt and shorts, will travel.

I'm seeing and hearing things now. Is that condensation on the piss-yellow wall, or a ten-foot iguana sticking its evil tongue out at me, taunting me through the tendrils of steam rising in the air? Is that the drip, drip of the leaky faucet, or a Charlie Watts backbeat rousing the crowd to their feet for the final encore? "*Oh, this could be the last time, this could be the last time,* maayy bee *the last time, I don't know.*" Before they became old men, Mick and Keef used to be able to harmonize pretty good, and that fake Southern accent always did crack me up. English guys crack me up in general.

Limey Bob, now that was a roadie's roadie. Whenever he said his name, it came out sounding like "Bub." He sometimes pretended to be one of them aristocrats, but he was really just a jerkoff like the rest of us. Back on my very first tour, he was the one who broke my cherry, who hassled me mercilessly, who taught me the Roadie's Rules:

1. If it's wet, drink it.
2. If it's dry, smoke it.
3. If it smells good, eat it.
4. If it smells bad, leave it for the musicians.
5. If it moves, fuck it.
6. If it doesn't move, load it on the truck.

Ain't a roadie in the world who can't recite those lines backwards and forwards. It's like a secret handshake—you can go into any bar anywhere in the world, walk up to any guy wearing a black T-shirt and shorts and say, "If it's wet…." If he doesn't reply, "Drink it," you know he's just a civilian posing. But if he gives you the right answer, you know he's a brother. A brother of the road.

And we brothers, we tend to die awful young. Limey Bob, he drank himself to death trying to set a new record for doing shooters one night—literally puked his guts out on the barroom floor. Poor bastard was stone cold dead for over an hour before it finally dawned on any of his equally drunk brothers to check on him slumped in the corner, insides oozing down his shirt. Now he's legend in the roadie world. Kind of a joke, too, truth be told.

I guess that's gonna be me after tonight. "Hey, man, did you hear about Cody the Roadie? Drowned in a fucking bathtub, just like Morrison." They'll raise a glass and drink a toast to my misfortune before moving on to the next bit of tour gossip, about the lead singer who nearly had his dick cut off by some psycho groupie, or the drummer who shat in the bidet, or the bassist caught in bed with the keyboard player. Every tour has its share of drama. I guess it's to be expected when you get so many dysfunctional people together in one small space … especially if some of them have egos the size of a stadium and others the brains of a gnat. Add in the assorted motley crew of hangers-on—the dope dealers, the groupies, the crazed fans—and it's no wonder that every tour spawns its share of mayhem, homicide, suicide, and tall tales … most of them true.

Something weird is happening to my face now. Or is it that I'm actually smiling? I guess that's a good sign. Maybe I *do* care after all. Maybe I should try to do something to get myself out of this goddamned tub.

No, that's not gonna happen. Shit. You spend your whole life effortlessly moving your limbs, and then the one time you need them to work, the bastards let you down. Maybe I just need to close my eyes and rest a bit....

> *Five little roadies looking for a score, one smoked some rotten hash, now there's only four. Four little roadies going on a spree, one bought a suit and tie, now there's only three. Three little roadies smelling like a zoo, one copped some hotel soap, now there's only two. Two little roadies having them some fun, one met a city cop, now there's only one. One little roadie, stoned as he can be, showed the rest his secret stash, now there's 43.*

Where am I now? This can't be heaven, it smells too bad. No, that's just my puke. Can't be hell, either: no fucking lawyers here.

Oh, right, still in that goddamned bathtub in that goddamned piss-yellow hotel bathroom in goddamned Amsterdam.

Still dying, too.

I wonder who will come to my funeral. That's one of my favorite mind games, actually. I change the list every day, depending on who I think gives a shit about me and who I think I've pissed off in the past twenty-four hours. Usually, though, the list is pretty short. Hey, I got an idea: laminates. I'll have the first funeral to issue laminates. Get a rent-a-goon to man the door and check everyone's name off on the list, then issue passes: Memorial Service Only. Cemetery VIP. All Access.

Yeah, that's good; I'll have to try to remember that. Funeral laminates.

Okay, let's see. There's Katie, of course. Katie is pretty much the only name that's always on my list. I never could get her to love me, but I always knew I could count on her. She knows the way I want to go out; we've even talked about it. No doubt she'll be the one to deal with the assholes in the black suits at the funeral home. "Oh, no, I don't think he'd want anything fancy," she'll say. "Just lay him out and dress him in his work clothes: black T-shirt, black shorts. And no expensive casket, either. A plain, simple box will do … as long as it's fireproof." Shit, a guy's entitled to a last wish, ain't he? Like Limey Bob always told me, a man should be able to put some "fun" in his own funeral. What's so wrong about wanting to include a little pyro in your final send-off, anyway?

Donnie will be there too, of course. I mean, he *woulda* been there. Damn, I never thought I'd outlive the Mick bastard. Hey, Donnie, heading up there to raise a brewski soon with you, bro.

Who else? Shithead Schiffman, he'll want to make an appearance, I'm guessing. Strictly for show, of course, but he's the last person I want there. Definitely leave his name off the list, get the goon at the door to block his ass from coming in.

Cocksucker.

And then there's Hinch.

Fucking Hinch. I never can decide if he'd have the balls to show up at my funeral. Sometimes I think he couldn't possibly pass up the opportunity, then I resign myself to the likelihood that he won't give a shit. My closest goddamn friend in the whole wide world and he won't give a shit.

Bastard!

Am I actually screaming now? I can't tell if that's my voice reverberating off the tile walls or if it's another hallucination. The air is sorta shimmery now, swirling in currents and eddies, enveloping me, welcoming me. Can't tell if I'm breathing it or drinking it. Shit, maybe I'm *smoking* it.

Too funny.

I just realized something. I'm higher now than I've ever been, and I've been pretty high in my time. Hey, maybe that's what dying is … maybe you just get higher and higher, until you run out of high. Maybe the infinite void is just an infinite high. Maybe the reason corpses lie there so still is that they're doing all their tripping inside; maybe they need all the energy they can muster just to keep that trip going, with nothing left over for things like moving and thinking and breathing.

Leave it to me to figure out the eternal truth just as I'm about to kick off. I've always had a lousy sense of timing. Maybe that's all it ever was; maybe it wasn't lousy luck after all. Like that stupid joke where you get someone to ask you what the secret of good comedy is and then you interrupt them by shouting out, "Timing!" Maybe timing really *is* what it's all about. Not the hokey-pokey, but timing.

Was that a giggle or a gurgle? I have no idea what this decrepit body of mine is doing any more. Can't tell if I'm farting or heaving, can't tell if I'm moving or if rigor mortis is setting in, can't tell if I'm making no sense or thinking more clearly than I ever did in my whole short, sad life.

Okay, feeling sorry for myself now. Good sign? Probably not. Actually, I think I've *always* felt sorry for myself. What was it that shrink called me? Oh yeah: the eternal victim. Fucking shrink. Why did I ever stop seeing her? Long time ago, can't remember. Can't really remember much of anything now....

What? Where? Shit, must have dozed off again.

Oh yeah, the funeral list. Amy. I guess Amy will be there. Little sister, she'd feel that sense of responsibility even if we barely know one another. But in her little straightjacket of a world, she'd be *expected* to attend. She and that asshole insurance salesman husband of hers. They'd probably leave the kids home, though. No need to see Uncle Cody in that box, and especially no need to expose them to Uncle Cody's rowdy friends.

Friends? Don't make me laugh. Not enough of them to fill a pill bottle most days. Drinking buddies, sure, I've got lots of those. But real friends? Count 'em on the fingers of one hand. Hell, count 'em on the fingers of one *finger*.

Hinch, you motherfucker!! You should have been my *friend*, not my boss. But instead you took and took and took. You took Katie's love and you took Donnie's life and now you're about to take what little is left of me. I only had half a century on this planet, you bastard, and I wasted so much of that time by giving it to you instead of keeping it for myself.

So I guess if this is the time of reckoning, if this is the time of ultimate truth, then the truth is that every time I saw you up on that stage

I wished it was me up there instead. Every time I saw you working that stadium crowd, every time I saw you balling a groupie, every time I saw that smarmy smile as you tooted a line or gave an autograph or granted an interview or signed a contract or cashed a check for an obscene amount of money I knew it should have been me instead and I knew that I could have done it so much better than you and I knew that I could have been so much of a better person than you.

But I never could stand up for myself, could I? So you took advantage of my weakness and you allowed me to turn into a self-loathing piece of shit barely human thing, dedicated to nothing more than hauling a piece of gear up on a stage or repairing a broken amplifier or driving five hundred miles in the middle of the night headed to yet another Holiday Inn on the road to nowhere. That's *your* legacy, Hinch. I hope you get to join me in hell someday.

God, I am so fucking tired. Tired of the road, tired of being used, tired of losing everything and everyone I love, tired of hating myself.

Most of all, I'm tired of trying to stay awake in this fucking bathtub.

Yeah, life's a bitch and then you die, but it's more of a bitch when you waste that whole life serving the needs of some selfish bastard who doesn't give half a shit about who you are or what you could have been. So next time you see a roadie crawling around on a stage somewhere in Sheboygan with a mag-light in one hand and a spare fuse in the other, show some respect. For we creatures of the road are the keepers of the truth, the one immutable, eternal truth, passed down from one generation to the next: The show is just that little distraction between load-in and load-out.

2

Transcript: Interview with Donnie Boyle, February 28, 1998

Yeah, Hinch was a real asshole back in those days. Still is, as a matter of fact. But Cody could be an asshole too, to tell you the truth. I guess you could say that about all of us.

Okay, ready? Let me know if I start rambling. This damn tube keeps getting in my way, sorry. Problem is if I take it out too long I start wheezing. Guess that's the price you pay for too much sex, drugs and rock 'n' roll. Or, at my age, at least too many of these damn cigarettes. I don't care what the fucking doctor says—I ain't quitting. Fuck 'em if they can't take a joke.

So, yeah, Hinch. Thomas A. Hinchton. Did you know that Aloysius was his middle name? No, not many people do. Not much of a middle name for a rock star, is it? I guess I first met Tommy when we were ten or so, back in '62, I think it was. We were classmates at Wrightsville Elementary, in York, Pa. That's where I'm from originally. Hinch, I'm not so sure. Somehow I have a feeling he was born out west and his family moved to York when he was just a baby. He never seemed like one of us, anyway.

What do I mean by that? I mean he was, I don't know ... different. Real tall, for starters. Even as a kid, he carried himself like he could see things a bit further than we could. And he always seemed to take things a little bit more seriously than the rest of us. Like we'd be playing dodgeball or something out in the schoolyard, and us kids would just be having a good time whomping the others with the ball, but somehow it seemed like it was, I don't know, *important* to him. He always had to win, too. Fact is, he *did* win, most of the time. And if somehow he didn't, he'd be making excuses about how the other kids cheated or something, then he'd play twice as hard the next time.

You'd have thought that kind of attitude would have made him unpopular, but in fact the opposite happened: it made the other kids gravitate to him, like they wanted his attention, wanted his approval. Maybe it's just that everyone loves a winner. In some ways, he was like the dog that always keeps his tail straight up—you know, the alpha dog—and the rest of us in the pack naturally looked up to him.

There was no special reason why, but Hinch and I just kind of hit it off at a young age and we started hanging out together, along with a couple of other kids. We weren't exactly a gang; we were more like what they call a posse today. I got the impression I was definitely his favorite, too—in fact, he used to call me his right-hand man. What that meant was, if a bunch of us wanted to do something, like go hang out at the candy store, I'd be the one to pass the idea on to Hinch. If he agreed, it was officially cool to go, and we went. But if he said, "Nah, I don't think so," well, most of the time, most of us wouldn't go even if we really wanted to. Stupid, isn't it, how kids will do almost anything to impress their peers.

So, yeah, Hinch very much called the shots even in those days. Not by being a bully, but just by the way he carried himself. Now, that said, I don't remember him ever going out of his way to impress any of the teachers. It seemed like all he cared about was being the most popular among the other kids; what adults thought of him didn't seem to matter at all.

A lot changed, though, when we graduated and moved on to junior high. That's because we'd been top of the heap at Wrightsville—the sixth graders were the oldest, of course, and so the younger kids all looked up to us, or feared us, or something. But now all of a sudden we were the new kids on the block, the littlest ones. And some of those seniors really were bullies, so it wasn't an easy adjustment. Mind you, Hinch wasn't about to take them on any more than the rest of us were; he just stayed within our small group, where he was king of the hill. I guess it was inevitable that he would eventually get called out, and one afternoon that's exactly what happened. But maybe I should back up a bit first and tell you how Hinch hooked up with the third member of our little band of musketeers.

You see, most of the kids in our junior high school class were the same familiar faces from elementary school, but for some reason they'd merged school districts or something and so now there were also a handful of kids who'd come from another nearby elementary. We pretty much stayed away from them, the way kids shy away from strangers. In fact, we poked fun at most of them, same as most of them did us, I suppose. One of them, I remember, had the biggest nose I'd ever seen in my life, and terrible acne, too, and there was another little girl who kept throwing up all over herself, grossing us out and making the classroom smell like puke till one day she got transferred out.

So, yeah, we pretty much steered clear of those kids, but there was one stocky little guy with curly red hair who seemed pretty normal, and for some reason I remember him trying to be friendly to me, though of course I couldn't be friendly back because he was officially one of the outsiders. But I'd see him across the lunchroom and he'd sometimes wave. If I thought nobody was looking, I might wave back, but that was about it. We never actually talked.

One day, though, the teacher was late coming into class and so we were all sitting there shouting and throwing things, carrying on like you do when the teacher's not there to tell you to shut up, when all of a sudden this red-headed kid starts pounding on his desk with his hands like he's playing drums or something. We all turned to look, and I could see that some of the kids in our group were about to start teasing him for being a show-off. But before any of us could get a word out, Hinch stood up and strode over to the kid, and there was this kind of magical silence that fell over all of us. What was Hinch going to do?

"Hey, that's 'Wipe Out,' " Hinch said. He made it sound like a challenge.

"Yeah, that's exactly what it is," the kid replied. I remember being pretty impressed with the calmness of his response. After all, this was Hinch he was talking to.

"Wipe Out" was one of the hottest records on the radio in those days. You remember it? No, it was probably before your time. But surfing music was all the rage, and the Surfaris, who played the song, were one of the top groups. They'd even been on *American Bandstand*—you know, Dick Clark's dumb-ass TV show—so they were really kind of a big deal. Although none of us had come within three thousand miles of a surfboard, we all thought it was a groovy record because it had this goofy voice and this amazing drum solo that kept getting repeated over and over again. And here was this kid actually playing it right in front of our eyes! We all held our breath as we waited for Hinch to speak.

Hinch paused for a long moment, staring the new kid down as he pondered his verdict.

"You know, that's pretty cool," he finally said.

There was this huge sigh of relief in the classroom, like in that old coffee commercial where the South American guy in the white suit approves of the beans. The new kid, now officially worthy, stuck his hand out. "My name's Cody Jeffries."

"Hinch."

"I know."

"And that's my right-hand man, Donnie Boyle." Hinch gestured toward me.

"I know."

And with that one simple exchange, Cody Jeffries became part of our in-crowd, rescued from the depths of a hell populated by a huge-honkered walking acne commercial and the Queen of Regurgitation. As the year went on and the other kids in our class pursued other interests and made new friends, our circle tightened until it was pretty much just the three of us: Hinch, Cody and me. Our bond was strengthened by Hinch's newfound interest in music, sparked, no doubt, by a competitive desire to one-up Cody. Hinch began by asking Cody to teach him the drum part to "Wipe Out," but it soon became obvious that he didn't have Cody's rhythmic instincts or skills, and he quickly tired of my observation that Cody simply played it better.

But Hinch wasn't prepared to give up that easily. Instead, he adopted a new strategy and showed up at my house one day with a brand-new Silvertone electric guitar and a tiny amplifier, which he proudly told me he had talked his parents into buying. Almost overnight he became obsessed with that guitar, and for the next few months, he carried it with him everywhere. "I'm going to be better than Dick Dale on this thing, you wait and see," he insisted. "I'll get Cody to be my drummer and we'll form a band and make hit records and be famous and everything."

"What about me?" I protested.

"No problem, Donnie boy. I'll teach you to play bass."

Now this was a pretty strong statement, especially considering that Hinch didn't even know how to play guitar himself at that point, much less bass. But there was a prevailing sentiment in those days that the bass player was always the least talented kid in the band. So if you had no discernible musical ability—which I certainly didn't—you became the bass player by default.

I don't know how, but somehow I managed to harangue my parents into buying me a crappy used acoustic guitar, on which I strung four bass strings and drilled holes to accommodate a five-dollar Lafayette guitar pickup: instant electric bass. Hinch and I would both plug into his little amp and, painstakingly, he taught me the simple bass lines to "Wipe Out" and a couple of other easy songs. In the meantime, Cody talked his folks into buying him a snare drum and cymbal and a couple pair of sticks—they weren't about to spring for a full set of drums, not right away, but his small kit was sufficient for our modest needs.

Slowly, all three of our lives became consumed by band rehearsals. Hinch lived in a nice big house—nicer than any of ours, anyway—but his folks wouldn't let us practice there. His mom and dad were always kind of a mystery to me; I hardly ever saw them and never got much of an idea about what they were like, or even what they did for a living. With Hinch's place out, we'd end up sometimes at Cody's house, but more often at mine. My folks just seemed a lot more forgiving about us making noise—and trust me, it was pretty much just noise we were making at that point in time. But my dad seemed to get a kick out of the idea that his son might be a budding rock 'n' roll star, even if it meant that my school grades were suffering as a result. That didn't make my mom all that happy, as you might imagine.

Within a few months, we landed our first gig: playing the Christmas party for Mrs. Ellison's seventh grade class. Our set consisted of exactly three numbers: the Monkees theme song; the Troggs' "Wild Thing"; and, of course, "Wipe Out," which Cody played fast and furious on his one little drum, smashing his cymbal so hard at the end of each chorus I thought it was going to shatter into a hundred pieces. We got a pretty good round of applause at the end, too. In fact, now that I think about it, we were a four-piece at the time: we'd hooked up with some other kid who stood in front and shook maracas. A week or so after the gig Hinch told this kid he sucked and fired him on the spot. I didn't think he was that bad, actually, and neither did Cody, but somehow our opinions didn't seem to count. I think it was just that Hinch couldn't stand anyone else being in the spotlight. He was like that, even back in those days.

Now, as I said, all throughout that first year in junior high, the kids in our class were being tormented by various seniors. Bullying those younger or smaller than you just seems to be in our DNA, at least when you're growing up.

The worst bully in the school was a kid named Vogel: Eddie Vogel. His dad owned one of the bigger farms in the York area, and I guess Eddie did a lot of work on the farm, because even as a thirteen year-old he had huge forearms and a neck like a bull. He was a nasty piece of work, too: he seemed to take a lot of pleasure in hassling every kid who had the misfortune of walking by him in the hallway. Eventually the intimidation turned to extortion, as he discovered that his extra size could be used to cadge our lunch money. "Hey, Boyle," he'd snarl as I'd squeeze past him on the stairs, doing my best to make myself invisible. "You look like you've got some extra spending money today. Come on, giff." He had this awful German accent, like the way Arnold Schwarzenegger talks, you know?

Sometimes you could wheedle your way out of it, especially if he got preoccupied harassing someone else. "No money today, Eddie, sorry; I'll pay you tomorrow." He might accept that—*might*—but you knew that you'd better seek him out first thing the next morning and make the promised payment before he came looking for you. We watched him kick the crap out of some poor kid one morning who tried ducking him, and we never forgot that.

Fortunately, none of us had done anything much to attract Eddie Vogel's attention, so we hadn't been especially singled out for these shakedowns, but all that changed after we played that Christmas party. "There they are, the little pussy group of musicians," he'd sneer when we'd walk past. "Who do you think you are, anyway? The Peedles?"

That was the way he pronounced "Beatles": Peedles. It used to make my blood boil. Sometimes I'd find myself wishing that John Lennon himself would turn up at our school so he could dispense some justice, Liverpool-style. 'Course, that never happened.

Vogel had been doing this to all three of us for a few weeks, extracting a handful of coins whenever he could, when one afternoon during Social Studies class some snot-nosed kid passed me a note saying that Eddie was "looking for Hinch."

This was the most dreaded of all messages, and at first I didn't believe it. "What do you mean?" I asked the kid from behind my notebook.

"It means Hinch promised to pay him today but didn't," he hissed back. "You better tell your friend he's gonna get his butt kicked!!" He seemed to take great delight in the prospect.

Within minutes, it seemed that everyone in the classroom knew. Everyone but Hinch, that is, who sat at his desk with a faraway look in his eyes, like he was rehearsing a guitar solo in his head.

"Pssst, Hinch!" I whispered as loudly as I dared.

He looked up. "What?" he replied, unfortunately in his normal speaking voice.

"Okay, what's going on here?" It was the damn teacher, planting her fat ass midway between my face and Hinch's left elbow. I made my excuses and she waddled back to her desk at the front of the room.

"It's Vogel—he's after you!"

The teacher turned around and fixed her porcine gaze upon us once again. Out of the corner of my eye I could see Hinch turn white. With Miss Lardass on to us, we couldn't communicate any further, but the moment the bell rang everyone gathered excitedly around Hinch's desk.

"Jeez, what the hell did you do to piss him off?" I asked.

"Oh, shit, I completely forgot. He got me in a headlock in the hallway yesterday and I told him I didn't have any money but would give him two dollars today if he'd leave me alone."

"And you didn't pay him?" one of the other kids gasped.

"No, dickweed, I didn't. I completely forgot, and I'm completely broke. Any of you got any money I can borrow?"

Everyone looked at one another but no one volunteered to loan Hinch the necessary funds. There were several reasons why. One, it was doubtful anyone had any spare money other than bus fare home, what with both lunch and recess long since gone. Two, it was unlikely that Eddie Vogel would forgive the debt at this late stage since Hinch had committed the cardinal sin of not voluntarily bringing him the offering earlier in the day. And, three, everyone wanted to see a fight.

I looked at Cody. "Sorry, Hinch, you know I'd give you the bucks if I had it, but I'm flat broke," he said, before adding, to my dismay, "But Donnie and I will walk you to the bus stop. We got you covered."

I gulped. Much as I enjoyed Hinch's friendship, I wasn't so sure I was willing to get my ass kicked for him, especially not by Eddie Vogel. Sensing my discomfort, Cody gave me a sharp elbow to the ribs.

"Uh, right. We got you covered. Like Cody said." The words sounded more like a squeak than a statement, but there they were, hanging in the air. Hinch looked at me dubiously, but nodded his head.

Heart in mouth, the three of us marched out of the classroom to the chants of "Fight! Fight!" I noticed that Cody took the lead, with Hinch treading cautiously in his wake. Me, I was happy that I was bringing up the rear. To tell you the truth, I was already eyeing the exits, looking for a possible way out if the worst occurred.

Miraculously, we made it outside in one piece and started down the school steps. The bus stop beckoned, just down the road, and for a brief moment I thought we might actually get home alive, but the dozens of kids milling up ahead told a different story. Magically, like a scene from *The Ten Commandments*, the crowd parted and out strode neither Moses nor Charlton Heston but Eddie Vogel. He looked grim.

"Hinch!" he yelled. "Get your scrawny ass over here so I can give it a whupping!"

A slight cheer of excitement went up. Where the hell were all the teachers when you needed them? Watching from the windows, no doubt, anxious to witness retribution being doled out to the school's budding rock star.

I thought I could see Hinch starting to tremble. He took a deep breath and opened his mouth as if to speak.

"Vogel, you fat German fuck! Get your own fat ass over here so I can rip you a new asshole!"

I'd never heard Hinch talk like that before. And there was a good reason why. It wasn't Hinch talking.

It was Cody.

Amazed, I stared at the little red-headed kid, who fixed Eddie Vogel with a gaze so ferocious I thought it might burn holes in his forehead.

"What the hell are you doing?" Hinch whispered frantically. "Are you trying to get me killed?"

"Don't worry, bro," Cody replied, calm as all get-out. "I told you, we got you covered. Just stand behind me. I'll take care of this fat prick."

With dozens of kids urging him on, Vogel strode the hundred feet across the road, snorting like a bull. For some reason, though—greed, maybe?—his anger still seemed directed at Hinch, despite Cody's verbal taunting.

Which was his big mistake. Dismissively, he pushed Cody aside and lifted a fist, readying it for launch at Hinch's slack jaw. But in the second or so it took him to put his arm in motion, Cody nimbly stepped behind him and cold-cocked Vogel in the back of the head, causing him to crumple to the ground.

"Fuck you, you Kraut bastard!" Cody screamed as he jumped on top of the helpless bully and pounded him over and over again, fists flailing like a windmill. "You leave my friends alone, you piece of shit!" In my young life I'd never seen anybody so angry, so totally out of control. Vogel rolled into a ball, trying desperately to ward off the hail of blows. Cody was on his feet now, delivering vicious kicks to the ribs; with each one he seemed more and more enraged. Even through the shouts of the screeching kids who were circling like vultures, I thought I could hear Eddie moaning in pain.

For the first time since we left the school, I heard Hinch's voice, now oddly subdued.

"Cody, stop! You're gonna kill him."

It was like a switch had been thrown; instantly, Cody obeyed, mid-kick. Just seconds before, his face had been twisted in violent rage; now, he flashed us a grin. Without saying a word to the sniveling heap lying on the ground, he threw one arm around Hinch, the other around me.

"I told you we had you covered; you know you can count on us," he told Hinch over and over again as we walked away to the cheers of the other kids. I felt embarrassed; I hadn't done a damn thing, but here was Cody talking as if the two of us had taken on the Aryan bully, thrashing him senseless through studied teamwork instead of the focused rage of one out-of-control teenager.

Now I know that seems like a story with a happy ending, but it really isn't. The next day Vogel's influential father got Cody suspended from school, and a few weeks later Cody got the snot kicked out of him when Eddie and a bunch of his friends ambushed him in a parking lot. Landed him in the hospital with a broken nose and a couple of busted ribs, too. That was the first time Cody took a beating for Hinch, but it sure wasn't the last time. Strangely, when Cody got out of hospital and finally did make it back to school, he wasn't treated as a hero—Hinch had already somehow taken that mantle—and Hinch didn't treat him especially nicely, either. In fact, after that day it was almost as if Hinch *expected* Cody to act like his bodyguard. Which Cody did, without complaint and without question. I never understood that. I guess there was a lot about their relationship I never did understand, not even all these years later.

So does that tell you what you wanted to know? I hope so, because I'm kinda tired and I think we need to stop. No, it's okay, I don't need any help up. Just turn that goddamn tape recorder off, willya?

3

My editor called again this morning. Same old shit: missed deadlines, don't burn your bridges, take responsibility for your actions, blah blah blah.

Then the shrill voice emanating from my cordless phone said something that caught my attention. "And if you don't get it done soon, Mr. Temkin," it squeaked, "you're going to have to return your advance."

Three words every author fears: Return. Your. Advance. Turning in a manuscript late—that's just par for the course. They know you're going to turn it in late, and you know you're going to turn it in late, and it's kind of a game you both play: Let's see just how far we can push things. Truth is, it almost doesn't matter how late you are, if the manuscript is good enough—that is, if it ends up actually turning a profit for the publisher. When that happens, all is forgiven. And it's that prospect of a massive profit that keeps most publishers from abandoning most projects they've signed, especially if the advance is a piddling one, which it usually is.

This time, though, Sol was able to actually negotiate me some real money, which means I'm treading dangerous ground. So I made nice with the little rodent of an editor, issued a few more promises I knew I couldn't keep, and ended the call as quickly as I could.

"Britney, I'm fucked."

"I know, babe. Often and with great skill."

Britney spread out languorously beside me, her magnificent breasts winking at me from beneath the sheet.

"I'm not joking," I told her, now thoroughly distracted by the sight of her erect nipples. "I think they're serious this time—I may have to give back the money."

"Well, in that case I guess I'll just have to find myself a new stud. One who can keep me in the style to which I am accustomed."

I laughed nervously. She was trying to sound flip, but both of us knew that she was telling me the absolute truth.

What the hell have I gotten myself into? Once I was a budding Master of the Universe. Now I'm just another fat, balding schlub, pushing fifty but still playing a young man's game, messing around with a girl half my age who is clearly only interested in the size of my bank account. Returning the advance was unthinkable; it would ruin me. I'd have to give up the condo, the hairpiece, the Corvette, the girlfriend. The first three I could do without. But where would I ever find an ass as perfect as Britney's? I tried focusing, something made infinitely more difficult by her hand slowly snaking its way down my chest toward the rapidly growing tent in the sheets.

Later, while Britney was in the shower, I rang Sol. Maybe he'd have an angle I hadn't thought of.

"Bubbie, what's going on?" he shouted. He always yelled when he talked on the phone; you'd have thought he was deaf. Actually, he *was* half-deaf, but I never felt that was much of an excuse. The fact of the matter is, he seemed to *like* talking loudly. Sol had always been like an uncle to me, albeit an uncle who'd been taking fifteen percent of my income for the last twenty years.

"Sol, I got another call today. They're talking about making me give back the advance." I knew I was whining, but I couldn't help myself. After what I thought was a melodramatic pause, I added, weakly, "They can't do that, can they?"

"Of course they can!" he thundered. I had to hold the receiver two feet away to avoid having my eardrum punctured. "What the hell is your problem, anyway? How hard can it be to get this book finished?"

"I told you," I stammered. "I'm getting stonewalled by Hinch's people. But I'm sure there's something going on here. There's something that just doesn't make sense."

"Fuck Hinch's people!!" he screamed, adding another exclamation point for emphasis. "Make it up if you have to. Just get the goddamned book done! If they get the lawyers on to you, we're both screwed." To my amazement, Sol was getting angry. In all the years I'd known him, I'd never heard him get angry before.

Now his voice turned icy cold. "You listen to me, you little shit, and listen good. If they make you give back the advance, I'll be suing *your* sorry fat ass for fifteen percent of it. After all I've done for you! Dammit, I put my reputation on the line negotiating that contract for you."

I paused to contemplate Sol's reputation, which, frankly, couldn't have been much lower to begin with. I started to issue a smartass response, but then thought better of it. Silently I ran through my options. Unfortunately, there didn't seem to be any.

"Sol," I whimpered like a zit-faced adolescent, "isn't there anything I can do?"

"The only thing you can do is finish that damn book," he snapped. "Either that or spend the next ten years in court being sued. It won't leave you a lot of time to keep *schtupping* that pretty young thing of yours, I guarantee you."

"I know, Sol, I know. She'll probably leave me anyway." I was having trouble holding back the tears now.

Sol sighed. "Look, Bernie, I gotta go," he said abruptly, clearly fed up with my complaining. "Just finish the goddamn book, willya?" With that, he hung up.

I looked up, stared around the room morosely. Britney emerged from the shower, wrapped in a towel, looking unbearably sexy as usual.

"That was Sol, I suppose," she said, absentmindedly looking at herself in the mirror.

"Yes. He says hello."

"Oh please, don't make me laugh," she snorted. "We both know how he feels about me. I sometimes wonder if he thinks he's entitled to fuck me fifteen percent of the time."

Something halfway between a chuckle and a wounded cry of self-pity burst out of my mouth. How could I possibly part company with such a beautiful and witty creature?

"Come on, let's go to Rodeo Drive and do some shopping," was all I could mumble.

"Really? Oh, babe, you're the best!" Letting the towel drop, Britney jumped onto the bed and gave me a big hug. I started to cop a feel but she shoved my hand away.

"Afterwards, stud-muffin. But I'll tell you what: Buy me something especially nice and I might just get out the Monica Lewinsky kneepads tonight."

I know, I know. But you should see that ass.

Most people are impressed when I tell them I've written two dozen books. But the truth of the matter is that you'd be hard-pressed to find my name on any of them unless you've got a magnifying glass handy. That's because

I've spent most of my literary career turning the random, disjointed thoughts of a bunch of empty-headed celebrities into something vaguely resembling English. Ghost-writing is a very specialized profession. It takes a certain kind of personality to gut one of those projects out: endless patience, combined with an ability to completely sublimate your ego. You have to spend literally months, sometimes even years, listening to the narcissistic babbling of some idiot, nodding your head thoughtfully even as you hear the same pointless story repeated for the twenty-fifth time. (Nodding my head thoughtfully, I have found, is the best alternative to nodding off completely.) Then you have to go home and listen to the whole goddamned thing all over again as you transcribe the tape.

And then there are the rewrites. Endless skirmishes over minutiae, minds being changed eighty times a day, never-ending comments to cope with, and not just from the celebrity you're writing about, but from their manager, agent, husband, wife, best friend, second-best friend, lesbian lover, gay partner, brother, sister, and third cousin twice removed now living in Miami Beach. And they're all battles that you know you are predestined to lose.

Still, somehow you suck it all up and eventually—if you have the self-control to keep smiling and stop yourself from telling these morons what you actually think of them—the book comes out and a trickle of small royalty checks begins coming in. Five percent of a million, as Sol likes to tell me, is a lot better than a hundred percent of nothing. Even if Sol is skimming his fifteen percent off the top.

That's been my writing career up until now. This book on Hinch was supposed to change all that, but that's going to shit and so I'll probably soon be back to my routine of sinking into the overstuffed wing chair of some retired sitcom character actor, lamely grinning as he tells me for the hundredth time about how he had a chance to boff Shirley Jones back in '72 but decided to go out drinking with the boys instead.

Whoops, I forgot about the money. No, there will be no overstuffed wing chair for me, at least not any time in the foreseeable future. First of all, I'll have too many court appearances to make. Secondly, it's an unwritten rule that any author who absconds with a large advance without delivering the goods—even if the legal system eventually lets him get away with it—is blackballed for life by every publisher in the business. I'll be lucky to get a job writing on the back of cereal boxes after this.

And I guarantee there won't be any Britney—or Tiffany, or Amber, or even a Mabel—hanging around when I'm doing that kind of work.

Come on, Bernie. Get a grip. This was supposed to be your big opportunity, your chance to finally move from the ghostly background into the bright light of success. Those were pretty much Sol's exact words when I signed that publishing contract two years ago. It was my golden contract, my twenty-fifth, and the first one that actually had my name alone on it; the first one that guaranteed me a sole credit as author. *Hinch,* by Bernard J. Temkin. Had a good ring to it, I thought.

Actually, years ago I was a fan of Hinch's. Back in the '70s, when I was in college, you almost couldn't pass a dorm without hearing the strains of *Keeping It Real* blasting through the windows. I even saw Hinch play live a couple of times, and I thought he was pretty cool—definitely an intriguing character lurching around the stage in too-tight gold lamé. In my idle moments I even sometimes imagined myself up there, spitting fire, tearing off ferocious guitar licks, posing in the spotlight. Mostly, though, I imagined the scenes in the dressing rooms and hotels afterward—the all-night partying, the hot groupies. It was a lifestyle that part of me hungered for, part of me feared. At one point I even went out and bought myself an electric guitar, inspired by Hinch and some of the other rock stars of the era. But it soon became clear that I had no aptitude for the instrument, and not enough balls to try and fake it. So back into the case it went, and that's where it remained until one of my ex-girlfriends discovered it years later and smashed it to pieces in a fit of rage. I should have been angry but somehow it seemed fair enough—a metaphor, a fitting ending to a misplaced dream.

Things would have been so much easier if this Hinch book had been just another ghost-writing assignment, which was, after all, the original plan. But when Hinch backed out, it was Sol who convinced me to go it alone and write an unauthorized biography instead. It was only after the contracts were signed that he revealed the true reason, which had nothing to do with his confidence in me.

It had to do with Jack Landis.

Jack Landis is richer than God. Nobody is quite sure where it came from, but his immense wealth has apparently continued to accumulate despite eight highly contentious marriages and divorces. It doesn't seem to matter: He was born rich, he will die rich, and in-between, he's gotten even richer. Beyond boasting an annual income in excess of the gross national product of most small countries, he owns a baseball team, two cable TV networks, four nuclear power plants, and a chain of discount shoe stores. And, for kicks, a publishing company.

Landis Books is not a purveyor of fine literature by any stretch of the imagination. Mostly they publish right-wing rants from the talking heads who appear on the two Landis Networks, poorly ghosted autobiographies from washed-up baseball players who have drifted in and out of Landis's employ, and horrendously boring tomes about the history of nuclear power and discount shoes. So where did a book about a fading rock star fit into that milieu?

It didn't. But Jack Landis always gets what he wants, and, as Sol discovered one sunny afternoon on the golf links, what he wanted was a book about Hinch. Why? Who knows. Maybe he used to be a fan, maybe he once owned a guitar company. Maybe it was just because. And somehow the fates drew Landis and Sol together—the story I got was that one of Landis's golf buddies didn't turn up that day and Sol just happened to be conveniently hanging around and managed to weasel his way into the foursome. However it happened, by the sixteenth hole Sol had convinced Landis that he represented the perfect author to ghostwrite a Hinch autobiography, and by the eighteenth hole they had settled on terms: a surprisingly decent royalty, and a cool million as an advance ... all this despite the fact that Sol didn't know Hinch from a nine-iron.

The next few weeks were spent in frantic negotiations between Sol and Hinch's manager Alan Schiffman as they tried to work out how to divvy up the pie. "Don't worry, bubbie—they need the money," Sol told me confidently. Which meant, of course, that Schiffman needed the money; Sol was quite sure that little if any of it would ever trickle down to the great rock star himself. For awhile they seemed to be making steady progress: two canny old *goniffs* circling one another warily, with Hinch and me caught in the middle. On Tuesday, Schiffman would insist on a 90/10 split, on Wednesday, Sol would counter with 60/40; on Thursday they'd seemingly meet halfway at 75/25. Then on Friday they'd have a falling-out and the whole infuriating process would begin all over again.

Finally, it seemed as if they had everything ironed out; I don't remember the exact deal, but it was considerably more than I'd hoped for, and, I'm equally sure, considerably less than what Schiffman wanted. Nonetheless, the two men shook hands and sent a green light to Landis's lawyers to draw up a contract.

It was only then that it finally occurred to someone to ask Hinch.

For the next excruciating six weeks, we all clambered right back onto the same sickening roller-coaster. One week Schiffman would tell Sol that Hinch was onboard and ready to meet with me; the next, we got word that Hinch was getting cold feet and might not go through with it after all. I was popping Xanaxes like they were breath mints, and even Sol—the man who'd seen it all—seemed to be thrown for a loop. Yet through all of this, Landis's representatives remained unnervingly calm. I guess they knew that, in the end, their boss always got what he wanted.

But Hinch didn't know, or didn't want to know. One blindingly bright morning, I was awoken at the crack of dawn—that is, shortly before noon—by the phone ringing. It was Sol.

"Bernie, listen. It's all over."

"All over?"

"Hinch says no book. Schiffman's pissed as hell, but he says he can't do anything. The project is dead." I actually heard defeat in his voice.

"Dead? But, Sol, what about the million dollars? I've already started doing all this research …" I began blubbering. What I meant was, I've already maxed out all of my credit cards in anticipation of the advance, but I wasn't about to say so.

"You sound like shit," he observed, correctly. "Just go back to sleep. We'll talk later."

Even my psychotropically infused system wouldn't allow me to return to unconsciousness, so I spent the next few hours frantically going through my research notes and tried desperately to come up with some kind of alternative plan.

I needn't have bothered.

By mid-afternoon, Sol was back on the phone, restored to his usual blustery self. Sure enough, he'd figured an angle—one that, he explained, would make me richer than I'd even dared dream.

"I just got off the phone with Landis," he bellowed excitedly, "and it's all set."

"What's all set?" I asked, confused. "Last time we talked—what, three hours ago?—you said the deal was off."

"Off, schmoff. Uncle Sol has come to the rescue, as usual. Come into the office, *bubeleh*—I want to tell you in person."

An hour later, disheveled and foggy-headed, I cleared off a seat in the agent's overheated warren, surrounded on all sides by a veritable wall of dusty books and contracts. It was all I could do to focus on Sol's gravelly voice as he regaled me with the story of his triumph, chest puffing out like a proud papa.

"It was as simple as taking candy from a baby," he crowed. "Landis wants a book about Hinch, right?"

"Right."

"So he's going to get a book about Hinch. It's just that it will be *about* Hinch, not *by* Hinch. I pointed out to him that an unauthorized biography might be an even hotter property than another one of those crappy as-told-to puff pieces."

"I don't understand," I said, even though I kind of did.

"What's not to understand? Instead of ghostwriting Hinch's autobiography, you are going to be the internationally renowned author of the soon-to-be best-selling book that tells the real story of what it takes to become a famous rock and roll star. All that's different is that instead of talking to Hinch himself, you'll simply talk to everyone *around* him. It's a much better opportunity, believe me. And best of all ..." He paused here, a devilish gleam in his eye. "... the money is the same."

My eyes widened.

"The same?"

"The same. You, my little *pisher*, are about to become a millionaire. Minus my cut, of course."

I'VE NEVER BEEN good about money. Maybe that's because I never had much of it, but when that first advance check arrived, I started spending like a drunken sailor too long out of port. First came the Corvette—a gleaming silver '73, just like the one I always dreamed of owning when I was in college—then came the beachside condo in Malibu. And then, of course, came Britney, the highest ticket item of all.

At first my future looked rosy. I had a flash car, a sumptuous bachelor pad, and a hot blonde who plied me with unbelievable sex as long as I allowed her access to my platinum Visa card. In the first couple of months after signing with Landis, I also had a series of what seemed like amicable phone conversations with Alan Schiffman, who, despite Hinch's personal refusal to participate, promised full cooperation from the Hinch organization. But it soon became painfully obvious that nothing of the kind was going to happen. Calls began not getting answered, promised interviews were called off at the last minute, and eventually one of the flunkies in the front office told me—strictly off the record—that Schiffman had put the word out that talking to me was grounds for immediate dismissal; worse yet, he had begun forcing his employees to sign legally binding non-disclosure forms. Why, I don't know. But I soon got an object lesson in how quickly and efficiently the ranks can close around a star, right down to a system of shunning that would have made the Pilgrims at Plymouth Rock proud. Thank God for Donnie Boyle and the transcriptions of the interviews I did with him last year, or I'd have nothing at all.

Yet the more Schiffman and the people around him resisted, the more I became convinced that something was going on here, something well beyond the bounds of the usual rock 'n' roll excess story. I had nothing concrete to base that on; it was just little comments that people made, rumors that were swirling around the industry. It had been years since Hinch had had a hit, or had made an album that sold beyond the fifty thousand or so core fans of his that remained—most of them in Europe and Japan. But even in the downside of his career, his name still meant something to most music fans, at least those of my generation. And then there was the simple fact that Jack Landis was no fool. He obviously believed that this book—*my* book—had the potential to be a best-seller; that would have been the only reason he put so much cold, hard cash on the line. But, as I'm starting to realize, even a Jack Landis—someone who always gets what he wants in the end—has limits to his patience.

Sol is right. The only way out is to finish the goddamn book. But he's wrong about one thing: I can't just make it up, or Schiffman will be the one suing my ass for the next ten years instead of Landis Books. The problem is getting at the truth, and it's damn near impossible if no one in the Hinch camp will talk to me. I can't even turn to Donnie Boyle anymore, God rest his soul. I grew to love the cantankerous bastard in his last days, not just for his willingness to stand up to Schiffman and talk to me, but for who he was—a straight shooter in an industry full of pathological liars and bottom-dwelling scum. When he finally gave in to that damned lung cancer last year, I should have taken it as a sign that this project was doomed.

What the hell. Maybe I'll try calling Schiffman again tomorrow. The prick hasn't taken any of my calls for months now, but at least I'm starting to get real good at banging my head against a wall. At least that's what his secretary tells me.

I wonder if she's cute.

4

Transcript: Interview with Donnie Boyle, March 11, 1998

Okay, Bernie, I'm ready when you are. No, wait, let me just move this goddamned machine out of the way. Fucking thing.

Alright, so we were talking about the fight with Eddie Vogel. Well, I think I pretty much told you all there is to tell. It was such a big deal at the time, and now it's only a memory. Like most of the stories in our lives, I suppose.

Looking back, I guess the seeds for everything that came afterwards were sown in those early days. By the time we got to high school, Hinch and Cody and I were tighter than ever. The band seemed to take up all of our waking moments—the moments we could get away with not having to sit in class or do homework, anyway—but somehow it always seemed to be more of an obsession with those two guys than it was with me. I mean, sure, I enjoyed plunking away on that bass and I definitely appreciated the admiring looks we got from the girls whenever we'd play one of our little local gigs—parties, school dances, things like that—but somehow it never really mattered to me how good I got on my instrument. I guess I just didn't have musician blood in me like the others did.

Take Hinch, for example. During that period of his life, it was almost like his guitar had become an appendage—you'd literally never see him without it. By then, he'd moved up to a cherry red Stratocaster—same kind of electric guitar that his idol Dick Dale played—and he'd gotten a matching Fender amp, too, so he was starting to sound pretty good. I have no idea how he talked his parents into springing for that kind of expensive equipment, but, boy, he carried that guitar with him everywhere he went, carefully tucked into its hardshell case with that big familiar F logo on the front. It became kind of a status symbol for him, I guess. None of the other kids in school owned a musical instrument anywhere near as classy, that's for sure.

Cody, too, had moved up in the world equipment-wise. In those days, the Beatles were all the rage, and so he'd gotten himself a small used Ludwig drum kit very much like Ringo's, silver sparkle and all that. But at the time he couldn't afford good cymbals, so he'd just beat on these crappy-sounding things that were really no better than garbage can lids. He'd smash the shit out of them, too, to the point where sometimes metal shards would actually start flying around and Hinch and I would find ourselves ducking the shrapnel. It seemed kind of funny at the time, but I suppose either of us could have just as easily lost an eye, so it came as quite a relief when Cody finally bought some decent-quality cymbals later on. Not only did they sound better; they were far safer.

Sorry, I go into those damn coughing fits whenever I start laughing. Keep this interview *serious*, willya?

Anyway, yeah, Hinch kept getting better and better on his guitar, and Cody, he kept getting better and better as well—and not only on the drums. The little bastard was actually constantly surprising us with his musicianship; he'd even started messing around with piano whenever he'd see one off in the corner of a place we were playing, and every once in awhile he'd pick up my bass, too. In fact, I don't mind telling you that he was every bit as good a bass player as I was.

Frankly, that was fine with me. Truth is, I was perfectly content just to play the parts they taught me, and no more. That's right, I said *they*. A lot of the time, it was Cody, not Hinch, who would figure out the bass lines of the songs we were covering and then teach them to me. I just didn't have the kind of ear to be able to do that for myself. Eventually Cody would start taking control of everything we were doing musically.

I can see by the look on your face that you're surprised to hear that ... but I'm getting a little ahead of myself. Give me time—I'll get there.

There was another reason why Hinch seemed to kind of stall at around that time, and her name was Katie. Katherine Mary Elizabeth Quinn, to be exact, or Katie Q, as we knew her. She was far and away the prettiest girl in our high school—long, silky soft dark hair, milky-white skin, with a classic Irish pug nose, and the bluest eyes you ever saw. She was smart, too, and funny, and, I don't know, she just kind of made you feel special when you were with her. To be honest, we all had a crush on Katie at one time or another—once I even spotted she and Cody sharing a kiss behind the football stands—but she only ever really seemed interested in Hinch, which meant that, for a while, at least, he had to split his time between her and that cherry red Strat. Eventually he figured out a balance, even if he had to do it by ignoring Katie a lot of the time, and slowly but surely the guitar became his main squeeze again ... though he always made certain to give Katie just enough attention to keep her from straying. Just enough, mind you—never any more than was necessary.

But in spite of that little diversion, Hinch pretty much stayed true to his guitar, and he kept plodding onward, picking up a new lick here, a fancy chord inversion there, becoming a solid and occasionally spectacular player. At a gig, you knew you could count on him one hundred percent—no mistakes, no fluffs, no screw-ups … even if that meant he usually just took the safe route and played the same every night. Once in awhile he'd pull a rabbit out of his hat and come up with a new ending to a solo, or a new phrase he'd throw in. We always knew when he would be throwing us a curveball, though, because he'd get this goofy grin on his face and his eyebrows would go up, like he was signaling us—and the audience—"Watch this." What was most impressive was that these experimentations of his would always work. That kind of made me suspect that he'd rehearsed it all out beforehand, that it really wasn't an improvisation at all, just something he'd unveil only after he'd worked out every permutation of it in advance. I always felt that if you threw Hinch into a jazz gig where he *really* had to improvise, he wouldn't have any idea what to do. Even all these years later, I still feel that way.

Gimme a sec, willya? Damn coughing fits. No, I'm okay, just keep the tape rolling.

Now Cody, on the other hand, Cody was *always* experimenting. Not only would he constantly be questioning everything at rehearsal: "Let's try it faster; let's try it slower; let's try changing the chords around"—something which used to drive Hinch crazy—he also liked slipping in these little surprises at gigs. He'd start pushing the beat at a certain point, or throw in a different kind of rhythm or accent. Sometimes he'd drag me into these escapades, too, yelling at me to play a different bass pattern, or do a harmony line behind Hinch's lead instead of exactly doubling him. Hinch's face would turn a bright shade of red when we'd do stuff like that—hell, it would almost match his cherry Strat—and there would often be a big argument in the dressing room afterwards, but I always felt that it was good that Cody challenged us to get outside our comfort zone. If it was up to Hinch, we'd just play the same parts—the safe parts—night after night, and we probably never would have developed very much as musicians.

Most people who saw us play live assumed, of course, that Hinch was in charge: after all, he sang most of the songs and did the flashy guitar work. But I'm telling you, behind the scenes, it was more often Cody calling the shots. And when it came to a showdown between the two of them, it was usually Hinch who would back down. I often wondered why. Maybe it was because he was a little afraid of Cody, having watched him take on Eddie Vogel and other assorted assholes who would hassle the band on occasion. Or maybe it was just that Hinch knew that Cody was turning into the superior musician.

Yes, that's what I said. I know that everyone thinks of Hinch today as a guitar hero, but I was there, and I'm telling you that back in those days, Cody—the same guy who later became known simply as "Cody the roadie"—was easily Hinch's equal, if not his better. He may not have had Hinch's sense of showmanship, but he had the fire in him, maybe even more than Hinch did. Hinch may have carried that damn guitar around with him wherever he went, but Cody carried the *music* with him wherever he went. Back in those days, there wasn't a moment when he wasn't tapping out a drumbeat on a tabletop, or humming a song, or listening to music, or thinking about music. I can still see Cody now, sitting on the floor next to his stereo, lifting up the needle to play the same part over and over again, listening intently until he had learned not just the part, but every nuance of the part.

Nuance. *That's* what I'm talking about. Sure, Hinch got to the point where he could play just about any guitar part he'd ever heard—and I'm talking heavyweights like Hendrix or Clapton or Beck here—but Cody was able to not only figure out *what* he was hearing, but every tiny detail of *how* the music had been crafted. It was a more painstaking process for him, but eventually he'd develop those skills for himself—not just copying people, but creating his own music.

Now don't get me wrong. I'm not putting down Hinch, or denying that he turned into a great performer who wrote some memorable songs. I'm just saying that at an early stage in the band's progress, he was actually the dark horse, not the guy you would have thought would grab the brass ring. Kind of like George Harrison in the Beatles, you know? Folks didn't pay much attention to poor George at first—it seemed like John and Paul were constantly overshadowing him—but eventually you couldn't help but notice that he had become a hell of a guitar player, and that he'd written some nice tunes, too. The difference was that Harrison shied away from the spotlight after all those years of putting up with the craziness on the road, while Hinch reveled in it. Maybe that's what ultimately made Hinch a star: his willingness to put up with all the bullshit that goes along with it.

Cody just didn't have the same tolerance for that crap that Hinch did … except when it was being doled out by Hinch himself. I told you before, I never was able to figure out the true nature of their friendship. That same protective streak that caused Cody to beat the shit out of Eddie Vogel never disappeared—in fact, in many ways, it kept getting stronger and stronger—yet Hinch would treat Cody in a way that Cody would never tolerate from anyone else. I don't know why he put up with it, but bad attitude from Hinch always seemed to just roll off of Cody's back.

Me, I guess I was somewhere in the middle. I could take a certain amount of crap, but I had my limits. Or at least I eventually found out that I had my limits. That came a long time later. For the most part, I was just the typical bass player, standing in the shadows and doing what I was told.

Anyway, by the time we hit senior year in high school, back in '69 or '70, Hinch and the Lynchpins—as we were known then—were a pretty big deal in York, Pa. All three of us turned 18 that year, so we started playing the local circuit on weekends, and it wasn't long before we became the hottest bar band in town. There weren't all that many places in York that offered live music, but we played the ones that did, and we filled them, too. Not because we were all that great at the time—truth be told, we weren't—but because of Hinch's personal brand of magnetism, which seemed to work on the guys almost as well as on the girls. People just couldn't stop themselves from watching him, especially when he was onstage doing his rock star moves. Charisma was just something that Hinch always had, and it came naturally to him, too.

I got to be real tight with Cody that year, mainly because Hinch was still spending a lot of time with Katie Q, and the more I got to know him, the more I liked him; he was just a solid kind of guy who seemed to live for music. We never talked about Hinch a whole lot, other than the usual good-natured moaning about how he got all the attention onstage. But we never resented him, because we knew that Hinch was the magnet that drew the crowds. And I guess that on some level we also knew that he could be our meal ticket, our ride to the top. Sure, Cody would bitch every now and then about musical differences with Hinch, but those arguments didn't last very long because, as I said, for some reason, Hinch would usually end up doing things Cody's way, even though he tended to resist new ideas at first.

Soon enough, we were graduating, and I don't think there was any question in our minds about turning pro after leaving school. It just seemed to be a foregone conclusion with Hinch, who was an only child, and with Cody as well, even though I know that he got some serious shit from his parents when he told them he had no intention of going to college. Personally, my folks couldn't care less. I was one of six kids, and my mom died when I was pretty young, so by the time I had that conversation with my old man, he was basically just glad to have one less mouth to feed. As I said, we were doing pretty okay by that time, playing the local dives, making a couple of hundred bucks a week apiece, so I was able to support myself once I moved out and started rooming with Cody in a tiny two-bedroom apartment downtown. Katie headed off to a college a few hours away, but she'd come home every weekend and stay with Hinch, who'd taken a small place of his own—I think the landlord was a friend of his family.

Of course, those were the days when the hippie thing was in full swing, and we were definitely counterculture: three long-haired musicians living off a diet of Spam and Kraft macaroni and cheese, flophouse mattresses on the floor, cheap incense holders, cinderblock bookshelves, the whole nine yards. But we had each other and we had our music and, as far as we were concerned, the world—or at least York, Pa., and its immediate surroundings—was ours for the taking. At the time, we were content with our status as top bar band and all the local fans and free beers that came with it, but all of that started to change when Cody came home one day with a cherry red Stratocaster of his own.

"What the hell are you doing with Hinch's guitar?" I remember asking him.

"That's not his guitar," he replied. "It just looks like his guitar. I spotted it in a pawnshop window and decided it needed me."

"I didn't even know you played guitar," I said.

"I don't," he said, flashing a toothy grin. "But I figure, what the heck, if a retard like Hinch can do it, so can I."

I remember laughing my ass off at the sheer audacity of it; I could almost picture the shit-fit Hinch would have when he saw the guitar in Cody's hands. And make no mistake—he did. It all seemed like good-natured needling at the time, but the truth of the matter is that, in many ways, that day signalled the beginning of the end. For Cody, for me, for the group as a whole. It took quite awhile to manifest, but that really was the start of all the bad things that would follow.

But, you know, that's a whole other story for another day. To be honest, I'm pretty wiped out from all this talking. Let's pick this up next time, okay?

And get that damn machine over here before I pass out.

5

I LEARNED TWO IMPORTANT things today. One, Alan Schiffman's secretary is not cute. And, two, my instincts were right: there *is* something going on here.

I woke up bright and early this morning, despite the fact that I spent most of the night tossing, turning and worrying. It feels as if I've spent the last few months passing through four of the five classic stages for dealing with tragedy—denial, anger, bargaining and depression—and now it seems that I've somehow finally moved on to the final stage: not just acceptance, but activism. At least that's how I feel today. Tomorrow I may revert back to the same old schlumpy Bernie Temkin I've known for decades.

God, I hope not.

But today ... today has been good. To my utter surprise, I practically leapt from bed, without even attempting to put the moves on a bleary-eyed Britney. As I stared at myself in the mirror while shaving, I realized that it had come almost as a relief not to be rebuffed by her (which seems to happen most mornings) or, on those increasingly rare occasions when she is responsive to my fumblings, to have to perform to her overly high—and, to my aging body, ungodly athletic—standards. Just avoiding sex—or even the semblance of desiring sex—seems to have imbued me with a new-found energy, an energy I've decided I can best put to use trying to extricate myself from the dreadful predicament I find myself in.

Gulping down a rapidly concocted smoothie as I head for the door, I catch a glimpse of my blonde angel softly snoring on the bed, a minute but distinct string of drool passing from her soft lips onto the pillow. *I'll miss her when she dumps me*, I think, paying homage to the inevitable. The only thing I can do now is to try to forestall things as long as possible. And that process begins by trying to salvage the book.

Cruising through Topanga Canyon with the top down, I briefly allow myself the luxury of believing that things will actually turn out all right. The combination of the warm California sun and the soft breeze blowing through my hairpiece seems to infuse me with new hope.

Maybe you can *find a way out of this*, becomes my new mantra. I have no idea where this expectation comes from, but it begins bubbling up from within, as unstoppable as a mountain stream beginning its long traverse into light and air as it rushes toward the river below.

Even the smog of downtown Los Angeles does little to dampen my rising spirit. Glowing with self-confidence, I march into the offices of Schiffman Entertainment International—a glitzy conglomerate of agents, managers, publicists, and accountants that proudly occupies the twelfth floor of a new high-rise on the corner of Wilshire and Figueroa.

"I'm here to see Trudy Cox," I tell the anorexic young receptionist. She seems barely out of her teens, and can't possibly weigh more than eighty pounds soaking wet.

"Is she expecting you, sir?"

"Not exactly, but she knows me," I bluff. I'm hoping that my months-long campaign of bullshit and sweet-talking will pay off and that Schiffman's sultry-voiced secretary will now be as intrigued to scope me out in person as I am her.

I'm duly announced and told to have a seat. While I wait, I note the frantic activity in the offices behind the reception area, phones ringing nonstop and metrosexuals of all persuasions running around like amphetamine-crazed headless chickens. It's not exactly the kind of thing you expect to see in laid-back L.A. At one point a shaven-headed flunkie—dressed from head to toe in fashionably chic black, of course—rushes in, deposits a stack of papers on the receptionist's desk, and sniffily instructs her to begin faxing them out A-SAP, emphasis on the "A." The papers appear to be press releases. I crane my neck and am about to stand up to try to get a better look when I hear a voice from behind me.

"Mr. Temkin? I'm Trudy Cox. We weren't expecting you."

I recognize the dulcet tones, but to my horror they are coming from the lips of a matronly woman nearly as old as me. From behind my Foster Grants, I take it all in: graying hair neatly pulled back in a bun, spreading middle-aged tummy held in check by a straining girdle beneath an austere business suit, all poised atop a pair of flat-heeled, distinctly 'do-not-fuck-me' shoes. This is hardly the stuff of fantasy.

In an attempt to disguise my disappointment, I adopt the persona of a smarmy game show host. "Trudy!" I call out in fake delight. "So nice to finally meet you in person! And, please, call me Bernie." I take a step forward and offer what I hope is a sincere smile along with my damp hand. She declines both.

"What can I do for you, Mr. Temkin?" she asks in a tone of voice that conveys a distinct lack of interest in the answer. "We're very busy today, as you can see."

"Yes, well, uh, I was in the neighborhood and …" I can feel the first rivulet of sweat begin the journey from my left armpit southward, my self-confidence evaporating with each new drop of perspiration. I sense that casual flirtation is not a tactic that will work with this woman. With no backup plan in mind, I find myself reverting to my usual bumbling self. "Well, er, as you know, I'm writing a book on Hinch and, well, um, would it be possible for me to, um, you know, maybe get a few moments of Alan's time?" Despite my attempt at bravado, the words tumble out in a torrent, my voice cracking at the end as if I were an awkward teenager trying to land a date for the prom.

"I'm sorry, Mr. Temkin, he's not here. And, really, you do need to call in advance to schedule an appointment if you want to see Mr. Schiffman." In a clear signal that our conversation is at an end, she swivels around and returns her attention to the receptionist.

Hopelessly, I address her broad back. "I know, and I've tried, but my calls don't get returned, and…." I'm running out of steam now and we both know it. Still, I push on, despite the growing awareness that my cheeks are turning a crimson red. "I guess I just thought that maybe …"

I trail off in the face of stony silence.

"Well, anyway, it was nice meeting you, Trudy, er, Ms. Cox," I mumble in the general direction of her fifth vertebrae. "I'll call next time, I promise." I manage what I hope is a wan smile. More likely I look like a grinning baboon.

The final nail in the coffin is the classic L.A. brush-off ("Have a nice day, Mr. Temkin"), accompanied by the sight of Trudy Cox's large and rapidly disappearing posterior as she purposefully strides out the door and down the hall.

I stand in the middle of the reception area, deflated, dejected, disconsolate, deflowered.

"Wow, that was cold."

The tiny voice is coming from the waif-like figure behind the reception desk busily inserting a press release into the fax machine. I turn to face her. Poor thing. She probably hasn't been here long enough to know that communication with me is strictly verboten.

"I'm sorry, are you talking to me?" I ask her.

"Um, yes—you don't see anyone else here, do you?" She reminds me of a pixie. A pixie with balls. I like that.

I reflexively look around the room. She's right, there's nobody else here. God, why am I such a dork?

"No, I guess not," I finally reply, trying to keep my embarrassment at bay. For a long moment we stare at one another. "Umm, I'm Bernie Temkin," I stammer at last. "What's your name?"

"I'm Chloe. And I already know your name, Mr. Temkin, remember? You told it to me as soon as you walked in here." She giggles. I find myself falling in love.

"Yes, of course. You're right. I...."

I'm speechless. This roller-coaster of ups and downs and ups again is really starting to get to me.

"Are you okay? You don't look so hot," Chloe says, a look of apprehension spreading across her face. "Why don't you sit down for a minute?" She takes a step in my direction.

"No, I'm fine, I'm just ..." Baffled at my inability to express myself, I start to wave her away, then think better of it. Why not seize the opportunity to feel her gentle touch, inhale her soft perfume?

Chloe takes my arm and steers me toward a chair. I was hoping for Chanel Number 5 but have to settle instead for Avon SkinSoSoft. No matter—the glimpse of the top of her tiny yet perfectly rounded breasts as she leans over to guide me into my seat quickly assuages any disappointment I may have felt.

"I think you must have been hyperventilating," she observes, sounding not so much like a trendy receptionist as a no-nonsense registered nurse. "That happens to my dad all the time, so I know how to deal with it. Would you like me to get you a paper bag to breathe into?"

Her dad! My hormonal instincts must be failing me; for a moment there I confused what was obviously daughterly concern with flirtation. I blink my eyes slowly as the realization of what a dirty old man I've become starts to sink in. I know I should be ashamed but I'm not; instead, curiously, the insight serves to invigorate me. I start to feel a trickle of self-confidence return.

Chloe stands a few feet away, arms crossed, eyeing me cautiously. I detect a gleam of amusement in her eyes.

"Really, I'm fine now," I offer. "But thanks. And, please, call me Bernie."

Another pregnant pause as we study one another. Suddenly the silence is shattered by the phone ringing. Chloe returns to her desk, still eyeing me intently.

"Good morning, Schiffman Entertainment. No, I'm sorry, he's not in. Would you like to leave a message?" I hear the voice on the other end of the line babbling intensely. "No, I'm afraid there's no one available for you to speak to, but we'll be issuing a statement shortly." More babbling. "No, I'm sorry, I can't read it to you, but we'll be faxing it out to the media shortly. Okay, I'll tell him you called. Bye!"

A few seconds of scribbling, then her gaze returns to me. "You writers, you're all so impatient!" she scolds.

"What do you mean?"

"Well, you guys have been calling and calling all morning wanting to know what's in our press release. Why can't you just wait for the fax to arrive? I'm sending them out as quickly as I can." There's a faint whine in her voice. For the first time since I've met her, Chloe begins to sound her chronological age.

As I study her face, the cobwebs start to loosen. Press release? It's been years since Hinch has done anything press-worthy.

"Um, well, I suppose it's because they—we—are on deadline," I say, trying to sound helpful. She shoots me a dirty look. I immediately begin backpedaling.

"Of course, you're right, though—we should wait until you're ready to make the announcement. Damn writers!" I try to conjure up a grin.

Chloe looks at me doubtfully as the phone rings again. "Hello, reception. Yes, Ms. Cox, I'll take care of it." Shit, I'd forgotten all about Trudy Cox. If she sees me still sitting here chatting up her receptionist, the next call will be to Security and I'll be exiting the building head-first.

"Sorry, Mr. Temkin—I mean, Bernie. I've got to go. And I think you should probably go, too."

I study her face for any signs of animosity. There aren't any, I note with relief. And then, as if reading my mind, she adds, with the hint of a smile, "It was nice meeting you, though. And ..."

I look at her quizzically.

"... good luck with your book."

Gathering up her sheaf of papers, Chloe heads for the door, cute little butt wiggling gently. Just as she reaches for the doorknob, two things happen which change my life.

One, she turns and winks at me.

And, two, a press release drops to the floor.

**REMAINDER OF HINCH TOUR CANCELLED
MILLENNIUM DOME CONCERT DATE WILL STILL BE HONORED.**

Los Angeles, California, December 15, 1999 — Schiffman Entertainment International announced today that the remainder of the current Hinch Live in Europe! tour has been cancelled due to illness. Singer/guitarist Tommy Hinchton is said to be suffering from nervous exhaustion and will be recuperating at an unknown location in Holland, where he and his band recently appeared before a sell-out crowd at Amsterdam's famed Paradiso Club.

"Tommy will be fine," said manager Alan Schiffman. "He gives so much to his fans, and it just reached the point where he needs a couple of weeks off." Local promoters will be offering refunds to those who purchased advance tickets for the cancelled dates in Groningen, Rotterdam, Arnhem, Dusseldorf, Munich, Frankfurt, Zurich, Copenhagen, Oslo, and Stockholm.

Hinch is expected to recover in time to make his scheduled appearance opening the Millennium Dome in London on New Year's Eve. "This promises to be the greatest gig of Hinch's long and storied career," Schiffman said, "and I know there's no way Tommy would miss it." A limited number of tickets for the Millennium Dome concert are still available through UK promoter Modern Style Events.

From the front seat of my convertible, I blink back the blinding California sun as I struggle to focus on the words before me. Nervous exhaustion, my ass. That's the oldest cop-out there is. Usually it's code for drug or alcohol rehab. But from everything I've learned about the man, Tommy Hinchton is that rarest of all commodities: a rock 'n' roll star who, despite having indulged in all the excesses of the '70s, is now apparently totally clean, even a bit of a health nut—something that has caused him to endure no small amount of ridicule in the often patronizing and always highly judgmental world of music journalism, not to mention some of his fellow rock stars. What's more, unlike many of his peers, Hinch has never smashed a guitar onstage, never destroyed a hotel room, never failed to show up for a gig, never even yelled at a paparazzi. In other words, he's as close to a normal, well-adjusted human being as ever trod the boards in the rock 'n' roll arena ... and that's saying a lot.

So I don't buy "nervous exhaustion." Something else has got to be going on here, and damned if I don't find myself determined to find out what it is. This is a new feeling for me, I have to admit. What do they call it again?

Oh yeah. Commitment.

THE FIRST THING I do when I get home is to call my friend Clive over at *Rolling Stone*.

"Clive, what's shaking, babe? It's Bernie."

"Bernie?" he repeats tentatively.

"Bernie Temkin. Remember?"

"Bernie. Oh yeah, Bernie," he says unconvincingly. A brief pause while he searches his memory banks. It has, after all, been a couple of years since we last crooked elbows side by side at some West Hollywood joint, and music journalists are notorious for large gaps in short-term memory due to excessive alcohol intake, Clive being no exception.

At last the synapses appear to clear. "Bernie! Hey, buddy, good to hear from you. What's going on?"

"Actually, I'm calling about this Hinch press release. You must have gotten it by now. You probably heard that I'm writing a book about him."

He hasn't heard. "Are you? That's great. Still a market for those seventies guys, I suppose."

I resist the temptation to point out that my million-dollar book advance represents twenty times what he earns in a year at the *Stone*, and that it is really only the fans of "those seventies guys" that still read magazines like his.

"Yes, I guess so," I say instead, adding for good measure, "Hey, a gig's a gig, you know?" Jeez, how phony can you get? I've definitely been living in L.A. too damn long.

"So what's on your mind, Bernie baby?"

"Um, well, as I said, I was calling about that press release on Hinch. I was wondering what you make of it."

"Press release on Hinch? I'm not sure I read it all that closely. Wasn't it something about cancelling tour dates?" I hear papers rustling in the background as Clive searches through the pile on his desk. "Oh, yeah, here it is. Hmmm. Of course, that's total bullshit about the Millennium Dome concert being the 'greatest of his long and storied career.' He's what, fifteenth on the bill? Still, as you say, a gig's a gig."

Sarcastic bastard. Somehow I restrain the impulse to tell Clive to go fuck himself.

"Anyway," he continues blithely, "if we weren't talking about Mr. Clean, I would say it was just another middle-aged rock guy in rehab."

Mr. Clean is the derisive nickname music journalists started tagging Hinch with back in the early '80s when he publicly swore off using drugs and alcohol, to the dismay of many of his fans. That was bad enough, but then, in a true fit of insanity, Hinch briefly agreed to become Nancy Reagan's "just say no" spokesperson. Some rapid crisis management by a high-priced PR firm was able to salvage his career to some extent, but the damage had been done, and even in recent years he had persisted in making public statements about how good he felt since getting on the wagon. Hinch was still famous enough to be chased by the paparazzi from time to time, and judging from his most recent photos, I had to admit the guy looked healthy enough; certainly there had been no reports of drunken rampages in nightclubs. I simply had no reason to believe the guy was in need of rehab, as I explained to Clive.

"Well, maybe you're right, but the real question is, who cares?" His response was predictable. People in Clive's position are renowned for their cynicism. They all seem to have chips on their shoulders, despite the fact that, as Frank Zappa once wryly observed, music journalists are nothing more than people who can't write, interviewing people who can't speak, for the benefit of people who can't read. Clive may have been a friend—sort of—but I had always considered him kind of slimy. As I mull the thought, his voice crackles through the speakerphone once again.

"Look, nobody really gives a shit about Hinch these days," Clive mutters acidly, "other than you, of course." I'm about to slam the phone down when he begins backpedaling. "Okay, well, perhaps that's stretching things a bit. But if he's not back on the sauce or the smack, maybe he just plain flipped out. Maybe this is the first press release ever issued that actually is telling the truth."

I'm reminded that there is a reason why I like the guy. "That's the least likely possibility, I agree," I say. "But beyond the fact that press agents always lie, I doubt it."

"Why?"

"Because Hinch has always struck me as being so … I don't know, *normal*." He *was* normal, at least for a rock star. Maybe not Donnie Boyle normal, but normal enough. And definitely not the type to suffer a nervous breakdown.

Another pause. Is Clive mulling it over in his mind, or is he just losing patience with me? The latter, apparently. "Look, Bernie," he finally says, patronizingly, "I can understand your hoping there's something juicy here because it will help sell books, but frankly I don't see anything in this. Either the guy is freaking out, or he's drinking too much, or smoking too much, or shooting up too much. Despite his public image."

Maybe he's right. Maybe I *am* making this into something it isn't. Maybe my hunch that there's something sinister going on is just wishful thinking. Maybe my book is doomed to have the same boring dénouement every rock star bio has: star gets messed up on booze/drugs/smack, star enters rehab, star gets clean, star lives happily ever after. The end, cue sound of public yawning.

Then all of a sudden Clive seems to get a brainstorm. "I guess there is another possibility," he offers tentatively. Metaphorically, the clouds begin to part.

"What? What are you thinking?" I blurt out, grasping at the proverbial straw. "Come on, tell me."

"Well, maybe it's just that the tour wasn't selling tickets and the promoters have pulled the plug. Claiming Hinch has nervous exhaustion might just be management's way of allowing him to save face."

Another old scam from the rock 'n' roll annals. Why didn't I see it? Because I'm a damn fool, that's why.

"You know, you might be right," I say glumly. If true, this does not bode well for my book, that's for sure.

Clive seems to pick up on my suddenly black mood. "Well, I'm not saying that *is* what happened—only that it's a possibility," he says softly. Do I detect a note of—dare I say it—compassion in his voice? "Tell you what," he adds. "If I get a few moments, I'll make a couple of calls and see what I can find out."

To my astonishment, I find myself practically bawling. Jeez, the prospect of having to pay back my advance really *does* have me stressed out. "Thanks, Clive—I owe you," I finally stammer, holding back the tears.

"No problem, Bernie. Good luck with the book. And let me know if you ever decide to write about a musician who's actually had a hit in the last twenty years."

Click. Dial tone.

Smarmy little cocksucker.

6

Transcript: Interview with Donnie Boyle, March 26, 1998

[INDECIPHERABLE] ...yeah, I think so too, must be this new doctor. Goddamn quacks, all of them. Move a bit closer so I don't have to shout so much, willya?

Okay. So, now, remind me, where did we leave off? It's been awhile. Right, Cody's red Strat. Yeah, I remember him bringing it home—it would have been sometime in early '71—and you can be damn sure I remember how pissed off Hinch got when he found out Cody'd taken up guitar. I think Cody was wise to keep it to himself while he practiced and gained some proficiency—he didn't spring it on Hinch right away. Swore me to secrecy, though I'm not really sure why. It certainly wasn't because Cody was afraid of Hinch; hell, he wasn't afraid of *anyone*. Maybe he just wasn't a hundred percent sure himself that it would turn into anything. I remember thinking at the time that the only reason he'd bought the thing in the first place was to mess with Hinch's mind. It did get serious, though, and it did have a big effect on the band... eventually. But in the beginning Cody was careful to hide that red Strat under the bed whenever Hinch came by.

With things starting to pick up for us gig-wise, I found my role in the band changing, too. Of the three of us, I was the only one with even a vague interest in the business end of things; Cody only ever cared about the music, and Hinch, the adulation, I suppose. At gigs, I'd be the one talking us up to the club owner between sets, trying to land return bookings, while Cody would be hiding away in whatever little cubbyhole they called our dressing room, practicing on his drum pads. Hinch? He'd usually be parading out front, pretending to be watching the other bands, but really he was there to be seen—especially by the girls. So I sorta became the band's manager, not because I wanted to, but just by default.

Fact is, I grew to kind of like it. It gave me something to focus on. I started reading all the music magazines and trade rags: *Billboard* and *Rolling Stone* and *Musician*. As I learned more about the business, I could begin to see a path to stardom for us, and I truly believed we had a real shot at it. Plus it was a distraction from practicing my instrument, which, unlike the other two guys, was something I'd really come to dislike. Deep in my heart, I knew I was only a mediocre bass player at best, and that Hinch and Cody were really just carrying me, but that was okay. As I said, I never had a burning desire to be a great musician, though I did always want to be a success.

The only tough thing about being the band's manager was collecting the money. See, I've never been especially physical. Maybe I wasn't quite as skinny as I am now, but even when I was younger I never had a lot of meat on my bones. It was a problem because the club owners were notorious for ripping off bands—it wouldn't surprise me if they still are—and if you didn't have someone who could step in and face up to them and their meat-headed bouncers, you could find yourself driving home after a four-hour gig with not even enough bread in your pocket to pay for gas.

Thank goodness we had Cody. The guy was absolutely fearless when it came to protecting our interests. Didn't matter how mean and threatening the bouncers were, Cody would get right in their face if I was having any trouble collecting. More often than not the bastards would back down once they saw what a crazy motherfucker he was. Sometimes, though, they didn't, and Cody got his ass kicked more than once. I'd jump in whenever I was needed, but truth is, I really wasn't much of a help in those kinds of situations.

Hinch could throw a punch if he had to, but somehow he was usually nowhere to be found when things turned ugly. I know it may sound strange, but Cody and I actually didn't mind that our guitar player was mostly absent when we got into brawls. We didn't talk about it all that much, but we knew he was our pretty face, and so I think we both realized that if he got his lip split or his nose broken, we'd be out of work for awhile. Hinch always was a lover, not a fighter, and I guess Cody and I accepted that in him. As long as he kept turning up the charm onstage, that's really all we asked of him, and he delivered. If the price we had to pay was the occasional ass-kicking, so be it.

Things began getting a bit easier for us when we began picking up gigs out of town—Philly, Baltimore, DC—because that meant we were finally able to afford a roadie. Believe it or not, the first guy we hired went by the name of Mike Testa. Swear to God that was his real name, as in "testing, one, two, three." The guy was a real bruiser, too. Six foot three, long, curly blond hair, biceps bulging out of his rolled-up shirtsleeves. He was well-organized and he got us from gig to gig, plus he served as our enforcer whenever a club owner tried to pull the old "I'm a little short" routine on us.

Cody and I loved having Mike drive us around and set up our drums and amps so that all we had to do was turn up and play, and so we had no problem with his insistence on a weekly salary as opposed to a cut of the earnings, even though that meant he often made more money than we did. But after awhile Hinch started to grow pretty resentful. Not because of the money, but because of the girls. You see, Mike was quite handsome—even better-looking than Hinch himself, if I'm honest about it—and once we began our set, there really wasn't anything for Mr. Testa to do unless a mic flopped over or a guitar string got broken. From the stage, Hinch could see him hanging out at the bar, the ladies flocking around him like moths to the flame. Sometimes the guy would disappear for a little while and we knew he was out in the van getting a quick blowjob. As I've said, once Hinch felt secure in his relationship with Katie, he seemed to think that gave him license to stray, and it wasn't long before he was bedding every willing female in sight—and, believe me, there were lots to choose from. But it started pissing Hinch off that our roadie was getting first crack at the local talent, often taking the tastiest girls for himself. Cody and I didn't give a shit; we thought, well, why the hell not? After all, we still had plenty to pick from. Mike just had much more opportunity to chat up the ladies, and we probably would have done the same if the situation were reversed.

But Hinch was starting to get seriously pissed off at this turn in events, not least because Mr. Testa was, shall we say, considerably better endowed than any of us. In fact, he had more to offer than most men on the planet.

Hell, let's be honest: Mike's dick was a thing of wonder. Not that I spent a lot of time looking at it—I'm as straight as they come—but I had ample opportunity to view his package, not just uncoiled in the men's room as he peed in the urinal next to me, but as it was being put to real use during our post-gig partying. See, in those days we rarely could afford more than one motel room when we were on the road, so there were many a night when all four of us would be in action at the same time, sometimes even swapping partners when the opportunity presented itself. I'm not talking full-blown orgies or anything—just nice scenes with the four of us and three or four sweet little things. You ever notice how some girls can seem so demure and all when you first meet them, and then, when you get them alone and naked, they turn into raging animals? Makes me long for the days when my own equipment used to work ... even if it never measured up to that of the formidable Mike Testa.

Damn, I hate getting old.

Anyway, yeah, those were good days, but it wasn't long before Hinch started lobbying for us to fire Mike and hire a more average guy instead, if you'll pardon the pun. Cody and I began getting weary of his complaining and so we eventually gave in, I'm sorry to say.

I probably should mention that we weren't known as "Hinch and the Lynchmen" by then, although I couldn't rightly tell you what we were called, because we went through an extended period where we were constantly trying out new names for the band. One week we'd be "The Hitmen"; the next, "Grand Slam." Eventually we started going under the name "Powdered Sunshine," even though none of us had ever been near a powder, or a pill, at that point. Beer was our thing: good old working-class brewski, pure and simple. Maybe the occasional bottle of cheap red wine, but mostly longnecks. We smoked a little pot, too, of course, but none of us had that kind of stoner personality—we were all too driven in our own way—and so we never really got into it, apart from the odd joint during rehearsal, or after a gig. The serious drugs would come later, along with the fame.

I know that a lot of people envy what we did for a living, but the rock 'n' roll life is actually pretty grueling, even if you do manage to achieve the money and the hit records and the groupies and all that. You still have the same exact problems that you did when you were first starting out, huddled together in a beat-up old van with no heat and no AC, playing shit gigs. The only difference is that as you get bigger, the problems get bigger.

I don't know why it took me so long to realize this, but it's only occurred to me in recent years that celebrity and sex and drugs are really just the trappings of success. They may seem like the prizes at first—that, and the money, of course—but over time you come to realize that those are nothing more than distractions, diversions, from what's really important. For true musicians, what's important is the music itself, not how many hit records you make, or how many magazine articles are written about you, or how many fans are calling out your name when you hit the stage. Sure, most people get into the business for those bullshit kind of reasons—at least initially—but if they don't evolve past that point pretty quickly, they tend not to stick around too long. Personally, I've come across very, very few true musicians who really care more about those things than the fulfillment that comes from playing a song well. There's just something about living a superficial life that gets old really fast.

Now that I'm a certifiable Boring Old Fart, I can see that I was never a true musician myself, because the music was never the main thing to me. What became important to me was the satisfaction of landing a prestigious booking, or having a promoter tell me I was a pleasure to deal with—even just having some sleazy scumbag of a club owner actually hand over the green without an argument. That's why I made a much better manager than a bass player.

Where was I? Oh, yeah. After Hinch forced us to fire Mike Testa, we lost touch with him for quite a while, which was a shame, because I really liked the guy. But then a few years later, damned if I didn't bump into him backstage at some big festival we were playing. He was still a roadie, of course. It seems like it's in their blood, those guys: it sure ain't very often that you hear of a roadie retiring and becoming a bank teller or something. Some of them graduate to tour manager, and every now and then one of them actually gets their big break—fifteen minutes of fame on the stage instead of behind it—but for the most part, once a roadie, always a roadie. They're like bikers—a bunch of kindred spirits that have their own little society, complete with secret handshakes and a language all their own. I guess it's not all that surprising, given that they live their lives in the seedy underbelly of the music business. As I said, very little of the rock 'n' roll life is actually glamorous; it's mostly just illusion, like a magician waving his wand while his other hand slips behind his back to grab some poor rabbit around the neck. Sure, there are moments of unbelievable highs, mostly when the lights go up and the crowd begins to roar, but afterwards it's just miles and miles and hours and hours of boredom, self-doubt, pettiness and recrimination. No wonder so many musicians slip down that rabbit hole of drink and drugs. Name the biggest rock star you can think of, living what you might think is the most incredible life. In reality, I'll guarantee you he's just like the rest of us … only less so.

Shit, now I sound like some kind of damn philosopher. You gotta stop me when I start spouting off like that, okay, Bernie? I don't know, a kick in the shins, maybe. Or a whack upside the head with a two-by-four. Anyway, I think I need to break for a while. If I don't take a few whoops on this frigging machine, I'm gonna pass out on the spot.

Now, IN THE early days, we used to rehearse in back of this small print shop on the outskirts of York. The guy who owned it was a buddy of mine, and he let us store our equipment there and hold band practice a couple nights a week, after hours. It was really just a crappy little room with the paint peeling off the walls and a naked light bulb hanging off the ceiling. Cody and I usually traveled to rehearsal together, but on this particular day we must have arrived separately, for reasons that escape me now. Maybe he was coming from work or something—he would do odd jobs at construction sites every now and then to pick up some extra cash, so sometimes he'd be a bit late. But I do remember the leaves on the ground—it was a crisp fall evening, and you could almost smell winter coming.

Hinch was already there when I arrived, noodling on his guitar as he sat hunched over on this ratty sofa we'd rescued from a dumpster somewhere. Katie Q was sitting by his side, along with a friend of hers—Tina? Dina? No matter. There were often chicks hanging around at our rehearsals. Whenever Katie was there, Hinch was on his best behavior; when she wasn't, he would flirt shamelessly with anyone of the female persuasion, and sometimes go home with them, too, at the end of the evening. But on this night I'm talking about, Katie was definitely there, so Hinch was being cool. I got my bass out—a black Epiphone I'd picked in a pawnshop in town—and began tuning up. A few minutes later, Cody strolled in. To my amazement, he was carrying his guitar case. Casually, he leaned it against a PA speaker, opened it up, and proceeded to extract the cherry-red Strat.

I don't think I'll ever forget the expression on Hinch's face. You would have thought he'd just gotten kicked in the balls.

"What the hell is that?" he snapped.

Cody turned to him, totally Zen-like. You could practically feel the calm emanating from his body.

"Well, what does it look like?" he replied laconically. I thought I could hear Tina/Dina giggling.

Hinch's face turned red, but he forced a smile. "Hey, I didn't know it was my birthday," he said, smartass-like, looking at the girls. "Thanks for the present, bro, but I've already got a guitar."

Grinning from ear to ear, Cody shot right back at him. "I got a news flash for you, good buddy: it ain't for you. It's for me."

Hinch's eyes turned steely; every muscle in his body seemed to tighten. "Now tell me, good buddy, what the hell does a drummer need with a real instrument?" He made sure to emphasize the "good buddy" part so none of us could escape the venom in his words.

Ignoring him, Cody gently placed the guitar on a nearby stand. "Back in a flash," he said. "I got something else to show you."

Hinch and I watched him stride out of the room purposefully. "What's going on?" he asked me as soon as Cody was gone, sounding like a petulant child.

"I'm not sure, H," I lied, "but I think we'll find out in a minute."

A moment later our drummer returned, weighed down by a beat-up old amplifier. As Hinch watched warily, Cody plugged his guitar in and slowly and deliberately proceeded to tune up.

Finally he seemed satisfied with both tone and intonation. There was a brief moment of silence during which Cody took a deep breath, as if readying himself for something momentous. Then, all of a sudden, he blasted out a lick that seemed to resonate with every molecule in that shitty little room. The moments that followed were nothing short of a revelation. Eyes tightly shut in concentration, mouth curled as if tasting the very notes he was wringing from his instrument, Cody tore off riff after riff after riff, each flawlessly executed and dripping with emotion. The air itself seemed to vibrate in sympathy.

I was totally blown away. I mean, I knew that Cody had been practicing, but I didn't know he had gotten *that* good. I looked over at Hinch. "What the fuck?..." I could hear him mutter.

When Cody finished playing—it might have been ten seconds, it might have been ten minutes—he opened his eyes and stared straight ahead, drained and devoid of expression. Hinch's jaw was hanging open stupidly. He never looked less like a rock star.

But, you know, I have to give him a lot of credit. After gathering himself for a brief moment, Hinch stood up straight and tall and began answering Cody back the only way he knew how—with his guitar. Blasting out a perfect rendition of *Purple Haze*, Hinch shook his long locks and gazed skywards as if appealing to the very ghost of Jimi Hendrix. Cody responded with a lightning-fast blues run from the bottom of the neck all the way up to the very highest note, sustained and screaming through the gloom of the stale air. For an instant it seemed as if the earth and the moon and the sun and the stars all hung motionless, frozen in time, watching and waiting and listening for whatever might come next.

The two knights began jousting in earnest, twin cherry-red Strats held aloft like lances. Hinch would blast out a staggering flurry of notes, and Cody would answer in kind, then vice versa. Though they avoided eye contact with one another, I noticed them both stealing glances at Katie from time to time, like they were trying to impress her. There was no question that Hinch's technique was more nuanced, more polished ... but there was also no question that Cody had more fire in his playing. Soon they were pushing each other to new heights, the blasts of their screaming guitars ricocheting off the walls. I stood there rooted to the floor, too dumbfounded—hell, too *intimidated*—to even consider picking up my bass and joining in the duel. Like me, the girls were transfixed, focusing their full attention on the two combatants. Our heads were swiveling back and forth as if we were watching a championship tennis match: serve, return, volley; serve, return, volley.

Then, just as suddenly as it began, it was over. Hinch unleashed a blistering delivery of Jimmy Page's "Whole Lotta Love" solo, note perfect like he always played it, but this time imbued with a rawness and passion that I'd never before heard him coax out of his instrument ... and Cody didn't even attempt an answer. At that stage in his development—and, remember, he'd only been playing the damn guitar for a few months—he knew he couldn't hope to match that.

Temporarily vanquished but not defeated, Cody put his guitar down and caught his breath, then, with a barely perceptible shrug of his shoulders, he pulled a fat joint out of his shirt pocket. Calmly, he lit up and took a deep pull before passing the doobie to Hinch: a peace offering. A couple of hits later, we were brothers once more. Cody returned to his usual place behind the drum kit and we began rehearsing like always ... sort of. On the surface, things seemed the same, but there was a new kind of vibe hanging over us; it was as if the air had been let out of a balloon.

From that point forward, everything changed.

And the one thing I'll never forget is the look Hinch had on his face all that night, and for a long time afterwards. It was partly an expression of deep hurt, partly an expression of betrayal, but somehow it was more.

It was a look of cold fury.

AFTER THAT NIGHT, Cody started bringing his guitar regularly to rehearsals, though never to gigs. But I noticed that he'd low-key it; most of the time it would just sit there in its case, all tucked up in a corner like a silent witness. Once in awhile he might pull it out for a few minutes to show Hinch or me some fingering or a little lick, but then he'd put it right back and return to his drum kit, doing what he always did. Cody seemed to understand instinctively that brandishing that Strat under Hinch's nose any more than that might be viewed as an act of provocation, like waving a cherry-red flag in front of a bull. I guess none of us really wanted to rock the boat very much. I know that Cody especially valued his friendship with Hinch, even if it was sometimes a one-way street.

Actually, "one-way street" could pretty much describe all of Hinch's relationships: not just with Cody, but with me, too, and certainly with Katie Q—something I know she found exasperating a lot of the time. Sure, he could be a good guy on occasion—mostly when being a good guy would somehow help his situation—but on the whole it always seemed like he took more than he gave, even when we were just kids. Worse yet, he always seemed to feel entitled to all he took. Maybe the sole exception was the way he interacted with his fans: he always gave them a hundred percent onstage. He was usually pretty good about signing autographs and things like that, too—especially if the request was coming from a pretty girl who wanted a signature scrawled across her left boob in Magic Marker. I suppose you could make the case that what he took from the fans was a lot of hero worship and a shitload of money, but he always pretty much gave them what they wanted in return, too.

Still, me and Hinch and Cody, we were pretty tight back in those days. Within reason, of course. Didn't mean there wasn't pettiness or little jealousies. That's just part of being in a band; it goes with the territory. No matter what went down, though, we still thought of each other as best of friends, and there were very few people admitted into our inner circle—Katie, maybe, and, for brief periods, a handful of others—but for the most part it was just the three of us, and then there was the world outside.

As we started establishing a reputation beyond York's perimeters, I began spending more and more of my time wearing my manager's hat. Musicians are like actors in that they never think they have enough work, and we were no different. I'd literally spend hours on the phone pleading for gigs, and I was really starting to get my shit together: I'd arranged for us to pose for some publicity shots and even had cards printed up, all professional-like. All that effort was starting to pay off, but as we began moving up the food chain, more and more of the club owners began telling me they wanted to hear a demo tape before they'd give us a gig, even a low-prestige mid-week date.

Of course, the prospect of going into a recording studio got Cody fired up right away. Hinch was willing, but a bit dubious, too. He'd take the high road, expressing these high-falutin' reservations about our ability to translate the energy and vibe of our onstage act onto tape, but you knew that was basically crap. The real reason was that he was afraid that Cody might outshine him in the studio. One day they were arguing about it and he actually blurted out, "How are they gonna know how good we are if they can't see me?" He passed it off as a joke, of course, but we knew different. It didn't matter. Cody and I were solidly behind the idea, so Hinch was outvoted, and we began scouting out local studios, checking out their equipment—of course, only Cody had any idea what any of that stuff was—and then I'd rap to the owner and see if we couldn't cut a cheap deal.

While all this was percolating, Cody dropped another bombshell on us: he'd started writing songs. I suppose it was inevitable, given how fast he was developing as a musician. Up until then we'd strictly been a covers band: our repertoire consisted of whatever happened to be the week's Top 40, augmented by some personal favorites of Hinch and Cody, mostly Hendrix and Cream tunes. I'd also do a specialty number or two at every gig where I'd sing lead, mostly just to give the other guys a chance to rest their voices. I'd pick songs with dead simple bass lines and only the merest hint of a vocal melody, which allowed me to shout them rather than sing them—not only did I have a pretty terrible voice, I found it incredibly difficult to sing and play at the same time. As a result, I usually just stood rooted to one spot, kind of like Entwistle did in The Who. The audience probably thought I was focused intently on the music, but I was more usually thinking about how good the night's takings might be and whether or not we'd need to unleash Cody to collect our earnings.

Now Cody, he had a pretty good voice, for a drummer. There wasn't a lot of power there—his tone was kind of reedy—but he had excellent pitch, and he'd figured out just how to blend his vocals perfectly with Hinch's, kind of like the way Keith always meshed so well with Mick. Cody would sing a few leads every night, but it really made no sense to have him do any more than that since his voice was nowhere near as good as Hinch's. Hinch was just a natural when it came to singing. His voice was totally unique, yet, as many critics have pointed out through the years, it was at the same time familiar and comfortable: He didn't actually sound like anyone else, but somehow it was like you'd heard him before. Plus he had a great sense of dynamics. He knew instinctively just when to bring things down a notch and when to let loose. That same instinct made his phrasing dead-on, too. By easing into some syllables and attacking others, he was a master of "selling the lyric," as producers like to say.

The truth of the matter is that most bands would kill to have a lead singer as good as Hinch, and the fact that he could play guitar like a demon and also get the little girls moistening their seats with a shake of his head made him the undisputed star of our band, at least when we were onstage. But things were often quite different backstage and in the rehearsal room, where more and more it seemed like Cody was calling the shots, especially when he started bringing in original songs for us to play.

Hinch resisted at first, of course. He saw this as yet another challenge to his authority, and he was none too pleased about it. But he also knew that cover bands only go so far; so long as we were nothing more than a live jukebox, we were doomed to the club circuit and no better. And, make no mistake, Hinch had plenty of ambition burning inside him. Maybe not as much as Cody, but it was undeniably there.

In that strange dynamic that existed between Hinch and Cody, head-on confrontation never seemed to work, and they both knew it. If one of them wanted to get the other to do something, it would be accomplished only by stealth, diplomacy, and, occasionally, subterfuge. Consequently, Hinch's initial form of resistance was to act off-handed and dismissive, as if he didn't give a shit whether Cody was writing songs or not. "Hmmm, yeah, that's not too bad," would be a typical comment from him, and then he'd begin tossing off riffs from the latest Doobie Brothers or Steely Dan tune, all casual-like. He may have thought he was being subtle but his message was unmistakable: He was telling Cody, "Your music isn't as good as theirs."

But Cody perservered in that annoyingly efficient way of his, and eventually we began incorporating one, then two, then three of his new songs into our set, though Hinch pointedly refused to sing on any of them, not even backing vocals. Fact is, those early songs of Cody's weren't all that good. But at least we were on our way toward escaping the bar scene.

Then one day at rehearsal Cody threw Hinch a curveball. "I got a new one for the band," he announced, "but the thing is, it's not quite finished."

Hinch gave him a sideways glance. "And you're telling me this because…?"

Cody paused for a moment. "Well, I guess I thought you might help me finish it, dickwad."

"Yeah, right, that'll happen," Hinch mumbled sarcastically before turning his attention to an invisible fleck of dust on his bell-bottoms.

Ignoring the comment, Cody pulled his red Strat out of its case and proceeded to play down what he had. Admittedly, it was just a fragment of a song, and it was kind of rough, but I thought it had a pretty good hook, and the melody seemed tailor-made for Hinch's voice.

When he was done, Hinch said nothing. I made an awkward attempt to bridge the silence, saying, "Hey, man, that really rocked," or something equally lame, but to no avail, as Hinch continued examining every square inch of his awful green velvet trousers. Realizing that to persist would only invite defeat, Cody made the sensible decision to return to his drum kit and count in a run-through of whatever Three Dog Night piece of crap we'd been rehearsing.

And that was the end of that … or so I thought. But the following week at rehearsal Hinch started casually playing a tasty little rhythm lick I hadn't heard before, softly singing a lyric in accompaniment. It was merely a verse, without a chorus or bridge—just a snippet of something.

"What was that, bro?" Cody asked, trying to hold back the shit-eating grin beginning to spread across his face. I suspected he already knew the answer.

"That, Mr. Mozart, is the missing piece of the puzzle you asked for." Hinch was trying to look bored but I could tell that he was excited, deep down.

After waiting just long enough to appear respectful, but not long enough to seem disdainful, Cody finally issued his ruling, co-opting not only Hinch's phrase but his tone of voice: "You know, that's not too bad." Four clicks of his drumsticks later we were off and running. It was no masterpiece, but it was a start, and, more importantly, the Hinchton/Jeffries songwriting team was born. Five years and a team of lawyers later the body was officially laid to rest … but that's a story for another day.

———

No, I'm okay. I just needed to take a breather; goddamn lungs aren't worth a damn any more. Anyway, let's finish what we were talking about. Now, soon after Hinch finished that song of Cody's, I noticed that there were very few times when Cody would come to rehearsal and present us with a fully completed tune. More often, there would be a part conveniently missing, which he would duly wait for Hinch to provide. Hinch would always be dismissive at first, and he very rarely would actually put any work into the song right there and then, but a week or two later he'd turn up with just the bit that was needed. Was it better than anything Cody might have come up with on his own? Hard to say. But that business of roping Hinch in by only presenting half-finished songs, that was so Cody. He truly was a master diplomat in those days: He knew how important it would be to the band's development to start performing original material, and he knew he could never effect that kind of change without Hinch's participation. It really was a stroke of genius.

Hinch, on the other hand, he never gave a shit about diplomacy. He knew that he was the only indispensable person in the band—I was a mediocre bass player at best, who didn't provide much in the way of either musicianship or showmanship, so I'm sure he thought that I could be easily replaced if need be. In fact, I think he thought Cody was just as replaceable, so he just barreled ahead, doing whatever he wanted. One night after a gig, he and I were shooting the shit—I don't know where Cody was, but he definitely wasn't part of this conversation—and to my surprise, Hinch confided that he'd been studying up some on the financial aspects of the music business.

"I read this article in a magazine," he told me, "where they were talking about this thing called publishing royalties. Seems that they can amount to a lot of bread—in fact, a whole shitload of bread." He paused expectantly. It seemed like he was looking to me for confirmation.

"Yeah, I think that's right," I said with as much authority as I could muster. I myself had only a vague idea at the time about how those things worked.

"According to this article, it's the songwriters who get the big bucks in any band," Hinch continued. "For instance, John and Paul make a lot more than George and Ringo. Mick and Keith pull in a lot more than the other Stones, too."

"Is that so?"

"Yeah. Interesting stuff."

The very next week Hinch turned up at rehearsal with not one, but two songs. Finished songs. No missing parts, no request for help or input from Cody. They were shitty songs with sophomoric lyrics, but they were complete, and, as the chord charts he handed out to us indicated, they were credited to "T. Hinchton" alone.

I exchanged glances with Cody as Hinch ran them down. Cody looked a little hurt, but he also looked resigned. Hinch didn't bother asking us what we thought of either song, and we didn't bother telling him, but we spent most of that rehearsal learning our parts until it sounded tight and polished. By the weekend, both songs were in our set. As I said, they were total crap, but Hinch did a lot of triumphant rock star posing as we played them and I've got to give him credit: He sold those dumb-ass lyrics as if they actually meant something. And in our set those songs would stay, too, for quite a while, until Hinch came up with a couple of slightly less shitty songs a few months later.

Cody may not have been happy with this turn of events, but, as I said, he knew better than to take Hinch head-on. So he just kept doing what he had been doing—turning up at rehearsal with half-finished songs, always leaving something for Hinch to contribute. Hinch seemed content enough with this arrangement, and he even started singing on a few of those collaborations, which made us all happy since we knew that any new song had a much better chance of getting into the set list—and being accepted by our fans—if Hinch was up at that microphone making goo-goo eyes at the girls. That's just the way things were.

Then one day in late spring I got a call from the owner of one of the demo studios we'd been casing. He offered me a deal too good to turn down: One of his bookings had gotten cancelled at the last minute, and so he was stuck with nearly a week's worth of empty studio time—"down" time, they call it—which he was willing to sell us real cheap. After checking with Cody, who assured me that their recording equipment was up to snuff, I called the dude back and sealed the deal. All of a sudden we were about to become a recording band.

Naturally enough, this precipitated a huge argument within our ranks. Hinch was adamant that we should record a bunch of cover songs and nothing else. Cody was equally determined to include several of the original songs he and Hinch had been laboring over in recent weeks.

I could see both their points. Hinch was absolutely right when he said that no club owner in our circuit would be the least bit interested in hearing anything other than cover tunes, and that to put even one original song on the tape might lessen our chances of landing a booking, which was, after all, the object of the exercise. On the other hand, Cody made the valid point that recording some of the new songs would provide us with a golden opportunity to get them out into the world and maybe even propel us to bigger things.

In the end, I had to side with Hinch. We only had a few hundred bucks in the band kitty at that point in time, and we had to make every one of them count. If the tape landed us new and better-paying gigs, I argued, we could consider using some of the increased income to fund a second recording session down the road, in which we could concentrate on our originals. Even outvoted two to one, Cody couldn't be budged, though—he always was one stubborn son of a bitch. Problem was, Hinch wouldn't back down either.

Eventually, a compromise was hammered out. The band would first lay down a set of cover tunes to everyone's satisfaction, which we estimated would take two or three days to record and mix. Then and only then would we attempt to record an original song. But there was a caveat: Hinch refused to allow me to spend any of the band's money on the recording of said original tune ... even though he stipulated that it had to be one of his songs, not one that he and Cody had worked on together. He'd play on it, he said, but he wouldn't pay for it.

To my astonishment, Cody told Hinch to fuck off. It was the first of two times that I ever heard him do that, and I haven't decided yet if I'm going to tell you about the other one. Hinch didn't give a shit, though. He just flipped Cody the bird and said, "Hey, do whatever you want with the extra studio time, bro. Just pay for it yourself and leave me out of it."

And you know what? Damned if Cody didn't do exactly that ... and damned if Hinch didn't end up eating his words. It was the pigheadedness of both of them which would ultimately take us to the next level. At last, we were on our way ... though none of us knew it at the time.

7

So much has been going on the last few days, I hardly know where to begin. It all started when Clive called back. Much to his chagrin, it turned out that his theory about Hinch's case of "nervous exhaustion" actually being a cover-up for slow ticket sales was wrong. In fact, most of the gigs were actually sold out well in advance and the European promoters had already collectively taken the first steps to file a lawsuit against Schiffman—a costly procedure that would not have been undertaken if they weren't serious.

On the one hand, it's gratifying to know that my instincts were correct, but on the other, my life has just gotten even more complicated. In a few hours' time I board a flight to Amsterdam, where Hinch was last seen. It seems I have no choice but to get on the damn plane; there's simply nothing more I can accomplish here in L.A., especially since being informed by the new pert receptionist at Schiffman Entertainment International that Chloe was no longer employed there.

Now the one ally I had in the Hinch organization was gone, "terminated" into the void. It looks like I'm going to have to get to the bottom of things all by my lonesome self.

And lonesome I shall be for some time to come, it appears. Britney declined my invitation to accompany me ... a little too readily, I thought. Using pressing schoolwork as her excuse—when did that ever stop her from a spur-of-the-moment shopping spree in Santa Barbara?—she dismissed my pleas with a wave of her hand. "No, you go—I'll be fine," she demurred. Well, of course she'd be *fine*. What Southern Cal babe with a body like that *wouldn't* be fine, especially when unencumbered by a jealous middle-aged chaperone? With me gone, Britney would be free to party with her unbearably good-looking young friends of both sexes, hopping from club to club doing belly-button shots until dawn, while I slogged through the cold, damp streets of Amsterdam searching for the answer to a mystery I wasn't sure even existed.

No, I was quite certain Britney would be fine. I wasn't nearly as convinced that *I* would be fine, and she did absolutely nothing to reassure me as I packed.

"Don't they have lots of diamonds in Amsterdam?" she purred, stretching out seductively on the bed as I folded underwear and placed it carefully inside my fraying suitcase. Lately she seems to be living in that damned bed.

"Diamonds? I guess so. Smuggled ones, anyway." I tried my best to appear uninterested.

"Bring me back a few, will you, sweetie?"

I glared at her, astonished. Could she possibly be that self-centered? With me, Bernie Temkin, the love of her life, about to board a plane to fly halfway around the world to probe the murky depths of the music business underworld and find God knows what, was that all she could think of?

"Why are you looking at me that way?" she said, pouting. "You know how much I love presents."

Pointedly ignoring her, I continued my task of furiously bundling socks into mismatched pairs.

"Oh, come on, stop sulking," she cajoled, crossing the room until she was right behind me. As her arms snaked around my mid-section, I could feel her hot breath in my right ear. "Think of how great the catch-up sex will be when you get back," she whispered before plunging her tongue in.

Normally at this point I would have been getting a raging hard-on. Now I felt nothing but rage. Red-faced, I continued folding and bundling.

This accomplished nothing other than to make Britney more intent on distracting me. Slowly and purposefully, she bent down to retrieve a stray sock, allowing me a view of her gorgeously round ass clad in sheer white panties. Standing up quickly, she caught me leering and laughed.

"I see I still know how to get your attention," she said, licking her lips. "Maybe we should just start the catch-up sex right now."

I have to admit it was a tempting proposition. How much could a few smuggled diamonds cost, anyway?

TWELVE HOURS LATER I landed in Amsterdam, head pounding from lack of sleep and legs aching from lack of circulation. I had spent the entire flight wedged into a coach class seat being kicked non-stop by the Brat From Hell behind me while his mother napped peacefully.

Typical.

Sol, my prince of an agent, had refused to even consider requesting that Landis Books pick up my travel expenses. "Try to see it from their point of view, *boychik*," he explained in his most patronizing listen-to-reason tone of voice. "They've already given you a million dollars and gotten nothing in return; in fact, they're on the verge of suing you."

"But couldn't you at least ask?" I kept whining, fully aware that he wouldn't.

"Bernie, you're a first-class putz," he finally sighed before slamming the phone down on me.

I wouldn't have minded the insult if it had landed me a first-class seat, but I had allowed the cheapskate in me to overrule all semblance of common sense, and now I was paying the *real* price, not in dollars but in weariness. I navigated my way through customs and immigration on autopilot and eventually stumbled my way out of the Schiphol. The taxi line was unbearably long so I cast about for an alternative. Bleary-eyed, I accepted the first ride offered me by a gypsy cab though I was certain I was going to be ripped off. I wasn't disappointed. After being taken on a lengthy yet decidedly non-scenic route that apparently ran through Istanbul, we finally arrived at my destination—a seedy-looking hotel near the Leidseplein that didn't look anything like the photo in the brochure. I shoved a fistful of Monopoly money into the driver's hand, cursing him loudly to the gods, and shuffled into the lobby, dragging my suitcase and sorry ass behind me. The desk clerk prided himself on his mastery of English, though he had neither command of the language nor my reservation, and so it was only after nearly an hour of pantomime arguing that I finally found myself in a tiny, airless room after climbing up five dimly lit flights of steps—no elevator, of course—carrying my own fucking bags. Within seconds of falling onto the bed, I was fast asleep.

It was four in the afternoon.

Which is why I found myself wandering around the streets of Amsterdam at two in the morning, freezing, wide awake and starving. I had picked up the phone in my room and discovered that, despite being located in the heart of the tourist district, my hotel offered not even the slightest semblance of room service, and it soon became clear that trying to explain the concept to the befuddled operator on the line would be a total exercise in frustration. After climbing down five goddamn flights of stairs in near-darkness, I stepped outside into the deserted plaza and surveyed the prospects. A few bars were still open, though I was pretty sure they could only provide nourishment of the liquid variety. But my craving right now was for food, and I wasn't especially fussy about what kind, either. Off in the distance I spotted a neon sign that appeared promising: *Leidseplein Kaffeeshop*, it loudly proclaimed as it blinked on and off, a beacon in the night.

Crossing the square at a fast clip, I had visions of ham and eggs swimming around my head, but after excitedly opening the door, I found myself in a tiny shop that offered nothing but overpriced espressos and a rather grim selection of unappetizing pastries. *No, this won't do at all*, I thought as I headed back out in search of real food, but then some primal low-blood-sugar instinct kicked in and transported me back to the pastry case, where I pointed to a brownie that appeared to have my name on it.

"Can I get one of those to go?" I asked the bored counterman.

He looked at me blankly.

"To go?" he repeated. Suddenly he seemed to understand; I could almost see the little light bulb go off over his sleepy head. "Ah, yes, to take away. One space cake, to take away ... to go. Any coffee with that?"

"Uh, no thanks." I turned to leave, stuffing the brownie in my coat pocket. "By the way, do you know where I could get some food around here?" I asked.

"Food? But the space cake, it is food, no?"

"Yes, I guess it is," I conceded. "But I mean real food. You know, like dinner."

"Ahh, of course, you are an American," he said, now interested. "For you, dinner is steak, rare, and with baked potato, yes?"

Salivating at the mere suggestion, I fairly shouted, "Yes! Steak with baked potato! Exactly!"

The pendulum controlling his mood suddenly swung to the other extreme. "But it is the middle of the night," he intoned sadly, stating the obvious. I hate people who state the obvious. "You cannot get steak in Amsterdam in the middle of the night, like you can in America," he added, unhelpfully.

My face fell as the counterman scratched his head, deep in thought. "I suppose you could find some *kroketten* in the *automatiek*," he finally allowed. "But they are filled in the mornings, so I don't think it would be very nice now."

I'd heard of the Dutch *automatiek*—street-side food dispensers not dissimilar to the Horn and Hardart's of my New York youth—and I'd been warned that their quality control often left much to be desired, especially at the end of the day, when the only things left for the wandering drunks were rancid croquettes and stale ramen noodles. I was hungry, but I wasn't quite *that* hungry.

"Nothing else?" I asked glumly.

"Hmmm," he intoned. He appeared to be meditating. Suddenly he opened his eyes wide as if struck by divine inspiration. "The Melkweg—they have a restaurant open all night. You should be able to get some dinner there. Maybe even," he added slyly, "steak and baked potato."

The Melkweg—Dutch for "Milky Way"—was a famous floating club I had planned to visit while I was in town anyway; it wasn't even supposed to be all that far from the Leidseplein.

"*Dank je wel*," I replied, showing off the little Dutch I'd learned from my guidebook. I gave the clerk a high-five and headed back out into the night, pulling the brownie from my pocket as I strode toward redemption.

THE MELKWEG IS not quite as nearby as I thought it would be, or perhaps it is the dizzying effect of the brownie which I at first misinterpreted as rapidly rising blood sugar but soon realize is the result of a massive infusion of the industrial-grade cannabis that put the space in the cake. By the time I arrive at the towering barge strung with Christmas lights sitting atop one of Amsterdam's fouler-smelling canals, I am stoned out of my head and suffering from the most severe case of the munchies ever known to man. Food is no longer the goal; it has become the sole focus of my very existence, a priority just slightly more important than breathing.

Judging from the cacophony emanating from its warehouse-like windows and throngs of Dutch youth hanging around the front entrance puffing away on every possible combination of tobacco, cannabis and hashish, the coffeeshop counterman was absolutely right about this being an all-night joint. I shove my way through the milling crowd, pausing only long enough to pay the cover charge and get my hand stamped with what appears to be an undulating crab. Once inside, I am faced with an even larger gathering assembled in a huge lobby area the size of an airplane hangar. On the periphery I can make out vendor booths of all varieties, selling everything from tie-dyed T-shirts to cheap glass jewelry to prerolled joints to the ubiquitous space cakes ... but, alas, not a hot dog in sight. I sniff the air like a bloodhound on the trail of a rabbit, trying to discern the scent of even a moldering kernel of popcorn, but all I pick up is incense and the musty scent of the unwashed sea of humanity surrounding me.

Interspersed between the vendors are a series of doors, and each time one opens, a blast of music pours out. In a stoned haze, I begin exploring, tentatively at first, then with a growing sense of urgency. Behind door one, a proto-punk trio thrashing away on a large stage at a deafening volume, crowd pogoing away in rhythm to the throbbing bass; behind door two, a Neil Young look-alike mournfully pumping a harmonium while occasionally emitting howls of anguish that resemble the bleats of a dying goat. Door three, country music being played badly by a motley group of middle-aged hipsters stuffed into Nudie suits two sizes too small, accompanied by whoops, hollers, and the occasional sound of a shattering beer bottle as shards of glass rain down on the enthusiastically inebriated audience. Door four reveals a tacky disco with dozens of spinning balls hanging from the ceiling, populated by a huge throng of Ecstasy-laden teenagers moving as one to the beat of an appallingly loud bass drum.

Dammit, where's that fucking restaurant?

I stagger back out into the central lobby and spy a set of stairs snaking up toward the second floor. Hanging on to the handrail for dear life, I ascend slowly. In the rarified atmosphere up here things are a little quieter, a bit more civilized. Perhaps it's due to the physical challenge of climbing the stairs, something which the most paralytic of the crowd are probably incapable of.

Around the balustrade are more doors, yet the sounds coming from behind them are slightly more sedate. Behind the first one I discover an undernourished waif dressed all in black seated on a tiny stage. Staring catatonically straight ahead, she trills a Dutch folk song while strumming a badly out of tune acoustic guitar, the stoner couples in the audience gazing adoringly up at her as they sit cross-legged on the floor. Door two reveals a mime in full makeup doing an embarrassingly poor rendition of climbing-a-ladder-while-trapped-inside-a-small-box, to the obvious annoyance of his miniscule audience.

But then there is door three.

Door three! Nirvana, salvation, the gates of paradise!

I open door three, and what lies before me is, wonder of wonders ... a buffet.

Not just any buffet, but the finest, most delectable collection of meticulously prepared culinary delights ever known to man. Or a pile of dog shit. Frankly, I don't care. It's food.

And there's no line! At breakneck speed I hustle inside, grab a plate, and begin piling spoonful after spoonful of meat, fish, rice, potatoes, vegetables, cold salads, warm salads, cheeses, fruit, bread, cake, pastry, pudding, whipped cream, ice cream, and custard cream, all mixed together into one revolting mess. I don't care. Scant seconds later I am standing at the nearest table, greedily shoveling stupid quantities of food into the slobbering maw that used to be my mouth. I am aware that the lip-smacking noises I am making are not just gross but downright obscene, yet I only vaguely hope that there are no civilized human beings—especially those of the opposite sex—around to hear, and see, me make a spectacle of myself. I am utterly disgusted at my own behavior, yet powerless to cease and desist.

But as the sheer quantity of inhaled foodstuffs expands my stomach to bursting proportions, rising ominously into the lower depths of my esophagus, I slowly begin to feel satiated. The pangs of hunger I have been living with for what feels like the last hundred and eighty-two years of my life begin to abate, and it is then, and only then, that I pause to take in my surroundings.

That's when I realize that I am the only person in the room who is not butt naked.

Actually, I exaggerate. But only slightly. I am the only person in the room who is neither butt naked nor wearing leather, chains, or nipple rings.

Confused, I swivel my head and for the first time discover that over at the far end of the room, hidden behind the buffet, is a modest stage area. And on that stage there are a number of people fucking.

No, only a few of them are fucking. The rest are enthusiastically licking, sucking, groping, stroking, fellating, cunnilinguing and dildoing. Gathered around them is a small but clearly interested group of voyeurs, men's penises in various states of erection, women's nipples in various states of hardness. Some are studiously masturbating, goofy looks of orgasmic glee on their reddened faces.

All of this is happening within a couple of feet of the buffet table, around which a slightly larger crowd of minimally clad couples have now gathered, politely helping themselves to what I note with dismay are modest, nay, dainty portions of food. I look down at the rapidly decomposing remains scattered willy-nilly on my plate and am thoroughly disgusted with both my greed and lack of culinary discrimination: remnants of pork fat oozing into coconut cream pie, rivulets of strawberry juice tracing paths through half-depleted mounds of mashed potatoes, marinated goat cheese melting into the last sad remnants of chocolate-laden creamed herring.

I begin to feel a strange combination of arousal and nausea. There's a couple doing disgraceful things to one another just inches from my left knee; another bumping and grinding uncontrollably to my right. I hear a loud moan come from directly behind me and turn around just in time to view a fully engorged penis encased in a cock ring shoot a stream of semen into the air, splattering the ecstatic couples underneath. I duck instinctively as the last, final spurt of ejaculate whistles past my ear like a tracer before landing squarely on my plate, where it comes to rest gently atop a piece of rum baba.

I stare, mortified, as it drips sadly, a mute testimonial to human depravity. An overweight chick in latex sidles up to me, pendulous breasts swaying in the nonexistent breeze.

Gesturing toward the defiled pastry, she asks me a question in a thick Dutch accent that, were I not to repeat it now, would be nothing short of unspeakable.

"Are you going to eat that?"

I shake my head numbly as she delicately picks up the rum baba and begins to nibble coyly at the edges. There is nothing left for me but to upchuck, which I do, copiously and violently.

THE REST IS A BLUR. Apparently I was forcefully ejected from the Melkweg, in violation of Dutch laws against projectile vomiting in the middle of a public sex show, and was escorted by a number of uniformed policemen back to my hotel room, where I spent the next twelve hours poised over my toilet wishing I were dead.

Finally I collapsed into a deep and darkly disturbing sleep, my body rebelling against every injustice that had been done to it since the moment of my birth.

When I finally awoke two days later I felt starkly depleted, but nearly normal.

The first thing I do is call Britney. Poor thing, she must be frantic, having not heard from me for more than three days.

"This is Bernie and Britney," the phone machine chirps happily. "Leave a message and we'll get back to you ... if we feel like it." At the time, I couldn't resist tacking on the smartass sign-off; now, it just makes me feel like even more of an asshole.

"Britney, baby, it's me," I intone reassuringly. "Sorry I didn't call earlier, but something came up"—actually, a *lot* came up—"and, um, I couldn't get to the phone until now. I know you've got to be worried, but I want you to know that I'm fine, and I love you, and ..." My voice trails off, unsure what to add. "Er, well, anyway, take care and I'll talk to you soon." God, I really *am* a dork. Take care? What does she have to take care of? She has my hotel number—I made sure to leave it with her and even wrote it on a slip of paper which I carefully taped onto our bathroom mirror—but judging from the message light stubbornly not blinking on the phone, she obviously hasn't called.

I check downstairs with the desk clerk and even though his English hasn't improved one iota, he eventually convinces me that yes, the message light is working, and, no, there have been no calls for me. Guess she's busy with schoolwork or something.

Or something.

Well, no time to dwell on that, Bernie boy. Time to get back to that positive thinking you displayed back in L.A. Time to get back to the plan.

Unfortunately, my plan, as it were, is quite thin on detail. Step one: call the Amsterdam office of Schiffman Entertainment International, where I fully expect to be rebuffed and treated with the same disdain that I encountered back in the States, only in a different language. Step two: get in touch with the local Dutch promoter to see if he can cast any light onto the whereabouts of Tommy Hinchton. Step three: well, to paraphrase Monty Python, there is no step three. Step four? See step three.

With a deep sigh I dial the number I have for Schiffman's local office. An infuriatingly brief conversation with an infuriatingly haughty receptionist (where *do* they find these people? Do they all come from central casting?) reveals that, no Alan Schiffman is not available, and, no, they have no information about Hinch other than what is in the press release.

Step two goes a little easier. The gruff voice that answers the phone at Hans Uhlemeyer Promotions clearly does not belong to a cute receptionist; in fact, I imagine the longshoreman at the other end of the line to have forearms the size of the QE II, but it turns out he speaks English reasonably well, and even seems like a pretty nice guy. I explain my reason for the call and ask if I can make an appointment to meet with Uhlemeyer to discuss the cancelled Hinch tour.

"Yah, I think so," he says affably. "Hang on." I begin readying myself mentally for the Dutch version of Muzak while I am put on hold but am instead surprised to hear a loud bellow rattle the earpiece.

"HANS!"

In the background, I hear muffled conversation. Hans is clearly interested, or is being persuaded to see me, I can't tell which.

"When can you come in?" the voice says.

I'm not really prepared for a meeting right now. On the other hand, I feel I've got to seize any opportunity that comes my way. Hey, the guy is actually willing to meet with me; that's more than I've gotten from Schiffman in two years of trying.

"Um, this evening?"

No response.

"In a couple of hours?"

More silence.

"Now?"

"Yah. Now will be good."

FIFTEEN MINUTES FROM now I am climbing the stairs in the narrow building (hell, *all* the buildings here are narrow) that houses the shabby offices of Hans Uhlemeyer Promotions. There's no longshoreman at the front desk, though; in fact, there is no front desk. Instead, the steps lead to a dingy hallway, the gloom of the late afternoon sun only vaguely illuminating the peeling wallpaper. Behind the lone door I hear voices. Tentatively, I knock.

"Yah, who is that?"

"Bernie Temkin. The American? I phoned a little while ago."

Muffled sounds, followed by the squeak of a chair scraping across a bare wooden floor.

"Yah, come in."

I open the door, hand extended in greeting. The next thing I know I am lying on said floor, seeing stars, blood gushing from my nose.

"ALAN SCHIFFMAN IS A NO-GOOD MUDDERFUCKING

PIECE OF SHIT!" the voice above me shouts. It hurts to look up.

Towering over me are two men, one clearly agitated, the other calmly shaking his fist as if to get the circulation going; I'm guessing he's the one who cold-cocked me. Idiotically, I find myself hoping that the bridge of my nose did some damage to his hand.

"What the fuck...?" I protest feebly.

"YOU TELL THAT SCUMBAG BASTARD PRICK THAT HE IS A DEAD MAN!" the agitated figure standing over me shrieks at the top of his lungs. Like a wounded animal, I roll over and assume the fetal position, shutting my eyes tightly. Why I do this I have no idea; it's not as if it would hurt any less if I couldn't see the oncoming kick in the nuts I was fully expecting to occur.

But there is no kick in the nuts, no follow-up blow to the head; only silence. Slowly I open my eyes and survey the scene. The shouter is dressed fashionably in a knit pullover and sports coat, with neatly pressed slacks. From my vantage point on the floor I note his finely polished shoes. His rather larger companion—still nursing his hand—is much more casual, clad in baggy T-shirt and ill-fitting khakis. Both men have thinning blond hair atop chiseled Aryan looks.

There is an awkward silence while we look each other over. Fashion Plate seems to be trying to decide whether to have me exterminated right there and then.

"Look, fellows," I whimper from the floor. "I don't work for Alan Schiffman. In fact, I barely know the guy."

"You're a lying American cocksucker," growls Fashion Plate in a thick Dutch accent that makes it sound as if I am a lying American cogsooker. Baggy T-Shirt moves a little closer. Involuntarily, I cringe. This, for some reason, causes them both to laugh.

"Look at him," says Baggy T-Shirt. "Look at the way he's screwing up his face, like a little baby."

"Yah," says Fashion Plate before dissolving into a fit of decidedly unmacho-like giggles. "Like a little baby American cogsooker."

I lay there looking at them both in disbelief. It's like a scene out of a Three Stooges movie. Any second now I expect Moe to sneak up from behind and bop them over the head with a hammer.

No such luck. Finally Fashion Plate leans over and pulls me up by the collar. "You're telling me the truth?" he asks, searching my face for any signs of twitchiness. I can't help but notice that he has the bluest eyes I've ever seen.

I meet his gaze head-on. "I'm telling you the truth. I'm just a writer writing a book. A book about Hinch." His face starts to darken. "But I don't work for Alan Schiffman."

Something in my face seems to reassure him. Relaxing his demeanor, he sticks out his hand as if we are now best buddies.

"So," he says, beaming, "I am Hans Uhlemeyer. I have two questions for you, Mr. American Writer. One, what is it that brings you to our fair country? And, two, where can we find Alan Schiffman?"

This sounds ominous to me. I can't help but notice Baggy T-Shirt beginning to move toward me once again.

"Don't mind Rudie," Hans purrs. "He's got a quick temper but he's actually a very nice fellow." Rudie's scowl begins to turn into a broad grin. They both continue to stare at me expectantly.

"Look," I say timidly, "I'm here because Amsterdam is the last place anyone has seen Hinch publicly. I'm trying to track him down so I can finish my book. But I have no idea where Alan Schiffman is. In fact, he hasn't talked to me for over a year."

"Over a year, you say?" Hans inquires with false politeness. "And tell me, have you talked to *him* during that time?"

"Well, no. I mean, how could I?" I'm flummoxed. Both Hans and Rudie seem amused by my discomfiture. "I mean, I've tried contacting him because of this book I'm writing, but he just doesn't return my calls. So, no, neither of us has spoken to each other."

This seems to satisfy Hans. "So, then, we are all allies, yah?"

"Allies, yah. I mean yes."

"And if you were to find Alan Schiffman, you would tell us where he is, yah?"

There seems to be no alternative answer to this question other than yah. Which is what I tell them. I mean it, too. I have no loyalty to Schiffman; in fact, I'd be quite happy if Rudie were to issue him the same greeting I just received. Just thinking about it makes me happy. Unfortunately, it also reminds me that my nose is throbbing and still bleeding profusely.

"Come, my American friend," says Hans expansively, putting his arm around my shoulder. "Let's get you cleaned up and then get you a drink. I have a feeling we have much to discuss."

As it turned out, we had quite a *lot* to discuss.

8

Transcript: Interview with Donnie Boyle, April 4, 1998

YOU EVER HEAR those demos we were talking about, Bernie? They came out on one of those "best of" box sets a few years back. Even before then, they were pretty heavily bootlegged. I'm telling you, what Cody did with those tapes was nothing short of astonishing. Even more amazing was that he kept his cool, considering the king-size chip Hinch had on his shoulder at the time. I don't know if it was resentment at the spotlight being taken away from him, or lack of self-confidence—you never really know what you sound like until you've listened back to a recording of yourself—but whatever it was, Hinch was a total pain in the ass the whole time. "Close enough for rock 'n' roll" became his mantra, though the whole point of the exercise was to get it *better* than just "close enough," as Cody calmly kept reminding him. How he remained so calm I have no idea, since deep down he must have been furious, especially since he was paying for a lot of the recording time out of his own pocket. But somehow he sucked it up and we got through the sessions without killing each other.

We were fortunate in that the nerdy-looking sound engineer who worked at the studio did seem to know what he was doing, and, more importantly, actually seemed to give a shit about getting it right. He and Cody quickly bonded, and though I tried my hardest to remain neutral, I had to admit I agreed with them way more often than I did with Hinch, who seemed interested in only one thing: getting the hell out of there as soon as possible. But Cody and the engineer—I can't remember his name, Frank or Fred something—persisted, and they managed to get things sounding pretty damn good after awhile. It was my first time in a recording studio as well, and I remember thinking that it was no place for someone as impatient as Hinch. Slowly it began to dawn on me that it was a process—sometimes an excruciating process—and that there's a reason why bands always sound so much better on record than they ever do onstage. It's not just a matter of how well you play, or how good the equipment is, or even how skilled the engineer is technically. It's got way more to do with the care taken, the time expended, and, most of all, everyone's degree of anal-retentiveness.

"Hit that tom-tom again," Frank Fred would say over and over again to Cody, sometimes for hours at a time, before leaving the sanctity of the control booth to confer with our unfailingly patient drummer in the studio. All of us in the booth—Hinch, myself, sometimes Katie Q, plus whatever other friends had been favored with an invitation—would have long ago developed a splitting headache at listening to that damned thudding, but Cody would keep whacking away at that tom-tom, and the engineer would keep moving microphones around and tweaking mysterious-looking knobs and faders. At first I couldn't hear any difference at all but damned if it didn't eventually start sounding like the most incredible tom-tom you ever heard, better even than we'd heard on some Kiss records.

Then it would all start all over again with the cymbals, or the snare drum, or my bass, or Hinch's guitar. Hour after hour of thwacking/plunking/twanging away until your head started throbbing and you just wanted to jam knitting needles into your eyeballs to make it stop … and then all of sudden it would start sounding amazing, and you'd think, hell, that was worth it.

I once read this article about a commercial jet pilot who described his job as millions of hours of boredom interspersed with a few seconds of sheer terror. That's actually pretty much what it's like for people who make records for a living, except that those few seconds are of elation rather than terror. When everyone gets their act together and plays as well as they can possibly play in perfect coordination with everyone else—something record producers like to call "nailing it"—everyone in the room knows it, and it truly is a magic moment. It's almost like a glow settles over everyone: musicians, technicians, and onlookers alike. Those are the moments you live for when you're in the studio, but the dirty little secret of the music industry is that it often takes many, many tedious hours to get to that point—sometimes even days, weeks, or months.

In our case, it took us almost four days to nail our first song—counting the time we spent getting sounds together, which nearly drove Hinch crazy—and then another day and half to get the rest of the cover tunes recorded. Cody was like a Buddha through it all, totally at peace yet quietly brimming with confidence. "Just hang tight; we'll get there," he kept repeating softly, keeping Hinch and me motivated, even when all we wanted to do was throw in the towel. I'm sure Hinch couldn't understand any better than I could why a three-minute song which took us three minutes to play, and play well, onstage, should be taking us three hours or more to get right. The reason came partly from nervousness, but also partly from the intense scrutiny that a recording receives as compared with a live show. Every error you make—every misplayed note, every flubbed beat, every slightly mistuned string—leaps out at you when you hear the tape being played back. It's different at a gig, where everyone is so excited by the spectacle; the lights, the antics of the lead singer, the musty smell of beer in the air, the promise of possibly getting laid at night's end. All too often, that's what fools an audience into thinking that they're witnessing a masterful once-in-a-lifetime performance instead of the depressingly sloppy shit that's actually being played onstage.

Maybe it was just a matter of being intimidated, but I think it was the lack of audience feedback that most threw Hinch when we were in the studio making that first demo tape. There was no cheering crowd to tell him how wonderful he was, or how exciting his solos had been, or how enthralled they were with his rock star posing. Katie was present for a lot of the sessions, it's true, and she was utterly supportive of all of us, but that alone was never enough for Hinch—he always needed lots of admiring women swooning at his feet to feel motivated. He had to have known how badly he was messing up every time we listened to another crappy playback but of course he couldn't bring himself to say so, hence the "close enough for rock 'n' roll" mantra. But Cody gently spurred him on, even when it appeared to me that Hinch was moments away from storming out of there, maybe even quitting the band altogether.

I was having my own problems in the studio, but it didn't bother me as much because I expected to make mistakes. That's why I didn't get nearly as frustrated as Hinch when I was listening to those early playbacks. Yeah, I wanted to get it right, but I knew my limitations. I also had the safety net of knowing that the band was not especially dependent on me, at least not in terms of my musical abilities. Somehow I knew that Cody would find a way around it. And damned if the little bastard didn't do just that.

"Do me a favor, Donnie," he said one night as we were packing up to go home. "Leave your bass here, will you? I'll bring it home with me later." He and I were still sharing digs in a tiny apartment in York at the time.

"Later? Aren't you coming to the bar with us?" I asked. We'd made plans to drop our gear off at the rehearsal room and then meet up at a local dive to get shit-faced.

"Of course," Cody assured me. "But I've got a little more work to do here before I knock off. Just leave the bass, okay, bro?"

I was perplexed as to the reason for the request but simply said, sure. Then Hinch and Katie and I waltzed out the door and spent the rest of the night getting so severely wasted I don't think we ever even noticed that Cody never turned up.

When I finally got home in the wee hours of the morning, Cody wasn't there. I paid no mind—he was a big boy and had stayed out all night plenty of times before—so I collapsed into bed. Hours later, when the brilliance of the noonday sun woke me, I saw my Epiphone case carefully tucked into a corner of the room. Rubbing my bloodshot eyes, I padded into Cody's bedroom to say hi. His bed appeared to have been slept in, but he wasn't in it, nor was he anywhere to be found in our small apartment. The still-wet towel in the bathroom and still-warm coffee pot on the kitchen counter told me it hadn't been long since he'd awoken and headed out, probably back to the studio. *What a glutton for punishment,* I thought. Feeling like a Mack truck had rolled over me, I headed back to bed and buried myself underneath a pile of blankets.

LATER THAT DAY, when the jackhammers in my head had finally subsided to tolerable levels, I picked up the phone and gave Hinch a call. Katie Q answered. She sounded slightly out of breath. "You guys seen Cody today?" I asked her.

"No, but let me give you to Hinch." I heard grumbling in the background as she passed the phone over.

"Man, have you got a bad sense of timing," he told me with annoyance in his voice, "and no, I haven't heard a peep from drummer boy. I'm guessing our budding Phil Spector must be back in the studio." Hinch had long been a fan of the eccentric producer's work, so it wasn't an altogether sarcastic comment.

"You're probably right," I replied. "I guess I'll head over there in a little while myself. What time do you want to meet me there?"

"Meet you there?" he snorted. "Hey, man, I'm done with that bullshit."

I pointed out that the songs we'd recorded still needed to be mixed.

"Screw the mixing," was Hinch's response. "That's Cody's department—him and that doofus of an engineer. I held up my end of the bargain, now he can take it from here." As far as he was concerned, he'd done all he was going to do and wasn't about to do any more. As usual, it was all going to fall on Cody.

When I got to the studio that evening, Cody and Frank or Fred or whatever the hell his name was were deep in conference. They both looked disheveled, as if they hadn't gotten much sleep, but they were also strangely manic. Coffee cups littered the room and I guessed they were the source of the mania—this was a few years before any of us could afford coke—but there also seemed to be a heightened level of adrenaline, so real you could almost taste it.

"Donnie! Glad you're here," Cody called out cheerfully when he finally spotted me standing in the doorway waiting to be noticed. "Come on in—I got some stuff I want you to listen to."

After a few mumbled directives to the engineer I was invited to sit in the place of honor, directly in front of the mixing board, precisely halfway between the two massive speakers mounted in the wall. A minute or so of tape chatter followed as the reel was rewound, then the familiar music began blaring forth at a ridiculous volume that practically had my hair blowing back like the guy in the Maxell commercial.

It was loud, damned loud … but it was also phenomenally good. Off at the side of my peripheral vision I could see Cody fidgeting excitedly. Midway through the playback of the first song I turned to him.

"What do you think?" he shouted.

"Too fucking loud!" I yelled back. His face fell. "But fucking fantastic, too," I quickly added. "What the hell did you do? We sound incredible!"

It was the truth. There was a cleanliness and a polish to our playing I hadn't heard before. Somehow the mix captured the power of Cody's forceful drumming as readily as the slightest nuance in Hinch's vocals, plus you could pick out every single note of his guitar, clear as day. Even my normally crappy bass playing somehow didn't sound quite so crappy now.

Suddenly Cody leapt up from his seat and planted a huge kiss on the astonished engineer's forehead. The two of them high-fived like a couple of football fans after a winning field goal, then began clumsily boogieing around the room as the music kept pounding away all around us, a true wall of sound. It was probably the most animated I'd ever seen Cody.

"Are you high or something?" I remember asking him as I sat there in amazement.

"High on life, bro," was his answer. "And on the music."

And indeed he was. In fact, as the playbacks of the completed tracks continued, his enthusiasm kept growing until it became downright contagious. To my surprise I found myself rising from my seat and joining Cody and the nerdy engineer in their ungainly dance to the gods of the muse, tripping over studio cabling as the three of us—idiots, all—stumbled around the room, grunting and laughing and clapping and cheering as the sheer joy of melody and harmony and rhythm washed over us.

Then, as suddenly as if a light switch had been thrown, it was back to work. There was only one day of studio time left, and several more tracks left to mix, including the one original song we'd recorded—an uptempo Hinchton/Jeffries collaboration. With Cody and the engineer once again huddled over the mixing board, deep in concentration, it soon became clear that there was nothing I could contribute. But before I headed out the door I had to ask one question, a question that had been bothering me ever since I'd heard the first few notes of that first mix.

"Hey, Cody, are you sure that's me playing bass on those tracks?"

Cody looked up, a sly grin on his face. "Why do you ask?"

"Well, to be honest, it kind of sounds too good to be me," I said.

"Would you like it to be you?"

"Well, sure, but ..."

"Okay, then it's you. Fair enough?"

"I guess."

Through the dim light I thought I could see him winking at me. Could have been my imagination, though.

WHEN I WOKE UP the next morning, there was no sign of our drummer. A little worried, I called the studio. Frank Fred answered. Yes, they'd worked through the night. With the allotted time rapidly running out, they had decided to continue plowing on until one or the both of them collapsed. Cody was busy at the moment but he'd tell him I'd called. And, yes, things were still sounding fucking amazing.

I didn't hear from Cody until late that evening. He sounded weary but that same undercurrent of excitement was in his voice. "We're just about done here, so why don't you and Hinch come by and have a listen to the final mixes?" he asked.

"Not sure if I can get Mr. Rock Star to join me, but I'll give it a shot," I told him.

To my surprise, Hinch readily agreed to accompany me, Katie in tow. As we drove through the darkened streets of York, Pa., radio blasting, windows down, Hinch's long, lanky hair blowing in the breeze, I remember a surge of optimism washing over me, a feeling of certainty that great things lay ahead.

When we got to the studio, we found the engineer splicing some tape together while Cody snored softly on the sofa. "He's pretty beat," Frank Fred told us, "but I think you'll be pretty happy with the final results." To Katie's horror, Hinch couldn't resist jumping on the unconscious drummer, hooting "Last call, Mr. Spector!" loudly in his face. Cody was pretty pissed, but I could also tell that he was glad to see Hinch.

"Fucking asshole," he sulked. "Just for that I should erase your parts."

Hinch laughed. "That, my brother," he crowed, "is the last thing you would ever do."

He was right. But what he didn't figure on was how much Cody would *add* to his parts. The engineer proceeded to thread up the final mix reel, which began with the same few songs I'd heard the previous day. Hinch listened closely, head down, but offered no comment despite Cody's obvious attempts to catch his eye. Katie Q seemed to really be digging what she was hearing, though, which seemed to come as a huge relief to Cody.

Then the new mixes started rolling by. To my ears, they sounded as good if not better than those I'd heard the night before, though I still had the nagging feeling that not all the bass playing had come from my two hands. And although the essence of what we had recorded as a three-piece bar band remained, I couldn't help but notice that Cody had added a number of new flourishes: an extra guitar lick here and there, even a touch of piano or organ on a couple of the songs. Even more impressively, he'd filled out his harmony vocals with lots of new parts, painstakingly overdubbed on one at a time. We didn't exactly sound like the Beach Boys, but there were definitely more than two voices on many of the tracks, and all the extra ones belonged to Cody Jeffries.

Cody had gone even more to town on the original song—the one that Hinch refused to play or sing on. In the absence of our lead singer, Cody had gone ahead and done the vocal himself: not just once, but perfectly doubletracked, with layer upon layer of harmonies added. The instrumental accompaniment was equally sophisticated, with lush underpinnings of keyboards and what sounded like a whole damn orchestra of guitars. Cody had even overdubbed Hinch's usual guitar solo, note perfect. I remember thinking that it was a textbook demonstration of how little Hinch was needed, at least in the recording studio.

I began studying Hinch's face for any sign of approval or disapproval. Whatever reaction he was having internally, he was doing a great job of keeping it under wraps. That was such a typical Hinch head game, making us wait for his final verdict.

It didn't come until after the last notes of the last song faded away and the played-out tape began flapping on the machine. At long last, Hinch raised his head and turned squarely toward Cody, who stared right back at him, though somewhat apprehensively. A long silence followed.

Finally Cody could hold back no longer.

"So?" he asked Hinch. "What do you think?"

Hinch fixed him with a steady gaze. "Sounds like the damn Eagles," he said, though not derisively.

And that, believe it or not, was all Hinch ever had to say about those demos, despite the monstrous effort our drummer had put into them. Cody and I chose to take it as a compliment, knowing how much Hinch was into "Witchy Woman," which was all over the radio at the time.

That's the way it all went down. Cody showed a side of himself I never knew existed and did an amazing job on those tapes—even if he did erase me and play all the bass parts himself, and even if Hinch gave him no credit whatsoever. The tapes did exactly what we wanted them to do, too—just about every club owner I sent them to offered us a gig, which then turned into repeat bookings once they saw how the little girls reacted to Hinch's playing and posing onstage. And despite all the *sturm und drang* beforehand, few people who heard the tape had much to say about the original song we included, not for a long time, anyway. Maybe that was because Cody had taken the wise precaution of putting it last on the reel, partly on the theory that people might not even listen that far, but mostly, I think, on the assumption that it might stick less in Hinch's craw. All I can tell you is that the whole experience was an eye-opener for me, and for Hinch too, I'm sure, because from then on, he was quite happy to let Cody do the heavy lifting—both figuratively and literally.

Okay, I think I'm all talked out for today. Later, bro.

9

AFTER DUSTING ME OFF and handing me a towel so I could mop up the blood still spurting from my nose, my two Dutch assailants had given me a critical evaluation.

"You look like crap, Bernie," Hans said thoughtfully, a concerned look spreading across his narrow face. "When was the last time you had something to eat?"

After my disgraceful display of gluttony at the Melkweg sex show, I thought I'd never be able to face another plate of food again, but the fact of the matter was that it had been more than forty-eight hours since I'd eaten anything, and I was actually starting to feel a little hungry, as I dolefully admitted.

Hans and Rudie exchanged glances. A half hour later the three of us were seated at a funky little restaurant where we sipped genever and leisurely worked our way through the most amazing meal I've ever experienced. The gentle spices and rich variety of the *rijsttafel*—the Indonesian rice table which the Dutch are rightfully so fond of—seemed to do wonders for my soul. I felt as if I'd died and been born again.

Over many glasses of pink gin I got a good education in the economics of live performance in the rock 'n' roll world. Behind every concert, my hosts explained, is a promoter—the guy who actually books the venue and the talent, prints and sells the tickets, pays for advertising and insurance, hires the stagehands and security, arranges for the backstage conveniences, and generally does all he can to make the artist comfortable and see that the audience gets a good show. That involves laying out a lot of money, meaning that the promoter is also the guy who takes all the risk. In return, of course, there's a potential reward in the form of a profit, but that's only if everything runs smoothly, which apparently rarely happens.

"It used to be a good way to make a living," Hans tells me as we order yet another round of drinks. "That is, until Peter fucking Grant came along."

"Who's Peter Grant?" I ask.

"He was Led Zeppelin's manager," he replies. "A three-hundred pound motherfucker who ruined the business, not just for me, but for all promoters."

"Fat English prick," adds Rudie helpfully.

I am confused. "What does Led Zeppelin have to do with anything? They broke up almost twenty years ago."

"Let me explain," Hans says, and explain he does. Led Zeppelin's formidable manager, it seemed, had completely changed the relationship between promoter and artist back in the early '70s, shortly after the band formed. Grant was an ex-professional wrestler and he had no compunction about bringing serious muscle with him wherever he went, setting the stage for the Schiffmans of the world. His attitude toward promoters was simple: You want my band, you pay through the nose. He knew that the hype around Zeppelin—not to mention the monstrous sales of their first album—gave him all the leverage, and he wasn't the least bit shy about using it.

Before Led Zeppelin and their menacing manager came along, Hans told me, promoters and artists shared the net profits from the concert 60/40, with the promoter getting the lion's share. That may have seemed a bit unfair, but, after all, the promoter was the one actually taking all the financial risk, and many of them had lost their shirts on poorly attended concerts, regardless of the reason.

But Grant insisted that the split be changed to 10/90, meaning that the most any promoter could walk away with was 10% of the gate—*after* expenses. And if a promoter didn't like it, tough shit. In fact, most of them didn't, which resulted in more than a few of them landing in the local hospital after making the mistake of expressing their discontent. Word quickly spread, and within a few short months, managers of other well-known artists—greedy bastards like Alan Schiffman—began making similarly lopsided demands. From that moment forward, the entire concert industry changed. The only way promoters could book the better-known artists and still hope to turn a decent profit was to raise ticket prices sky-high and cut every conceivable corner, from hiring inadequate security—can you say Altamont?—to providing dangerously unsafe stage conditions. Standing outdoors in the middle of a raging thunderstorm while handling thousands of volts worth of amplified equipment is a risk no sane licensed electrician would ever take, yet bands are apparently forced to do just that on a regular basis. It's in their contract—a contract drawn up by a group of money men who couldn't care less about the artist's safety or comfort.

"Yah, it's turned into a miserable business," Hans moans as he drains his glass once again. "And it's made worse by cogsookers like Schiffman."

"Fucking Alan Schiffman," repeats Rudie glumly. "I ever catch that cogsooker, I wring his neck until his eyes pop out."

The image somehow cheers us all up, and we clink glasses in a drunken toast. In a fit of bravado brought on by inebriation, I decide to raise a tricky subject.

"So, tell me, my Dutch friends," I begin. "What *is* the deal with Alan Schiffman?"

Hans looks at me blankly. "Deal? I do not understand."

"I mean, why exactly do you hate his guts?"

Before Hans can open his mouth to respond he is rudely interrupted by an enraged Rudie, who begins pounding the table with sufficient force to cause nearby diners to duck under their tables in alarm. I very nearly join them.

"THAT FUCKING COGSOOKER! IF I EVER CATCH HIM I SKIN HIM ALIVE AND MAKE HIM EAT HIS OWN SHRIVELED-UP DICK!" he shouts at the top of his lungs.

"Okay, Rudie, okay," soothes Hans. "Come on, calm down or I have to tell the bartender no more genever."

The threat of being cut off causes Rudie to reconsider, and he begins to relax slightly. Very slightly. I can feel my hands still shaking and for the rest of the evening the hair on the back of my neck refuses to return to its normal resting position. Still, I plow on.

"You were about to say?" I ask Hans, all the while keeping one wary eye on his red-faced compatriot.

"Well, Bernie, the thing about Alan Schiffman is that he makes Peter Grant *als een Sint*—look like a saint." Hans studies me carefully, clearly interested in my reaction. "For many years I have been doing business with him, and always he wants more. Back when Hinch was a big star, okay, I give him more because then I can make more. But now, Hinch is not such a big star, so there is less possibility of making guilder, or even these new fucking Euros. When we go to Schiffman's fancy office in Los Angeles earlier this year I try to explain that to him like a gentleman, but he says nothing. Next thing I know one of his men has me by the throat, the other one shoves a big gun in Rudie's face. Rudie, he does not care,

I can see he is ready to kill Schiffman anyway. But I like Rudie, so I tell him, stop." He beams proudly at his associate, who is still muttering away to himself. "So if I want my friend to live another day, I have no choice but to sign Schiffman's *stuk stront* contract. You know the meaning of those words?"

I shake my head.

"It means piece of shit. Like Schiffman."

At this, the two men burst out in laughter.

"The contract," Hans continues, "it says I must pay big money, many Euros, for Hinch to make an appearance in Amsterdam, even if he does not make show."

"What do you mean?"

"It means Schiffman gets his money whether or not Hinch actually gives a performance. Tell me, how can I make any money if the rock star does not perform?"

I have no answer. "Is that what happened?" I finally ask. "Did Hinch not turn up for the concert?"

"No, he turned up," Hans replies. "He turned up for his sound check and so I paid his manager the full fee right then and there, in cash, just like the contract said. That night, I had more than a thousand fans packed into the Paradiso, paying good money for their bier and genever. And then Hinch comes out on the stage and everyone is waiting for him to *Maken tonen*, to make show."

He pauses for emphasis.

"But he does not make show. Instead, he staggers around for five minutes while his band is standing there waiting for him to start playing the first song. But he doesn't play a note, not one single fucking note. Instead, he sits down on the drum riser and falls asleep."

"Hinch fell asleep? On the stage? In front of the audience?" I am staggered.

"Yah, like this." Drunkenly, Hans and Rudie begin making loud snoring sounds. They're finding it a lot funnier than our fellow diners.

"How on earth can you fall asleep in front of a thousand screaming fans?" I ask, posing the obvious. "Was he drunk? Maybe he just passed out."

"No, he wasn't drunk," Rudie replies. "I was close enough to him to smell his breath. He was sober as a baby."

"Rudie is in charge of security at my concerts," Hans explains. "He was the first one onstage to try to get Hinch to wake up and play."

"Yah, but he wasn't playing a note, not that night," Rudie says. "And, yes, I was close to him. Very close." He leans in toward me conspiratorially. "So close I could see the track marks on his arm."

Hinch a junkie? I can't believe it, and I tell them so.

But they are adamant. "Oh, you'd better fucking believe it," says Hans confidently. "Rudie here, he knows a junkie when he sees one. And the thing about junkies is that once they've gotten their fix, they can fall asleep anywhere."

I look over at Rudie, who nods soberly in agreement. "It's too bad," he says. "Last time Hinch did a concert for us—was that a year ago, Hansie?—he was completely clean. And he did a good job for us, too—he played a great show and the crowd, they were happy."

"Yah, we even managed to make a little money on him last year," Hans says. "Maybe that's because Schiffman wasn't backstage with him then. You know, I've sometimes wondered what he was doing here, and without his *stuk stront* bodyguards to protect him, either. I've never seen him at a gig before, have you, Rudie?"

"No, never before," Rudie replies. "But I tell you what: I see him again, I rip out his eyeballs and feed them to the pigeons in the Vondelpark."

This is, of course, grounds for more hilarity and another toast. I decide to brave the waters again.

"So … you still haven't told me what happened after Hinch fell asleep," I venture cautiously. "Or what it is that Schiffman did that night to piss you off so much."

The two Dutchmen appear to instantly sober up. "What happened was that Rudie had to get the roadies to drag Mister Fucking Rock Star off the fucking stage before the fans tore him to pieces," Hans says angrily, small flecks of foam beginning to appear at the corners of his lips. "And what happened was that I had to give the money back to a thousand angry customers. It was all Rudie could do to keep them from tearing *me* to pieces. But that wasn't the worst part."

"What could possibly be worse than that?" I ask, willingly playing the straight man.

"The worst part is that Schiffman ran off with the entire fucking fee, even though the only thing his piece of shit star did was fall asleep on my fucking stage and embarrass me in front of all of Amsterdam. And now I am out thousands and thousands of Euros. And for that reason Alan Schiffman is a dead man."

Donnie Boyle had told me a bit about promoters, and what he had said made me wary of feeling much sympathy for them. According to Donnie, they're nothing more than leeches who take every available opportunity to screw the very artists who provide them with their livelihood. But, dammit, I liked these two guys—even though just a few short hours ago they had tried to kill me. They were, at the moment, the only friends I had on this side of the world.

And after all I'd been through, I needed friends more than just about anything.

THAT I HAD FORMED an uneasy alliance with the two menacing Dutchmen wasn't actually the biggest news of the evening; much more surprising was the revelation that Mr. Clean was a junkie. Or at least he had been at the time of his last public appearance, at the Paradiso club more than a week ago. Since then, no one had seen hide nor hair of Hinch, or Schiffman; in the general melee that followed the impromptu cancellation of the concert, they had slipped out the backstage door while Hans and Rudie were busy dealing with the angry crowd.

I needed time to think, to try and make sense of all this. But first I needed to speak with Britney. Staggering back into my dreary hotel room at three in the morning, I reached for the phone and dialed, remembering, even in my drunken state, that Amsterdam was nine hours ahead of L.A. Or was it nine hours behind? No matter. Either she'd be in, or she'd be out.

She was out. Or she was in and let the phone machine pick up. I had no way of knowing which it was, but in the darkest recesses of my mind I imagined the worst: images of my blonde bombshell lying in our bed as the phone rang, being entered from behind by some smirking mustached porn star. Or from the front. Or from the front *and* from the behind, by matching mustachioed porn stars. This, I came to realize, was how little I trusted my darling wench, so certain was I that in my absence she could not possibly help herself from inviting sexual violation in unspeakable ways by the throngs of inordinately endowed virile young men lining up to enjoy the pleasures of her flesh.

It was in this demented state that I finally drifted off to sleep. My last image before succumbing to Morpheus was that of Britney kneeling before a nodding-off Hinch who was barely capable of acknowledging the exquisite blow job being enthusiastically rendered.

Eight or ten hours later I awoke to the sound of a thunderstorm raging outside, each pelting raindrop drilling another painful rivulet into my throbbing brain. The pink gin had given me the mother of all hangovers, yet I felt strangely calm. *Perhaps Hans and Rudie have provided me with the final missing piece of the puzzle*, I mused as I brushed the cobwebs from my teeth. *Perhaps all that remains now for me to bring the book to a successful conclusion is to locate the rehab center Hinch is in and get an exclusive interview with him.* I imagined myself bursting in like Superman, rescuing the bigshot rock star from his unwanted exile, aiding him in his time of need; then getting the scoop like Clark Kent and becoming his confidante and best buddy, soon to be making joint appearances on *Lifestyles of the Rich and Famous*.

Alas, it was not to be. When I met up with him later that afternoon, Hans ruefully informed me that he had already used his extensive contacts with the constabulary all over the country to check every rehab center in the Netherlands, only to learn that there hadn't been a single admission of anyone even vaguely matching Hinch's description.

Maybe he's left the country, then, I offered. Not possible, said Hans. His circle of regularly bribed government officials included key members of the Royal Dutch Customs and Immigrations Service; keeping them on retainer made the job of safely importing and exporting dubious characters like musicians much easier. There was absolutely no question about it, Hans insisted: Neither Hinch nor Schiffman had left the country since their entry some ten days ago.

Which left all three of us firmly back at square one. Where the hell could you possibly hide an internationally renowned rock star and his glaringly well-dressed scumbag of a manager in a small, mostly rural country like Holland? The answer was: almost anywhere.

"Let's try to think this through logically," I said. "If you had to hide somewhere in a strange country, where would you go?"

"I would look for the biggest city," Hans replied. "That's the best place to be anonymous. That's why I'm convinced Schiffman is still in Amsterdam."

"If you're right, wouldn't he be holed up at the office he has here? I mean, sure, I called and they told me he hadn't been in but they were probably lying to me."

"No, they were telling you the truth: he hasn't been in his office once," Hans said. "We have people watching the building around the clock and I would know if he paid a visit."

"Look, your theory makes sense ... if it were just Schiffman on his own," I pointed out. "But you said Hinch was with him. He's got a pretty well-known face, especially here, where you were just promoting his concert by plastering posters all over the city."

"That's true," replied Hans. "But in the *landelijke omgeving*—the countryside—a tall American with long hair would stand out even more. Everyone in the small towns knows when there is a stranger in their midst, and the tourists, they usually don't venture outside Amsterdam or Den Haag."

"Was it just the two of them that have gone underground? What about the rest of the band, or their road crew?"

"As far as we know, it is just the two of them," said Hans. "The other guys in Hinch's band, they locked themselves in the dressing room like scared little rabbits when the riot started, then quickly left on the tour bus—we saw them. The crew stayed behind to protect the equipment. Later, after the *politie* had cleared the hall, they packed up everything in their truck and drove off. I don't think there was too much damage to their precious gear, apart from a guitar or two being smashed up."

"I was telling Hans we should hold on to the equipment as ransom," Rudie interjected, "but he wouldn't listen to me."

"Too much trouble," Hans said. "It would have meant warfare between our stagehands and their roadies, and I'd had enough violence for one night. After all, I'm a peaceful man. Right, Rudie?"

"Yah, Hansie. You are peaceful. Not like me."

"Besides," added Hans, "I don't want their fucking equipment. I want my cash. If I can't get that, I want Schiffman's head."

"Me, I want both," Rudie confided with a wink.

"You said the band members left in the tour bus, and the roadies left in the equipment truck," I continued. "So what kind of vehicle did Hinch and Schiffman leave in?"

Hans and Rudie stared at one another. "*Domkop!*" cried Hans. "Of course. How could I be so stupid? They left in the limo that Mr. Fucking Fancy-Pants American Manager arrived in. Now all I have to do to find that scumbag...."

"... is to call the limo company." I hate finishing other people's sentences, really I do. But I couldn't resist taking advantage of the opportunity to show off a bit. Hans didn't even seem to mind, so revved was he.

Unfortunately, his frantic phone call led to yet another dead end. The driver, it seemed, had reported back to the office later that same evening and turned the car in without comment. The dispatcher refused, correctly, to reveal the name of the driver, but Hans got out his little black book and soon was able to reach someone who knew someone who knew the owner of the company. Rudie was then dispatched to have a "private conversation" with the driver to elicit further details. Should the driver prove reticent or uncooperative in any way, Hans assured me, he would quickly regret it at Rudie's hands. Having been on the receiving end just the day before, it was a business I wanted no part of. Yes, I was anxious to find Hinch and solve the mystery of his disappearance, but I had no interest in being implicated in assault and battery.

Instead, I had a plan of my own. In one of our last interviews, Donnie had explained that touring bands often head straight to the next venue immediately after leaving the stage; that way, they can sleep on the tour bus and save on hotel expenses. I guessed this was where the crew and band members had gone … especially if they were looking to leave town in a hurry because their star had pissed off the promoter. According to the Schiffman Entertainment press release I kept carefully folded in my pocket, the next gig on the original itinerary was in Groningen, about two hours away.

"While Rudie has his conversation with the limo driver," I told Hans, "I think I'm going to head north, to Groningen."

"What's in Groningen?" he asked me.

"Well, if my hunch is right, the band and crew at least."

"But the gig there was cancelled. In fact, the whole tour has been cancelled."

"I know that, Hans. But if you're right about Hinch and Schiffman having not left the country, I have a feeling that's where the rest of the entourage is waiting."

"What makes you so sure about this?" Hans demanded.

"A friend. A friend by the name of Donnie Boyle."

10

Transcript: Interview with Donnie Boyle, April 14, 1998

I REMEMBER THE NIGHT we met the Trucker brothers clear as if it were yesterday. It was the summer of '73 and we were doing a week-long residency at some dive down in Manassas, alternating sets with a local band fronted by the fattest lead singer I'd ever seen—he looked like two Leslie Wests put together. Clearly the guy was in no physical shape to do what he was doing: he'd get so red in the face, it seemed as if he was about to keel over. It was almost laughable, but it was also brutal. You could see the sweat pouring out of him and the veins popping out on his forehead. He was ugly, too, with a scraggly beard and slimy black hair halfway down to his ass, and he couldn't sing worth a damn, which made you wonder why on earth anyone would stick him front and center. The audience would just stand there staring at him, horrified, like he was a creature in a zoo.

Somewhere behind his huge beer gut you could just about make out the band's two guitarists. Beyond their obvious lack of talent, they had nothing to offer visually, either. They'd just stand there, rooted to the stage, their faces hidden behind ridiculous amounts of hair. You remember Cousin Itt from *The Addams Family*? That's who those guys reminded me of. Not only did they look the part, they played like they couldn't see their fretboards. It was really pretty comical visually ... but pathetic musically.

The only saving grace was their engine room—the bass and drums—and damned if that band didn't have the tightest, hardest-hitting rhythm section I ever heard. We all thought so, even Hinch, who begrudgingly admitted that, yeah, they definitely had something going on.

Sometime that night we struck up a conversation with them, as musicians do. It soon became obvious that the singer and his two overly inbred cousins—the guitarists—were total assholes with major chips on their shoulders, but Joe Dan and Vernon Dean Trucker turned out to be a couple of nice guys, though they sure didn't talk a whole lot. Joe Dan was the older of the two, and it seemed that the best he could manage was the occasional friendly grunt, but, boy, could he hammer those drums! Vernon Dean was no slouch on the bass, either—he was definitely more melodic and precise than anyone we'd ever encountered on our local circuit. He was way better than I was, that's for sure, plus he could sing, with a high, pure voice that was made for harmony. Mentally, he had a little more on the ball than JD—you could occasionally get him chattering away for a few minutes on some topic or other—but mostly they were just two good ol' boys from down in Mississippi who lived to play rock 'n' roll.

More out of sheer boredom than anything, we started hanging out with the Truckers. They were actually pretty funny in an aw-shucks kind of way and we started getting in the habit of grabbing a bite to eat with them at the local all-night greasepit after finishing our long sets. They were both covered in tattoos and they had a real rock star swagger about them, plus they were good looking, which caused them to get most of the attention from the waitresses—something which irritated Hinch no end. It turned out they'd only hooked up with this particular band a few months before, but, despite the fact that the gig paid pretty good bread, it was clear that they were already looking to move on.

Hinch and I liked their company well enough, but it was Cody who seemed the most enthusiastic about spending time with them, talking mostly about music—what else?—and life on the road. As the week wore on, we got more and more comfortable with each other, and on the last night of the gig, we all got together for a monstrous jam onstage, Cody and Joe Dan clearly enjoying the challenge of double drumming as we played a couple of Allman Brothers tunes. Hinch blew both guitarists out of the water, of course, but they seemed oblivious. All eight of us were pretty drunk, to tell the truth, and we all had a damned good time. The next day, as we slowly made our way northward in our beat-up old van, Cody said he hoped we'd get a chance to play with the Truckers again. Hinch snorted that it wasn't likely to happen unless we were ever willing to accept another shithole gig in Manassas—something that he definitely wasn't interested in doing—but Cody just said you never know and gave me a sly wink.

Now, you have to understand that when Cody Jeffries got an idea in his head, he was relentless. Our demo tape, the one he'd poured his heart and soul into, had landed us a ton of gigs, but every now and then some club owner with ears—that rarest of all rarities—would comment about how different we sounded live. "You guys are good," he might say after listening to our first set of the evening, "but from the sound of that tape I was expecting a whole bunch of musicians, plus a lot more going on in the way of vocals." It was true. Cody's overdubs had done so much to supplement our sound, he'd almost changed the kind of band we were, though our essence—Hinch's singing and playing—remained constant. But Cody would make a point of repeating comments like that whenever they'd get made. "It just goes to show what kind of potential we have, what we could accomplish if we were more than a three-piece," he'd say in the van or in the dressing room.

Hinch was having none of it. "Look, Cody, this band is what it is," he would say. Then he'd add, with a twinkle in his eye, "It's me and two backing musicians, and you just happen to be lucky enough to be a part of it." This would earn the inevitable "Fuck off, dickwad" from Cody, after which Hinch would argue that we each stood to make more money if the paycheck were split just three ways instead of four or five.

"But what if expanding the band meant that the paychecks were that much bigger?" Cody would reply, at which point Hinch would end the discussion simply by staring off into space—his signal that he was through talking.

Actually, by this time we were splitting the bread much more than three ways, anyway. Fighting and clawing our way to the top of the club circuit meant more gear to haul and more miles between gigs, so we not only had a full-time roadie—this knucklehead bodybuilder who went by the name of Muscle Beach Len—but our own little light show and PA system, both designed and run by this geek named Crazy Quentin, a real Mad Hatter–type character. In his spare time, Crazy Quentin was a genius. He read books about nuclear physics and dabbled in crystal meth—a drug none of us were the least bit tempted to try, not after seeing what it had done to his personality. Len, on the other hand, had no personality. If he wasn't setting up or breaking down equipment for us, or driving our van to or from a gig, he was sitting in his crappy, paint-peeling-on-the-walls hovel of an apartment, drinking beer and staring at a TV with the picture on and the sound off. Though he was thick as a brick, we all liked him—even Hinch—because he was utterly dependable, having no life whatsoever other than working for us. And, from Hinch's viewpoint, the added bonus was that, though big and muscular, he wasn't particularly good-looking, in contrast to his predecessor, Mike Testa.

With everyone's knowledge and consent, I was taking a little extra off the top, too, in my role as quasi-manager. Hinch grumbled about it from time to time, but Cody argued that it was only fair, since I was devoting so much of my time to getting us gigs and looking after the business end of things. So, between my share and the bucks we were throwing to Muscle Beach Len and Crazy Quentin, it was already like we were splitting every paycheck four ways. How much more of a difference would it make if it were five ways?, Cody would needle Hinch, especially if we were making more per gig?

But Hinch would not be swayed. Things were going good, and he was a creature of habit who had no interest in rocking the boat.

That's when Cody devised the Great Mono Swindle.

Mono, as in mononucleosis. Though he had always been in perfect health, all of a sudden one night our drummer boy managed to get mysteriously ill. We had a rehearsal planned for the next day and he didn't show up, which wasn't like him at all. He called Hinch later that evening, claiming he was feeling like shit, complaining of a sore throat and chills and saying he was really tired. Despite that, he did turn up at our next gig, and he looked okay to me, but it seemed like his playing was dragging a bit as the night wore on. Katie Q was there and she seemed quite concerned. With a trace of alarm in her voice, she told us that Cody appeared to have the same symptoms as her college roommate Monica, who had been laid low for months with mono. We all urged Cody to go see a doctor, but he said no, he'd be fine. Normally, we would have shrugged off this kind of macho approach, but the problem was that we had a really big gig coming up later that week, with a tour to follow. We knew all too well that if we cancelled at short notice, we would be blackballed by the club owners on that circuit, who could be vindictive bastards if you left them in the lurch.

"What the hell are we going to do about Cody?" Hinch asked me when we had a moment alone.

I looked at him blankly. "Don't know, H."

"Well, you're the damn manager, so think of something," he growled. See, in Hinch's mind, Cody had somehow become the enemy. He'd led us to this point in our career where the gigs were really starting to matter, and then he'd given in to some human frailty that stood in the way of Hinch achieving his goals. Hinch really could be a self-centered prick sometimes.

I decided to have a heart-to-heart with Cody when we got back to the apartment later that night. Maybe I could get him to seek some medical help, or maybe together we could figure out a back-up plan of some kind.

As it turned out, I needn't have wasted my time.

"Don't worry; I've got it covered," Cody cheerfully informed me with that shit-eating grin of his. "Remember Joe Dan Trucker? He's available to do the gig, and the tour, too."

I remembered, of course. That great jam session we'd had at the end of the residency in Manassas was still one of the best nights of making music I'd ever enjoyed.

"But, how…?"

"Look, bro, it's a done deal. Don't sweat it."

Further interrogation revealed precious few details, other than that Cody had stayed in touch with the Trucker brothers and learned that they had finally quit the crappy band with the obese lead singer and his two asshole cousins and were currently "between gigs," as overly optimistic musicians like to say. According to Cody, it was just our good fortune to have caught Joe Dan in this window of availability before he and Vernon hooked on to another band, as they undoubtedly would soon be doing.

First thing the next morning, I called Hinch with the news.

"S'good," he mumbled, distracted. Presumably Katie Q was there with him. "I have to admit that cat really could play," he added, "though if he's going on the road with us, he'd better be cool with the chicks." The howl of laughter I heard at that last comment confirmed my suspicion. Or maybe it wasn't Katie but some part-timer he'd picked up. In any event, Joe Dan Trucker was going to be our drummer, at least for the next couple of weeks, and Hinch was okay with it. That's all that mattered to me.

We had a couple of days' rehearsal with Joe Dan before our next gig, and despite his claims of frailty, Cody showed up to lend a hand. He didn't actually sit behind Joe Dan's huge kit—far more elaborate than anything Cody owned—but he issued directions to the impassive drummer, filling him in on cues and things like that. By the end of the second day, we were like a well-oiled machine. In fact, we sounded *better* than we had with Cody drumming. Hinch didn't actually say as much to me, but I could tell from the look on his face that he felt the same way, and we even took it up yet another notch at the gig itself. Like I said, it was an important gig for some reason—a showcase for a bunch of club owners or something like that—and with Joe Dan behind the drums we really kicked butt that night.

Later, as we packed up our guitars, Hinch and I did our usual postmortem, dissecting the high and low points of our performance. There had been a couple of false starts and a few sloppy endings, but nothing more than what you'd expect from a first gig with a new player, and the consensus was that, overall, we'd done well. The only thing missing, we agreed, was Cody's harmony vocals, even though I'd tried my best to chip in and sing a few of his parts, though without a lot of conviction, I had to admit. But the evening was deemed a success, and we decided that we both felt pretty good about the upcoming tour.

I call it a "tour," but it was really just a dozen dates I'd strung together over a two-week period as we made our way west to Pittsburgh before taking a right turn on up to Cleveland. They weren't exactly prestige gigs, but the venues were decent-sized and the money was okay, so it was definitely worth doing. The first couple of dates were warm-ups at a club in Penn Hills. Now, Cody had promised us that he absolutely, positively, would stay home and rest in order to get himself better, and for those first two nights he actually kept his word. We played great, with Joe Dan getting more and more comfortable with the set list, and Hinch seemed considerably more relaxed, too. I'm guessing that was due to Cody not being there to give him a hard time, though that translated mainly to Hinch spending less time at sound checks and more time flirting with the local babes.

But when we got to the club in Pittsburgh the next day, damned if Cody wasn't sitting at the bar, pulling on a long-neck Bud all casual-like, as if he spent every evening of his life there.

"What the fuck?" said Hinch. He seemed more surprised than annoyed, though.

"Come on, H, how about a little love?" Cody responded, unperturbed. He got up from his bar stool and moved toward Hinch, arms open wide as if to give him a hug.

"Keep those cooties away from me, man!" Hinch said in mock horror. "What the hell are you doing here, anyway? You're gonna catch some serious shit from Katie Q when I tell her."

"Who says you got to tell Katie?" Cody said, though he knew there was no way Hinch wouldn't be spilling the beans.

I don't know why Hinch was so surprised. I could have predicted that Cody would have turned up at some point, though I was still buying his "mono" story enough that I didn't think it would be this soon into the tour.

"What's going on, bro?" I asked him worriedly after Hinch had gone back to the van to get something from his case. "You know that we've promised JD the full two-week gig. He'll kick my ass from here to Altoona if we break the deal."

"Don't worry, I'm not here to take my job back," Cody laughed. "Can't I just be a fan for a change?"

"I know you, you bastard," I replied. "It can't possibly be as simple as that."

Just then we were interrupted by Muscle Beach Len, strolling in with Joe Dan.

"Hey, little buddy, what's up?" Len boomed, slapping Cody on the back so hard it nearly sent him flying across the room.

"Hands off, Len," Joe Dan said ominously. It was the longest sentence I'd ever heard him utter.

Len gave our new drummer a long look. I hadn't known the dumb ox to be especially violent, but he definitely had the muscle to put a serious hurt on someone if he wanted to. After a moment's consideration a big grin spread across Len's face.

"Hey, man, just having some fun. Lighten up, willya?"

Joe Dan stared at him stonefaced as Len headed off to the sound board, cackling softly to himself.

"I think you hurt his feelings," Cody laughed.

"Ah, fuck him if he can't take a joke," Joe Dan finally blurted out, which was the new longest sentence I'd ever heard him say. JD always was as economical with his words as he was with his playing. And just as precise.

You would have thought Joe Dan would be at least a little intimidated by Cody sitting there watching him play the entire night with us, but if he was, he certainly didn't show it. In fact, I noticed that he and Cody were doing a lot of bonding, hanging out together in the dressing room between sets while Hinch worked the local lovelies at the bar.

We finished our last set well after midnight and, as we were packing up, I asked Cody what his plans were. It was a good three-hour drive back to York and I was concerned about him making the trek all alone.

His reply was pure Cody. "Actually, bro, I thought I'd hang with you guys for the next few dates. Don't worry—I already talked to JD and he said he was okay with me bunking in with him, so it won't cost the band any extra bread."

Of course he had every angle figured: that was pure Cody. I tried putting up a token protest, citing his health, but Cody wouldn't take no for an answer, and, anyway, who was I to tell him what to do? My business card may have said "Manager," but we were friends first and foremost, and this was as much his band as it was mine—probably even more so.

I looked to Hinch for some support but got nothing more than a terse, "Hey, he's a grown boy. Whatever." And so Cody followed our van back to the hotel in his creaky old Pinto, with Joe Dan Trucker riding shotgun. As we milled around the lobby waiting for the sleepy-eyed desk clerk to sort out our room keys, Hinch was nowhere to be found; undoubtedly, he'd scored with one of the local lasses and would be spending the night in a bed elsewhere. With nothing better to do, I looked around our dismal surroundings. That's when I happened to notice Cody's guitar case sitting on top of his duffel bag. It gave me pause because he'd never brought his guitar to a gig before, not ever.

"What's so interesting?" a voice asked.

It was Cody; I must have been so transfixed, I never even noticed him sidling up to me.

"Nothing. I mean ... well, what's your axe doing here?"

"No biggie," he said. "Got to keep the fingers in shape, you know."

"Uh huh," I said, suddenly suspicious.

Cody was nonplussed. "Hey, it'll give me something to do while I'm hanging out," he said. "Thought I might even write a song or two while I'm on the road with you. That's why I brought my amp along, too."

Yep, there it was: his beat-up old amp, parked next to the drum cases. I knew then that it was only a matter of time before he made his next move.

Sure enough, a few days later, as we were all having breakfast at the local IHOP, Cody suddenly announced that he was feeling a whole lot better and planned on sitting in for a song or two at that night's gig.

"No way, C," Hinch said. "You may be on the mend, but drumming's still way too strenuous for a sick dude like you." I studied his face for any sign of true concern, but came up blank. No, Hinch's real message was *Joe Dan's a better drummer than you.*

"Totally," Cody replied, nodding his head in agreement and acting all sincere and deferential. "You're right; I'm definitely still way too weak to get behind the kit...."

Hinch looked at him suspiciously.

"... which is why I thought I'd just play a little rhythm guitar instead."

Now Hinch looked at *me* suspiciously.

"What do you know about this, Donnie?" he demanded.

"Me? Nothing."

Hinch turned to Cody again.

"What the hell is going on here?"

"Nothing, man, nothing," Cody insisted. "I'm just trying to find something to do to help the band out." At first he wore a look of contrition, like a kid caught with his hand in the cookie jar. Then he moved in for the kill. "You know, my being onstage would mean that you'd have decent backing vocals again," he added softly. Cody knew how much Hinch dug having a harmony voice behind his, and with a tone-deaf Joe Dan incapable of singing at all and me doing a lousy job of covering Cody's vocal parts, this was clearly meant to be the carrot on the stick.

There was a long pause while Hinch weighed his options.

"Well, alright, have your fun," he said finally. "But just for a couple of songs. And remember," he added, only half-jokingly, "rhythm only. No solos, no posing."

"Deal," Cody said somberly, offering to seal it with a handshake. "No solos, I promise."

As soon as Hinch's head was turned, he slipped me a big wink.

That night, Cody sat in on just two songs, just as he had agreed. The next night, he played on four of them, and the night after, half a set. By the last few gigs of the tour he was onstage with us from start to finish. At first, he kept his promise to Hinch: he mostly stuck to playing rhythm, with the occasional tasty little lick thrown in, and his steady backing vocals were really welcome, especially to me since I could give my throat a rest—I simply wasn't used to singing more than one or two songs a night. Then, slowly but surely, Cody began playing harmony lines behind Hinch's solos. Cody knew those solos inside out because, as I've said, they were mostly predictable and rarely varied from night to night. But he was careful to stand at the back of the stage, next to Joe Dan's drums, and not in the spotlight with Hinch, and so there were no objections voiced by our front man; in fact, there was even the occasional gruff, "Sounded good tonight, C—I dug what you were playing."

We were now nearly at the end of our tour, and somehow we'd morphed into a four-piece. Between Joe Dan's solid drumming and the added dimension of Cody's second guitar, we had turned into one kick-ass unit, and I noticed that the crowds were bigger and more enthusiastic than ever before. The club owners were noticing, too. After every gig, I was being offered return bookings, and when I said we'd need to get paid more money next time around, I was meeting no real resistance—a total surprise, given the way club owners were notorious for cheaping out at every possible opportunity. I guess it was just testimony to what a great little band we had become.

On the next to last night of the tour Hinch and I found ourselves hanging out at the bar together, talking about Cody and the way he had manipulated things so that he was able to switch from being our drummer to our second guitarist, and score us an even better drummer in the process. Even Hinch had to admit that Cody had pulled off a masterful coup.

"Yeah, he definitely is a schemer," he told me as we knocked back another brewski. "But you gotta be careful, Donnie boy, because schemes can sometimes take on a life of their own."

"What are you talking about, Hinch?" I asked him with a dopey grin.

He suddenly grew quiet. "Nothing. I'm just saying."

But he wasn't saying anything. If I wasn't so buzzed, I might have seen that Hinch was trying to send me a warning signal. No matter. Between the great gigs and the ton of new bookings that were coming in, I was happy.

It wasn't long before the other shoe dropped.

Now, the last night of the tour had us playing this big hall in Cleveland. It was the biggest gig we'd had yet, both prestige-wise and attendance-wise, and we were psyched. By that point, we were totally in our groove, completely confident that we were going to kick some major ass every time we took the stage. But we were also starting to get a bit homesick—even Hinch, who had been having these long heart-to-heart phone calls with Katie the last few nights instead of running around partying like a madman—so we were looking forward to getting off the road and sleeping in our own beds for a change. I'd made sure to give the band a solid week off before we resumed doing any more gigs, and I think we were all looking forward to enjoying some down time.

I think that's why we were like lightning in a bottle that particular night. From the moment we hit the stage, Hinch had the audience in the palm of his hands as he posed and strutted around like the star he was always destined to be. Joe Dan was smacking the hell out of his drums, while Cody simply stood quietly in the background, adding his little touches and flourishes and keeping the whole thing together. I have to admit I was having a great time, too, for once not worrying about how many clunkers I might hit on the bass or how squeaky and out of tune my vocals might be the few times I approached the microphone.

Somewhere around the third or fourth tune, I heard a shout come from the audience. It was a voice I recognized, vaguely, and through the glare of the lights I could just about make out where it came from. The face was also kind of familiar, though it took me a minute or two to place it.

It was Joe Dan's brother, Vernon Dean, and he was a-whoopin' and a-hollerin' and a-carrying on like he was at some wild midnight ramble in the bayous of Louisiana instead of a beery nightclub in Cleveland.

It didn't seem especially strange at the time. I guess I thought, well, why shouldn't baby bro make a point of coming by to watch JD play with us? After all, they'd been on the road together for years; this might have been the first gig either of them had ever taken without the other. Vernon was sure giving us a lot of support from behind his little table, anyway. People were looking at him kind of funny, but there was no question that he was helping rev up the crowd.

When we got offstage after that first set, dripping with sweat and flying high on adrenaline, ol' Vern was waiting for us in the dressing room. Weaving unsteadily and waving an open beer bottle over his head, he wrapped JD up in a great big bear hug, then greeted us all like long-lost brothers. "Man, you guys totally rocked tonight," he said over and over again as we high-fived, chest-bumped, and did all the dumb-ass macho things guys do.

After a little while, Hinch and JD headed off to the bar to scout out the local talent. I was being buttonholed by some sleazy promoter with bad breath who was babbling on and on about how great we were and how he wanted to add us to this tour he was putting together, and damned if we didn't start negotiating a nice little fee right there and then. Out of the corner of my eye I could see Cody and Vernon huddled together in a corner of the dressing room talking excitedly, I presumed, about music.

Just before we headed back out for our second set, Cody pulled me aside and asked me if I'd mind sitting out a couple of numbers so that Vernon could jam with the band. "It'd mean a lot to him," Cody said earnestly, "especially since he and Joe Dan haven't played together for awhile."

So far as I knew, it had been only a few weeks since the Truckers had last shared a stage, but it was honestly no big deal to me so I said, sure, and handed my bass over to Vernon, who mumbled a quick thank-you. As the band kicked into a ferocious "Johnny B. Goode"—the Old Faithful of barband standards—I plowed through the heaving crowd to the back of the room. It was the first time I'd ever gotten to sit in the audience and hear our band play, and I have to say I was impressed. Real impressed. Beyond Hinch's flamboyance and Cody's musicality and JD's rock-solid beat, there was a polish and professionalism that I guess I hadn't really appreciated until that moment. And I had to admit that Vernon was doing one hell of a job holding down the bottom end—he was even helping Cody out on some harmonies, and their voices meshed beautifully.

After a few numbers, Hinch strode up to the mic and asked the audience to give Vernon a big hand, which they did. It was my cue to return so I made my way back to the stage. Vernon was still there, perspiration pouring off his scraggly beard as he pumped his fist in the air, riding high not just on the cheers of the crowd but the sheer joy of the music he'd just been a part of. As he clambered off and I strapped my Epiphone back on, I remember feeling almost embarrassed to be reclaiming my role in the band. It was almost like I was standing outside myself, as if in a dream. After years of being in the center of a gathering storm, I finally had a chance to step back and witness the magnificent power that had arisen from all the hundreds and thousands of hours that Hinch and Cody and I had put into this thing. I think that was the moment when I first realized that my rightful place was not up on the stage with them, but on the sidelines, where I could best contribute to all we had accomplished together. It was something I thought long and hard about that night, especially during the long drive back to York.

A couple of days later, we held a band meeting. Hinch, as usual, waffled around the truth. "Look, it's not you, Donnie. It's just that the Trucker boys are inseparable. They're giving us no choice—it's like a package deal. If we want JD in the band, we have to take Vernon as well. Plus the guy can sing pretty good: it'll mean we can have three-part harmonies...." His voice trailed off.

Cody was a lot more straightforward. "You know as well as we do that it's what's best for the band," he told me. "Your heart's not in playing bass; it's in making deals and being our manager. But, look," he added—and I know he meant it—"if you really feel strongly about staying in the group, I'll go back to playing drums."

I looked over at Hinch, who was staring down at his feet and shuffling uncomfortably.

"No need, buddy," I said, a smile starting to slide across my face. "I just wanted to make you guys sweat a little. You've got yourself a new bass player."

And that, my dear Mr. Temkin, is the true story of how I became full-time manager of the soon-to-be world phenomenon known as Hinch. Years later, I asked Cody if replacing me with Vernon Dean Trucker was part of the Great Mono Swindle from the beginning and he swore it wasn't.

To this day, I'm not sure if I believe the fucker.

11

GRONINGEN IN DECEMBER is not my idea of a good time. In fact, it may be one of the dreariest places I've ever visited, and, to paraphrase Mark Twain, I spent the longest winter of my life one summer in Seattle. Actually, Groningen reminds me of Seattle, at least in terms of the brisk winds constantly blowing in off the sea and the somber-faced, flannel-shirted college students lounging idly in the many brightly colored *koffiehuisen* that do little to warm the ambience of the cold, gray city.

Hans and Rudie had been reluctant to let me out of their sight, but I argued that it made sense for me to make this trip alone because the band and crew—if I could find them—would recognize their faces. Before they dropped me off at the train station, however, Hans insisted I take his cell phone so we could stay in contact. "If I don't hear from you, I have to send Rudie to find you, yah?" he warned. I didn't mind, actually, because I had no intention of not staying in touch, especially at the first sign of trouble. As I examined the tiny phone and tried to figure out what all the different buttons did, it occurred to me that there seem to be more of the damn things here in Europe than there are even in ultra-hip L.A. I have to make a note to myself to pick one up when I get back home. Even if you can barely hear the person at the other end over the crackle and static, I have to admit they look pretty cool.

No sooner had I purchased my ticket and settled into my seat than the phone rang. It was Hans. "Okay, Bernie, I spoke with the local promoter and he gave me the name and address of the hotel where Hinch's band and crew were supposed to be staying during their three-day layover in town. Mind you, he hasn't heard a word from any of them, not even the road manager—just a fax from Schiffman's office instructing him to cancel the gig. And of course he still hasn't gotten his deposit back."

"Any word from Rudie?" I asked, hoping I would be spared the gory details.

"No, not yet. I imagine he's occupied at the moment," came the cryptic answer. *Yeah, probably occupied kicking the shit out of the poor guy.*

"Well, let me know," I replied. "Just don't let me know too much. And remember, stay away from the genever."

He laughed hoarsely and the line went dead. Three hours later I found myself standing in front of the Hotel Schimmelpenninck Huys, an imposing 12th century building not far from Martini Plaza, where the Groningen gig was to be held.

My first thought was, nice digs. My second thought was, what the fuck am I doing? Even if my hunch was correct and the band and crew were staying here, everyone in Schiffman's employ had been instructed not to talk to me. Besides, I had no plan. Images of Trudy Cox's expansive ass reminded me what had happened the last time I came into contact with Schiffman's minions without a plan.

Come on, Bernie, a little voice inside me urged. *You didn't come this far to turn back now. The sooner you find Hinch, the sooner you can get back to the City of Angels and the welcoming arms—not to mention the other body parts—of Britney.*

It was enough—just enough—to propel me through the front door. I still had no idea what I was going to do once I got inside.

EVERYWHERE I LOOK is sheer opulence. The Hotel Whatsitsname is the very embodiment of an old-world elegance that immediately makes me ashamed to be an ugly American. I am embarrassed at everything about my appearance, mortified by the breakfast stains on my shirt, chagrined at the wrinkliness of my chinos, humiliated by the scuff of my shoes. Nonetheless, I plow on and proceed to make an absolute fool of myself at the registration desk.

"Can I help you, sir?" says the immaculately groomed hotelier. Outfitted in immaculately creased trousers and immaculately shined shoes, he is wearing—I swear to god—a morning coat and cravat. Beau Brummel here looks like he just stepped out of the pages of *GQ*, had the magazine been published in the late eighteenth century.

"Yes, er, I'm here for a meeting with one of your guests," I stammer inelegantly.

"We have many guests staying with us, sir," he replies with the smug politeness inbred in royalty and hotel desk clerks. "Perhaps you can provide me with a little more information."

"Yes, of course," I mumble. I decide to take a stab in the dark despite Hans's certainty that Hinch and Schiffman are not staying here. "The last name is Hinchton. He's a famous musician. A rock star, actually."

"Ah, a rock star. Yes, we get many of those, although I am afraid I am not familiar with this particular one. However, let me check the guest register." He turns his back on me and heads to a nearby computer terminal. I feel sure I see a smirk appear on his face the moment he thinks I'm not looking.

A moment later he returns. "I'm sorry, sir. There is no one registered here by that name."

"I see," I say solemnly, trying not appear any more inept than I have already proven myself to be. "He must be traveling incognito, then. You know, because of the fans."

"Yes," the desk clerk says, humoring me, "those troublesome fans. Will there be anything else, sir?"

"Could you check another name for me? His manager. The last name is Schiffman. Alan Schiffman."

"Certainly, sir." Another brief pause as he goes off to once again smirkingly check his computer. "Sorry, sir," he reports unctuously a moment later, "no one here by that name either."

I offer sweaty thanks and start to make my retreat when I once again hear the clerk's dulcet tones. This time he is addressing my back.

"Did you say you were looking for musicians, sir?"

I do a quick pivot. "Yes, that's right."

"Well, sir, we do have a number of gentlemen staying with us this week who appear to be in the music trade. Perhaps they can help you locate your friend. You'll find them in the hotel bar ... as usual." These last two words are delivered almost in a whisper, but the sadness in his voice is apparent. Nothing can bring down the tone of a classy hotel faster than loading it up with musicians. And where else but the bar *would* they be congregating?

Red-faced, I thank the desk clerk once again and find my way to the drinking area at the far end of the lobby. It is not quite seven in the evening, but a loud chorus of drunken voices is already wafting across the room.

My quarry, it appears, is almost in sight.

THE BOOZER, AS to be expected in a joint like this, is tastefully appointed, replete with dark wood-paneled walls accented by burgundy velvet drapery. A dozen or so small tables, each dimly lit with a single glowing candle, surround a long mahogany bar, along which sit a handful of besuited businessmen solemnly nursing martinis and scotch-neats. The ambience is intimate and reeking of class, or at least it would be, if not for the group of drunken yobbos half-hidden in the gloom, making a racket which shatters the sombre atmosphere like a sledgehammer on a fine piece of stained glass. They are, I have no doubt, the "gentlemen in the music trade" to whom the desk clerk was referring.

Normally, there are few things I hate more than mingling with a bunch of drunken strangers, as I keep telling Britney. Just what pleasure she derives from hanging out in noisy bars filled with inebriated morons yelling in one another's ears—even though none of them can possibly hear what the other is saying—escapes me. Of course, I'm not a hot young blonde in her twenties being hit on every ten seconds, but still I fail to understand the allure. Never mind. I've traveled halfway across the world to try and salvage my book—no, my life—and the journey has brought me precisely here, to the bar of the Hotel Schimmelpenninck Huys, and right now my quest depends upon socializing with this loud, obnoxious group of drunks. I know myself well enough to realize that if I stop and think about it I'll lose my nerve, so I force myself to plow straight ahead. I don't even have time to come up with a cover story, or an opening line.

As I draw nearer, I size up my adversaries. There are only five of them, actually—far fewer than I expected, judging from the decibel level. But all are shouting loudly at one another, as if they were in a crowded disco fighting a deafening four-on-the-floor beat instead of a sedate hotel lobby filled with the soothing tones of canned Muzak. The three roughnecks at the bar are all bleary-eyed, unshaven and identically clad from head to toe in black—the roadies, I'm guessing. Bantering with them are two well-dressed young men seated at a table a short distance away. Judging by their carefully coiffed hair and impossibly tight trousers, they must be the musicians.

I wade right in, taking quick note of the brand of beer they are drinking. Positioning myself a foot or two to the right of the group, I call to the bartender and order a Heineken.

"Here's to the Dutch, and to their beer," I exclaim in a toast, turning to the nearest celebrant, beer bottle held aloft.

He's clearly surprised by my intrusion into their private party, but not annoyed. I can also see that he's impressed with my choice of drink. "To the Dutch, and their beer," he parrots, elbowing his nearest neighbor in an entreaty to join in.

"Are you guys in town for the gig?" I ask, trying to sound as hip as possible.

"Gig? Nah, we're here for the shoe salesmen convention," he sneers, smartass, in a European accent I can't quite place. "The same one you're attending, I suspect."

The others howl in glee and my face begins to redden. But if there was anything Donnie Boyle taught me, it was that needling is a way of life for the touring musician and crew. I realize then and there that if I am not to be ground up by their sarcasm, I have no choice but to join in. "I *thought* you looked familiar," I reply in what I hope is a breezy tone. "You were running the 'Sizing Up Your Customer' workshop, am I right?"

Another whoop of drunken laughter. "More like 'Sizing Up Your Customer's Knob,'" pipes up another roadie in a Cockney accent. "'Size It Up and Suck It Off.'"

"What are you—a size twelve?" adds one of the musicians in a mincing tone as he rises to his feet. "Slip right into *this* and see how it fits," he says, pointing to his ass as he sashays around the bar, fluttering his eyelashes seductively at the roadies. I see my opportunity and seize it.

"Bartender, give that lady a drink!" I call out. "In fact, give *all* these ladies drinks—they look thirsty. And horny."

There is, I have found, no more universal currency, no more immediate way of making a roomful of new best friends than buying a round, and the ploy works just as well in this high-class hotel as it does in the lowest of low-class dives. Sure enough, for the price of a half-dozen bottles of beer, I appear to now be fully accepted into the giggling fraternity.

After taking a long chug of his Heineken, the Cockney roadie—the largest of the three, with a shiny shaved head and imposing beer gut—turns to me and says, "Right, Mr. Shoe Salesman. So what is it that brings you to the Hotel Skinnypenis Whores?"

"Actually, I'm here to do an interview," I reply, grinning at his not-so-clever wordplay, sophomoric as I find it to be.

"A reporter from *Shoe Salesman Weekly*!" calls out Euro-roadie. "Paging Mr. Thom McCan!"

"Hush, puppy," warns the no longer mincing musician, joining in the game.

"Bally good show," adds the other musician, adopting a snooty English accent.

I still haven't heard a peep from the third roadie, who sits at the end of the bar sourly nursing his drink. He appears to be a few years older than the others, and with his big, bushy beard and thick glasses, he seems to not quite fit in. I decide to take the bull by the horns.

"And you, my friend?" I say, addressing him directly. "Have you nothing to say for yourself? Perhaps you are just here to watch the Florsheim show."

There is no laughter, only an embarrassed silence as he glares at me. "That's Silent Stu," explains one of the other roadies. "He can't speak; he's mute."

I am mortified at the gaffe I have made. Fortunately, just before I can blurt out an apology, one of the musicians chimes in, a puckish grin on his face.

"He's stone deaf, too. That's why he's our sound man."

Everyone explodes with laughter as Silent Stu starts sputtering Fuck Yous at his tormentors.

"Nice one. Okay, you nearly got me," I say good-naturedly, waving my beer bottle at the hapless sound man in a gesture of truce. He shakes his head forlornly; I get the sense he has long been the butt of the others' jokes. Clearly, he doesn't like playing the role of buffoon, but he seems to be stuck with it, at least for now.

Reasonably sure that I have passed muster, I decide to press on with my charade. "Seriously, I *am* here for an interview. I'm looking for a fellow who goes by the name of Hinch—a pretty famous rock star. Can any of you guys help me out?"

"Hinch? Never heard of him," says Euro-roadie, evoking a wry laugh from the others. When the chuckling dies down, the large English dude gets up from his bar stool and saunters over, then suddenly whirls around and gets right in my face.

"Who wants to know?" he demands threateningly.

Frantically improvising, I blurt out the first thing that comes into my head.

"Clive Swindon. With *Rolling Stone*."

Fucking Clive will have a fit if he ever finds out I was impersonating him, but hopefully he'll never find out … at least not until long after my book comes out.

Fortunately, they seem to buy it, and everyone relaxes. "*Rolling Stone*, huh?" says the burly British roadie, whose name, I soon learn, is Big Vic. "Any chance you can get my mug on the cover?" he smirks.

"No chance whatsoever," I answer, just as smartass. "But I might be able to get your picture in *Shoe Salesman Weekly*." That seems to do the trick. With a laugh, Euro-Roadie reveals himself to be the suitably named guitar tech Pauli Footpedal, and the other two, as I correctly guessed, are Hinch's rhythm section: Scott the drummer and Jacques the bassist. Scott is from Minnesota and has been with Hinch the longest—going on five years, he tells me. Jacques is, like Pauli, a Swiss native who is doing his first tour with Hinch, both men having met the rock star at a local tavern near his palatial home in St. Moritz. The two musicians are a study in contrast: Scott, short and stocky, with Midwest farm boy features and the trace of a mullet; Jacques, tall and thin, with jet-black hair shaped in an unfashionable poodle cut, his face accentuated by an impossibly perfect dimple set in the exact center of an impossibly square jaw.

Of the two, I like Scott the better, mainly because Jacques is clearly a publicity hound ... and hound me he does, incessantly. The first thing he does upon hearing the magic words "Rolling Stone" is to attach himself firmly but metaphorically to my hip, where he is to stay for most of the rest of the evening. The second thing he does is to reach into his jacket pocket and produce his demo CD, which he forces into my unwilling hands, insisting that I play it for Jann Wenner immediately upon my return to the States. "He'll thank you for it—I swear!" Jacques proclaims over and over again. *Does this guy carry his demo CD with him wherever he goes?* I wonder.

"I bring this with me wherever I go," he says, answering my unspoken question. "It's a reflection of who I am as a musician and the unshakable faith I have in the beautiful music I want to share with the world. I even play all the instruments on it."

"Badly," whispers Scott in my other ear. "Don't listen to it on a full stomach: you have been warned."

Momentarily breaking free of Jacques' grasp, I turn my attention to the roadies. "So, how's the tour been going so far? I hear you guys had a rough time of it in Amsterdam."

"Amsterdam sucked," growls Pauli.

"Ahh, I've seen worse," says Big Vic, who is clearly the veteran in the crew. "Bullshit Dutch police. If we'd been playing my home turf, we would have had a chance to put the boot in, and the coppers would have left us to it." Silent Stu, living up to his nickname, scowls silently into his beer.

"Have you guys been hanging out here ever since the gig?" I ask, wishing I had a reporter's notebook on me so I could look the part.

"Yep, almost two bloody weeks now," says Vic. "Got no place else to go, now that the rest of the tour's been cancelled."

"At least the Dutch beer is cold," adds Pauli, holding up his now-empty bottle, "unlike the warm piss Vic here grew up on." I take the hint and order another round. Jacques returns to my side and begins yapping again about the stunning clarity of sound on his demo, which I have managed to already conveniently misplace.

I do my best to politely ignore him. "I guess you'll have to suffer through the warm beer at the end of the month when you get to London," I say to the roadies. "Hinch is still playing the Millennium Dome gig, right?" They look at me a bit dubiously. "I mean, that's what the press release says, anyway." I pull the dog-eared piece of paper out of my pocket and begin waving it around as if it is a letter of introduction. Even as I do so it occurs to me that trying to shore up my credentials as a bona fide reporter is probably completely unnecessary, given the fact that they're all too drunk to notice, or care.

"That's what we've been told," Pauli says after taking a long pull off his bottle. "So until we get instructions from our crew chief to move on, this is where we'll be waiting."

"Is he here? Perhaps I could talk to him."

"No," Big Vic tells me. "Actually, we haven't seen him, or Hinch, or Hinch's candy-ass manager since the Amsterdam gig."

"So Hinch isn't staying here? Or his manager?"

"No, no chiefs here," he says. "Just us Indians."

"Well, there is *one* Indian missing," Pauli interjects. "Remember, we haven't seen Cody since the gig, either."

I nearly choke on my drink. "Cody?"

"Yeah, that's right," sighs Vic as he drains the last of his beer. "Cody the Roadie, the longest-serving member of our happy little family. But he's an old buddy of Hinch's, so he's probably just off partying with them, lucky bastard."

I summon the barman for yet another round in hopes that my generosity will dispel any suspicion over the question I'm about to pose.

"So," I ask as casually as I can manage, "do you have any idea where

I can find Hinch? I'm supposed to be turning in this interview soon, and...."

Just then Silent Stu slams his Heineken bottle down on the bar, startling us all. "Who the fuck is this guy, anyway?" he asks no one in particular. "You all read that memo Mr. Schiffman sent about us talking to reporters. I'm not about to get my ass fired just because you morons can't keep your mouths shut."

There is a long moment of silence as everyone considers this.

"Come on, Stu, the guy's from *Rolling Stone*," protests Jacques.

"I don't give a shit," snarls Stu. "I'm not about to lose my job over this asshole. He can keep his fucking beers." Am I detecting a Boston accent? New England, almost certainly.

Big Vic turns to me. "Sorry, mate, but he's right. We've been told not to talk to any reporters. Good luck with your interview anyway."

Everyone except Stu walks over to shake my hand and thank me for the drinks. *Goddamn Schiffman has shut me down again*, I think angrily as I turn to leave.

"Wait!" The voice coming from over my left shoulder is that of Jacques. "You forgot this!" He presses another copy of the demo CD in my hand, stealing a glance back at the others as he does so. "Maybe I can do you a favor," he whispers. "You know, a favor for a favor."

"Sure. What do you have in mind?"

"I think I know where Hinch is," he murmurs under his breath. "If I tell you, do you promise to give my demo to Jann?"

My ears perk up. "Yes, I promise," I lie.

"Well, my guess is that Hinch has gone back home, to Switzerland. I know that's where I would be if I were him. Do you know who his wife is?"

I do. The Countess Miranda de Couqueville, to whom Hinch had been wed in an ostentatious public ceremony some two years previously, is a famous model and one of the most beautiful women in the known universe. She's also half his age and, according to the tabloids, notoriously tempestuous ... and promiscuous.

Jacques studies me as if I am some kind of test-tube experiment. "Tell me, if she were waiting in your bed every night, would you want to be anywhere else?"

"No," I reply honestly. "But I have it on good authority that Hinch is still in Holland."

"Fuck good authority," he says. "Hinch's wife is, shall we say, incredibly uninhibited between the sheets—so I'm told." He winks lecherously. "If his dick can still get hard, I guarantee you that's where he is. And if he isn't there ... well, trust me, you stand a good chance of finding out about her proclivities firsthand."

I stare at him as the enormity of what he is telling me sinks in. If what he is saying is true, all I have to do is get on a plane and head to glamorous St. Moritz: there, either I will find Hinch and get to finish the book, or I have a shot at sex with a nymphomaniac supermodel. It is a temptation impossible to resist.

"You *will* get this demo to Jann, right?" Jacques says, interrupting my reverie.

"Absolutely. And thanks."

As a bellman hails me a cab, the dark gloom that was once Groningen has magically transformed itself into the brightest of thousand-watt spotlights. Everywhere I look I see the face of an angel—an angel named Miranda—moaning softly in pleasure as I, Bernie Temkin, schlub from the Bronx, have my way with her in the bed of an international rock star by the name of Hinch.

I GET BACK TO the station just in time to make the midnight train back to Amsterdam. It's only when I settle into my seat that it occurs to me to check the cell phone. There are eight messages waiting for me, all from Hans.

"Hey, it's Bernie. What's up?" I ask casually once he picks up.

"Why the hell haven't I heard from you?" he screams down the line. "If you're trying to pull a fast one on me, I promise you Rudie will make you regret that decision."

"No, it's nothing like that," I protest. "This is just the first chance I've had to call. I'm actually on the train on my way back to Amsterdam."

"What did you find out?" If he's calmed down any, it's hard to tell from the tone in his voice.

"Well, Hinch's musicians and most of his crew are here, all right, but there's no sign of Hinch himself, or Schiffman. They don't seem to have any idea of where those two might be, either, though one of the musicians seems to think Hinch may have headed back to his home in St. Moritz."

"Impossible," sniffs Hans. "There's no way he could have left the country without my knowing about it."

I decide this isn't the expedient time to let Hans know about my plan to fly to Switzerland in the morning. "What did Rudie find out from the limo driver?" I ask instead.

"Not much. The driver claims he dropped Hinch and Schiffman and two other members of their crew off at the Schiphol before bringing the car straight back to the office."

"Do you believe him?"

"Well, Rudie does, so that's good enough for me."

"I hope he didn't have to resort to any...." I let the words trail off.

"Violence?" Hans laughs. "From our pleasant little Rudie? No. But he did make it clear to the driver that he knows where his wife works, and where his children go to school, so I think we got the truth from him."

"Where does that leave us?"

A deep sigh. "Nowhere, unfortunately. From the airport they could have taken a commuter flight anywhere within the Netherlands without needing any paperwork, or they could have hired a car. Who knows? I've got my contacts checking the local airline passenger lists and the car rental company records, but that could take a few days."

"Well, if it helps, one of the guys with Hinch and Schiffman is an American roadie by the name of Cody Jeffries—he's an old friend of Hinch's who actually used to be in the band. The other one is their road manager—they clammed up before I could get his name. None of them has been seen since the gig in Amsterdam."

"Hmmm. Good information. Nicely done, Bernie."

With Hans seemingly in a better mood, this seems like as good a time as any to bring up the Switzerland thing again.

"Look, Hans, I know you've got a lot of faith in your contacts, but I'd like to pursue this lead anyway. I was thinking I'd catch an early flight to Zurich, then jump on a train to St. Moritz. I want to check out Hinch's place. Even if he isn't there, it would give me good background for the book."

"I think that would be a total waste of time," he growls.

"Perhaps. But you seem to have everything under control, so I don't know if I can be of any more help to you here in Holland right now. I promise you, if I find out anything about Schiffman or where he is staying, I'll let you know right away."

"Maybe you should take Rudie with you for protection. Trust me, these are dangerous people we're messing with."

No, that's the last thing I want. A threesome with the gorgeous

Miranda de Couqueville and a cauliflower-eared Dutchman is not my kind of sexual fantasy, not in my wildest dreams. "Hans, I really don't think that's necessary," I argue. "In all likelihood, the only thing I'll encounter at Hinch's home is a cranky housekeeper who won't even let me in the door. You keep Rudie close by, where he can do his job helping people tell the truth." Even as I say the words, I can't shake the image of a terrorized limo driver who'll probably be spending the rest of his days living in fear for his family's safety.

"Okay," he finally capitulates. "As you Americans like to say, it's your funeral."

"Hopefully not."

"Just do me a favor," Hans says before signing off. "Hang on to that cell phone. I have a feeling we're going to be catching up with that slimy motherfucker Schiffman sooner rather than later."

12

Transcript: Interview with Donnie Boyle, May 2, 1998

Dammit, Bernie, I feel like shit. That little stay I had in the hospital kind of threw me for a loop. They got me on some new drugs now and it's messing me up even worse than this damn emphysema. Fucking doctors. If they can't cure you, they try to kill you.

So, yeah, we were talking about the Trucker boys, right? Well, all I can say is that getting Joe Dan and Vernon in the band proved to be just the kick in the ass we needed, and at just the right time, too. For one thing, it allowed me to concentrate full-time on getting us gigs. For another, it marked the end of our days in York.

Truth is, we'd been thinking about leaving for some time. Cody, certainly, had been lobbying for us to move to a big city to improve our chances of breaking big. But he was talking pie in the sky—New York or Los Angeles—and there was no way we could afford to live in either of those high-rent places. Then there was Hinch's relationship with Katie Q, which had us all pretty perplexed by that time. I mean, the guy had no scruples whatsoever about cheating on her—he'd ball any halfway decent chick who showed the slightest bit of interest in him, and, believe me, there were lots of them—yet he had this almost compulsive need to maintain daily contact with Katie, at least on the phone. But she was attending college in Philly and so she could only make it back to York to physically be with Hinch on weekends and holidays, which left him plenty of latitude.

So with JD and Vernon now in the band, there was the little problem of finding a place for them to stay, and, being manager, that became *my* problem. The tiny apartment Cody and I shared was barely big enough for the two of us, so that was out, and Hinch made it abundantly clear that he had no interest in having any roommates, so at first I had to stick the Truckers in a motel room. They didn't appear to mind all that much—they'd been on the road for so long by that point, it probably seemed like home to them anyway—but the band was footing the bill, and we didn't have the bucks to keep them there long-term. So the topic of housing was very much top of the agenda at our next band meeting, and this time around, it was Hinch who proved to be the catalyst.

Cody began, as usual, by going on and on about how great it would be to live in New York or L.A., talking excitedly about all the great places there were to play and how all the major record labels were based there.

"Nah," said Hinch with a wave of the hand. "I got a much better idea. Let's move to Philly."

Cody laughed, thinking he was joking. "What's in Philly?" he asked. "Besides Katie Q, I mean."

"You got a problem with Katie being in Philly?" Hinch growled.

Knowing he'd struck a raw nerve, Cody simply shrugged his shoulders.

Hinch continued, "Look, they've got a pretty decent music scene going on there, and it's affordable. Plus, it's that much closer to the Big Apple, so Donnie here can start earning his keep by getting us gigs on the New York circuit. Isn't that right, Donnie boy?"

I was a bit pissed off with his implication that I had somehow not been doing enough up until then but I had to admit that, yes, Philly would be a lot more affordable than either Manhattan or the Hollywood Hills, and that, yes, living there would give me considerably more opportunity to get us into the well-known New York venues: telling owners we were a "Philly band" would sound a lot less provincial than having to explain where York, Pa., was.

Plus there was the steadying influence of Katie, which I thought would be good for our front man. I was just surprised that Hinch was prepared to place himself more in her orbit and limit his opportunities to stray. I looked over at the Trucker brothers, who were sitting there impassively, offering no clue as to what their thoughts were—if any.

Cody continued to put up a half-hearted struggle, arguing that if we were going to make a move, we might as well go all the way, but Hinch was having none of it, and I found myself taking his side, both for financial and logistical reasons. Finally, the discussion—such as it was—came to an end, without either Trucker contributing a single word.

"I guess it's settled then," I said, looking around the room as four heads nodded in agreement. "Philadelphia, here we come."

In those days, rents in Philly were pretty cheap, and it didn't take us long to find a suitable place—a big run-down house with an attached mother-in-law apartment, which Hinch and Katie moved into. There were four bedrooms upstairs and a big eat-in kitchen downstairs that we all gathered in every morning for breakfast, plus a ramshackle living room, one corner of which served as a comfortable space for Cody and Hinch to do their songwriting. Cody even found an old upright piano advertised in the *Pennysaver*, which we had Muscle Beach Len haul over in our van. A lot of great songs would get written on that piano over the next couple of years.

At first, I tried managing the band from the sanctity of my bedroom, but the house quickly became party central, what with Cody constantly practicing and one or both of the Trucker brothers carrying on drunk as a skunk. It didn't help any when Katie began bringing by her friends from college, several of whom began carrying on noisy and jealous affairs with various band members. I have to admit I found myself entangled with one or two of them myself, back in the days when I could still handle it.

But that house was clearly no place to conduct business, and I was determined to do things right. I took my job seriously, see. Like Cody, I made it my goal to do everything in my power to propel the band as far as I possibly could. Maybe that's why he and I were always the closest in our triumvirate; Hinch always seemed to think he had fame and fortune coming to him. The Trucker brothers? Basically, they didn't give a shit. As long as they could play music, get drunk, and get laid—not necessarily in that order—they were happy.

So I rented a small office above a downtown storefront, and sat behind my rented desk in my rented chair and mailed out demo tapes and promo packages and pestered every club owner whose name and phone number I could locate and began the grind of lining up work. Eventually my persistence and our growing reputation began to yield results, and slowly some of the better gigs started rolling in.

But the pay in those clubs, even the ones in the bigger cities, was garbage; it was rare that we'd take home more than a couple of hundred bucks... assuming that the club owner was being honest about the door count, which few of them ever were. After paying the two roadies and putting gas in the van, not to mention covering the rent and household bills, there was barely enough left over for anyone to live on.

The big breakthrough, when it came, literally arrived at our doorstep in the form of one Janet Jaworsky, a rather dumpy, plain-looking friend of Katie's who had bad skin and wore thick glasses. She also had mammoth breasts, which, frankly, were her main redeeming physical feature.

Now, Janet had developed a bit of a crush on Vernon Dean, who was inclined to small women with big knockers, which she was and had, and so she had come over this one particular night to share a bottle of cheap red wine with our new bass player.

As they settled on the shag rug in front of the TV and began chugging down the vino, I happened to wander in. Katie Q, who was curled up on the sofa with Hinch, introduced me. "You know," she said, "you and Jan really should talk, because she's the head of our entertainment committee."

"Is that right?" I said, addressing Miss Jaworsky, who appeared to already be quite drunk. "And what exactly does an entertainment committee do? Plan birthday parties?"

I could tell from the expression on her face that Janet didn't appreciate my patronizing attitude, but she was also finding it difficult to get appropriately angry, what with Vernon earnestly fondling her in-between slugs of wine.

Disentangling herself from him momentarily, she smoothed her hair back and fixed me a reprimanding look. "Actually," she said, "we book concerts for the college."

"S'right," mumbled Vernon, distractedly nuzzling the nape of her neck. "I been talking to my sweet little jaybird here about getting us on a bill with one of them big groups."

"Big groups? Like who?" I asked.

"Well, not them," she replied. "They're too big now. Though they played at our college a few years back."

I had no idea what she was babbling about. "Excuse me?"

"The Who, silly," she giggled, now losing all pretense of propriety as Vern began tickling her. "But we do get some big acts in, like that cute Peter Frampton guy. And that new, hot singer from New Jersey, what's his name? Springstreet?"

I snapped to attention. Over on the sofa, I could see Hinch do the same. Frampton was already a big rock star from England, and the music press—which I read compulsively—were trumpeting Bruce Springsteen as if he were the second coming of Christ.

"Um, do you mind if I ask what kind of money you pay those guys?" I asked Janet while doing my best to appear professionally disinterested.

Vernon stopped sucking on her fingers just long enough to answer. "Thousands," he whispered between slurps. "Tell him, babe."

Rising unsteadily to her feet, Janet Jaworsky gave me a haughty look.

"That's right. Thousands. Even for the opening acts."

Thousands? For a single gig? I was dumbfounded.

"And," added Vernon, now standing directly behind her, arms wrapped tightly around her waist, grinding slowly with his hips as if about to take her doggy-style right then and there, "she's gonna be getting us a gig soon. Ain't that right, babe?"

From the depths of her mounting sexual ecstasy, Janet struggled to preserve one last shred of dignity. "Well, I'm definitely going to propose it to the committee," she told me, attempting to be business-like despite the red flush spreading across her face. "You should give me your card."

As I reached for my wallet to fish one out, she held up her hand to stop me.

"Not now, Mr. Manager," she said. "Later. After your bass player fucks my brains out."

I turned to Vernon, who looked like he was about to have an orgasm on the spot. "Honey," he said to her, "I thought you'd never ask."

THE NEXT MORNING, over breakfast, I finally got to hand Janet Jaworsky my business card. She and Vernon had spent the last twelve hours a-rockin' and a-rollin' in his hardly soundproof bedroom, and if the volume and frequency of her shouts and screams were any evidence, he had done his job well. A week later, she called my office, all prim and proper—a far cry from the sex-crazed co-ed who'd kept us awake all night while she ravaged our bass player. "Okay, you're in," she said. "The boys will be opening for the Edgar Winter Group in six weeks' time. I'll be mailing you the contracts tomorrow."

"Mind if I ask what the fee is?"

"Um, let me see. Oh yeah, here it is. Thirty-five hundred. Is that okay?"

I gulped. "Three thousand five hundred? Yeah, I guess that'll do."

That was more bread than we were making in a month slogging around the clubs—way more. And we'd be performing to a crowd of several thousands, instead of the two or three hundred upstanding citizens who frequented the dives we'd been playing.

Everyone in the band was over the moon about this, of course, and there were more than a few wisecracks about Vernon's sexual prowess. "Shit, you should have let me fuck her," Hinch said, good-naturedly. "They'd be paying us at least *ten* grand."

Vernon just sat in the corner, flashing the same kind of shit-eating grin I'd seen on Cody's face so many times before. Our new bass player had pulled off a feat even Cody couldn't have managed. He was a sparkplug, our Cody, but he never was a sex symbol. This was the first time I realized that he was starting to become the odd man out in our newly reconfigured band. Still, Cody had a lot more tricks up his sleeve.

"We're going to have to rework our set," he pointed out at our next band meeting. "Those college audiences will want to hear original music, not a bunch of tired old Top 40 tunes."

"Bullshit," huffed Hinch.

"I'm serious, bro. We need to put together an hour of original music."

I'd read the same thing in music press concert reviews and I turned to the Trucker brothers for corroboration, but it turned out that neither of them had ever been within a mile of a university. No surprise there, I suppose.

Still, Hinch insisted that we could do the gig with a condensed version of the same set of mostly cover music we'd long been playing on the club circuit. Like I said, he was very much a creature of habit and so he was starting to get pretty pissed off at Cody's suggestion that the set list be revamped.

"Look," I said, trying to act as peacemaker. "We can settle this easily enough by seeing for ourselves. Vernon, do you think Janet can score us some tickets to a gig at her school?"

Vernon picked up the phone. "No problem there, Donnie," he said with a grin and a wink. "I reckon that little girl will do just about anything I ask of her."

God, he made it sound so dirty.

THE CONCERT WAS AN EYE-OPENER. The British band Mott the Hoople were headlining, but we were far more interested in watching the opening act—an obscure five-piece out of Boston named Aerosmith.

Damn, they were good. Even Hinch had to admit they had potential, though he kept calling their flamboyant lead singer "Mick, Jr."—a sarcastic reference to the guy's obvious copping of the whole Jagger persona. JD and Vernon stood there bopping their heads in unison for a couple of songs, then trundled off to the bar, Janet in tow. But Cody, he didn't say a word during their entire set. He simply sat there watching them, transfixed, taking it all in. One of their songs—"Dream On"—was vaguely familiar, having been a minor hit the year before, but everything else in their set was new to our ears. As Cody had said, it was all original music: not a cover song to be heard.

But the biggest difference between this gig and those we'd been playing in noisy, smoky clubs for the past five years was the audience. They actually paid attention. Maybe it was because they were educated college kids and not working stiffs; maybe it was because they were mostly high on pot and not alcohol—the sweet smell of cannabis was the first thing that hit you when you entered the cavernous gymnasium, with hardly a beer bottle in sight—or maybe it was just because we were in a different league. But, here, the audience *listened*. To them, the music was something to be experienced and absorbed, not just aural wallpaper to serve as background noise while they shouted at one another across a raucous barroom.

That, for all of us, was the biggest revelation. By the end of the evening, Hinch had to concede that we would indeed have to rethink our set list. Cody seemed to be the most affected, though; in fact, it probably wouldn't be stretching things to say that he was positively transformed by what he had witnessed that night. For a long time afterwards, he couldn't stop talking about the way that several thousand people in one room could share such a positive experience, all through the liberating power of music. I guess that, somehow, it had never occurred to him that music could be as important to other people as it was to him.

The next few weeks of preparation for the gig were pretty intense. Every free moment was spent in rehearsal, as the emphasis shifted from the cover tunes we'd come to know so well to the original songs that Cody and Hinch had been writing—the same songs which had been given short shrift on the demo tape and in the sweaty clubs the band had been playing up until now, where the audience had limited interest in anything that was unfamiliar.

I have to say that everyone reacted well to the pressure. There was little infighting and surprising consensus in terms of deciding the set list and order. The Trucker boys, as usual, didn't have much to say, but they'd offer the occasional comment every now and then, and their suggestions were almost always good ones. Hinch and Cody began writing a bunch of new songs in preparation for the gig, but I noticed they continued to operate the same way as before, with Cody making sure to always leave something for Hinch to finish, and Hinch bringing in completed songs that he wouldn't allow Cody to put much of a fingerprint on. Still, I had to admit that some of the new material was really good, a definite step up from the tunes they had written previously. I remember thinking at the time that this increased sophistication reflected not only their growing abilities as musicians and songwriters, but also their common desire to forge new paths and not just follow current trends. It was, I felt, a healthy direction to be going in.

Throughout all of this, Vernon and Janet seemed to be solidifying their relationship: in my naiveté, it seemed like they were actually becoming a couple. Maybe it was just wishful thinking on my part, because the more we talked, the more I realized that Janet knew a lot more about booking gigs than I did, and I was eager to learn from her. One thing I was intensely curious about was how her school was able to pay musicians such big bucks. Turned out it wasn't just her college: it was pretty much every university in the country, at least those that had decent enrollments and hip student bodies. As she explained it, the tuition that the parents of these kids shelled out every year included a sizable contribution to what they called a student "union," which was responsible for providing recreational and social activities to kids who were presumed to be stressed out from their studies. Never mind the fact that most of those students were in fact spending most of their time getting high on pot, acid, and every other kind of drug they could get their hands on—the college charters allowed them to form their own unions and provided them with ample funding. Some of those funds were used to buy ping-pong tables and subsidize the cost of the food being sold in the student cafeterias, but the majority of the money was spent putting on special events like large concerts, which could offset their costs and perhaps even turn a profit through ticket sales. And these entertainment committees were shrewd enough to realize that the best way to attract musicians to play in the often out-of-the-way places where the campuses were located was to offer huge fees—in some cases, way more than bands would even get from playing big concert venues in major cities.

What's more, even though each committee had considerable discretion as to who they booked into their college—which is how Janet had been able to sneak us in as a support group even though we weren't all that well-known—they were organized on both a state and national level. Janet was already a member of the Pennsylvania committee, and she had hopes of being nominated to the national committee in her senior year. I was rooting for her, that's for sure: As far as I was concerned, as her stock rose, so would ours.

Which is why, as I said, I was happy with the idea of she and Vernon being in a relationship. I even took him aside at one point and told him so.

"Why, Donnie, I didn't know you cared," he drawled, beaming that gap-toothed grin at me. "But I think you may have gotten our little filly wrong."

"What are you talking about, Vern?"

"Hell, boy, she's just a star-fucker. A groupie. I'm just another notch on her hitching post."

I shook my head in disbelief. "I don't know, Vern—she sure seems into you."

"I'm just flavor of the month, Donnie boy. I got that sweet little thang all figured out. You mark my words."

That was all he had to say about the subject, though it was a conversation I'd replay in my head many times in the years to come. But I had no time to dwell on the sexual proclivities of sweet Miss Jaworsky.

We had a gig to do.

13

If I was dismayed by the climate in Groningen, I am absolutely numbed by the cold in St. Moritz, not to mention the prices. I knew this was a playground for the rich and famous, but I never realized just how much gouging goes on when the perceived affluence of the consumer exceeds the greed of the vendor. Twenty of those newfangled Euros for a frigging cheese sandwich—more than twenty bucks! Eight for a beer, five for a bar of chocolate, twelve for the flimsy reporter's notepad I thought to purchase in a news agent's shop. And I thought L.A. was an expensive town to live in.

Oh well, I'm here now and I have no choice but to go with the flow. Hopefully I'll manage to get out of this money pit before I run through the pitiful little that's left of my book advance. Which reminds me: I still need to call Britney. Needless to say, the message light in my claustrophobic Amsterdam hotel room was still resolutely unlit when I got in late last night and crashed for a few hours before packing a small bag and heading for the airport. I left yet another message on our answering machine, this time giving her Hans's cell number before breezily reporting my snap decision to fly to Switzerland for a day or two. Of course, I left out the part about the Countess de Couqueville, just in case I get lucky. Not that I think it's likely to happen—it's just ... well, you never know.

I'm sure glad I brought my laptop with me. Not only has it allowed me to go through the transcriptions of my interviews with Donnie Boyle—and I'm still convinced they will yield some kind of clue that will lead me to Hinch—but I was able to connect to the Internet at the airport and do a little advance research. Despite the fact that Al Gore claims to have invented it, this WorldWide Web thing does seem to hold some real promise.

Hinch's sprawling estate, I learn, is not in St. Moritz proper, but on the slopes of the nearby village of Celerina, just to the north, where, according to the *People* magazine website, he has a "stunning view of the Swiss Alps off to the east and the Engadin valley below." He's rumored to have paid just over four million dollars for the place back in '86 when he finally made the decision to emigrate following years of bad publicity over the Nancy Reagan thing. In those days, he was single and developed quite a reputation as an international playboy; since then, he's remarried and divorced three times.

Which makes him a rank amateur compared to his current wife, who has worked her way through no fewer than six husbands in her brief twenty-seven years of existence. Born to wealthy parents in Brazil, the vixen originally christened Miranda Esteban has lived at various times, and with various significant others of both genders, in Paris, Rome, Milan, Monaco, New York, Miami, Palm Springs, and, for some unfathomable reason, Little Rock, Arkansas. Hinch is the first rock star she's ever dated and/or married, but she's been linked to various European royalty as well as assorted industrialists, politicians, media moguls, film producers, and professional athletes in eight different sports. Mostly, she's a professional jet-setter; what little gainful employment she's had has been as a fashion model, her smoldering beauty gracing the covers of rags like *Vogue*, *Glamour, Cosmopolitan* and *Mademoiselle*. Other than that, she appears to have lived most of her life in nightclubs getting shitfaced and acting in a thoroughly unseemly manner. Rumor has it that she's bisexual and bipolar, a heavy drinker and a cokehead, a porn aficionado and a slut, none of which has prevented her from producing four healthy children, including an infant son she bore Hinch earlier this year. She must have the constitution of an ox, because none of this has done anything the least bit deleterious to her astonishingly perfect body. Yes, her oversized boobs may be mostly saline and her luscious lips botox-enhanced, but she is still, according to numerous polls and any red-blooded male you care to ask, the most desirable female on this spinning globe we call home.

And in just a few short hours, I'll be meeting her. Hopefully.

Maybe Hinch, too.

IT IS LATE AFTERNOON by the time I arrive in Celerina and check into the modestly appointed tourist hotel I've chosen for my stay—just four hundred Euros a night, a bargain in these parts. I drop my bags off in the musty room and race out the door after applying the tiniest splash of cologne, hustling in hopes of completing the journey up the treacherous mountain roads that lead to Hinch's mansion in the last fleeting daylight.

Some forty-five minutes later I steer my rented Citroen up to an imposing gate with its wrought iron neatly carved into a large letter "H." There is an intercom box off to the left, and I am about to press the button when I notice that the gate is ajar. Throwing caution to the winds, I opt to drive straight through; perhaps, I reason, it will fool whoever answers the door into thinking that I actually belong there.

I park the car off to one side of the circular driveway, newly cleared of the snow that has been gently falling all afternoon. Gravel and ice crunch beneath my feet as I trudge up to the massive doorway that will admit me either to heaven or hell, depending on how the gods favor me this day. A shiver runs up my spine, and not just from the cold, as I ring the bell.

No one appears. I strain to pick up sounds of life from within; there are none. Cautiously I begin to explore the exterior, peeking through one triple-glazed window, then another. Is that a faint light I see? Yes, that's definitely a table lamp, glowing softly in the gathering gloom.

Suddenly the door flies open.

"Who the fuck is that?" yells a foghorn. "Are you here with the stuff? I have a gun and I'm not afraid to use it!"

I can make out the words though they come out not in a human voice but in something closer to an unearthly shrieking, like the sound an alley cat might make if it were in extreme pain while simultaneously scraping its claws against a chalkboard.

"Uh, hello?" I venture cautiously from behind a hedge. "No need to use that gun, I can assure you."

"I said, who the fuck are you?" the voice repeats, a little more loudly. "Show your goddamn face!"

"I'm right here," I say as meekly as possible, stepping forward to reveal myself, hands aloft in the classic pose of surrender. "I'm not an intruder, I promise you. My name is Clive ... Clive Swindon."

"I haven't seen you before. Where's my stuff?" the voice demands.

"Stuff? I don't know anything about any stuff. I'm a reporter with *Rolling Stone* magazine, in the States. I'm here to interview Hinch."

"Patrick didn't send you?" says the voice disappointedly, now somewhat abated in volume but still possessing the harsh timbre of a wounded crow in heat. Shielding my eyes against the brightness blaring forth from the floodlight mounted above the doorway, I am finally able to identify the source of the caterwauling. It seems to be a barefoot female figure in a state of disarray, hair blowing wildly in the wind, hands clutching a threadbare robe around her to ward off the bone-shattering chill. I move closer and can finally make out her face.

My god. It's none other than the Countess Miranda de Couqueville.

Any second now I expect her to slam the door shut, but for some reason the Countess relents. "Okay, Mr. *Rolling Stone* man, I guess you'd better come inside. Stay out here much longer and your dick might freeze up and fall off."

Charming.

"Wait here," she commands once we are in the warmth of the vestibule. "I have a call to make." I am assaulted by the unmistakable odor of cat's piss. Off in the distance I hear a baby crying.

Once again I am subjected to the harsh grating of the Countess's voice, this time at a distance. "Sarah!" she yells at the top her lungs. "Get Patrick on the fucking phone! And tell Giselle to shut that brat up!"

"Yes, ma'am," a tiny voice replies. "Right away, ma'am."

The scuffling of feet and Miranda pokes her head back into the hallway. I notice that she has taken a moment to comb her hair and apply a smear of lipstick.

"Alright, follow me and take a seat," she instructs as she ushers me into the living room. "I'll have my useless piece of shit maid fix you a cup of tea. Unless you'd like something stronger, that is."

"No, tea will be fine. I...."

"Sarah!" More yelling. "Some fucking tea for our guest! And a brandy for me ... a double."

Sarah races in, skittish and gray as a mouse. "Yes ma'am," she gulps. "Tea, and a brandy."

"A *double* brandy, you bitch. And, for the second time, tell that fucking nanny to shut that goddamn baby up."

"Yes, ma'am, of course, ma'am." The voice trails off as sorry little Sarah scurries off to run her errands. As I glance around the room, I am shocked at how shabby and depressing it is—not at all what I was expecting of a rock star's mansion. There are a handful of gold records hanging crookedly over the fireplace, and some of the paint is beginning to peel off the walls. For the first time I realize that we are surrounded by cats of all sizes and varieties. Some are lounging on chairs; others are scratching themselves behind the ears or licking their balls. You know, all the things cats do when they are bored, which is always.

Idly removing one particularly large gray feline from her lap, the

Countess turns her gaze to me. "You just can't get the help these days," she sighs. I am having enormous difficulty reconciling the grating voice with the beauteous creature before me; even wrapped carelessly in a disheveled silk robe, there is no question that this is a gorgeous, utterly desirable woman, albeit one with the voice of Foghorn Leghorn.

There's a moment of awkward silence, and then the beleaguered maid enters again, bowing and scraping, bearing a pot of tea and a large brandy for Madame. The cats scatter in her wake.

"Where's the fucking bottle?" asks Her Majesty without a trace of grace. "If I've told you once, I've told you a hundred times, bring the fucking bottle along with the glass! You think you can keep it for yourself? No way, you little bitch. I *own* that bottle; I own every fucking bottle of fucking brandy in this fucking house. In fact," she points out to the quaking maid, "I own *you*."

After a brief chorus of "Yes, ma'ams, sorry, ma'ams," Sarah scuttles off to retrieve the bottle, eyes firmly cast downward, presumably lest she turn into stone.

Once again Miranda returns her attention to me. "They steal, you know. Every one of them."

I am about to utter words of sympathy despite the fact that I've never employed, much less owned, a servant before, when Sarah reappears with impressive alacrity. As she gently places the bottle before her mistress, I notice her hands are trembling.

The Countess continues her haranguing. "What about that phone call to Patrick?" she demands. "Why haven't you called him yet?"

"I have called, ma'am," Sarah quakes. "There was no answer. I left a message."

"Well, keep trying. Bitch." With a wave of her arm, Sarah is dismissed. Idly I wonder what her living quarters look like. It wouldn't surprise me if it were a dungeon.

There is a brief pause while I sip my tea and Miranda slugs down her double, then immediately refills her glass, studying me closely the entire time.

"Well, I will say this," she observes. "You sure look like a faggoty reporter. Why can't I ever get a *real* man to appear on my doorstep? It would be nice to meet someone who looks like they can keep a hard-on going for more than a minute and a half." She punctuates the complaint with a loud belch.

Shocked as I am by her coarseness, I find myself also feeling somewhat flattered that she feels comfortable enough in my presence to confide such personal details. As she leans back in her seat, sighing deeply, her right breast falls out of her robe. Christ, it's even more magnificent than I imagined. I find myself wondering if the left one is even half as good.

Too late I realize I am staring, my mouth hanging open like a cow in mid-moo. "What are you looking at?" Miranda demands, quickly returning her stray breast to its comfy home inside the robe. "What do you think this is, a fucking peep show?"

"Sorry, so sorry," I mumble, thoroughly chastened.

Still, she seems more amused than angry. "I don't give it away for free," she says, a little more softly. "Everything in this world has a price. Right, Charlie?"

"Clive."

"Clive, Charlie, whatever."

She gulps back her second brandy and stares at me. *She's nuts*, I think. *Gorgeous, but nuts.*

"Alright, Mister Reporter, tell me about this interview," she suddenly barks, breaking the silence.

"Well, actually, I was sent to interview Hinch. Is he here?"

She laughs. "My asshole husband? I haven't seen him since he walked out the door a few weeks ago with that creepy new road manager of his."

"To begin the tour, you mean?"

"Whatever it is he does when he goes away," she says with a sneer. "He calls it work; I call it banging groupies."

I almost start to say *well, it's a tough, dirty job, but someone's gotta do it*, but I have a feeling the humor would go over her head. Instead, I go for the phony sympathy. "It's got to be tough for you," I commiserate, furrowing my brow in what I hope is a look of deep concern.

"I don't miss him, if that's what you mean. In fact, the next time I see that prick will be the last time, because I plan on filing for divorce. Just wait till my lawyers get their hands on that sweet little bank account of his! He's already afraid of his own shadow, the big pussy. Well, I'll give him a good reason to be afraid. He'll be sorry he ever met me, you wait and see."

Somehow, I suspect Hinch already feels that way but I decide not to share that thought. "What was it about this new road manager that you didn't like?" I ask instead.

"Everything. He's ugly. Big scar across his face. And he's bald. I hate bald, ugly people." *Good thing I remembered to wear the toupee.* "The old road manager who used to come around," she continues, her speech starting to slur, "he was tall and handsome and pretty to look at. I wanted to fuck him, of course, but I also liked him, you know? He was nice to me, so I liked him, and Hinch liked him also. But this new one, I didn't like at all, and neither did Hinch. I could see Hinch was very unhappy to see this bald, ugly road manager, but he left with him anyway to go off and bang groupies."

"So you don't have any idea where Hinch might be?"

"No, and I don't give a shit, either. So we'll just have to change the focus of your little interview, won't we? It's been way too long since *Rolling Stone* has run a feature on the Countess Miranda de Couqueville, don't you think?" She flutters her eyelashes at me.

I melt.

DURING THE NEXT several hours, I am exposed to at least half a dozen Mirandas as I pretend to take notes. There's the coquettish flirt, the self-pitying whiner, the spoiled brat, the cruel slave owner, the neglected wife, the charming psychopath. She is by turns insightful, obtuse, erudite, moronic, breezy, and disagreeable. One moment she is giggling like a little girl; the next, raging like a bitter old hag. My head is spinning faster than Linda Blair in *The Exorcist* as the clinically insane woman sitting before me puts on a show of personalities that rivals both Ringling Brothers *and* Barnum and Bailey.

Still, I want her.

As she shifts around in her seat, I take every available opportunity to feast my eyes on every square inch of her flesh, at least the bits I can see. Sadly, the right breast fails to make a reappearance, nor is it joined by its companion, but as the Countess crosses her legs I get a tantalizing yet all too fleeting glimpse of the dark bush at the apex of her exquisitely creamy thighs. Her calves are perfectly shaped, with ankles so slender they would make even Oscar Wilde's heart beat fast; and her arms toned, smooth and soft, glistening slightly in the flickering candlelight that illuminates our surroundings, delicate fingertips gently caressing the brandy snifter I long to be.

Her face, too, is an endless sea of mystery that churns the waves of desire welling deep within me. Impossibly high cheekbones, eyes like fiery orbs, sensuously flaring nostrils, ruby red pouting lips, soft darting tongue, all framed in a spray of jet-black hair so soft that it invites stroking just as the nape of her delicate neck invites kissing.

"Sarah!" she suddenly screeches, rudely interrupting my lusftful inventory. "Get the fuck in here!"

The meek chambermaid pokes her head in the door uncertainly. "Yes, ma'am?" she squeaks.

"What the fuck is going on with Patrick? How come his guy hasn't shown up yet?"

"I just got off the phone with him, ma'am. They were delayed with the snowstorm. He should be here any minute."

"He'd better be," Miranda growls, "or it's your ass on the line."

Just about on cue, the doorbell rings and Sarah goes off to answer it. A moment later she returns and hands a small envelope to the Countess.

"About fucking time," snaps Miranda. "Now get the fuck out of here."

I start to rise, mumbling my thanks for the tea and hospitality.

"Not you, dickhead. Her." She points to Sarah, who gratefully scampers off, barely suppressing a huge sigh of relief. "You, I have plans for. Besides, there's a blizzard going on out there. You'll never get back down those mountain roads tonight."

I retreat to my chair, the blood pounding in my ears at the prospect of what may lie ahead. Visions of last night's dream flood back into my consciousness as I picture myself entering Miranda's lithe body, providing her with wave after wave of orgasmic pleasure that transcend any that Hinch or the original Count de Couqueville or any of her dozens of previous conquests were ever able to deliver. I feel my manhood beginning to grow hard in anticipation. *If only I can make it last more than that minute and a half*, I think.

Once again my horny daydream is interrupted by a sound of the most intrusive variety. This time the Countess is blowing her nose, noisily and sloppily, into a silk handkerchief which she then drops on the floor. As I watch it fall to the ground, foul contents exposed to the air, my ardor begins to cool. Looking up, I notice a small booger on the end of Miranda's perfectly upturned nose. I'm debating how best to alert her to this social *faux pas* when she lets out a fart. Not a small, delicate ladylike fart which might easily be ascribed to one of the ranging cats, or simply ignored, but a blast which defies polite circumspection.

"Sorry," she mumbles. "Phew, that's a bit smelly." She begins waving the air with one hand while removing a brown and white feline from her neck with the other. Unfortunately, her gesture only has the effect of worsening the olfactory offense. My erection subsides.

My erstwhile hostess is now ignoring me completely, so intently is she focused on unwrapping a small glassine envelope contained within the larger one Sarah brought in a few moments ago. Reaching into a drawer, she extracts a small mirror, atop which sits a single-edged razor blade and a rolled-up banknote. With total concentration she lays out a dozen thin lines of white powder, then promptly inhales them all, several hundred dollars gone up her nose. I am reminded of the old rock 'n' roll aphorism about how a cocaine habit is God's way of telling you you're making too much money.

With a deep sigh she throws her head back. For the first time in ten minutes she seems to notice me. "Mmmm, good shit," she says. "Want some?"

"Um, no. No thanks," I mutter.

She looks at me as if I have lost my mind. "Are you sure?"

"Yes, thank you. I mean, normally I would, only I'm working. You know, doing this interview."

"Oh well," she shrugs. "More for me, then." Five minutes later all the coke is gone and she is laughing hysterically at absolutely nothing. "Fucking cats," she roars when one starts to sit on her head. "Hinch hates them, you know. Claims he's allergic or something."

"Why do you have so many of them around, then?"

"To annoy him, mostly," she answers. "To watch him sneeze and sputter. I can't stand the little fuckers myself." Another whoop of uproarious laughter. Suddenly Miranda leans forward, eyes burning intensely. "I have a baby, you know," she confides with a totally unnecessary degree of urgency. "I'm a mother. I'm not just a motherfucker, I'm a mother, too." She giggles at her own unfunny joke.

I chuckle politely, not sure what to say.

"Do you want to see him?" she suddenly asks.

"Your baby? But it's nearly midnight."

"Fuck what time it is: I want you to see him." She begins to holler at the top of her lungs: "GISELLE!"

Overhead I hear the shuffling of feet. A moment or two later another scared rabbit—I mean servant—races in, this one a middle-aged woman with blond curls and a puffy red face. She looks as if she's just been awoken from a deep sleep, which I'm sure she has.

"Yes, ma'am?"

"Bring the baby downstairs. I want my friend Charlie here to see him."

"Clive," I protest. She pays me no attention whatsoever.

"But the baby, he is fast asleep," says the nanny in a soft French accent.

"ARE YOU TALKING BACK TO ME?" shrieks my genial hostess to the terrified nanny.

"No, ma'am, of course not, ma'am," Giselle avers while curtsying. "I'll go get the baby now."

As she leaves the room Miranda cuts another fart, this one even more powerful and offensive than the first. "Fucking nannies, fucking maids, fuck them all," she grouses, her head weaving like one of those bobble-head dolls.

I am speechless. This has got to be one of the weirdest evenings I have ever suffered through.

"I hate babies," she suddenly announces out of nowhere.

"You do? Why do you keep having them, then?" This is an indelicate question, I know, but I have a hunch she won't take offense.

She doesn't. "My lawyer," she explains. "He told me a long time ago, always have a kid with each guy you marry. Makes it harder for them to get out of paying through the nose when it's time for the divorce."

"That's a reason to bring a baby into this world?" I ask, astonished.

"Good as any," she answers blithely. "And, believe me, I will make Hinch pay handsomely."

After a moment of fumbling around in another drawer, Miranda pulls out a lethal-looking glass pipe, then extracts a second glassine envelope and fills the bowl with its contents. "Pure opium," she proclaims to me proudly. There's a passing moment of hysterics until a cigarette lighter is located, and then, without further ado, I find myself sitting in an opium den opposite a crack ho who happens to be married to one of the most famous rock stars in the world and the subject of the book which has come to consume my life.

Christ, the fumes are noxious! It's hard enough to tolerate the harsh second-hand smoke; her lungs must be lined with leather to be able to absorb the full impact of the black, smoldering narcotic. I watch in morbid fascination as the Countess repeatedly lifts the pipe to her lips and notice, for the first time, the trace of an unsightly mole on her left cheek and the barest shadow of stubble on her crossed legs.

The unventilated room is rapidly filling with toxic smoke when, to my horror, Giselle walks in, holding Hinch's infant son, bundled in a gray wool blanket. At first, Miranda doesn't even notice their entrance. After a moment she raises her head slightly and mumbles something burbly that sounds like "My baby, this is my baby," before her head falls back and she passes out. Within seconds, my dream girl is snoring like a stuck pig, saliva leaking from both sides of her lipstick-smeared botox-injected mouth. It's quite possibly the most revolting thing I've ever seen.

"Take the child back upstairs," I quickly instruct Giselle. The relief on her face is unmistakable. Just as quickly as she appeared, she disappears. I remove the pipe from Miranda's faltering grasp and toss it on the table.

Every last ounce of my desire has evaporated and been replaced with disgust. The Countess Miranda de Couqueville may be the hottest woman I've ever laid eyes on, but I've got to get the fuck out of here.

OUTSIDE, THE BLIZZARD is raging and the mountain roads are every bit as treacherous as I have been warned. More than once I find myself beginning to slide off the edge of a cliff as I carefully steer the rattling Citroen around heart-rending hairpin turns, but somehow I manage to make it back down to the village in one piece. For hours afterward my hands cannot stop shaking, but I think I'm more frightened at what I witnessed back at the mansion than at the perils of the journey back. My perfect woman has been revealed as grossly imperfect. How can a woman so physically alluring be at the same time so emotionally repellent? It's a new concept for me, and one that I'm having a lot of trouble wrapping my head around. Somehow in my mind I've come to equate beauty with perfection; I've just assumed that the unattractive women I've met in my life had to be just as flawed on the inside as they were on the outside.

As I lay on my hotel bed, I think of Britney. Is there anything about her that I actually like, other than her pert titties and glorious ass? I'm trying hard to come up with something when fatigue suddenly overtakes me and I begin to drift off to sleep. The last thing I see before I close my eyes is a small sign over the door. It reads, "It is not permitted to bring pets or musicians in the room."

With the slightest hint of a smile playing about my lips, I fall into the deepest slumber of my life.

14

Transcript: Interview with Donnie Boyle, May 6, 1998

YOU KNOW, AFTER our last conversation I got to thinking some more about Janet Jaworsky, or JJ, as we came to know her, and I realized that she really was like a guardian angel to us. Not only was she the driving force in getting us our first-ever concert date, back in the spring of '74, she somehow always seemed to be there whenever we needed to move on to the next level, at least in the early years. I wonder what the hell ever happened to her? Probably married with two kids and a nice home in the suburbs. Geez, if only her old man knew some of the wild things she'd gotten up to back in those days. ...

And, yeah, it turned out that Vernon was absolutely right about her. My first clue came the day of the gig. We got there good and early and had a chance to mingle a little with the guys in the Edgar Winter Band while their equipment was being set up onstage. They'd been friendly enough, if a bit standoffish. But then they started showing their true colors. Our contract stipulated that we'd have a full hour to sound check after they completed theirs—the opening act always goes last because they take the stage first during the concert itself—but the Winter guys began running way overtime, leisurely joking and wisecracking their way through most of their set. They even tried out a couple of new songs, which meant that they were essentially rehearsing on our time.

I tried finding someone from the college to intervene, but the only person I could get a hold of was this utterly disinterested security guy who told me in no uncertain terms that not only didn't he give a shit, but we all had to clear out at 5 PM whether we were done or not. In the end, we only had ten minutes to sound check, which barely gave Hinch and the boys enough time to run through a couple of songs. Making matters worse, the Winter roadies refused to move any of their massive backline equipment offstage, which forced Muscle Beach Len to set up our gear in front of theirs. That meant that our guys had to play all crowded together on the very lip of the stage, leaving

Hinch almost no room to maneuver from his front and center position.

This was actually standard operating procedure for a headlining band that wasn't familiar with the support group, though I didn't know it at the time. It was nothing more than rock 'n' roll hazing—a psychological ploy to try to throw the opening act off so they give a bad performance. We may have been babes in the woods, but we were still all pretty pissed off about it, I can tell you.

With all that going on, the guys only had a couple of hours to grab a quick bite and change their clothes before they had to take the stage. The auditorium was still filling up as they launched into their first song, and Cody and Hinch seemed slightly nervous to begin with, but things soon settled down. Frankly, I had seen them play better during some recent club dates. Still, all things considered, they did a pretty good job that night, despite the lack of stage area to work in, and so the audience was pretty hyped up.

I was watching from the wings, standing next to Muscle Beach Len, who was focused intently on the band's every move, flashlight at the ready so that he could dash right out and provide assistance if the slightest problem arose. About halfway through the set, I happened to notice Edgar Winter himself standing off in the wings over on the other side of the stage. Given all the shit that had gone down earlier, I was surprised to see him there, and even though my attention was on Hinch and the boys, every now and then I would steal a glance over at the albino rocker to see his reaction. Edgar seemed to be enjoying himself immensely. At first I allowed myself a flush of satisfaction at the idea that the band—*my* band—had so impressed the veteran musician. But somehow I couldn't shake the feeling that he was enjoying himself a little *too* much.

That's when I looked down and saw the back of sweet Janet Jaworsky's head rhythmically bobbing up and down as she crouched on her knees in front of him.

Guess old Vernon knew what he was talking about, I thought, curious to see if he was witnessing the same thing I was. He seemed oblivious, though, lost in the music, keeping the groove locked with his big brother, who was happily flailing away behind his huge drum kit. Finally Hinch stepped up to the mic, thanked the audience for coming, and launched the band into what I knew was the final song in our carefully thought-out set list. It was an all-out rocker he and Cody had written in the last few weeks, designed to bring the crowd to their feet.

And damned if it didn't do just that, Bernie boy. The audience had been pretty enthusiastic all night but now they kicked into another gear, boogieing in the aisles and letting out a huge roar as the climax of the song was reached and the final power chord hung in the air. I was ecstatic—we'd pulled it off! And the band knew it, too: I could see it in their eyes as they rushed past me, drenched in sweat and pumped up with adrenaline, heading for their dressing room to towel down briefly before reemerging to do a well-deserved encore.

But then, nothing. Though the crowd stomped their feet and waved their cigarette lighters aloft in the smoky black air, there was no movement either backstage or onstage. Then, just as quickly, it was over. The house lights went up, signalling the start of intermission to the disappointed crowd.

What the hell? I was furious. Pushing past the various hangers-on at the side of the stage, I fought my way to our dressing room, only to find my entrance blocked by two big goons wearing black T-shirts. I recognized them immediately as members of Edgar Winter's road crew.

"Sorry, no one gets in or out," said the bigger and uglier of the two, crossing his arms.

"I'm their manager, you idiot," I barked, frantically waving my all-access laminate in his face.

He and his compadre exchanged knowing looks, looks which told me I was about to get my ass kicked. But I was determined to hold my ground. Reaching between them, I pounded on the door.

"It's Donnie! Let me in!"

Fists cocked, the goons advanced on me menacingly. "Open the damn door!" I shouted again, even louder.

All of a sudden, with a loud bang, the door flew open and Cody burst out, followed closely by Joe Dan and Vernon, who neatly gang-tackled Goon #1 while Cody took down Goon #2 and began whaling on his surprised butt. What followed was a whirlwind of violence, the only sound that of fists slamming into flesh, accompanied by a chorus of animal-like grunts and yelps of pain. This was as nasty a brawl as I had ever witnessed, even in the shittiest bars we'd ever played, and for a brief moment I contemplated diving in, though from the look of things Cody and the Truckers didn't seem to need much in the way of help.

"Stop it! NOW!"

The voice, shrill and harsh, belonged to Janet, who, having apparently completed her blowjob duties, had just made her way backstage. We were all so surprised by the ferocity of her command, everyone just kind of froze, like you'd see in a cartoon. It was funny in a way, really.

Now she addressed the two roadies as they lay on the ground, bleeding profusely.

"Listen to me, you assholes. Edgar needs you onstage, right now. If you want to hang on to your pathetic jobs, I think you'd better get going. *Now.*"

The goons took a minute or two to weigh their options, which, I guessed, included taking on this very angry little chick. Slowly, they peeled themselves off the floor and started heading for the stage area, glowering at Cody and the Truckers as they retreated. Through the broken door leading to the dressing room I could see Hinch rooted to the ground. At first I thought he was laughing, but I was wrong. He was seriously pissed off; in fact, he was angrier than I'd ever seen him.

"Those motherfuckers locked us in our dressing room," he said, fairly spitting out the words, "and they wouldn't let us out."

A red-faced Cody chimed in. "The audience wanted an encore. Dammit, we *earned* an encore."

Janet stepped forward and gently put her hand to his cheek. "It's the way of the world, sweetie," she said soothingly, causing Cody to get even more red in the face, this time from embarrassment. "Opening acts don't do encores unless the headliners want them to," she explained. "The good news is that you guys played well enough for Edgar to view you as a threat."

She turned to Vernon and slid her arm through his. "The bad news, my darlings, is that the cost of repairing this door is going to come out of your paycheck. Now let's all go home and celebrate."

THAT NIGHT, JANET positively outdid herself. Unashamedly flirting with all of us except Hinch—only because he was accompanied by a clearly disapproving Katie—she spent considerable time making out with Cody on the sofa before deciding to spend the night in Joe Dan's room, along with Joe Dan *and* Vernon. What the hell, they were brothers: I guess they were used to sharing. The next morning, as we all nursed hangovers from hell, I noticed Cody seemed a bit down in the dumps.

He didn't want to talk about it, though I suspected he was more upset about JJ's choice of sleeping partners than he let on. Poor guy, he seemed to have developed a slight crush on our bed-hopping little trollop. Cody always was a bit too sensitive when it came to women.

What do I mean by that? Well, look, Bernie, I'm a happily married man now and I don't want to get myself into a shitload of trouble, but the truth of the matter is that none of us had any trouble getting chicks in those days. If Hinch wasn't with Katie Q on any given night, you could be almost certain he was with someone else—sometimes even two or three chicks at a time, which was something he got increasingly into. Even for the rest of us, who didn't have Hinch's good looks and charm, it was generally no problem getting laid. Musicians always have been babe magnets; there's something about that bad boy image that women seem attracted to. It's as true today as it was then, but people were a lot freer in expressing themselves back in those days, before there were things like AIDs.

I soon came to realize that not all groupies were the same; in fact, they tended to come in three different varieties. There were the fans, who basically were attracted to the fame, the idea of breathing the same air as someone they idolized. These chicks sometimes took a bit of work to score with, because once they wormed their way inside the inner circle and faced the reality of the situation, they would often freeze, like deer caught in the headlights. If you were persistent enough, however, and paid them enough attention, they would usually bow to the pressure and spend the night ... or at least a few worthwhile hours. And as demure and sweet as they seemed to be when your first met them, they would usually turn out to be raging monsters once you got them between the sheets. The problem was afterwards, when some of them would turn into stalkers.

Then there were the trophy collectors. These were the pros, whose goal was to bed as many musicians as possible. They were often engaged in competition with one another, and of course the more famous the musician, the greater the bragging rights—the more prestigious the trophy. You might think these would be the oldest of the girls we'd encounter, but quite often it was the opposite. Many of them were just teenagers, in fact, and more than a few of them were jail-bait. They always lied about their age, trying to make themselves seem like they were sophisticated and in their twenties, but you'd usually know from the impossible smoothness of their skin or the gravity-defying perkiness of their breasts that they were barely out of junior high. These girls would have to have an especially amazing ass, or a particularly luscious mouth, for you to get tempted, but sometimes you'd just give into that primal lust anyway and take your chances. The trophy collectors were very proficient at what they did—they knew all kinds of positions and especially prided themselves on their blow job technique—but the sex tended to be very mechanical; you always felt like you were being graded and compared to their last conquest.

Finally, there were the nurturers, the chicks who saw it as their duty to welcome you to their home town and make you as comfortable as possible. They tended to be the oldest of the groupies—sometimes they were even the moms of the fans or the trophy collectors—but they were always a welcome sight, even if they weren't necessarily the best-looking of the bunch. That's because these were the women who would be happy to do your laundry or buy you booze or wipe your nose if you had a cold ... all before hopping into bed with you and giving you the kind of warm, touchy-feely sex that only a girlfriend—or, in their case, temporary girlfriend—could provide. You could very easily get attached to one of these chicks, even develop feelings for them, but deep down you also knew that no groupie was actually girlfriend material, if for no other reason than that they had been performing the same exact "services" for the last band that hit town.

So groupies were simply a part of the way of life, and a welcome one at that, but none of us ever really took them seriously. No one except Cody, that is. Whereas Hinch and I—and certainly the Trucker brothers—saw these flings as nothing more than a way of letting off steam, Cody always viewed them as, well, *relationships*.

Now I know that's a very popular concept today—every woman says they're dying to meet a guy who actually wants to be in a relationship with them, but things were different back in the '70s, when, more than anything, women wanted to be *free*. Free to work at whatever job they wanted; free to pursue whatever interests they wanted; and free to fuck any guy they wanted. For most women—at least the ones we knew—that meant no commitment, no kids, no ties: they would just keep trying out different men like they were trying on different shoes. So when Cody would start getting all soppy-eyed, talking about how he was starting to fall in love with this girl and how he wanted to settle down with that one, they usually would go running, even if they kinda liked him. I tried explaining this to him more than once, but he stubbornly clung to the illusion that the right woman for him was out there on the road somewhere and that he'd find her eventually.

"Sure you will," I'd say to him sarcastically. "In the meantime, keep fucking as many of the wrong ones as you can, because when you do stumble across the right one, she's going to have your dick in a sling."

He'd flash me that lopsided grin of his and then keep on doing what he was doing, getting his heart broken a dozen times a week. That Cody, he always was a glutton for punishment.

WITH THE COLLEGES out for the summer, we returned to our usual routine of playing the club circuit, continuing to build up a loyal following as the band got even tighter and more polished. It was a trying time, though, especially for Cody, who was still lobbying hard for the band to play all-original music—something that was impossible to do in bars, where audiences would often turn hostile if they weren't hearing tunes they were familiar with. On the positive side, our net was being cast wider and wider, with gigs starting to come in around the New York area. I'd sent our demo tape to the owner of a chain of clubs on Long Island called the Oak Beach Inn, and on the strength of that, he'd booked us into each of his five venues on successive weekends, culminating with a big Labor Day bash at their place in the Hamptons. It seemed promising, though what was bugging my ass was that I hadn't been able to land us any gigs in the city itself, even in a support slot. Still, the little tours we were doing were beginning to get longer and longer, and we found ourselves spending three, sometimes four weeks on the road at a time, staying in cheap motels and Holiday Inns. Whenever we were back home, JJ would stop by the house, doing her thing with the boys in the band—even with Hinch on occasion, if Katie Q wasn't around. Still, even as Janet was screwing them all silly, she was turning into a true friend and ally, and even Cody seemed to start to get it.

One August morning JJ announced to me that she had received her coveted appointment to the national college entertainment committee. She hoped, she explained excitedly, that this would open up the door to our landing well-paying college dates all over the country. It was music to my ears, but things didn't quite turn out that way. That's because we were now at the point in our career where we were firmly caught in the Great Rock 'n' Roll Spiral, which goes something like this: In order to be a rock star, you have to play original music. However, in order to have somewhere to play your own songs, you have to land concert gigs. And in order to land concert gigs, you have to have a booking agent. But in order to get a booking agent, you have to have a record contract. And in order to land a record contract, some A&R guy—the "Artists and Repertoire" record company flunky whose job it is to scout out talent—has to see you playing a concert gig so they can determine how your songs go down with an actual audience. But in order to land a concert gig—well, you get the picture.

Okay, maybe it's not quite Catch-22, but it's pretty damned close. And there we were, stuck in this crazy closed loop. Every college Janet or I approached asked who our booking agent was, and every booking agent we approached asked who our record label was, and every record label we approached said that their A&R man needed to see the band at a proper gig—if not a college concert, then at least a slot at a well-known New York club like Max's Kansas City or CBGBs—before they'd even consider signing us. Yet even those dives were impossible to get into without a booking agent ... who was impossible to land unless we had a record deal, and on and on and on.

It was all so damn frustrating. I knew we had a kick-ass band with solid musicianship and great showmanship and, based on the one experience we'd had, I knew we were perfectly capable of winning over a college audience. I also knew in my heart that the songs that Hinch and Cody were writing were as good as most of the crap coming over the radio waves, probably a lot better. But we were caught in this ridiculous cycle, and I was searching desperately for a way to break out of it.

I dunno, Bernie, maybe there is something to that Zen thing, because the answer presented itself just as I stopped searching for it. It was Labor Day weekend—that ritual end to the summer—and after all the hazy, hot months spent in pursuit of that Magical Gig From The Sky, I'd pretty much resigned myself to putting the guys through another long, cold-weather slog around the smoky, noisy bars of the Northeast. I hadn't given up on *them*, mind you; maybe I'd just given up on myself.

That's the state of mind I was in when we showed up at the Oak Beach Inn East: tired, discouraged, resigned. The band had done well at the other OBI clubs the previous four weekends, with the size of the crowds increasing noticeably with each gig. Still, we were unprepared for the huge crush of people awaiting us that night. Judging from the sheer number of Birkenstocks alone—not to mention the deep Coppertone tans and expensive resort-wear on display—this was not our usual audience. No, these were definitely New York City people, and not just any Manhattanites. These were the socialites and jet-setters, the corporate muckamucks and their surgically enhanced wives and mistresses: the privileged few you'd read about in the papers as they frolicked in the playground of the wealthy.

And, man, were they ready to party! As good as the band had gotten since the addition of the Truckers, I almost couldn't believe the response they received that night. It was like they could do no wrong—every number was followed by a huge wave of applause, and everyone was dancing and sweating and drinking their sweet asses off. Okay, maybe you saw more martinis in people's hands than long-neck beers, but there was no lack of enthusiasm coming from any quarter, and the appreciation radiating from the audience kicked the band into a higher gear. It might have been their best gig ever, at least to that point.

Afterwards, the dressing room was packed to the gills with well-wishers. It reminded me of that crazy scene in the Marx Brothers movie where Harpo is walking on top of trays being carried by waiters and finally the maid comes to clean the room and when she opens the door, a flood of people come pouring out like water. There were insane rich people everywhere, all gushing with praise for my little band: drunken socialites sticking their tongues in my ear, prep school hoo-hahs pressing their business cards in my hand, inebriated masters of industry slapping me on the back as if I were a member of their yacht club; there was even this one insufferable geek with bushy eyebrows who spoke with a weird accent and insisted on telling me every last excruciating detail about the diamond trade even as I was being pulled in ten different directions by twenty different people.

And then there was Joe Finnerty.

"Excuse me," said this tiny, wobbly voice with a pronounced lisp when the madness had died down a little. "I take it you're the band's manager?"

He offered his hand: just as tiny, just as wobbly. I shook it. Cold and clammy, it was like holding a dead mackerel.

My first instinct was to turn my back on him: another weirdo. But something in his soft voice told me he had something to say that I wanted to hear.

"Yes, I am. Donnie Boyle."

"Hello, Donnie," he responded shyly, almost demurely. "My name's Joe. Here's my card."

I took the elegantly engraved business card and looked at it while fishing in my pocket for one of my own. Joe Finnerty, President, Noteworthy Records, it said. There was a hokey-looking musical note in the lower left-hand corner which made me a bit dubious, though there was also a recognizable midtown Manhattan address on the right-hand side which lent him some legitimacy. I gulped—surreptitiously, I hoped.

"Noteworthy Records, huh? I'm not sure I've heard of them." As soon as the words came out of my mouth, I immediately regretted it. I mean, I *hadn't* heard of them, but then there were lots of small labels I had never heard of. And the last thing I wanted to do was to appear argumentative or uninterested.

It seemed to wash right over him. "Well, we're kind of new," he replied evenly. "We may not be in the same league as the big labels yet, but I have big plans … and I think your band might well fit in with those plans."

Just then JJ appeared, weaving slightly. She had accompanied us to the gig, along with Katie and a few other friends, all of whom had spent a relaxing afternoon on the beach while we were setting up and sound checking.

"Who's got big plans?" she said. She was obviously buzzed but I still resented her butting in.

But Finnerty seemed amused by her and they began chatting excitedly about the band. Annoying as her unexpected appearance was, it gave me the chance to think about how I should best play this out. *Don't show your excitement*, I decided. *Play it cool.*

JJ and Finnerty had shifted gears now and were talking about songwriting. "Oh, they've got tons of original songs," she was telling him. "Hinch and Cody—they're the two guitarists—they're writing new material all the time."

Joe turned to me. "Is that true, Mr. Boyle? Because your group will, of course, need material if they're going to make a record for me."

I gulped again. This was exactly what we had been waiting for! JJ continued babbling, ignoring the fact that Finnerty had posed the question to me and not her. "Oh, the band have been writing songs for years," she enthused. "In fact, they've easily got an album's worth of original material, all ready to go."

He peered down at her. "Who exactly *are* you, my dear? I thought Mr. Boyle here was the band's manager." I noticed that he was studying her face, instead of her bra-less boobs, which were bouncing provocatively beneath her tight orange T-shirt. *Okay, there's the proof*, I concluded. *Finnerty's got to be gay.*

"Well, I work with Mr. Boyle," she asserted. "In getting the band gigs, that is."

I felt like strangling her, but somehow kept my cool. "Are you a booking agent?" he asked, looking somewhat amused.

Before Janet could insert her foot further into her mouth, I interjected. "No, not exactly. But she has helped us get some gigs. Not this one, though. College bookings."

Now Finnerty was interested. "College bookings, you say?" He turned to JJ once again. "Which colleges have the band played?"

Janet improvised. "Well, they did an amazing gig at Temple University in Philly last spring, and I've got a whole bunch of dates lined up." Now I felt like smacking her. Getting caught in an outrageous lie was no way to start a relationship with a record label.

"That's good to hear," Finnerty said, "because as a next step I'd like to see the band performing some of their original material before a live audience." He returned his attention to me. "Don't get me wrong, Mr. Boyle—I love your band. They have real stage presence, and there's no question that they can get a crowd fired up. But most of what I heard tonight were songs by other artists."

He was right. The OBI management had specified that we had to play "mostly" cover tunes, which meant we had only been able to sneak in one or two of Hinch and Cody's songs the whole night.

"You understand," Finnerty continued, as if lecturing a novice, "most of the money is in the song publishing."

"I know, Mr. Finnerty," I was quick to assure him. "And Miss Jaworsky here is right; the band does have a lot of strong original material."

Finnerty turned to JJ once again. "Here's my card, young lady. Please be certain to let me know when your next college booking is confirmed, and I'll do my best to attend. Now, do you think it would be possible to introduce me to the boys in the band? I'd like to have a little chat with them as well."

Flashing me a wink, Janet took him by the arm and began heading across the dressing room. "It would be my pleasure, Mr. Finnerty. Let's start with Hinch, shall we? I'm guessing you'll probably want to meet him first."

I could see Joe Finnerty practically salivating: Janet had read him exactly right. And, intrusive as she had been during that first improvised meeting with the head of our future record label, there was also no question she had sold the band better than I had; in fact, she had totally charmed the guy. Hopefully Hinch, Cody, and the Truckers would do the same. I doubted that any of them would cross the line with Finnerty that he clearly wanted them to—I was quite certain that Cody wouldn't, anyway—but maybe that wouldn't matter. Brian Epstein, it is said, never stopped lusting after John Lennon, yet he did great things for the Beatles despite the fact that their relationship apparently always remained strictly professional. Perhaps the same would happen here.

Or maybe Hinch or one of the Truckers would sleep with the guy. Honestly, it didn't really matter to me one way or the other … as long as we landed that record deal. That's the way I thought back in those days—hell, that's the way *all* of us thought. A recording contract was the Holy Grail of rock 'n' roll; the prevailing wisdom was that once you had signed with a label, you were made in the shade. But, as we were to learn the hard way, it's not the endpoint at all; in fact, it's just the start of a whole series of problems, promises, commitments, and entanglements that only rarely lead to fame and fortune. Still, that piece of paper seemed like the ultimate goal, and at last it appeared to be tantalizingly within our reach.

If only Janet Jaworsky could come through for us one more time.

15

My return to consciousness in the morning is brutal. A tentative peek out the curtains is met by an assault of painfully bright sunshine, despite the fact that it is several degrees below zero outside. The overnight coating of snow has given Celerina the look of a Hallmark Christmas card, and I am reminded that the holiday of good cheer and overly commercialized gift-giving is just two days away. Back in the Bronx, the Temkin family didn't actually celebrate Christmas—our sour-faced rabbi would never approve—but I will give my parents credit for at least tacitly acknowledging the holiday, at least when I was small enough to have felt left out. I'd get all the usual crappy Chanukah gifts—chocolate coins wrapped in gold foil and the stupid dreidel that you'd spin for about five minutes before deciding it was the most boring game you'd ever played in your entire short life—but on Christmas Eve my brothers and I would also get to hang up stockings on the fake mantelpiece above our fake fireplace, with the fake logs that glowed red yet put out no heat whatsoever when you plugged them in. That way we'd get to spend the same sleepless night as our non-Jewish friends before rising at dawn in a state of frenzy. We'd empty the stockings in eager anticipation, only to find that they were filled with nothing more exciting than Pez dispensers and more of those fucking gold foil coins. Sometimes there would also be an actual present or two stacked on the floor, carefully wrapped in holiday red and green. Even if they were disappointingly of the functional variety—ugly sweaters and scratchy wool socks—they were generally enough to satisfy our childish need to be part of the mainstream.

So here I am forty years later and five thousand miles away, having just escaped the clutches of a drug-crazed sex kitten, on my way back to the filthy streets and foul-smelling canals of Amsterdam. My, how time does fly when you're having fun.

Thoroughly living up to their reputation for cleanliness and order, the Swiss plowing crews have done a remarkable job of clearing the roads, and I am soon at Zurich airport awaiting my flight, which is equally remarkably scheduled to take off on time. Once we get in the air, however, it is a different matter: the plane is filled with large families with squalling children, and the air traffic controllers who rule the skies above the Netherlands are either on strike or celebrating the holidays prematurely because we circle Amsterdam endlessly before finally being granted permission to return to mother earth.

By the time I get back to my tiny hotel room, it is mid-afternoon, and so absorbed am I with the mechanics of unpacking my bag and running a lukewarm bath (there is apparently no option for actual hot in this pathetic excuse for a hostelry), I don't notice for a long while that the message light on my phone is blinking. There are twelve messages from an increasingly frantic Hans, whose cell phone was unusable in Switzerland and dead by the time I touched down in Holland—have to remember to charge those damn batteries!—but there was also, miracle of miracles, a message from Britney.

Sort of.

"Hi, babe, it's me," squeaks the perky voice through the receiver. Too goddamn perky if you ask me. "I got your messages, but I've been so busy here with..." a telling pause, "... uh, schoolwork that this is the first chance I've had to call back. Anyway, everything is good here in sunny California and I hope you're having a good time and that you haven't forgotten about my diamonds." This last statement is followed by a cute giggle designed to wrap me once again around her sexy little finger. I keep listening, waiting for more. There is silence on the line, but I still hear her breathing as if she is thinking of what else to add. "So, er, I guess we'll, like, talk soon, and ... oh yes, you've had a couple of calls here. One from your editor asking about the manuscript and one from some woman who I don't know— um, let's see, I wrote the name down somewhere here, are you cheating on me?" Giggle. "... oh, and there was also a message from your friend Clive, I wrote down his number, too. Oops, sorry, can't find that piece of paper right now." Giggle giggle. "Okay, gotta go, talk to you soon, love you, bye."

My darling, dear airhead Britney. I've been gone a week now, and this is the first moment she's had to call? Busy with schoolwork, my ass. She's been busy partying that sweet tushie of hers with her muscle-bound friends from USC, I'm sure of it. Plus there have been three messages for me and she can't even remember where she wrote down the numbers.

Figures.

This crude reminder of my life in L.A., as it is, has a real sobering effect on me. In fact, I find myself getting depressed again. Forty-eight years on this earth and all I have to show for it is a condo in Malibu, a Corvette, and an airhead girlfriend who can't even take messages properly. Doesn't seem like much of an inventory for nearly half a century of breathing Bronx soot in and Los Angeles smog out.

Still, it could be worse: I could be married to Miranda Esteban, a/k/a the Countess of Cockteasers. Suddenly my life doesn't seem so bleak, at least not in comparison to Tommy Hinchton's. Britney may be an empty shell, but at least she isn't a raging virago. Not yet, anyway.

I pick up the phone and dial the condo. As usual, no answer. "Britney," I tell the machine in as forceful a tone as I can muster, "it's Bernie. Sorry I missed your call yesterday, hope you're okay. Listen, call me back as soon as you can, alright? And see if you can find that piece of paper with the numbers on it, 'kay? Okay, bye." It is only after I hang up that I realize I have failed to end the message with our usual "love you" tagline. Can this mean I'm no longer in love with Britney? I suppose anything is possible.

In an effort to distract myself from the troubling thought, I'm about to fire up my laptop and look up Clive's office number when Hans's cell phone, now sitting snugly in its wall charger, begins shrieking at me.

"Bernie?" it says when I pick up. "Where the hell have you been? I've been worried about you." It's worry wart Hans, as usual.

"I'm fine, Hans. I just haven't been able to call you, that's all. Your phone didn't work in Switzerland."

"It didn't? So much for the fucking EEU." Why Hans would figure that the formation of the European Economic Union would somehow cause his cell phone to function in Zurich is beyond me, but I decide not to get into it with him. "So," he says, "where are you?"

This, I have decided, is the question for which the cell phone has been invented. It's as if purchasing one of the damn things obligates the user to utter those magical three words at least once during every conversation, upon penalty of law.

"I'm back here in Amsterdam, at the hotel." I report dutifully. Tempted as I am to ask the same tedious question of Hans, I demur.

"Well, when were you planning on calling me?" he says petulantly. "This isn't some kind of game we're playing, you know."

"I know, Hans, I know. Look, I only got in a little while ago. I was just about to call you, I swear." Though not normally superstitious, I find myself crossing my fingers.

"So how did it go with Hinch's wife? Did you get any information out of her?"

What does he think I am, another Rudie? "No, not really," I sigh. "She hates Hinch's new road manager almost as much as she hates Hinch. And she's planning on divorcing him—Hinch, I mean. That's about it."

"Well, did you at least get laid, then?"

"No. I mean, I could have if I wanted to. Probably. I just ... well, I guess I didn't want to."

"You didn't want to fuck Miranda de Couqueville? Are you crazy?"

"Maybe. It's just that ... well, it's a long story."

"I know: she's a bitch and a cokehead. So what? That hasn't stopped everyone else in the business from laying her. Or so I hear."

All of a sudden I feel incredibly unclean, despite having just stepped out of the bath. "Well, I feel sorry for Hinch, is all I can say. It must be hell being married to her," I tell him.

"Don't waste your time feeling sorry for rock stars; there are plenty of other people in this world who deserve your sympathy more." Hans is right. In fact, I'm actually feeling a lot sorrier for myself than I am for Hinch. Hans must be hearing it in my voice, or maybe he's telepathic. "Do you know what tonight is?" he suddenly asks.

"Friday?" I say.

"Well, yes, it's Friday, but it's also Christmas Eve. No wonder you feel depressed—you're a long way from home and you probably miss your family."

I somehow don't feel this is the right time to explain that I'm a nice Jewish boy from the Bronx and that my only family right now is a 21-year-old blonde in Malibu who's probably making her own brand of Christmas merriment with some surfer dude at this very moment.

"I don't think that's it," I finally say, without elaborating.

"Come on, join Rudie and me for a nice dinner and some genever; it will make you feel better," he coaxes. "We can get Rudie talking about how he plans to slice Schiffman's balls off and serve them on a platter: that will make *him* feel better."

Much as I don't feel like laughing, the image brings a smile to my face. At last, some Christmas cheer, albeit of a dubious variety. For all of the hassle they've put me through, I find myself wishing that Schiffman and Hinch, wherever they are, are having a miserable Christmas Eve, and I decide, then and there, to make mine a merry one.

"Okay, Hans, you talked me into it. Break out the bottle; I plan on getting wasted tonight."

ROADIE

We meet at a cozy little restaurant called *De Groene Lantaarn*—The Green Lantern—which I am delighted to see is filled with locals, with nary a tourist in sight. From the tiny verdant light in the window to the faintly dingy atmosphere inside, it radiates comfort and warmth—the two things, I realize with a start, that I find myself missing the most. Hans and Rudie are already seated behind a small table when I arrive. "*Prettige Kerstfeest*," they call out, to which I offer a wan "Merry Christmas" in return. It suddenly occurs to me that I am bone-tired. This trip has taken more out of me than I realized. I guess I'm just getting too old for this shit.

But the genever and the heaping plates of home-cooked food have a mysteriously revivifying effect, and we are soon sharing tales of our lives' journeys, stories which transcend any barriers of culture or language. Hans, I learn, comes from a family of newspapermen; he was in journalism school when the rock 'n' roll bug first bit, causing him to abandon his studies for the rough and ready life of the promoter. He and Rudie were childhood friends; Rudie's dream, to be a policeman, thwarted when his mental deficiencies—which he cheerfully acknowledges ("I just don't think as good as other people")—prevented him from passing the qualifying examination. Until Hans gave him a job as chief of security and general right-hand man, Rudie had been aimless and adrift; since then, the two men had forged a firm friendship built upon a bedrock of physical violence tinged with an odd sense of fair play. That explains why they've both developed such a sense of outrage at Schiffman: not so much for the money he stole from them as for the sheer injustice of what he had done to the fans who were denied the concert they paid good money for. In that sense, they are very much like the vigilantes of comic book lore minus the costumes, though when I try to explain my theory it seems to go right over their heads. Expanding on the theme, I point out the improbability of their having picked a restaurant named after one of those super-heroes, but they look at me blankly, completely unaware of the masked character with the omnipotent power ring.

"You look a bit different tonight," Hans says between mouthfuls of rookwurst as he gives me the once-over.

"Really? Nothing different I can think of," I reply nonchalantly.

"I know. It's your hair," he proclaims triumphantly. "It's missing."

Okay, I'm busted. I looked at the damn toupee laying on top of my dresser like a dead raccoon when I got out of the bathtub this afternoon and for the first time in years thought, *Fuck it; it's just not worth putting on any more.*

"I'm surprised this place is open tonight," I say, trying to change the subject.

"Why wouldn't it be open?" Hans asks.

"You know, because of the holiday. You won't find many restaurants open in the States on Christmas Eve."

"I don't understand," Rudie says as he slurps his soup. "People have to eat, don't they?"

"Sure, but on Christmas Eve people like to be home with their families. So they can wrap the gifts for the children, things like that."

"Oh, the little ones," says Hans. "Here, they get their gifts much earlier, on Sinterklass Eve. December 5th, right, Rudie?"

"Yah," he agrees. "When Sinterklaas and Black Peter come from Spain with all the presents."

"Spain?" I ask. "Why Spain?"

"I don't know," says Rudie as he scratches his head. "I guess that's where he lives."

"Santa Claus? He lives in the North Pole."

Rudie flashes me a lopsided grin. "Well, your Santa Claus may come from up there, but our St. Nicholas, he is much warmer-blooded."

"Yah, and he has a tan, and he eats paella," adds Hans.

We all laugh. "So Santa Claus does not visit the Netherlands on Christmas Eve?" I ask. "We're taught that he travels all over the world on that night."

"No, here he comes earlier, because the Dutch are special," Rudie replies proudly. Judging from the wide-eyed look of innocence on his face, I am convinced that he believes in Santa.

We toast Old Saint Nick with a clink of glasses. It occurs to me that one of the benefits of tonight's conversation is that we haven't once mentioned Alan Schiffman, or the twisting off of his head and/or slicing off of his genitals, which comes as a vague relief, to me anyway.

As if reading my mind, Hans suddenly gets serious. "So where do you think Schiffman is spending *his* Christmas Eve?" he asks.

"Hopefully lying at the bottom of some sewer, covered in shit," Rudie offers helpfully.

We all pause to consider the distasteful imagery, then reconsider as plates of *oliebollen* are served—stodgy fried desserts that can't seem to make up their minds whether they are zeppole or cinnamon buns. *How on earth do the Dutch remain so thin?* I wonder between bites. Rudie cleans his plate of the heavy morsels, then half of Hans's, then orders seconds, washing it all down with cup after cup of thick, dark coffee. *Well, maybe not all of them.*

We sit back in silence and for the longest time we are each lost in our own private reverie. Outside, the stars are winking and the frosty white glow of the moon is bathing the canals and narrow streets of Amsterdam in a fluorescent sheen. In the warmth of the dim light which softly illuminates our small green universe, I study both mens' faces, searching for a clue as to what they are thinking. Rudie, I'm guessing, is still conjuring up new and imaginative ways to eviscerate Alan Schiffman. But Hans, Hans is much more difficult to read. His thin, narrow face is devoid of expression, yet his sad eyes are filled with a tenderness I haven't seen before. I get the sense he is thinking of family. Hans is not the typical self-serving, money-grubbing promoter that Donnie spoke of so often, of that I am sure. This is a man I feel I can trust, with my life if necessary.

I only hope it doesn't come to that.

16

Transcript: Interview with Donnie Boyle, May 9, 1998

WELL, OLD JANET did come through one more time, and what she did for us simultaneously catapulted us another rung up the ladder and opened the door for a whole host of problems that were to entangle the band for decades. You know that saying about being careful about what you wish for because you just might get it? That's pretty much what happened to us.

Whether it was her gift of gab or the other ways that she used her mouth—you know what I'm talking about, right, Bernie?—within just a couple of weeks of our first crossing paths with Joe Finnerty, JJ had landed us another college gig. This one was also on Long Island, at a state university up on the fancy North Shore, in a place called Stony Brook. The town was small and kind of quaint, but the campus itself was a huge mud pit at the time, with construction going on everywhere. The university had a similarly schizophrenic reputation. It was renowned for churning out civil engineers and tech-heads—they even had one of the first computers, this humongous thing housed in a building all its own—yet the student body seemed to largely consist of potheads taking liberal arts courses. What that meant to us was a rowdy, stoned-out audience—just the kind of people who enjoyed our no-nonsense brand of rock 'n' roll best. It also meant that the school had a huge budget for concerts, which allowed them to book all the top acts.

That's why I was surprised when Janet called and told me that the gig would not pay us one thin dime; in fact, it was going to *cost* us—a cool grand, no less—to play there. When I protested, JJ got this icy tone in her voice I hadn't heard before.

"Look, Donnie," she explained, "first of all, I was only able to land us this gig because someone owed me a favor." I could only imagine what she had done to garner such a favor, but wisely decided not to go there.

"Secondly," she continued, "we're not even the opening act; we're third on the bill. Anyway, the whole point of the gig is to showcase for Finnerty, not to rake in the bucks. Am I right?"

I couldn't argue with her logic, but then again I wasn't expecting to have to spend money to do the showcase either, and I told her so, in no uncertain terms.

"Well, actually, to be honest with you, their concert committee did offer me three hundred bucks," she replied, somewhat contritely. "But I turned them down."

"What?" I shouted. My Irish blood was beginning to boil. Even a few hundred bucks would help offset the costs of getting to the gig, plus, of course, Muscle Beach Len and Crazy Quentin would have to be paid.

"Calm down, asshole. I got us two hundred tickets in lieu of the fee, so we can pack the crowd. And they promised to reserve the front few rows for Finnerty and his guests."

I sighed. Obviously the deed was done, and my complaining about JJ's negotiating skills wasn't going to get me anywhere. "How do we even know Finnerty is going to show?" I asked.

"You leave it to me, Donnie. Give me a grand for expenses, and I guarantee he'll be there. What's more, I guarantee he'll offer you a contract."

Bullshit, I thought. Even back then I was worldly enough to know that verbal guarantees were worth the paper they were written on. And that grand JJ was asking for was a huge sum of money for us in those days. I started thinking that I was being scammed. Maybe JJ and Finnerty were in on this together; maybe this was just a hustle to extract some money from us. Then I calmed down and realized I was probably being paranoid; hell, if they *were* a couple of hustlers, they'd have to be a lot smarter than to play their con on a bunch of starving musicians. Besides, Janet had a pretty good idea of how limited our funds were. I decided to humor her.

"So tell me," I said, trying to sound cagey, "what exactly do I get for that thousand dollars?"

She immediately took offense at the tone in my voice. "Don't patronize me, jerk-off," she growled. "What you get is Joe Finnerty sitting front row center, along with however many guests he wants to bring along in the stretch limo I plan on sending for him. And what Finnerty gets is two hundred screaming, rabid fans sitting all around him pretending the band is doing the greatest gig in the history of the world even if they actually suck that night. Fans that I will personally select for their enthusiasm and lung capacity—including some very pretty boys to keep Mr. Finnerty happily horny and distracted—all supplied with free tickets and chauffeured in on the half dozen buses I plan to charter."

I had to admit that I was impressed. Backpedaling furiously, I stammered an apology and promised to mail her a check in the morning.

"The check's in the mail?" she smirked. "That's the second oldest cliché in the music business. Don't bother, Donnie—I'll come around and collect it in person, first thing tomorrow morning."

Before I hung up, I asked her what the oldest cliché was.

"Come on, you know it, sweetie," she said, giggling. "It's something you yourself whispered to me not so long ago."

"I did?"

She laughed out loud.

"I promise not to come in your mouth. Remember?"

I did. It was a promise I hadn't been able to keep, either.

I MIGHT NOT have been true to my word, but Janet was, and we did the gig with Joe Finnerty in attendance, surrounded by his entourage: a half dozen male friends dressed in hues of lavender and shocking pink. Though their allotted time onstage was brief, Hinch and the band slammed through a power-packed set that featured the very best of their original material. They looked good, too—damned good—with Hinch in a fringed vest and too-tight leather trousers, shaking his long blond tresses as he pranced around the stage like he owned it, Vernon off to his left wearing shades and his best I-don't-give-a-shit sneer, musclebound JD behind, his sweat flying everywhere as he pounded out a ferocious beat. Hell, even Cody busted a move or two from his usual position at stage right. They managed to rouse the crowd into an encore, too, which they actually got to play this time by virtue of merely retreating to the wings next to the protective shelter of Muscle Beach Len instead of all the way into their dressing room. According to Janet, who sat next to Finnerty, he and his friends were up and bopping during the entire set, enjoying themselves thoroughly, spurred on, no doubt, by the honest enthusiasm of not only the student body but the two hundred ringers surrounding them. Less than a week later, Joe invited me up to his office to talk deal, and by the end of the month, Hinch Reload—the name given the band by Cody right after the Truckers joined—had a recording contract.

That was the good news. The bad news was that, during the course of those negotiations, I made just about every mistake it was possible to make, and we were to pay the price for my missteps for years to come. My first mistake—though on this one I have to pass some of the blame on to Janet, who really should have known better—was to treat the gig as a showcase for Noteworthy Records alone. What we should have done was to spend *five* grand and send five limos to five different record labels. That way, we could have possibly initiated a bidding war, which would have driven our price up exponentially and also would have resulted in much better terms. But we didn't, and so we found ourselves in a position with no leverage: like all unsigned bands, we were desperate for a recording contract, and Noteworthy was the only label offering us one. That alone put us at a tremendous disadvantage.

My second error was not hiring an expensive hotshot attorney to do the negotiating. Instead, I trusted Finnerty, who I thought then—and even, to some degree, think today—was basically fair-minded. Sure, we had a lawyer look over the final contract, but he wasn't a music business specialist, just some local yokel in Philly that a friend had recommended. If I were closing a real estate deal to buy a nearby strip mall, this fifty-buck-an-hour shyster probably would have been just fine, but he was completely over his head trying to parse a complicated recording contract.

Now, the contract itself wasn't that horrible: The per-record royalty we were to be paid was actually pretty reasonable, given that we were a new band with no history of sales, and the hundred grand advance Finnerty was offering was decent money, again given our status as nobodies. But there was a ton of fine print mumbo-jumbo in there about promo copies and residuals and recoupables and manufacturing fees, and I couldn't make head or tail of any of it, and neither could our lawyer, and that really should have been a red flag to me. Honestly, there's no defense for my stupidity, other than that I was under a lot of pressure from the band to get the deal done and sign the damn thing. It wasn't just that they were eager to get their hands on that hundred grand, it was more that they craved the status that having a recording deal would afford them, the thrill of seeing their names on an actual album that people could go out and buy. Plus we all knew that having a record out would at long last allow us to crack the well-paying college circuit and get to play all-original material every night for appreciative audiences.

There was one thing I did right, though, and I don't mind telling you that I'm kind of proud of it. It stemmed from a casual conversation I had with Finnerty one afternoon during the course of the negotiations. He was telling me how he was convinced that the album was going to be huge and how it was going to put us, and Noteworthy Records, on the map. For some reason, his child-like enthusiasm tapped a vein of suspicion that I didn't even know I possessed.

"That's just it, Joe," I blurted out without thinking about what it was I was actually saying. "What if you're wrong? What if things don't work out?"

"That simply won't happen, Donnie," he said quietly. "I won't let it happen."

"But we can't control everything, can we? What *if* something happens? Something unexpected?"

"Like what?" he asked.

"I don't know. Maybe an act of God, like a natural disaster or something." The truth was, I *didn't* know; I was really just babbling. But there seemed to be some primal instinct inside me that wanted to preserve an escape route just in case things didn't fall into place the way Joe kept telling us they would.

Finnerty sat back in his chair, deep in thought, staring out the window. "Look, Donnie," he finally said in a soft voice, "I want you, and the band, to be completely comfortable with our arrangement. I have total faith that the record you'll be making for us will be a big hit, and that it will be the first of a long string of hit records. But I'll tell you what. If that first album somehow doesn't come together the way I think it will, or if it isn't a hit—let's say if it doesn't chart in the Top 20 within six months of its release—I'll let you out of the contract and you'll be free to go elsewhere. That's how sure I am."

I was impressed. "You'd do that for us?" I asked. "In writing?"

"Absolutely, my good man. I'll call our attorney and have him add the amendment right now."

That clause—two simple sentences inserted in the middle of a forty-page contract—was to save our collective asses time and time again in the years to come. It's one of the best things I ever did for Hinch … not that he ever appreciated it. But let's not go there right now. Let's just say that I didn't mess up our first record contract completely.

Just mostly.

THE INK WAS HARDLY DRY on the contract before everyone started spending their money; in fact, if any of us had halfway decent credit in those days—

which we didn't—I'm sure it would have all been spent beforehand. Now you may think that the hundred grand advance we got is a lot of bread, and I guess it was—at least in those days. But by the time the lawyer got paid and I took my cut and set aside the roadie's retainers for the month we'd be in the recording studio, the four band members only got about fifteen grand each, which was hardly a fortune. Still, they acted like they were on easy street. Hinch and Vernon both went out and bought huge stage amplifiers—a necessary expenditure since we would soon be playing larger venues than the clubs and dives we'd been stuck in for years. Joe Dan already had pretty much acquired everything he needed equipment-wise—his drum kit was enormous and nearly new when he first joined the band—so he was able to spend all his dough on drugs and booze, and brother Vern did his best to match him on that front. Hinch immediately began making plans to take Katie to Hawaii for the two weeks we had freed up in our schedule before recording was due to start; upon their return, he blew what little he had left on a bunch of flashy stage costumes, all custom-tailored by this Jewish guy that Finnerty had recommended.

Cody, on the other hand, invested every last penny of his share in a whole bunch of new instruments: guitars and effects pedals, a Hammond organ, an electric piano—even a couple of synthesizers that sported a bewildering array of knobs and switches.

"What the hell are you planning on doing with those?" I asked him good-naturedly as he began hauling them out of their boxes and setting them up in the living room.

"What do you think, dickwad?" he answered with a grin. "I'm going to learn how to program these suckers."

"Yes, but why?"

"To make us sound better. I've got some ideas on how we can take things to the next level sonically."

I'll give Cody credit: he was always thinking ahead. But I knew Hinch wouldn't be too happy about this latest development. "Don't fuck with the formula" was his mantra, and I wanted Cody to be prepared for resistance from our front man.

"Hinch isn't going to want to take things to any new level," I pointed out. "You know that as well as I do."

"Of course I know that," he laughed. "Don't worry about Hinch; I can handle him."

And handle him he did. Things played out pretty much as I predicted:

Hinch taunted Cody mercilessly about his ideas at first, but Cody kept plodding on, and little by little the stack of new instruments began getting integrated into the band's sound. And if Hinch had been the only obstacle, I have no doubt that most of Cody's new toys would have found their way onto our first record, too, but he wasn't. There was a new roadblock in Cody's way, and his name was John Thomas Wallingford

Wallingford was our new record producer. He was also the craziest fucking lunatic I've ever met in my life, which is saying a lot. But that was something we didn't know when Finnerty first informed us that he had acquired the Great Man's services for our debut album. JTW, as he liked to call himself ("JTW here," was the way he always answered his phone, though with his snooty upper-class English accent, the "here" always came out in two syllables, as in "he-yah"), had worked at the best British studios—even well-known places like Abbey Road—and had produced a bunch of Number One records in the early '70s. He had a reputation as a hit-maker and was therefore a hot commodity in the industry back then. As most labels do with most new artists, Noteworthy Records had refused to give us any kind of creative control over the album, so we were glad that they'd gone out and paired us up with a producer that had such a strong track record. Unfortunately, he turned out to be a madman, and an extremely costly one at that. In my naïvete, I didn't realize it at the time, but it turned out that every penny of his outrageous fee came out of our pockets, as did the ridiculously expensive hourly rates levied by the ridiculously expensive midtown Manhattan studio Wallingford had hired for us to record in. Way too late, I discovered that we owed Noteworthy a hundred grand to repay those expenses on top of the hundred grand they'd already advanced us, and that's not counting the share of the promotional costs that we were also responsible for.

We were nearly a quarter of a million dollars in debt before our first record even got released. Welcome to the wonderful world of economics, music biz style, Bernie boy.

Our first meeting with the fabulous Mr. Wallingford was deceptively uneventful. I will say this for the guy: he was one sharp dresser. Wearing wraparound shades and clad in a leopard skin coat, leather trousers and snakeskin boots, the producer turned up at the recording studio the first day of the sessions, said hello to everybody, slapped the engineer on the back, and disappeared out the door.

We didn't see him again for three days.

The next time Wallingford showed up he stayed a little longer. Five minutes longer, to be exact. That's because almost as soon as he arrived, a phone call came in for him, and he spent four minutes arguing vehemently with whoever was at the other end of the line about the detailing on his car. A minute later he was out the door again.

"What the hell?" I asked the engineer, who had been patiently working with us to dial in sounds to Cody's satisfaction.

"That's just the way JTW works," he said. Apparently he'd done a number of records with Wallingford before and was used to his modus operandi. "He needs to be inspired. When he feels the time is right, he'll be here, don't worry."

I tried not to worry, though we only had four weeks of studio time booked to make the record, and I was hoping our producer would actually turn up before it was completed. I phoned Finnerty and expressed my concerns.

"Oh, that's just the way John works," Finnerty said, parroting the engineer. "He'll do a great job for you in the end, don't you worry about it." Had I known at the time that we were the ones footing the bill for Wallingford's long absences I would have been considerably more forceful. Instead, laboring under the delusion that it was Joe Finnerty's long pockets and not our considerably shorter ones that were financing the project, I merely grumbled politely and hung up.

On day eight—the start of our second full week in the studio—John Thomas Wallingford finally came to stay. Or so we thought. Things started promisingly enough: Without any pretense of small talk, he officiously instructed the guys to run through all their original material so he could evaluate each song. I have to admit being impressed when Wallingford pulled out a notepad and began scribbling furiously. *Finally*, I thought, *he's actually doing his job*.

And he *was* doing his job, at least within the very loose definition of record production. Like film directors, record producers come in all stripes. There are the ones that meddle incessantly, making the artist feel like sidemen on their own sessions, doing their best to give everyone present an inferiority complex, courtesy of their own megalomania. At the opposite end of the spectrum are those that are completely hands-off, allowing the artist and the recording engineer to take control of the ship ... though of course claiming full credit—not to mention healthy royalties—if the record becomes a hit. And there are a million variations in-between. There are the rah-rah cheerleaders that try to charm the artist into giving their best performance, and then there are the intimidating goons who threaten to beat the crap out of the artist if they *don't* give their best performance. There are the consummate musicians only interested in harmony, counterpoint, and rhythmic variation—even if everything sounds like shit—and there are the geeky nerds with no musical ability whatsoever who are only interested in pushing the frontiers of sonic exploration ... even if the musical content is shit. Then there are the drunks, dopers, letches, and junkies just looking to score; the record company pencil-pushers pretending to be inventive when in fact they don't have a creative bone in their bodies; the hopeless dreamers with no social, organizational or administrative skills whatsoever; and the unknown ciphers who have no business in a recording studio or anywhere else civilized people congregate.

And I'm just talking about the *good* ones here.

Seriously, there's no way to accurately describe what it is a record producer actually does, other than to collect a fee for delivering a product to the label, in addition to which they take home a percentage of the goodies if and when shady accounting practices allow the record to show profitability afterwards—which is rare. And if I had to describe John Thomas Wallingford's style of record production, I would have to say that he was all of the above.

Most of all, as I told you, he was a fucking lunatic.

This became immediately obvious when the band started running down their original material for his comment. I sat in the control room with him and the engineer, so I was privy to their conversation as the band played in the studio. It went something like this:

Wallingford (who was British): "Did you catch last night's match?"

Engineer (who was not): "No, we don't allow smoking in here."

Wallingford: "Eh? Oh, I see what you mean. Yes, yes, very droll. I was referring to the match in the World Cup Finals, if you must know."

Engineer: "I don't follow soccer."

Wallingford: "Soccer? Dear boy, it's football."

Engineer: "I don't follow football either."

Wallingford: "Ah, pity, that. What about cricket? Do you follow cricket?"

Engineer: "No, not cricket, either. No sports."
Wallingford: "No sports? Dear boy, how can one exist without sports?"
Engineer: "I work here. That's sport enough."
Wallingford (after long, thoughtful pause): "Hmmm. Well, what about wine? Which do you prefer—red or white?"
Engineer: "I don't drink."
Wallingford: "You don't drink? Dear boy, how can one exist without drink?"
And on and on.

I sat at the back of the room grim-faced. This was the guy who was supposed to be crafting a hit record for us? I sauntered up to the mixing console and stole a glance at Wallingford's notepad, interested in seeing the notes he was scribbling. It was filled with doodles: mostly crude drawings of penises entering even cruder vaginas.

"Uh, John, can I have a word?"

He looked around the room in confusion. "John? Who's John?"

I continued staring at him.

"Oh, you mean *me*. Dear boy, I haven't been John to anyone since my blessed mum passed away some years ago. Please, do call me JTW. All my friends do."

I was starting to get more pissed by the minute. "Look, John, or JTW, or whatever it is you want to be called, are you listening at all? My band is playing their hearts out in the other room for your benefit and you don't seem to be paying the slightest bit of attention."

He grew affronted. "Not paying attention? Whatever do you mean? Every atom of my being is completely and utterly focused on the musical masterpiece unfolding before me. I am taking it all in, soaking up the slightest nuance like a sponge. I am completely and thoroughly engaged, minutely aware of the tiniest quaver, the most delicate semi-quaver, the finest gossamer spread of every *demi*-semi quaver." Arms outstretched toward the heavens, he drew himself up to his full height—Christ, the guy was tall—and fairly bellowed his parting line:

"I, dear boy, am *creating!*"

The ferocity of his response rattled me. Maybe I *had* misjudged him. Maybe, as the engineer had explained, this is just the way the guy worked. Having never seen a record being made before, I had no idea if this was actually how it was done.

"Well, I'm sorry if I got you wrong," I said sheepishly. "As long as you're paying attention."

He waved his hand dismissively. "No problem, dear boy. Allow me to make it up to you by buying you a drink."

I thought he meant later. But no, he meant right now. And with that, he began making his way unsteadily to the control room door. "Tell the musicians that I very much approve of what I am hearing and that when I return I'd like them to play it all a key higher and a tad faster," he instructed the engineer before returning his attention to me. "Come on, my friend. Let's go get that drink."

He disappeared out the door. Slack-jawed, all I could do was follow. As I headed into the hallway, I heard the engineer addressing the band over the talk-back mic.

"Okay, guys, let's take a break while JTW and your manager hit the boozer. Who wants Chinese and who wants pizza?"

It was an omen, a sign of the insanity that the next three weeks were to become.

THE APTLY NAMED WALLINGFORD—"John Thomas" being Victorian slang for penis—was without a doubt the horniest man I ever met. It soon became clear that, whenever he wasn't actually having sex, he was thinking about having sex. We in the band all talked clumsily of getting laid, but he dazzled us with his impossibly large repertoire of British colloquialisms for the carnal act: to boff, to bonk, to boink, having a shag, having it off, giving her one, dipping the wick, doing the nasty, doing the old in-out, having a bit of slap-and-tickle, having a bit of the other, getting a leg over, getting a proper seeing to, throwing a knee-trembler, even the charmingly quaint "bit of rumpy-pumpy." And in the three weeks he spent with us, he was to bring into the studio a procession of models, starlets, stewardesses, cocktail waitresses, secretaries, receptionists, teachers, librarians, nurses, and supermarket checkout girls that was as staggering for its number as it was for its diversity. Young or old, large or small, it didn't seem to matter. Just wall to wall women: a dazzling array of blondes, brunettes, redheads, latinas, asian chicks, black chicks, all appearing and disappearing at various times of the day or night, sometimes waltzing in on his arms, other times just manifesting as if they had been beamed down from the Starship Enterprise. Much of the album was made with one or more of these glorious creatures writhing on Wallingford's lap, nibbling his ear, rubbing his back, stroking his long, greasy hair. The lounge near the common reception area became his private boudoir, everyone instinctively respecting the hand-lettered "OCCUPIED: KEEP OUT—JTW" sign whenever it hung on the door, the sounds of panting, thrusting, and slurping coming loudly from within. If the lounge was occupied by other clients—there were four studios in the complex, each with its own control room—he'd either adjourn to an unoccupied one, or commandeer the long-suffering studio manager's office, who dared not refuse him since he brought in so much business.

Wallingford wasn't the least bit averse to sharing, either. "Take your pick, lads—I am not a greedy man," he'd proclaim to the band, sweeping his arm munificently at the bounty of booty that was draped across every available space in the control room. Hinch, of course, was in seventh heaven and had no hesitation whatsoever in partaking heartily whenever Katie Q wasn't around. Vernon and Joe Dan made full use of the facilities, too. Every so often I even saw Cody, red-faced, emerge from the bathroom accompanied by a buxom beauty, though he always seemed way too embarrassed about it.

The fact of the matter is that all that sex did have a positive effect on the music being made because it gave the guys an audience they wanted to impress. Posing is an important part of rock 'n' roll. It's like a male peacock strutting his feathers: it inspires grand performance, which I came to learn was that unfathomable "something" that made the difference between a good record and a great record. And, as I was to discover, it's much more difficult to coax a great performance out of an artist in the oddly alien atmosphere of a recording studio than it is onstage at a real gig. Like gambling casinos, studios are devoid of any kind of natural lighting—hell, they're devoid of natural anything. Everywhere you look there is darkness punctuated by tiny blinking lights and LEDs, and the very air is permeated with the smell of new carpeting and suspect plastics outgassing into poorly ventilated spaces occupied by way too many people. The end result is that you feel as if you're suspended in nothingness: you could be almost anyplace or no place all at the same time, and you never have any idea if it's noon or midnight out in the real world. In fact, when you're in the studio for weeks at a stretch, as we were, you have no idea that there *is* a real world. You lose track of everything—weather, current events, friends, family, social obligations. It becomes all too easy to forget the trivialities of life, like paying your gas bill on time, which can lead to major problems when you finally reemerge into the humdrum realities of everyday existence. Instead you come to feel omnipotent, as if you are the king of all the artificiality surrounding you, as if you are in total command of the fluctuating signals being captured on tape, bound for immortality, when in fact you abdicate control of almost everything to your producer and manager ... who all too often are woefully incapable of even looking after themselves, much less you.

Actually, that was probably Wallingford's greatest asset as a producer: keeping things loose in the studio. To be fair, he was brimming with creative ideas, but the problem was that he was constantly running in a hundred different directions at once, sparked, no doubt, by the immense quantities of drugs he was consuming. At first he was relatively circumspect about his pill-taking and the white lines of cocaine that mysteriously appeared on the mixing console, initially shared only with the engineer and a favored female companion or two. But as the days wore on, he grew less discreet, sometimes leaving piles of powder out in plain sight. JD and Vernon took to coke like they'd been weaned on the stuff, and once he'd been advised on the positive effects it had on maintaining a boner, it wasn't long before Hinch joined them with great enthusiasm. Only Cody seemed to disdain the drugs on offer ... most of the time. In the chaotic waning hours of our last few sessions, even he took to rolling up a dollar bill or two, probably out of frustration at the way things were spinning out of control. Me? I have to admit that I dabbled once or twice, but I really didn't like how coke affected me—it made my thoughts race by too fast to absorb them—so I mostly stayed in the back of the room and watched as our dream of making a hit record evaporated into the ether.

WITH THE END of the booked studio time—our ostensible deadline—drawing near, the craziness began increasing in intensity. The stimulating effects of the mounds of coke, augmented by the stash of crystal meth which Crazy Quentin was foolish enough to bring by and share with JTW one memorable night, meant that the sessions were running longer and longer, often sixteen or eighteen hours at a clip. At times, Wallingford was completely out of control, staggering around the control room waving a small but lethal-looking handgun at anyone who approached him while he was "creating." Hinch and the Trucker boys were going with the flow, but I could see the mounting look of frustration on Cody's face as his hope of recording a masterpiece was disappearing rapidly.

That's not to say that JTW didn't allow Cody, or the others, to participate in the making of the album. "What a splendid idea, dear boy!" he'd crow whenever Cody or one of the others offered a suggestion, beaming broadly from behind the shades that he wore day and night, indoors and out. Wallingford was actually very good about appearing to allow everyone to contribute, and, in many cases, the idea being offered would find its way onto tape. The problem was that the next idea to come along would inevitably crowd the first one out, and so even the best suggestions would often get lost by the wayside, replaced by something more recent, even if it didn't have nearly as much merit. That's how spontaneous—some might say unfocused—JTW was.

That lack of focus, unfortunately, was starting to rub off even on Cody, who began getting sucked into the whirlwind of drugs and sex and unfettered madness that Wallingford was whipping up all around us.

"Donnie, I don't know what the hell is going on any more," he said to me one night, shaking his head in bewilderment.

"None of us do, I'm afraid," was my weak reply. "All we can do is to keep going, and hope for the best."

Of course, I was calling Finnerty almost daily to express my concern, but he kept reassuring me that this was simply the way Wallingford did things, and that we'd be pleased with the results in the end. Then he'd rattle off a list of the producer's recent hits, citing their chart positions and unit sales as if they were batting averages. "Well, it's your money," I would sigh before hanging up, not yet realizing that it was actually *our* money. And the next day, and the next, and the next, the lunacy would begin all over again.

One night, JTW arrived shaking with rage, infuriated by some perceived slight tossed his way by the producer in the studio next door, with whom he'd been feuding. "That motherfucker!" he roared. "Where's my fucking gun? I'm going to shoot his balls off."

Our engineer had taken to hiding Wallingford's gun after the producer went home each night, so he professed ignorance. "Last time I saw it, it was sitting here on the console, pointed at me," he complained. "You could have killed me, you know."

If he was looking for sympathy, he didn't get any. "If I had shot your nose off, you bastard, it would have served you right for tooting so much of my stash," Wallingford snarled.

At first, I was tempted to help him find the gun, thinking about all the album sales that would be sparked by the resultant publicity. Unfortunately, common sense prevailed and I decided instead to try to calm him down.

"What's wrong, JTW? How could anyone possibly upset a paragon of virtue like you?"

He failed to detect the sarcasm in my voice. "Quite right, dear boy, quite right. But I still need to teach that cunt a lesson."

Slowly, a smile worked its way across his face. If I could have seen his eyes behind his mirrored shades, I might have even detected an evil gleam.

"Christ, I'm randy," he announced suddenly.

I'd learned that this was British slang for "horny," not an announcement that he'd changed his name. Wallingford looked around the room, sizing up the half-dozen or so willing females in attendance.

"You, darling, and you," he said, pointing to the two sluttiest-looking among them. "Later tonight we are going to have a shag the likes of which you have never experienced. Until then, your job is to sit beside me and keep me stimulated."

Wordlessly, they crossed the room, waggling their gorgeous asses as they did so, and took up their assignment: one began rubbing his back, the other plunked herself down on his lap and stuck her tongue in his ear.

"Right, dear boys," he called out on the talkback to the band waiting impatiently in the studio. "Let us make a record!"

That was a particularly productive evening for us all, Wallingford's plan for revenge having refocused his remaining functional brain cells to an unusual extent. His instructions to Hinch during a vocal overdub were clear and concise; his suggestions to Vernon about changing a bass line nothing short of brilliant; his direction to Cody about adding a keyboard part sheer inspiration. Finally, I could see where the man's reputation had come from.

Exhilarated and rejuvenated by the flow of creative energy, we worked straight through till dawn. Unusually, at no time during the eighteen-hour session did Wallingford retire to the lounge to ball, boink, screw, or have it off with either of his two anointed beauties, nor did he give in to the temptations being offered by the other lovely ladies in the control room, although Hinch and JD did, more than once. As we were all packing up to leave after a long, long night, I was about to compliment our producer on his focus and self-restraint when he briskly informed us that he would be retiring for a short while with his two concubines for a fuck of mind-boggling proportions, and that he wanted us all to wait until he returned because he would have big news for us then.

Though we were all exhausted, we all willingly complied. What was John Thomas Wallingford about to do? The only thing we knew was that it would involve the producer next door, and we couldn't wait to learn the specifics.

Forty-five minutes later, Wallingford reappeared with a girl on each arm, red-faced and dripping with sweat. As soon as he saw our expectant faces, he burst out in hysterical laughter. "I showed that bastard! I showed 'im!" he crowed, getting redder in the face by the minute.

"What'd you do, JTW?" Hinch asked, a touch of awe in his voice.

"Well, my boy, what I did was, I shagged the tits off these two birds"— he said, pointing to the two girls, who, to my untrained eye did not appear at all titless. "I must say, they did a spectacular job of keeping my juices flowing all evening," he added, nodding to the pleased-looking wenches in acknowledgement before pausing for dramatic effect.

"And?" Hinch wanted to know. I did, too.

"Well, laddie, in celebration of this landmark evening I decided to do my shagging in the studio next door. In the control room. On top of their pile of tapes, to be precise."

If the control room next door was anything like ours, it had dozens of huge two-inch reels of tape lying around, stacked on the floor. The suckers cost a couple of hundred bucks each, and a band typically ran through twenty or thirty of them in the course of recording an album.

"Despite the prodigious efforts of these fantastic birds, I'm proud to say that I exerted amazing self-control—Tantric, one might even say," JTW bragged. "Finally, though, I couldn't hold back any longer. And at that precise moment...."

We all sat there wide-eyed as he held us in suspense.

"... I pulled out and spunked all over their fucking tapes like a fire hose," he chortled with glee. "And trust me, lads, it was absolute gallons!"

At the word "gallons" he began sputtering so uncontrollably we thought he'd burst a blood vessel. Alarmed, the two girls rushed to help him up off the floor where he collapsed in a heap, laughing hysterically. It was contagious, too—for the next ten minutes we were all doubled over with laughter until our sides ached, and for years afterward we would refer to that first album as our "absolute gallons" record. No one got the inside joke but us, of course, but that didn't matter. It was the most lasting memory we would have of those insane weeks we spent in the studio with John Thomas Wallingford.

AMAZINGLY, WE NEVER heard another word about the incident. I'm guessing that either the producer next door was so irate he decided to pack up and move to another studio, or perhaps he was just so used to those kinds of retaliatory tactics that he simply took it in his stride. But our long days and nights with JTW were coming to a close, despite the fact that we appeared to be nowhere near finished. Booking more studio time was not an option because we had a spate of gigs waiting—we hadn't played live in nearly two months, and there would be a lot of pissed-off club owners ready to sue my ass, or worse, if we failed to meet our commitments.

On the next to last day, I found myself alone in the control room with Wallingford and decided it was time to have a heart-to-heart talk—or some reasonable facsimile thereof—with him.

"Dear boy, you have absolutely nothing to be worried about," he told me, deftly blowing smoke up my ass. "I'll take the tapes with me and finish them off in the next week or two. All that's left to do is a little mixing and some spit-and-polish work; I won't need the boys for that, it's something I can do by myself."

He was going to finish our album on his own, without us being there? I knew Cody would go ballistic at the mere suggestion.

"Ah, your charming tousle-haired rhythm guitarist," JTW said when I reminded him of Cody's abiding interest in the quality of the recording. "He *is* a delight, isn't he? And so full of wonderful ideas." He paused to snort a line. "Don't worry, I will speak with him personally right now and assure him that I wouldn't dream of doing anything he wouldn't approve of." Another toot. "I think it's marvelous that he takes such an interest, you know. I wish all my artists were that involved in what I do for them."

Already he was turning things inside-out. I knew it, and he knew I knew it, but if he was willing to take Cody head-on, that was fine with me. To tell you the truth, I was dreading being the messenger of what I knew Cody would view as catastrophically bad news.

With that, Wallingford headed off to the studio floor, where he proceeded to hold a long conference with the band. I decided to wait in the control room and watch the fireworks from afar.

"Do you want me to turn on the microphones so you can hear what they're saying?" the engineer asked me.

"No, don't bother," I told him. "It'll be more fun this way."

But the expected explosion didn't occur. Through the glass, I could see Cody frowning, but the only arm-waving was coming from Wallingford, who seemed to be spinning a tall tale that had them all enthralled, Hinch especially. The Truckers, as usual, were saying nothing; most of the conversation was between JTW and Hinch.

After a couple minutes of this, one of the babes in the control room blurted out, "This is boring."

I turned around to face a vacant, gum-chewing peroxide blonde who didn't look more than fifteen. "Who *are* you, anyway?" I asked.

"I'm JTW's friend," she replied sullenly. "I'm a singer. He's going to produce my next album."

At this all the other ladies in the room began hooting with laughter. Even the engineer was chuckling softly. I was just about to give her a brief lesson in the realities of life—or throw her the hell out of there, I don't know which—when the control room door opened and in walked Joe Finnerty.

"Donnie, so good to see you!" he declared, embracing me as if I were his long-lost son. "I figured you must be getting close to wrapping things up, so I decided to stop by and have a listen ... if you don't mind, that is."

Well, I kind of did mind, but I wasn't about to say so, not to the guy who I thought—however mistakenly—was paying the bills. "It's okay with me," I stammered, "but I don't know how JTW will feel about it."

"How is John?" Finnerty asked, apparently oblivious to the fact that Wallingford hated being called John.

I was about to answer when Wallingford reappeared. "Joseph!" he boomed at the top of his lungs. "My dear, dear friend—what an honor to have you here." In the blink of an eye JTW had transformed from raging madman to congenial host. "Come, have a seat, make yourself comfortable."

Finnerty settled into the chair next to Wallingford, right alongside the engineer, who had offered the record company executive the briefest of nods in acknowledgement. "I presume the tracks are all done?" Joe asked innocently.

"Absolutely, dear boy, absolutely!" the producer lied. "All that remains is a tiny bit of tweaking and some remixing, but we're at the finish line and I guarantee you multiple hits and big, big sales from this fantastic band you were discerning enough to sign."

Finnerty remained expressionless; I guess he was used to Wallingford's brand of bullshit. "Well, I was hoping to hear the finished product," he said.

"Of course, of course," JTW exclaimed, gesturing through the control room window for the band to come in and join us. I saw Hinch look up from the heated conversation he was having with Cody and they all began trudging in. "Not all the songs are done, mind you," JTW continued, "but I have pretty much completed what I think will be the first single. Let me go find the tape for you."

Wallingford excused himself and went into a huddle at the back of the control room with the engineer, who began poring through the pile of tape boxes. Moments later, he was threading one of them onto the big machine while JTW fussed around with the light dimmers, turning them all down to a faint glow for dramatic effect. A few seconds later, music began pumping through the massive speakers: our first-ever record.

Or was it? Cody, seated on the sofa behind us, looked at me in alarm; I in turn looked at Hinch, who seemed catatonic with shock, staring down at the floor. Even the Truckers stopped their clowning for a moment and adopted expressions of bewilderment.

This wasn't the music we had recorded so painstakingly for the past four weeks! I mean, it sounded something like one of the songs Cody and Hinch had written, but only barely so. There were violins singing, trumpets blaring, clarinets tootling, bells and whistles and, for all I know, Mairzy doats and dozy doats and liddle lamzy divey. Oh, every once in awhile you'd hear Hinch's voice poking through the haze, or a signature drum fill pounded out by Joe Dan, but for the most part it was an unfathomable mess.

"What the fuck??"

It was Cody, rising to his feet, hands clenched, lips drawn taut. I knew what was coming and got up to block him.

"Don't make a scene in front of Finnerty," I hissed at him. "Later. We'll sort this out later, after he's gone."

Cody, temper now at a violent pitch, seemed apoplectic. At times like this I knew he was capable of almost anything. We'd never fought before, the two of us, but we were perilously close now.

"Come on, Cody—it's me," I pleaded. "I'm not the enemy here."

He raised his fist menacingly. I knew I wasn't the intended victim, but I was the only person standing between him and Wallingford, and so I braced myself for the inevitable blow. Fortunately, at the very last minute Cody somehow came to his senses and slowly sank back down into his seat. To my relief, I saw that Finnerty, still listening raptly to the playback with his eyes closed, had missed the whole confrontation. To my horror, he seemed to be enjoying what he was hearing.

When the tape finished its awful serenade, we all sat there in stunned silence.

"You know, that's quite good. I *like* that."

All heads swiveled to find the source of this insane comment. Shit! It was Finnerty.

Everyone began talking all at once. Cody and Hinch jumped to their feet in protest, but somehow we were all shouted down by Wallingford, who, by virtue of being seated nearest him, had Finnerty's full attention. "Delighted, dear boy!" we heard him boom. "I knew you'd love it. Lots of hard work from the lads here plus a little mojo dust from the old master"—he pointed at himself, puffing his chest out like a bantam rooster—"and you've got yourself a number one hit."

Finnerty appeared capable only of hearing one voice—that of our producer. "Great work, great work, I knew you'd give me a hit," he kept saying. He looked around the room expectantly, waiting for us to join in the praise. Instead, all he got was silence ... and five glum, angry faces.

"Boys! What's the problem?" he asked innocently.

"I'll tell you what the fucking problem is ..." It was Cody. Of course. This time I decided to be the one doing the shouting.

"No problem, Joe," I called out, fixing Cody a look to kill. "We're still just getting used to JTW's mix, that's all. Everything's cool."

Wallingford moved in swiftly to close the sale, and he did so with such breathtaking skill Willy Loman himself would have been impressed. "You know how artistes are, Joe—they're just adapting. The boys really care about their music, you know. I respect that. As I said, we still have some tweaking to do, so this isn't the final final. Once I incorporate all their ideas, you'll be even more pleased with the finished product, I promise you."

Finnerty looked relieved. "Oh, good," he said. "Just make sure the master you deliver me is as strong as that one was."

With that, he glided out of the room, satisfied smile on his face, and we were left alone with our tormentor. Cody advanced on JTW, fists at the ready.

"You'd better have a good explanation for that, you Limey bastard," he snarled through clenched teeth, white with rage.

Putting his hands up to protect his face, Wallingford began backing away. "Dear boy …" he began. He never got a chance to finish the sentence. Before any of us knew what happened, Joe Dan Trucker—our nearly always silent drummer—had cold-cocked the producer in the back of the head, sending his sunglasses flying into the air. He sprawled face forward on the carpeting beneath the mixing console, blood spurting from a split lip. One of the girls in the back of the room screamed.

"Get the fuck out of here—all of you!" I thundered. The wall of female flesh began retreating out the door, grabbing at purses and lipstick, high heels clattering on the wood floor.

The engineer, looking terrified, was helping Wallingford to his feet now. "Look, guys, I was only doing my job," he stammered, anticipating, I suppose, that he'd be the recipient of the next blow.

With Cody and JD still appearing ready to beat the crap out of anyone who came within ten feet, I decided to take control.

"Everyone shut the fuck up and sit down!" I yelled. I don't think any of the guys had ever seen me so angry. Once I saw all their asses firmly planted on the sofa I turned to our producer, who seemed to have regained his composure despite the blood streaming down his face. "Wallingford, explain yourself," I said, "or I'll unleash the hounds again." It was meant as a light joke in an attempt to relieve the heavy atmosphere, but he knew I meant it.

"It was just an experiment," he whined. "I stayed late one night after you guys had gone home and decided to try out an idea. There was an orchestra in the next studio and I hired some of the players to do a few overdubs. That's all. I thought you'd like it."

"Well, we fucking don't," Cody barked, though he remained seated.

"No, apparently not," JTW admitted. "But the president of your record label does, and that should count for something."

An angry Joe Dan got to his feet once again, this time accompanied by little brother Vern. Hinch, I noticed, still maintained his hang-dog position, head down.

Wallingford moved swiftly behind the engineer for cover. "Look, lads, I told Finnerty it wasn't the finished product, and it isn't. I'll fix it, I swear to you. But it is a direction I think you should consider going in … that is, if you want a hit single."

Once again, voices began rising in anger, Cody's the loudest. And once again, they were shouted down. This time not by Wallingford, nor by me. This time the voice that drowned out all the others was Hinch's.

"Pipe down, all of you!" he yelled, raising his head to survey the room and ensure we all complied. "Listen, you prick"—this directed at JTW—"what you did really sucked. You had no business springing that on us in front of Finnerty."

Wallingford looked contrite. For a moment I thought he was about to apologize.

"But," Hinch continued, turning to Cody and the Truckers, "I also think he's right. We *should* consider going in that direction."

"Goddammit, he put fucking strings on our song!" Cody protested.

"I know, bro, I know," Hinch said soothingly. "It doesn't sound like us. But maybe it sounds like something better." I was flabbergasted. For once, their positions as pioneer and resistance leader had reversed.

Wearily, Cody shook his head, half in disbelief at what he was hearing, half in defeat.

"All I'm saying," Hinch continued, "is that maybe we should give the guy a chance, even if he is a class-A asshole. Maybe he actually does know how to make a hit. He's done it before, after all. And we haven't."

Still wiping the blood from his mouth, I saw JTW preparing to speak. "If I were you, I'd be very quiet right about now, Mr. Wallingford," I warned. He shut up.

Cody continued to protest, weakly. "But, Hinch, it sounded like shit on a plate," he complained.

"Maybe you're right. But maybe shit on a plate is what the public wants. And maybe that's the price we have to pay to get our music out there, to play what we really want to play, to land the big gigs. We've all sacrificed a lot to be in this band. Maybe this is just another sacrifice we have to make."

I couldn't believe my ears. This was Hinch talking? But it was, and I had to admit that what he was saying actually made sense.

Cody took a moment to let it all sink in. "Alright," he finally growled at our producer. "We'll try it your way. But there are lots of changes I want made to that bullshit mix before I'll agree to it."

"Absolutely, dear boy, absolutely!" Wallingford gushed. Miraculously, he had turned into JTW again. "I shall slave night and day to get it sounding exactly as you like."

None of us believed him. But what choice did we have? Now that he'd heard it Wallingford's way, Finnerty would never allow the record to come out any other way, and we all knew it.

"Now, then, let's get back to work," JTW announced brightly. "After a line of blow and a quick shag, of course."

AFTER THAT NIGHT, we never saw John Thomas Wallingford again. He never turned up at what was supposed to be our final mixing session, and neither his version of the single nor any other version was ever released. For the next eight months, Wallingford bounced around from studio after studio all over the U.S. and Europe, dragging our tapes around with him, supposedly putting on the "final touches" that he deemed necessary to complete them. With his producer holding the master tapes hostage, Finnerty had no choice but to push back the release date of both the single and the album time and time again, right up until the morning he dropped dead of a heart attack.

That's when John Thomas Wallingford dropped out of sight completely, along with our tapes. For awhile, Finnerty's cadre of flamboyant assistants tried running Noteworthy on their own, until they ran it straight into the ground. Worse yet was the complicated web of legal entanglements that Finnerty left behind, many of which are still being sorted out today, more than twenty years later. No one knows who owns the assets of Noteworthy Records—if there are any—and no one knows where our tapes are or even if they still exist.

Thank god I put that clause in our contract relieving us of all future responsibility if the record wasn't a hit—a goal it never achieved, obviously, since it was never released. That little loophole ended up being worth a quarter mil to us because it meant that we never had to repay a penny of the money we owed. It also allowed us, bloody and bruised, yet a good deal smarter than we had been before, to march onward to the pinnacle of our career ... and to the calamitous fall that would follow.

17

My plan for Christmas Day was a simple one: sleep. When I got done sleeping, I thought perhaps I'd turn over and sleep a little more. Between my hangover from last night and this infernal jet lag—which I still haven't gotten over, despite being here more than a week—all I wanted to do was be unconscious for as long as was humanly possible.

Of course, it was not to be. Within what seems like moments of closing my eyes—okay, maybe it was seven hours later, if you want to believe the damn clock—Hans's obnoxious cell phone begins shrieking at me again. *If it's the last thing I do, I have to figure out how to turn that fucking thing off*, I think as I blearily pull the covers over my head.

But I haven't figured out how to turn it off, and Hans is nothing if not persistent, so eventually I have to get up and pad across the room to either answer it or smash it with an axe. Unfortunately, there is no axe at hand.

"Bernie, you lazy bastard, it's almost noon. About time you got up!" says Hans in a tone that I can best describe as chirpy, despite my predilection for applying the adjective solely to attractive young women, preferably of the blonde variety.

"H'lo, Hans," I mumble groggily. "Don't you ever sleep?"

"Sleep? Nah. Sleep is for pussies. Like you." I hear the sound of him and Rudie cackling.

"Yeah, okay, whatever. Listen, is this important? Because I really need to take an aspirin or something." Already I can feel the jackboots marching in lockstep inside my cranium.

"Yes, it's fucking important. We finally have a lead on Schiffman. And word about Hinch, too."

The news jolts me fully awake. "Really? What? Where?…"

"I'll explain it all when I see you. Right now I need you to pull on some clothes and meet us at the *Politiestation*—the police station, yah?—in Beursstraat. The taxi driver will know where it is."

"The police station? Are you guys in trouble?"

"No, but Alan Fucking Schiffman is. Just get here as quickly as you can. And bring your passport with you—you may need it."

With that, he hangs up. Ten minutes later I am seated in a rundown taxi with bad shocks, bouncing around mercilessly on my way to wherever. My head is still pounding like a steamshovel but the aspirin I gulped down on the way out the door is starting to kick in. The streets and canals of Amsterdam, eerily deserted on this holiday morning, fly by in a blur. The taxi driver seems to know exactly where he is going, as if he's been there many times before; idly, I wonder how many tourists he's had to shuttle to the police station to report being mugged, or worse. *This is such a faded gem of a city. One facet shiny, the other impossibly seedy.*

Speaking of seedy, I soon notice that we are entering the heart of the Rossebuurt, Amsterdam's famed red light district. It's one of the places I'd hoped to check out on this trip—what the hell, I'm only human—but I certainly never expected to be here on Christmas Day. The grimy neighborhood, nearly devoid of human life, has the look of post-nuclear aftermath, as underscored by the handful of Neanderthal-like males prowling the alleyways like the undead, driven by the most primeval of instincts. Most of the windows where the ladies normally display their wares are deserted, though a few are occupied by bored-looking, mostly unattractive women—atheists, perhaps?—making a feeble attempt to appear seductive despite being attired in housecoats and fuzzy slippers.

The cab driver pulls up in front of a modern gray building, windowless and completely anonymous except for the small blue *Politie* sign hanging out front, and announces that we have arrived at our destination. "You are having a problem with one of your girls, maybe?" he leers at me as I pay my fare. I immediately decide to halve the tip I was planning on giving him. "Up yours," he shouts as he pulls out with a skid of tires, flipping me the bird as he does so. *The universal language for cheap bastards like me*, I think as I head inside, anxious and uncertain about what awaits within.

THE FIRST THING I am struck by is how immaculately clean the place is, in stark contrast to the unrelenting dinginess outside; it's as if the police force has determined that the best way to counteract crime is with disinfectant. The second thing I notice is how incredibly polite and courteous the cops are, at least to me. My American passport and casual mention of the name Hans Uhlemeyer seems to have granted me not just immunity from suspicion, but an elevated status that is almost godly.

"What can I tell you?" shrugs Hans when I finally locate him in the bowels of the maze-like structure. "A lot of cops are music fans. Of course, I make sure they get plenty of free tickets—good for me, good for them. Plus, they like Rudie—he's become their, how do you say, *mascotte*."

"Their mascot?"

"Yah, mascot, that's right," pipes up Rudie, who is walking toward us with two steaming hot cups of coffee. "Here, Bernie, you take this—you look like you need it more than me." He hands over the styrofoam vessel, then passes the other one to Hans.

"Why are we here, Hans? Has Schiffman been arrested?"

"No, not yet, anyway." He smiles. "But this is maybe even better. It appears that our good friend Alan Fucking Schiffman has made his first mistake—one which has gotten him in a lot of trouble. Our rat has finally come out of his hole, and now that he is on the run, it's only a matter of time before we catch him, yah, Rudie?"

"Yah, Hans." Rudie seems to be almost salivating.

I wait for them to volunteer more information, but they have apparently told me all they intend to, at least for now.

"And??" I ask.

"You Americans are so impatient," scolds Hans. "Soon you will know the entire story. First we have a little entertainment for you."

"Entertainment? In a police station?"

He smiles enigmatically and says only, "Wait here. And give me your passport."

I hand it over and he studies it carefully. "Nice photo," he comments sarcastically. I remember well the day I had it taken, at a Long's pharmacy on Ventura. Britney and I had had a fight earlier that morning—about money and/or her fidelity, no doubt—and so I ended up looking like a sweaty, pissed-off psychopath in heat, bald pate glinting in the lens, causing what appears to be an unsightly white tumor to dominate my forehead. You know, a typical passport photo.

"Thanks a lot," I reply with what I hope is an equal dose of derision.

"You know, I could easily get you an EEC passport," Hans remarks casually, before adding, with a twinkle in his eye, "With your good looks, you could almost pass for a Dutchman."

"Why would I want an EEC passport?"

"No special reason. Might just come in handy one day at the airport if the immigration line is shorter."

"Seems like a lot of trouble to go through just to save a few minutes standing in line."

"No trouble," he says. "My friend Aachie, he could make one for you in minutes."

"Yah," interjects Rudie. "Aachie, he is a master at forging identity documents."

"Do you guys know you're in a police station?" I remind them incredulously.

Hans laughs. "We are among friends, Bernie. And the police are well aware that people can be whoever they want to be."

"As long as they have a friend like Aachie," Rudie adds.

At that moment a door opens and a cop waves vaguely in our direction. Wordlessly, Hans gets up and strides down the hallway, carrying my passport with him. I look over at Rudie with a quizzical expression.

"They need to keep a record of who they allow in," he explains as we wait for Hans to return. "Paperwork is a very important part of being a policeman, you know."

"Allow in where?"

"To the interrogation room. Relax, Bernie. You're going to enjoy this."

A moment later, Hans reappears, accompanied by a fresh-faced young officer who looks like he only just graduated from the academy that morning. "Mr. Temkin? Please come with me," he instructs as he returns my passport, nearly genuflecting as he does so.

I follow him through the doorway, with Hans and Rudie trailing closely behind, and find myself in a small room—almost as tiny as my hotel quarters—facing a large pane of one-way glass. Through the glass I see an unfortunate individual with rotted teeth and a two-day growth of stubble on his chin, bloodshot eyes set deep within his craggy face. Hunched over in his seat, disheveled and gaunt, he has the appearance of someone who has had neither a decent meal nor seen the sun in decades, like an underfed mole trapped above ground, darting eyes searching for a subterranean hole to escape into.

Sitting across from this wretched soul are two well-scrubbed gentlemen in polyester sports jackets and perfectly pressed slacks—police detectives, as Rudie cheerfully informs me. Hans reaches over to the wall and turns a dial, allowing us to listen in on the conversation.

They are conversing solely in Dutch, of course, so most of it goes completely over my head, but my ears perk up when I hear the words *rock starre Hinch* and *Amerikaans manager Schiffman*. What connection could this pathetic creature possibly have with either man?

That's the first question I ask Hans when we retreat back into the hallway after a few moments of eavesdropping.

"That," explains Hans, "is Hinch's drug dealer. Or Schiffman's. No matter. He is our *kaartje*—our ticket—to finally nailing that motherfucker."

"Will you please, *please* tell me what happened?" I am nearly crawling out of my skin with the need to know.

At long last Hans takes pity. Motioning me over to sit beside him on a long wooden bench, he finally spills the beans. "Well, Bernie, last night as the three of us were enjoying our genever, there was quite a lot of excitement going on here in the Rossebuurt. A shooting, in fact, which is actually quite rare in our fair city." He studies my face for signs of surprise. Finding none, he continues. "The amusing little fellow you just observed being interrogated," he says, "goes by the name of Wolter. Wolter the Wolf, he likes to call himself."

"*Wolter het wezel*," chimes in a passing police officer.

"Yah, that is better," agrees Rudie with a laugh. "Wolter the Weasel."

"It seems," continues Hans, ignoring the interruption, "that our Wolter got himself in a bit of trouble last night. He had a visit from one of his customers who was not very happy about the quality of the heroin he had purchased previously, and an argument ensued."

"I imagine that happens all the time," I interject.

"Yes, it does," says Hans, giving me a stern look that fairly screams *shut up and let me talk*. "But what does not happen all the time is that the customer pulls out a gun out of the silver briefcase he's carrying, attaches a silencer to it, and announces that he is going to execute Wolter on the spot."

"What did the guy think he was, some kind of vigilante?" I ask, enthralled. Comic book images of Red Ryder fly around my head.

"I don't know that *Englische* word, Bernie. But what I do know is that if you interrupt me one more time I am going to set Rudie on you."

"Sorry," I stammer as Rudie rises, a half-smile on his face, and I am. Not just because I don't want to be on the receiving end of one of his wallops, however good-natured, but because I really do want to hear the rest of this story, and how it connects up with Hinch, or Schiffman, or both.

Hans squints at me for a long moment as if making up his mind.

"Okay," he finally says, apparently satisfied with the contrite expression on my face. "So here's what happened. Customer comes to Wolter's place, just a couple of blocks from here, complains that the shit he bought was not pure enough, announces he's going to execute Wolter and proceeds to fit a silencer on his gun. But just before he's about to put the gun to Wolter's head, he stops and asks him a question. And here is where it becomes interesting, because the question he asks is, 'Has Hinch been back to buy more shit from you?'"

My jaw drops open. "Hinch?"

"Yes, he was very clear about that. Hinch. Tommy Hinchton, the rock star you have been looking for, managed by Alan Schiffman, the thieving prick *we* have been looking for."

"Why on earth would the customer ask that question?" I ask.

"Because, my dear Bernie, the irate customer was Hinch's tour manager—the very same bald-headed scar-faced tour manager who had last visited Wolter the night of the Paradiso gig to buy smack for his rock star employer. And what's more, he wasn't alone when he paid his courtesy call last night. He had a gentleman accompanying him. A well-dressed gentleman in an expensive suit who spoke in an American accent. A gentleman by the name of...."

"Alan Schiffman."

I hate finishing sentences, and Hans especially hates me finishing *his* sentences, but this time he lets me off with a free pass. Wide-eyed, we look at one another. "Are you sure?" I finally ask.

"The police are sure. They have been showing Wolter photographs all morning and he has positively identified both Schiffman and Hinch's tour manager, a charming thug who goes by the name Henry Ryker."

"Jesus Christ," I mutter. I don't know, it just seems like the appropriate thing to say on Christmas Day.

"Wait, Bernie, because it gets better. You see, Wolter used the momentary distraction to knock the gun out of the tour manager's hand and produce his own pistol, which he kept on his person for precisely such a scenario. A gunshot went off—Wolter isn't sure if it was Ryker's gun, as it fell to the floor, or his own—and the two men turned to flee ... but not before Schiffman himself pulled a gun out and also fired at Wolter, barely missing him."

"Hang on, you're saying *Schiffman* had a gun?"

"Sure. Why are you so surprised? This is a nasty business we're in; I've told you that many times."

"It's just that...." I don't know what to say. I mean, sure, the guy is a total scumbag—Donnie Boyle had me completely convinced of that—but I didn't figure him toting his own heat. Schiffman always struck me as the kind of guy who had others do his dirty work.

"Look, I have Rudie here, but I still carry a gun with me," Hans explains. "For protection, you know?" He pats his side pocket, grinning conspiratorially.

"What, even here in the police station?"

"Shh, don't tell, or they'll all want one," he jokes in an exaggerated whisper. "Anyway, I still haven't gotten to the best part of the story."

"There's more?"

"Yes, there's a delightful postscript to this story. You see, Wolter's next-door neighbor is, shall we say, a woman of the streets. And at the moment of this ruckus with Schiffman and the tour manager, she was busily engaged plying her trade. Imagine her outrage, then, when she was rudely interrupted by the sound of a bullet flying through her bedroom wall and landing squarely in the ass of the large gentleman lying on top of her."

Like schoolchildren, we begin to giggle at the ludicrousness of it all. In fact, so infectious is our mirth that within moments, the three of us are howling in fits of hysterical laughter so raucous that policemen begin pouring into the hallway from the doors all around us, concerned, I suppose, that they have a pack of lawbreaking hyenas in their midst. "*Wat is zo grappig?*" I hear one of them say. "*Gekke Amerikaan,*" another replies.

Yes, at that moment I am a crazy American, in the company of two crazy Dutchmen, giddy at the rapidly approaching prospect of fulfilling our quest. And it's all come courtesy of a weasel, or wolf, by the name of Wolter.

WHEN WE FINALLY calm down and catch our breath, the enormity of what has transpired begins to dawn on me. "So this fellow who was shot—was he badly hurt?" I ask.

"It doesn't look that way," Hans says. "He's still in hospital, but they don't seem to think it's too serious. Of course, they haven't told Wolter that—they've told him the guy was killed, which is why he's singing like a bird."

"Do they know who it was who actually shot the guy?"

"No, they're waiting for the ballistics results. They've got two of the three guns—Wolter's and Ryker's—so if the bullet they pulled out of the guy's ass doesn't match either of those, I suppose they'll assume it was Schiffman's gun that did the damage. Either way, it really doesn't matter: the cops will want to find him regardless. The only difference will be the seriousness of the charges they'll file against him."

"Do you think they'll be able to track Schiffman down?"

"So many questions, Bernie! But yes, I do think one of us—either we or the cops—will find Schiffman soon, because he is running scared now. And once the newspapers come out tomorrow morning, he'll be even more panicked. This is going to be headline news, you know."

"Why? It sounds like a pretty minor shooting incident to me."

"You fucking Americans," Hans sighs. "You call every shooting minor unless it involves dozens of people, or the president himself. But here in Holland, every shooting is big news, because we don't have cowboys running around in the streets with guns, like in your *gekke* country. So, yes, this will be in all the papers, and when that happens it will cause Schiffman to either do something even more stupid, or perhaps just turn himself in."

The logic, as Hans explains it, makes perfect sense to me. Still, I have a sneaking suspicion things won't go quite as easily as he predicts.

"Well, I guess this at least proves that you were right about them still being in Amsterdam," I point out.

"It proves that at least Schiffman and the tour manager are still in Amsterdam," Hans replies. "The police aren't so sure about Hinch, or the other roadie. What was his name again?"

"Cody. Cody the roadie." They don't seem to get the joke; I guess maybe it's not as funny in Dutch.

"Yah, well, all we really know now is that somehow Hinch got away from Schiffman and Ryker. We don't know whether this Cody fellow is with Hinch, or with the other two."

"He's with Hinch," I say. "I'm sure of that."

Hans looks at me as if I have something to hide. "How can you be so sure? Is there something you haven't told us?"

"No, other than the fact that I spent months interviewing Hinch's former manager, who was childhood friends with both Hinch and Cody. There is absolutely no doubt in my mind that, whatever is going on, Cody is with Hinch."

"If you say so. Can you give the cops a description of Cody?"

"I've never actually met him," I admit. "In fact, I only ever saw him once, at a distance. But, sure, I think I remember enough about him to give them the basics."

"Good," Hans says, "because the sooner the police catch up with Schiffman, the sooner I get my money back."

"And the sooner they can find Hinch, the sooner I can finish my book," I add.

"Yah, and the sooner that happens, the sooner we can get rid of your fat American ass," chimes in Rudie, prompting another burst of laughter.

Hey, it's good to see people who enjoy their work.

18

Transcript: Interview with Donnie Boyle, May 15, 1998

YEAH, I KNOW, the fucking machine is back. Thought I was rid of the damned thing once and for all. These goddamned doctors, they don't know their heads from their asses ... and they don't seem to have much of a clue about my lungs, either. So, yeah, I'm back to sucking on this damn plastic pipe. What the hell, I figure if that's the price I've got to pay to keep going, fair enough. I just don't want to end up as an invalid, that's all.

I think we left off last time with Joe Finnerty kicking the bucket, right? I can joke about it now, but that really was a shame. Like I said, I thought he was basically a decent guy. Inept, perhaps, but decent. The biggest consequence to us was that our debut album never saw the light of day, though maybe that was just as well: for all we knew, it could have completely sucked. Of course, it's just as possible that our insane producer might have fixed it up in the end—Lord knows he spent enough of our money to polish it into solid gold. I guess the world will never know, huh?

What amazed me the most was that, somehow, the album never materializing actually worked to our benefit. People were combing record stores looking for it, to no avail, which made it a desired commodity ... even if it didn't exist. And that in turn made JJ's job easier. Once she had landed herself a position on the national concert committee and we'd signed our deal with Noteworthy, she was able to start cranking on our behalf like a woman possessed, booking us tons of gigs from coast to coast. No sooner had we emerged from the cocoon of the recording studio than we were slammed into a solid five months of well-paid touring, opening for the likes of Foghat, Blue Oyster Cult, the Scorpions, even Aerosmith, whom we had first seen in a support slot themselves. And this time we weren't limited to the Northeast and mid-Atlantic states, where we might have started wearing out our welcome. Instead, we were going national, playing colleges in and around San Francisco, L.A., and

San Diego before swinging back to Philly via the deep South. Vernon and Joe Dan were totally in their element down there, partying hearty with the hundreds of long-lost cousins who magically appeared at every gig we played from San Antonio to Virginia Beach. And with every performance, the band got tighter and tighter, the show more professional, the musicianship more polished. We earned encores everywhere we played, and our newly enlarged road crew made sure that the headliners didn't get their pound of flesh from us. Most of the time, the extra muscle wasn't even necessary; it seemed that word was spreading around the circuit that we were no longer wet-behind-the-ear rookies to be messed with. Instead, we were increasingly viewed by the headlining bands and their road crews as veterans worthy of respect.

Gone, too, was the need to strong-arm local promoters for our hard-earned pay. I'll say this for the colleges: unlike the sleazebags who ran the dives on the bar and club circuit, they did everything on the up-and-up. Whatever cash guarantee had been agreed upon was handed over promptly and without argument, and checks were mailed on time and with good funds backing them. Touring was starting to become a pleasure, at least from my perspective.

But perhaps not from the band's point of view. Ever since their exposure to hot and cold flowing drugs in the recording studio, they had changed. Coke and speed were starting to make their evil presence felt, and the guys had also taken to drinking expensive brandies and whiskies instead of long-neck beers. Thankfully, these latest affectations of the rock 'n' roll life seemed to have only minimal effect on Cody and Vernon, but the more drunk or coked up Hinch got, the more insufferable he became in his vanity. Even Katie couldn't stomach him at those times—in fact, once or twice she left him, though he somehow always managed to sweet-talk himself back into her good graces.

It was Joe Dan who was becoming the real problem. Though mild-mannered when sober, he had shown himself to be a mean drunk, and an even more vicious cokehead. Hostilities and fighting were starting to become an everyday occurrence, to everyone's chagrin. But we didn't seem to know how to stop it, either.

The main target of JD's venom was Muscle Beach Len. He'd had it in for Len ever since that stupid incident in the club when Len had slapped Cody on the back and sent him flying halfway across the room. I know the big ox meant it in a well-intentioned way; unaware of his own strength, he'd simply hit the guy a little too hard. I'm not sure why that triggered such a protective instinct in our drummer—Cody, was, after all, a big boy and more than capable of taking care of himself—but from that day forward JD appointed himself Cody's unofficial protector, same as Cody had done for Hinch back when we were school kids. It was odd, and it made for some pretty uncomfortable moments, too.

Things came to a head one night when we were all sitting around the dressing room after a gig. The whole band was hanging out, relaxing, along with our road crew and a bunch of girls. Hinch, Joe Dan, and Vernon had been slurping from a bottle of Courvoisier and somebody had brought by a shitload of coke, which, arrayed in neat little lines on a small mirror, was being eagerly passed around the room.

Soon the cognac and the toot began having their effect, and couples began pairing off. Usually the main competition between the girls was for Hinch, but on this particular night there was absolutely no question who he was going to be sleeping with, because there was this one chick who literally stood head and shoulders above all the rest. She was positively Amazonian, with a killer body that she was not the least bit shy about showing off. She was bold, too: the minute she entered the dressing room she had planted herself on Hinch's lap and they'd been slurping one another's faces ever since.

Cody, as usual, sat by himself. Most of the time, he tended to shy away from the groupies. If there was a girl hanging around who looked the least bit intelligent, he might try engaging her in a conversation about music, or current events, or something equally boring. Most of the time he and the girl would end up parting ways a short time later with an awkward handshake, but sometimes they'd end up going off together for the night. Even if that happened, it was no guarantee that he'd scored: often, the next day, he'd tell us about how they sat up until dawn talking about the meaning of life or some shit instead of balling their brains out like a couple of normal twenty-year-olds would. Then we'd hit the road and he'd start moping around, pining for the girl he'd left behind … right up until the point where he'd get to chatting with another musician who'd offhandedly mention that he'd gotten the best blow job of his life from the lady in question. This in turn would send Cody into a deep funk which could last for weeks, until he found himself another incarnation of the Virgin Mary to place up on a pedestal. The whole thing was kind of tedious, and so we'd all gotten pretty uninterested in hooking Cody up, because we knew it would only lead to drama.

Perhaps that's what caused the groupies to tend to steer clear of Cody, even though he was in the band and hence a bigger "catch" than me or one of the roadies. Or maybe it was just that he didn't have rock star looks. Hinch, of course, was born to be a celebrity—he would have carried himself like a god even if he pumped gas for a living—and the tattoos and unkempt beards on the Truckers seemed to drive the girls wild. I myself had pretty long hair in those days, and I'd even grown a mustache because I thought that's how managers were supposed to look. When I see photographs of myself from that era, I realize that I looked more like a sleazy '70s porn star. What the heck, that had the desired effect on the girls, too. But Cody, he still looked pretty much the same as he had when we first met in elementary school: short and squat, with tight-cropped curly red hair. The only difference was that he'd started wearing glasses, onstage as well as off. I suppose he thought they made him appear intellectual, but in fact they just made him seem even geekier than he actually was. And since he only ever wore loose T-shirts and baggy, faded jeans instead of the body-hugging satin and leather that Hinch and the Truckers paraded around in, nobody except us knew that Cody's compact body was powerful and muscular. Nor did anyone outside of our little inner circle realize that he had a macho side which was fearful when aroused. To the girls that populated our dressing rooms and hotel lobbies, Cody was just a rather pathetic little nerd who was seen as a candidate only for a pity fuck.

As a result, once Hinch's choice of partner—or partners—had been settled for the night, it was usually Vernon and Joe Dan who got second pick. Being brothers, they rarely had any problem settling any disputed claims; if all else failed, they'd simply share the girl, same as they had Janet Jaworsky.

Anyway, on this particular night, with all of us pleasantly buzzed, Muscle Beach Len announced that he was going to act as matchmaker for the Truckers. It was just a bit of nonsense, the kind of bullshit game that bands on tour play to pass the time. Now, like I said, Joe Dan didn't like Len much, but he didn't weigh in against the proposal, either; he just sat there staring at Len through hooded eyes. Len was a bonehead, but he had a pretty decent sense of humor and he had us in stitches as he found reasons for eliminating each of the girls from contention, one by one. Personally, I think he was just trying to set aside a couple of them that he wanted for himself—by tradition, the roadies always got the leftovers that the band weren't interested in—but none of us really cared, as long as he kept us entertained.

After a bunch of mumbo-jumbo, Len managed to whittle the list down to just two girls, and then he made a big show of acting undecided, like he was having a lot of trouble figuring which would be the best match for which Trucker. "Okay, let's see," he intoned, mock-seriously. "Now, Crystal here, she's got a big bottom, which would seem to indicate she's gonna be the best fit for our bass player." He paused for effect, looking around the room to make sure we were all paying attention. "But then again," he proclaimed, "that same chunky caboose looks like it would stand up well to a hearty pounding from our huge-ass drummer."

A few chuckles from Hinch and the road crew; an embarrassed grin from Crystal. I looked over at Joe Dan, who was still eyeing Len warily, still not saying a word.

Len continued improvising. "On the other hand, my special powers of extra-sensory perception tell me that Amber here uses the rhythm method, which means she's a natural for our drummer ... though I'm guessing those pert little titties of hers need the kind of gentle strumming only our bass player could impart."

We all howled with laughter—even Crystal and Amber.

When the hoots had died down, Len hunched over and began stroking his chin like he was deep in contemplation. We all watched expectantly as an evil grin slowly began spreading across his face. I'd seen that grin before, and it generally led to something bad, like a flareup with another member of the crew, or, worse yet, with one of the Truckers. It was definitely a red flag, and in retrospect I should have done something to shut him up there and then, but with several brewskis bubbling in my gut, I confess to having been a bit out of it myself.

"I got me an idea," Len finally announced. "Maybe we should let the girls pick. Women's lib, you know?"

The two girls in contention gave him a blank look. These were definitely not bra-burners, though from the look of things they didn't exactly seem like they needed the bras they were wearing, either.

Len rose to his feet to deliver the punch line with exaggerated formality. "Okay, ladies, tell us," he said. "Which one of you would like to get JD, and which one of you would like to get VD?"

You could almost hear the air being sucked out of the room.

A clueless Len sat back down, triumphant smile on his dumb-ass face. Obviously this was the first time the offensive acronym had occurred to him.

The silence was broken by a red-faced Vernon.

"What did you say??" he spat out, each word tinged with challenge.

I looked over at our normally placid bass player. I expected him to be pissed. He wasn't. He was *livid*.

We all started talking at once, trying to defuse the explosion that we knew was coming. All of us, that is, except Muscle Beach Len, who continued to sit there wearing a shit-eating grin.

"I said," Len repeated calmly, enunciating each word, "which one of you ladies would like to get VD?" He looked around the room as if expecting the rest of us to be as pleased as he was.

Nobody moved. You could cut the silence with a machete.

And then, like a flash, the room erupted.

"Nobody talks to my baby brother like that!" shouted JD, hurling himself across the room at Len's throat. Before any of us could raise a finger to stop him, Joe Dan was pounding the crap out of Muscle Beach Len. A split second later, Vernon was on top of him too, fists flying like a windmill in a hurricane. The girls started screaming hysterically. It all appeared to be happening in slow motion, yet in what seemed to be an instant, two of our new roadies succeeded in pulling Joe Dan and Vernon off of a visibly injured Len.

That was scary enough, but what happened next was downright terrifying. Without missing a beat, the two roadies then proceeded to methodically kick the shit out of JD and Vernon. These guys had only been working with us for a few months—not nearly long enough to bond with Len, who was an anti-social jackass to begin with—but here they were, not just defending him but taking vengeance on his behalf.

Hinch, Cody, and I, of course, immediately jumped to our feet in an attempt to break it up. We didn't get very far. Our path was blocked by the largest of our three new roadies—a guy the size of a small Mack truck, who had instinctively positioned himself directly between us and the carnage going on at the other end of the dressing room. Crossing his arms defiantly, his body language made it abundantly clear that he had no intention of moving. Not for us, not for anybody.

Even with the three of us trying to barrel him over, the guy didn't budge an inch. It was like trying to upend a bulldozer.

"Stand back, motherfuckers," the roadie growled in warning. "Stay out of it."

"What the hell are you talking about?" I shouted. "Your guys are beating on my drummer and bass player."

"I said stay out of it," man-mountain repeated, this time a little louder. "Or I'll have to put a hurt on *you*."

Hinch and I exchanged panicked glances. We were concerned about our own safety, of course, but mostly I think we were worried about what Cody was going to do.

"Just stay right where you are," warned the roadie once again, this time focusing his gaze on an infuriated Cody, the one he correctly deemed most likely to interfere. Hinch and I both looked at Cody imploringly. To my great relief, common sense prevailed. Sighing a deep sigh, he simply put his hands up in surrender. It was the right decision. Clearly, there was nothing to be gained by the three of us getting involved in this melee.

Over on the other side of the room, things were going badly for our bandmates. Vernon, who was slightly built, was no match at all for the goon who was whaling on him, and even though Joe Dan was considerably bigger than his assailant, his drunkenness negated any advantage he may have had. The two Truckers were getting a serious ass-kicking by our own road crew and there was nothing we could do to stop it.

Finally, one of the girls who had run out of the room screaming reappeared with a bunch of security guards and everyone was separated. Fortunately, JD and Vernon suffered only cuts and bruises, but Len was spitting blood and had to be carted off to the local hospital, where X-rays revealed several broken ribs and a perforated spleen, which laid him up for months and ended his roadying days forever. Right there and then, I fired the three guys who had turned against us, and they took it calmly enough, but as they walked out of the room one of them turned to me and with a nonchalance that chilled me to the bone said something I'll never forget:

"You need to get your musicians under control, Mr. Manager. You'll be able to hire another road crew but you need to know that there ain't a single one of us who wouldn't do exactly what we did tonight, because we stand together. We are the heart and soul of this operation; your boys are just the window-dressing. The sooner you understand that, the better off you'll be."

It was at that moment that I came to a full realization of what the brotherhood of the road means. And it was at that moment I knew that the troubles were just beginning for Joe Dan Trucker.

I REMEMBER THE spring of 1975 as a time of turmoil. It wasn't just that one incident with Joe Dan; there was discontent flowing all around. All of a sudden, we had no road crew, and with each passing week, it seemed more and more likely that our album would never be released; in fact, with Joe Finnerty gone we didn't know if we even still had a record deal, or, if we did, who it was with. And, with us having outgrown the bar circuit and the colleges about to let out for the summer, we didn't know where future gigs were going to come from. Plus, Cody and Hinch were growing increasingly estranged. After having come down on opposite sides of the fence following the Wallingford debacle, I think each felt somewhat betrayed. They began sniping at each other, and one day it came to a head when they got into a huge argument over something trivial, like the tempo of a song or some shit like that. It was only the gentle intervention of Katie Q, who took Cody to one side and quietly calmed him down, which prevented the argument from erupting into a fistfight—something which would not have ended well for Hinch, I am sure. After that, Cody started becoming distant and disengaged, though he often talked of his desire to produce our next album "instead of some record company hack," as he put it—meaning JTW or someone with a similar pedigree.

Vernon also became increasingly isolated, torn between loyalty to his older brother and the dawning realization that JD was turning into a major-league asshole. For the first couple of weeks after the incident with Len, I threw a few extra bucks to the headlining act's road crew to help us load in and pack up, but it soon became clear that there was no love lost between them and JD; obviously, word had quickly spread among the black T-shirted brigade. Even when I was able to hire a new crew, they not only steered well clear of our drummer but made a point of having as little contact as possible with the rest of us, as if we were guilty of harboring the enemy. Hinch in particular took offense at that, believing that our roadies, like our fans, should worship the ground he walked on; when it became clear they didn't like him any more than the rest of us, he became resentful and churlish. Everything around me was starting to crumble, and I had no idea how to stop it.

Leave it to JJ to once again come to our rescue. One bright morning in early May, she called to report good news: good news for her, and potentially great news for us. With graduation just weeks away, she'd decided that working in rock 'n' roll was what she wanted to do with her life. To her parents' dismay, she had abandoned her plans of going to graduate school; instead, she'd landed an internship at Talent Unlimited, one of the oldest and largest booking agencies in the country, where she hoped to be able to get us signed. Then one night toward the end of our tour, she called again with even better news: She'd set up a showcase for us at Max's Kansas City in the heart of the Big Apple so that one of the agents she worked with could come see us.

His name, she told me, was Alan Schiffman.

19

The morning of *Tweede Kerstdag*—the day after Christmas—I awaken bright and early and head down to the nearest *nieuwsagent* to scan the papers. Incredibly, there is barely a mention of the shooting in the local edition of the English-language International Herald Tribune, and even the local Dutch papers have buried the story—what little I can make out of it, anyway—in the back pages. What's more, there isn't a single picture of Schiffman anywhere, not even one of Hinch.

"What gives?" I ask Hans when I get him on the phone.

"Not sure," he answers tersely. "But I hope to find out soon."

We arrange to meet for lunch, which gives me a couple of hours to kill before heading downtown. I'm about to pull out my laptop and go over the Donnie Boyle transcriptions for the umpteenth time when I begin getting this nagging sense that I've forgotten to do something important.

Of course—Britney! How the hell could I forget to call to wish her a happy holiday? As I learned the hard way when we started living together—the first and only time I neglected to max out the credit cards on expensive gifts—Christmas is of the utmost import to Valley Girls, at least in the commercial sense. I immediately begin dialing home without even stopping to think about the time difference. By the time I realize it's two AM in L.A., the phone is ringing. *What the hell*, I decide. *Might as well let it ring.*

On the sixth ring, my dream girl actually picks up.

"H'lo?" she murmurs, sounding like she's got a cloth sack over her head.

"Britney, it's Bernie," I fairly shout. "Sorry to wake you, babe."

"Who's this?" she asks sleepily, despite my pronouncement.

"Bernie. It's Bernie. Remember? The guy you live with?"

"Bernie!" Now she sounds fully awake. And pissed. "Do you know what time it is?"

"I do. I'm sorry. I just really, really wanted to hear your voice, and, you know, I haven't been able to reach you all the other times I've called."

"Oh. Well, listen, this isn't actually a good time for me to talk."

I hear some muffled sounds in the background.

"Isn't a good time? Why not? Do you have company?"

"Uh, no. I mean, yes. It's not what you think—it's my girlfriend Tiffany, she slept over last night because we got kind of drunk and …" Her voice trails off.

More muffled noises. I'm almost sure they're of the male variety.

"Britney, what's going on?"

"Huh? Nothing. Why are you always accusing me of something?"

"I'm not accusing. I'm just asking. Why can't we talk? I just wanted to wish you a Merry Christmas."

"We can talk. It's just … well, it's late, you know. And I'm still kind of drunk. And very sleepy. But Merry Christmas to you too. I'll call you tomorrow. Bye."

The phone goes dead in my hand. Numbly, I shake my head. That bitch! Cheating on me, and on Christmas day, of all days. I feel betrayed, jealous, angry, hurt, all mixed together in one poisonous cocktail. *Well, it's what you expected, Bernie boy*, I pout silently. *And to think, I was tempted by one of the most beautiful women in the world and I resisted in order to be true to you.*

Ahh, who the hell am I kidding? I went to St. Moritz hoping to get laid, and if Miranda hadn't been such a total pig, I probably would have fucked her silly without the slightest pang of guilt. I go over to the bathroom mirror and stare into my bloodshot eyes for the longest time.

It's a sobering moment when I come to the conclusion that the guy staring back at me isn't someone I like a whole lot.

BY THE TIME I get to the restaurant, Hans and Rudie are already seated at a corner table, looking dejected. I'm guessing they're already on their third or fourth genever.

Without the slightest trace of a smile or welcome, they wave me over. "Sorry I'm late, guys," I begin.

"We have more important things to worry about than you being late," Hans snaps.

"What's up?"

"What's 'up' is that we've found out why the newspapers are sitting on the story, and it's not good, not good at all." Hans stares down at the table glumly. I start to prod him for more details, but a scolding finger and a sideways nod from Rudie warns me it's best to just leave things as they are for the moment. I pick up the menu and begin to peruse it, though I'm not the least bit hungry.

After a moment or two, Hans continues. "I talked to my brother, who works in the Amsterdam bureau of the Tribune, and he tells me that all the papers have been told to, how do you say, place a lid on the story. They're being permitted only to report that there was a minor incident in the Rossebuurt on Christmas Eve, no more."

"But why?"

"Because the case has been turned over to the *Korps landelijke politiediensten*, our national police services force, like your FBI. Apparently it's no longer a local matter, but something now of national interest."

"Why? Just because Hinch is an American rock star?"

"Bernie, you always have so many fucking questions! It's fucking irritating, you know that?" Hans is starting to lose his temper, so I immediately begin backpedaling.

"Sorry, Hans." I apologize softly. For the next several minutes, we all study our menus wordlessly, though now I'm sure none of us is hungry.

At long last, Hans breaks the silence.

"The reason the KLPD is involved," he explains tersely, "is because it turns out that the fat-ass motherfucker who was busy laying the whore in the room next door from Wolter was the Turkish ambassador to the Netherlands. I guess they're worried that if they don't cover it up, the whole thing will turn into an ugly international incident."

"Yah, 'Turkish Ambassador Shot In Ass While Fucking Prostitute On Christmas Eve' would make a hell of a headline," says Rudie, trying to inject some levity into the situation.

I start to giggle, but Hans shoots us both down with an angry glare. "It's not funny, Rudie," he growls. "They've decided not to press charges against either Schiffman or Ryker. They just want the whole thing to go away. Which means we can't rely on the police to help us find Schiffman, nor can we count on the newspapers to help flush him out."

"Wow, that totally sucks," is all I can say, lame as I realize the words are.

"Don't worry, Hansie, we'll find him anyway," Rudie adds sympathetically. "And when I do...."

"I know, Rudie. You'll tear his dick off and serve it to him, sauteed in a balsamic reduction," Hans deadpans. It's good to see his warped sense of humor return. Glasses of genever raised in a grim toast, our mood lightens considerably, for no reason other than that we are joined in a common cause and determined to see this through, whether or not the Turkish ambassador is able to keep his pants on.

AFTER LUNCH, WE NEED to make another stop at the police station, Hans informs me, in order to help the drugs squad make their case against Wolter the weasel, now the sole person charged in the incident. As we navigate the winding streets in Rudie's cramped Renault, I ask a question that has been bothering me since I first met my two Dutch companions.

"Tell me, why is it that you didn't get the police involved sooner?"

"Sooner?" Hans says. "When sooner?"

"Well, how about when Schiffman—or his tour manager—first ripped you off?"

He laughs. "You are so naïve, Bernie. As I told you, I signed a legally binding contract obligating me to pay in full if Hinch showed up—even if he didn't play a note."

"But you were forced to sign that contract at gunpoint."

"Yes, but that was an American contract I signed on American soil," he points out.

"So why didn't you contact the American cops then?"

"Look, for all I know, the gun being pointed at me was a perfectly legal, registered weapon," he explains calmly. "Schiffman would have just claimed that I had threatened him and that his bodyguard pulled it out in self-defense. So the only thing I would accomplish by calling the cops would have been losing the chance to ever promote concerts for Schiffman's clients again. And up until now, those concerts have been money-makers for me."

I shake my head, mumbling something about the injustice of it all.

"Come on, Bernie," Hans says. "I keep telling you, this is a nasty business. It comes with the territory. If I want justice, I have to dispense it myself—with the help of my friend Rudie here, of course." He rubs his compatriot's head affectionately.

Despite the throngs of tourists milling about, enjoying the unseasonably warm winter day, we arrive at the police station with remarkable speed. I notice that Rudie parks directly out front, pulling a blue *Politie* tag from his glove compartment and hanging it on his rearview mirror before exiting. "One of the perks of the job," he tells me with a wink.

Once inside, we are escorted to the offices of the *Narcoticasquad* with alacrity. Judging from his effusive greeting, the middle-aged detective waiting for us is already quite familiar with both Hans and Rudie.

"Bernie, I would like you to meet my good friend, Inspecteur VandeVoort," Hans says, introducing me with a courtly bow.

"A pleasure, Mr. Temkin. I understand you are here all the way from Los Angeles, and that you are writing a book about our rock star friend Mr. Hinchton?"

I'm a bit taken aback by how much he knows about me, but I answer politely in the affirmative.

"Please don't feel as if we are viewing you as a suspect in anything, Mr. Temkin," VandeVoort assures me with a smile. "I simply make it my business to investigate associates of Mr. Uhlemeyer here. It is as much a personal courtesy as a professional duty."

Pleasantries over, he turns to business, chattering away in Dutch with Hans and Rudie. The only words I can really make out are "Wolter" and "heroin," but I pretty much get the drift of what's going on: VandeVoort wants to know everything he can about Hinch's drug connection and any relationship the promoter might have with the weaselly wolf. At one point, Rudie reaches into his pocket and produces a glassine envelope which he duly turns over to the detective. I can't help but notice the look of surprise and delight on VandeVoort's face as he slowly turns the envelope over, studying it intently before placing it carefully in his briefcase.

After fifteen minutes of chit-chat, they begin wrapping things up with small talk. Despite my limited command of the language, it seems clear that Hans is asking after the detective's family and offering him free tickets for the next Uhlemeyer Promotions event—an offer which is received with hearty handclasps, embraces, and *dank u*'s all around.

"Wow, you guys should get a room," I wisecrack as we walk out the door.

"*Welke middelen?*" says Rudie with a perplexed look on his face.

"Never mind," I reply. Best to leave sleeping dogs lie, I always say.

As we step out into the fresh air, I offer to buy a round of drinks at the nearest bar. I'm curious about that business with the envelope and feel the best way to approach the subject is over a tall glass of pink gin.

"It is no big deal," says Hans when I broach the issue cautiously. "VandeVoort just wanted to know if we had any proof that Hinch's drugs had actually come from Wolter. They're building a case against him and want to make sure he does hard time."

"And did you?"

"Did we what?" Hans raises his glass to the light and swirls it around thoughtfully.

"Have any proof?"

"Yes, Rudie had the proof. We often find envelopes in the dressing room, because that's where the musicians do their drugs before taking the stage. This time, there was only one, but before we called in the riot squad, I made sure Rudie picked it up because some of the younger cops don't know about our special relationship with their bosses."

"Actually, I collect the envelopes," Rudie says with a trace of embarrassment.

Hans frowns. "I keep telling him, this is not a good idea. Some day, Rudie, this collection will land you behind bars. But does he listen to me? No."

They sound like any bickering couple anywhere in the world, but I am careful not to express that thought out loud. Instead I ask an obvious question. "Those are the envelopes the drugs come in, I presume?"

"Look at our little Bernie here," Hans says. "He's starting to catch on. We're proud of you, *kinder*." He reaches over to pinch my face playfully. I am glad it is not Rudie doing that.

"Okay, okay," I say, blushing. "But why did the detective seem so surprised when you handed it over?"

"Oh, he wasn't surprised that I found an envelope. He was surprised at the *kind* of envelope I found," Rudie says.

I'm confused, and I say so. Hans provides the explanation.

"It's because every drug dealer puts their own unique stamp on the envelopes they sell their heroin in," he tells me. "It's important for satisfied purchasers to know who to go back to when they want more—it helps build repeat business." Hans gestures impatiently to Rudie. "Give our friend some of those envelopes so he can see for himself."

Rudie opens a small briefcase and pulls out a small stack of them, in all different colors. As he hands them to me, I see how literal his description is: each envelope is emblazoned with a crude marking in watery ink, made with the kind of cheap rubber stamp you'd find in the desk of a fifth-grader. One has an ink-smeared image of a dragon; another a two-headed viper. Some of these Rorschach images are so poorly executed as to be almost comical: the one meant to be an eagle looks more like Tweety Pie; another one that's supposed to be a snarling tiger resembles nothing more fearsome than a yawning pussycat.

"This one, of course, has Wolter's stamp," Hans says, reaching into the briefcase and producing a small blue envelope bearing the grubby visage of a howling wolf. "It's similar to one of the envelopes we found in Hinch's dressing room."

"Is that unusual?" I ask, still mystified.

"Not at all," Hans replies blithely. "We often find Wolter's envelopes backstage at concerts, because he's one of the biggest dealers in Amsterdam. What VandeVoort was surprised at was the *color* of the envelope we found."

My mouth is hanging open expectantly. As usual, Hans drags it out as long as he can; he seems to really enjoy keeping me in suspense. Bastard.

"And?..." I ask when I can hold back no longer.

"Ah, my detective friend, you want to know more?" he teases. "Okay. So, the other thing you need to know about drug dealers here in Amsterdam is that they use different colored envelopes to indicate the potency of the heroin. Blue is standard street strength; brown is for smack that is a bit more stepped on, for someone who is only sniffing or has just started shooting, so they have little tolerance for the drug. Red indicates something stronger, for the experienced junkie. What we found in Hinch's dressing room was a white envelope."

"And what does that color signify?" I ask, playing right into Hans's hands.

"White, my friend, indicates pure heroin, as it arrives, straight from the boat, completely uncut—at least in theory. Wolter is one of the few street dealers in Amsterdam who sells smack in white envelopes, because if he gets caught with them on his person, it means a very stiff prison sentence. Usually the only people who buy those envelopes are other dealers, who cut the smack themselves with milk sugar before reselling it."

The hair on the back of my neck begins to stand up.

"What if someone were to shoot up some of the heroin in a white envelope without cutting it first?" I think I know the answer but I can't help asking the question anyway.

"That would be a very unfortunate individual," says Hans. "Unless they had the constitution of an ox, they would probably find themselves very, very dead."

THE FIRST THING I notice when I get back to my room is the message light blinking. Since she's the only one who knows my hotel number, I assume it must be Britney calling me back. Heart pounding, I dial the code that allows me to retrieve what I assume will be a brutal message.

I'm not disappointed.

"Bernie, it's me," she announces in a cold and detached voice. "I want you to know that I did not appreciate you waking me up last night, and that I especially did not appreciate your suspicious manner. If you can't trust me, then I'm not so sure we should be together. To be honest, I'm not so sure I trust *you* all that much."

Okay, I guess I had that coming.

"So," the voice continues, "I'm going away for a few days, till after the New Year, with some friends. To, um, think things over. And I suggest you do the same."

Well, I guess I'll do just that. If I can fit it in between trying to find a missing rock star and finishing the damn book, that is.

"Oh, and you had two more calls from your editor, and another phone message from that woman," says the voice. "You know, the one you never told me anything about. The one *you're* probably having an affair with. Let's see, I wrote her name down somewhere here. Katherine something. Here it is: Katherine Sommerville. Didn't leave a number—she said she'd try calling again."

Never heard of her; in fact, I don't know anybody by the name of Katherine, not even a former classmate. Must be some telemarketer, I decide.

"Anyway," the voice concludes, "I have to go now. I guess we'll talk next millennium. Oh, and…." Long pause. Can there possibly be an apology forthcoming?

"… I need you to increase the credit limit on your Discover card. Sorry, but I maxed it out again. Okay, bye."

With that, the message ends abruptly. Not a tinge of regret, not a word of query about how I might be doing, not a trace of sympathy about what I might be going through thousands of miles away from home and in desperate need of a hug. Just, *I'm pissed at you, I'm outta here, and by the way, let the credit card company know that I plan on buying more skimpy bikinis with which to entice other men.*

It's odd; I should be feeling angry, but I'm not. Mostly I'm feeling relieved.

Women.

20

Transcript: Interview with Donnie Boyle, May 20, 1998

I'D LIKE TO BE ABLE to say that I didn't like Alan Schiffman from the start, but the truth is that he conned me in the beginning, same as he conned everyone else in our little circle. Actually, he was pretty innocuous at first—even charming, in a sleazy kind of way. Dressed in a double-breasted silk suit and wearing gold pinky rings, he turned up at our showcase at Max's, escorted by a visibly excited JJ. Afterwards, they came backstage and she introduced him to everybody. Schiffman seemed reasonably pleased with what he had seen and heard, though he didn't exactly go overboard with praise. I think that Hinch especially was thrown off by that because he'd started to get used to the brand of bullshit that people were regularly tossing his way. With Schiffman, though, there seemed to be a certain caution in the way he treated us. Of course, that only made Hinch want to impress him all the more, like the way a beautiful woman reacts when a man fails to start hitting on her immediately.

"What the hell is wrong with that guy?" he asked me after JJ and Schiffman had headed off into the night.

"I'm not sure what you mean, H," I replied. "He said he'd try to line up some gigs for us."

"I know, Donnie, but where was the *love*?"

"Ah, fuck him if he can't take a joke." This from Cody, who had become increasingly jaded of late.

"No, man, I'm serious," Hinch protested. "This guy's major league, and we should have blown his socks off."

As Cody walked away, shaking his head in disgust, I realized that I had no answer for Hinch. JJ had taken me aside earlier that evening to tell me not to worry, that Schiffman was always standoffish even when he was actually enthusiastic about something, but I didn't think Hinch wanted to hear that right then.

"Let's just see what develops," was all I could tell him. Fact is, I was curious to see myself.

Well, things did develop, but a lot more slowly than any of us would have wanted. We were like a freight train leaving the station, pulling away slowly at first until we built up a head of steam, then eventually chugging along at a good clip until we began hurtling down the tracks nearly out of control. But those first few months were agony: Gigs were few and far between, although Schiffman did book a handful of the larger ones for us directly, bypassing JJ in the process, which she was none too pleased about. Still, he continued to hold us at arm's length, and even though he was happy to take his commission on the few bookings he did make, he rarely showed up at our gigs and there was no offer of a contract with Talent Unlimited, no commitment to representing us exclusively. It was disheartening, to say the least.

Then, as summer began winding down into autumn, the locomotive started to gather speed. The colleges were back in session, and between JJ's solid connections on that front and the added clout that being affiliated with a major talent agency gave her, the gigs began rolling in. I noticed that Schiffman began turning up at our East Coast appearances with greater regularity too, and slowly but surely he started taking the reins from JJ. He began by doing what I had been unable to do: getting us into the notoriously difficult to crack New York City circuit, first as an opening act, then as headliners. Then, on our next swing out west, he managed to land us slots at some of L.A.'s top clubs—legendary places like the Whiskey and the Roxy, gigs that we had dreamed about playing when we were kids just starting out. On our last night in L.A., I was surprised to see Schiffman waiting in the dressing room. He'd changed his image, I noticed: for one thing, his hair was newly greased back, making his nose, which already seemed too large for his face, even more prominent. He probably thought this made him look cool, but to me he looked like a character straight out of *Midnight Cowboy*—a cleaned-up Ratso Rizzo.

"Hey, Alan, I didn't expect to see you all the way out here," I said when I spotted him, raising my hand, palm out, for the obligatory high-five.

"Um, well, I was in town for some meetings," he mumbled, ignoring my arm as it hung in mid-air. "TCB, you know." God, the guy was so *lame*.

"I didn't figure you for an Elvis fan," I said jokingly, referring to the ostentatious "Taking Care of Business" acronym famously appropriated by Presley's Vegas backing band.

"Huh?" he answered humorlessly. "Is Elvis in town?" His head swiveled around the room like a machine gun turret. I thought I saw him reaching reflexively into his pocket for a business card.

"Elvis? No. I just meant…."

The door flew open and Hinch raced in, sweaty and hyper from playing the last encore of the night.

"Alan! Hey, man, good to see you!" he exclaimed. The two men went into an awkward bear hug, Schiffman recoiling slightly from the drenched guitarist. "Did you catch our set?" Hinch asked eagerly.

"I did, man, I did. From the first note to the last," Schiffman lied. "You guys rocked."

"Did you really think so?" Hinch asked, sucking up as usual.

"Yeah, man, you were good," Schiffman replied noncommittally. Hinch beamed like a love-struck teenager. *How pathetic*, I remember thinking.

Just then Cody shoved past, nearly bowling both men over on his way to the backstage toilet. "Sorry, guys," he explained breathlessly over his shoulder, "but I'm bursting to take a leak."

Hinch reached out a hand to steady Schiffman, who was glaring angrily in Cody's direction. "Your rhythm guitarist is kind of clumsy, isn't he?" he asked. It struck me as more of a statement than a question, but what bothered me more was Hinch's response.

"Yeah, he's a bit of a dickwad, but I keep him around for laughs," he said offhandedly. With someone else, you might assume it was a joke. Not so Hinch.

"Well, I don't always find him funny," Schiffman growled. For the first time, he seemed to notice my face reddening with anger. With a look of defiance, he threw an arm across Hinch's shoulder as if they were best buds.

"Come on, Tommy," he said. "Let me buy you a drink."

With that, Schiffman crossed the room and marched out the door without giving me or anyone else a backward glance, Hinch trailing along after him like a faithful puppy dog.

It was, I have come to realize with the passing of time, the moment when everything we had struggled so hard to achieve started to turn to shit.

THERE WERE PLENTY of cracks in the band by then, as I believe I've told you. Hinch and Cody were no longer writing songs together, and even though Cody was still doing his best to steer the band musically, Hinch seemed less and less interested in what the guy had to say. In turn, Cody was disgusted with the way Hinch was throwing himself at Schiffman; to his way of thinking, "assholes in suits," as he liked to call them, were the enemy, the reason why the band was still suspended in the lower echelons of the music business instead of already at the top of the ladder. Schiffman, in Cody's mind, was no better than people like Joe Finnerty or John Thomas Wallingford. To Cody, they were all parasites who lived off the talent of true musicians like himself.

The Truckers, for the most part, remained silent and somewhat removed, although they both had occasional skirmishes with Hinch and Cody, exacerbated mostly by their excessive drinking and drug-taking. Joe Dan's constant battles with our road crew—now a motley and mostly interchangeable group of over-muscled boneheads—were taking a toll, both on him and on the rest of us, and Vernon's loyalties were becoming more divided than ever. To me, Vernon was the hardest to read, because, unlike his big brother, he actually had a brain in his head and a degree of sensitivity underneath all those tattoos. And while he was a great believer in blood being thicker than water—he had, after all, been on the road with JD for years before we met them—he could also see the damage his brother's drunken behavior was causing. I think he'd also developed a genuine affection for Cody, not to mention respect for the guy musically, so he didn't want to endanger his standing within the band. More than anything, Vernon and JD loved the rock 'n' roll life, and even though we hadn't hit it big yet, we were living large and enjoying many of the perks, including a seemingly unlimited supply of groupies and drugs. It was a complicated, confused dynamic, and I had been struggling to hold it all together even before Schiffman showed up. His appearance had made things even more convoluted, and even though I welcomed the bookings he was getting for us—not to mention the status and added income they provided—I was beginning to resent his shadowy presence.

Slowly, insidiously, the tables began to turn as I saw Schiffman start to woo Hinch instead of the other way around. It didn't seem to be a sexual thing this time, as it probably had been with Joe Finnerty, because Hinch and Schiffman had practically made screwing babes a competition sport. Following every night of drinking and debauchery the two of them shared—none of the rest of us were ever invited—they would regale us with tales of marathon sex that left even veteran groupie-samplers like us wide-eyed.

"Are you sure Alan's not just after that pretty mouth of yours?" I asked Hinch one afternoon.

"No way, dude," he replied, unabashed. "Believe me, with all the orgies we've been staging, he's had plenty of opportunity to stick it in me if he wanted to. The man obviously prefers pussy, same as I do. So give it a rest."

I did. Besides, even if they did have a thing going on, it was really none of my business. What worried me a lot more was the way Schiffman was methodically feeding Hinch's already overdeveloped ego.

"You were great, Tommy—you totally kicked ass," Schiffman would say to Hinch after every gig, making a point of ignoring the rest of the band, who had probably been just as great, and just as kick-ass.

"Hey, man, what about me and my bros?" Vernon or JD would mock-complain, doing their best to look affronted.

"You guys were okay, too," Schiffman would reply offhandedly before sliding into what I guess he thought was hipster talk. "You're doing a solid job of backing up my main man here, no doubt about it."

If Cody was anywhere within earshot, he'd snort in derision and storm out of the room; the others might laugh it off, but I could tell it was starting to get to them. Hinch never said a word in their defense, either, which pissed me off, but, then again, he'd always been that way: all for one, one for one.

But for all the flattery and sweet nothings being whispered in Hinch's ear, there was still no agency contract forthcoming, which I found puzzling. I tried raising the issue once or twice with Schiffman, but he just waved me off. "Why are you so concerned?" he'd say. "I'm keeping your boys working steadily, aren't I?" I couldn't disagree; in fact, it was probably advantageous to us not to be tied to any one agency, but on the other hand I had no doubt that Schiffman didn't have an altruistic bone in his body. Something didn't add up here, and it was starting to bug me.

I decided to try asking JJ.

"It doesn't make sense to me, either," she confessed. "I've mentioned it to Alan a couple of times and he just keeps telling me he's working on it. If it's any consolation, you're not the only client he has who isn't operating under an exclusive contract."

"Why would he do that?" I asked. "He's leaving the door open for us to sign with one of his competitors."

"I know. I guess he figures if you're satisfied enough with his services, you won't do that."

"But JJ," I reminded her, "we're in the *music* business. If someone isn't screwing you, you know something's wrong."

She sighed, a deep, world-weary sigh. "You're right, Donnie. But as long as he keeps getting you gigs, I don't think you have much to complain about. Now me, on the other hand, I've got a lot of bones to pick with Alan. For one thing, he's stopped paying me sub-commissions on the bookings he's getting you, even though I'm the one who landed you as a client in the first place. I'm starting to think the guy's a real prick."

"Of course he's a real prick," I said. "He's an agent."

Long pause.

"Oops. Put my foot in it again, didn't I?"

"Well, I can tell you this much," JJ replied testily. "It'll certainly be a long time before you put your *dick* in it again."

A FEW WEEKS LATER, to my amazement, Schiffman invited all of us, including Katie, to spend Thanksgiving with him and his family. I didn't even know the guy was married, much less a father, but sure enough he had the obligatory trophy wife and three kiddies, all tucked away in a small suburban estate in Connecticut. Hinch was the only one of us even vaguely enthusiastic about going, but JJ, who was also invited, convinced everyone else that it was in our interest to show up and be on our best behavior. Cody, of course, was the one most vehemently opposed, and this time with good reason, since he usually spent the holiday with his parents and sister, but in the end he grudgingly agreed to come along. I think that he, like the rest of us, was a little curious about what Schiffman's home life might be like.

It was surprisingly normal, to be honest with you. His wife, Cherisse was a pleasant and gracious hostess. I got a kick out of watching Vernon and a thankfully sober Joe Dan play with Schiffman's children—they were really just a couple of kids at heart themselves. Even Cody behaved himself admirably, at one point sitting down at the grand piano in the lavish living room to regale us with a couple of new love songs he was working on. I couldn't help but notice that he was staring directly at Katie the whole time. She seemed to take it in stride, though I could tell from her squirming that she was pretty uncomfortable with the attention she was receiving.

Even after the toddlers had been tucked into bed by their nanny and the after-dinner drinks started to flow, things remained civilized, even convivial. For the first time, Schiffman wasn't focusing all his charm on Hinch alone; in fact, he seemed to be carefully apportioning his time with each of us individually. I got the impression he was taking our measure, one by one.

When my turn came, he sank down alongside me on an overstuffed sofa and handed me a glass of wine.

"Vintage 1934," he announced, holding the glass up and slowly twirling it like a real connoisseur. "Do you like fine wines, Donald?"

"Please, Alan," I protested as I took a sip. It tasted good, but then I didn't know shit about wine. "It's Donnie. No one's called me Donald since I was in kindergarten."

He laughed. "You're quite right, Donnie. My error. Anyway, I hope you're enjoying yourself here."

"Of course, Alan. It's very kind of you to invite us all."

"My pleasure. You know I have very high hopes for that band of yours."

"I'm glad to hear that," I said, and I was. Maybe it was the wine, maybe it was just the false sense of serenity I had been lulled into, but I couldn't help myself from continuing. "Which makes me wonder …"

"… why I haven't offered you an exclusive agency contract," he said, finishing my sentence. "Am I correct in my assumption?"

The last thing I wanted to do at the moment was offend the guy, but the words just kind of blurted out of me. "Well, yes," I stammered. "I mean, I don't want to tell you your business, but I can't help but think that it would have been in your best interest to do so months ago. That is, if you like us as much as you say you do."

As soon as the last part of the sentence left my lips, I was sorry. *He said he had high hopes for the band. Why am I questioning it?*

To my relief, Schiffman pretended to ignore my indiscretion. "It's a fair enough question, Donnie," he said. "Frankly, if I were in your shoes I'd be asking the same thing."

He paused, then looked furtively around the room as if he were about to confide a deep, dark secret.

"All I can tell you right now is that a contract will be forthcoming in the very near future. Confidentiality precludes me from saying any more. But I want you to know that I am working on a very big deal that will totally reshape my future, and yours. Is that a sufficient enough answer for you?" He leaned back and smiled with contentment, reminding me of a greasy Cheshire Cat.

"Sure, Alan. I don't mean to be cornering you, certainly not here, what with all the hospitality you've shown us."

"Don't be silly. You're doing your job, and doing it well. No offense taken." He patted me on the knee as if to try and comfort me. For some reason his gesture made me feel like taking a hot shower. I don't know why—here he was being all nice and everything, yet I couldn't shake the feeling that I was somehow being manipulated. *You're getting paranoid, Donnie*, I told myself. *Give the guy a chance.*

"So," he continued, changing the subject. "Tell me again how you met Hinch. I love hearing about your exploits as kids growing up in, Pennsylvania, was it?"

For what seemed like the tenth time I began telling Schiffman about the early days. He'd asked me the question before, and I'd always answered him, but it had always seemed to go in one ear and out the other. Tonight, though, was different. Tonight he was paying close attention; I almost felt as if he were taking mental notes. For nearly a half hour he probed, like a reporter conducting an interview. When I told him all there was to tell—and I had no particular reason to hold back anything, so I pretty much told him the whole story—he seemed satisfied. Then and only then did he get up and return to the party, turning his attention next to Cody ... or was it Vernon? No matter; he made a point of spending quality time with each of us in turn, including Katie Q.

Later, we compared notes and discovered that we'd all gotten the same treatment: a personal grilling, accompanied by a "confidential" assurance that an agency contract would be forthcoming.

"I still say the guy is an asshole," Cody said as we rode back to Philly in the band van.

"Well, he may be an asshole, but he's an asshole who's getting us lots of good gigs," pointed out Vernon, ever the pragmatist.

"I wish you peckerheads would just lay off," snapped Hinch, who we thought was sleeping in the back, curled up with Katie. "The guy just opened up his home to us and everything. Jeez, give him a break, will you?"

"I will say this," Joe Dan declared sleepily. "His wife's got a great ass."

From the seat behind him, Katie delivered a swift kick. We all knew she disapproved of our brand of locker room humor; we just didn't know she was awake.

"Sorry, Katie," our drummer said, before adding, under his breath, "but it's the goddamn truth."

A FEW DAYS AFTER CHRISTMAS, JJ called with the news we'd been waiting to hear ... sort of.

"Your agency contract is finally on the way," she told me breathlessly. "Only it isn't with Talent Unlimited."

"Huh?" I said. "Who else would it be with?"

"Big news, Donnie. Schiffman is leaving the firm. He's landed major backing and is striking out on his own, setting up his own office in L.A. I guess this has been in the works for awhile, which is why he didn't want you guys signed—it makes it a lot easier to start fresh with his new agency without the threat of lawsuits hanging over everybody's heads. But you're going to be his first client, and he's genuinely excited about having you."

I was having a lot of trouble digesting all she was saying. Talent Unlimited, after all, was one of the oldest and largest booking agencies in the country, and so far they'd done okay by us. Did I really want to commit us to a new company, especially one that was probably going to be on the TU shitlist for years to come?

"Janet, you've always been straight with us," I said, and I meant it. "Tell me, is this good news, or bad?"

"Are you crazy? This is the best news you could possibly get. A hot-shot new agency setting up shop in the heart of Tinseltown, and the president of the company wants your band as his first signing? Wake up, Donnie, and smell the goddamn roses."

"I'm trying, JJ, I am. But there's something about the guy that just gives me the creeps. I don't know what it is."

"Look, as you yourself so wisely told me not long ago, all agents are pricks. It comes with the territory. But you're far better off having a prick who really wants you—and can make things happen—than a prick who's just saddled with you and can't move mountains."

"Are you saying Alan Schiffman can move mountains?" I asked her. "Because so far all I've seen are a few small molehills ... and a bunch of smoke and mirrors."

She sighed. "Look, Donnie, Schiffman Entertainment is about to take the industry by storm. We can do it with you, or without you.

Fortunately for you, Alan Schiffman would prefer to do it with you. But if you don't want to go for the brass ring, believe me, there are plenty of other acts who do."

Much as I disliked the patronizing tone in her voice, I had to admit that I did like the sound of the "we" in her answer. "Does this mean you're relocating to L.A., too?" I asked.

"In time, probably. But for now he's asked me to run the New York office for him. Is that good enough for you?"

It was. *We've ridden this far with Janet*, I thought. *If she's onboard, I guess it's worth taking a chance.*

"Okay, sweetie," I said. "Tell Alan he's got himself a client."

THE INK ON THE contract hadn't even dried when Schiffman sent us all first-class plane tickets to come visit him in La-La Land and pose for a bogus signing ceremony; the plan was to plaster our photos all over the next issue of *Billboard*, thus providing tremendous publicity both for us and for his new company.

He really laid it on thick, too, sending a stretch limo to pick us up at the airport and whisk us straight to his new office. I have to admit that I was blown away by the opulence of his new digs. I'd only visited him once or twice at Talent Unlimited, and while his corner office there was spacious and well-appointed, it was clearly that of a middle manager, not an executive. At Schiffman Entertainment there was no question that he was king. Even knowing nothing about interior decoration, I could see that all the furniture had been carefully chosen to match and blend with the plush carpeting and wall hangings; clearly a lot of thought had gone into every detail, from the fine wainscoting to the delicate porcelain vases filled with fresh flowers. As with almost everything in L.A., the object was to impress, and impress it did. *I have arrived*, proclaimed the four walls of Alan Schiffman's private domain. *Maybe if you breathe the air in here long enough, you will too.*

Hinch, I could see, was totally in awe. "Jeez, can you imagine what this desk cost?" he whispered to me after we were ushered in. "And that antique lamp—check it out! It's gotta be worth a fortune!"

Schiffman's office furniture made far less of an impression on Cody, but he was absolutely fascinated by the humongous state-of-the-art sound system installed there. With an air of affability, the agent proudly showed off all the advanced features of the futuristic contraption, as complicated and involved as anything I'd ever seen in a recording studio. When Schiffman threaded up a reel-to-reel of Steely Dan's latest album and began blasting it through his refrigerator-sized speakers, we were all silenced into submission, Cody most especially.

"Dude, that was awesome!" he exclaimed after the tape had finished. Rarely had I seen our boy wonder so excited.

The two Truckers, as usual, sat in silence, though I could see their heads and beards swiveling as they took it all in. *Now this is a step up*, you could almost hear them thinking. *Imagine all the booze and drugs we'll be able to buy with the money this guy is going to make for us.*

When the phony signing ritual was over and the photographers had left, Schiffman had us all pile into the limo for a tour around Beverly Hills. We gawked and gaped like a bunch of goddamn tourists from Podunk as he pointed out the homes of some of our favorite movie stars, then he took us up the Hollywood Hills to the mansion he'd rented for us to stay in over the weekend and dropped us off while he headed out to some important meeting with some important muck-a-muck. For the next few hours, we wandered from room to room, mouths hanging open in dumb amazement, practically pinching ourselves at our good fortune. There was a swimming pool, an indoor bar, even a small movie theater stocked with first-run releases. Later that evening, Schiffman sent the limo for us and we dined at Spago's, then headed to the clubs, only this time we didn't have to worry about playing in tune or winning over the crowd. Instead, we could concentrate on partying our asses off and hitting on the multitude of babes who were scattered around the room like so many gorgeous decorations. At dawn, we scooped up as many of them as we could and headed back to the Hollywood Hills, where the debauchery continued until, bleary-eyed and hungover, we finally slunk off to the airport for our early morning flight back to a cold and dreary Philadelphia.

Schiffman saw us off at the gate. As we groggily made our way to the departure lounge, I saw him take Hinch aside and whisper something in his ear. Later, as we cruised at eight miles high, I asked Hinch what Schiffman had said to him.

"He asked me if I really wanted to leave L.A., and I told him no." Hinch paused and scratched his head thoughtfully. "Then he said, good, because this is the life he had in mind for me."

I sat there, slack-jawed while Hinch yawned and stretched, then drifted off into a contented slumber. *The life he had in mind for me.*

What kind of life, I wondered, did Schiffman have in mind for the rest of us?

•

THE WHEELS ON OUR JET had barely touched down on the tarmac when the lobbying began. Everybody in the band—not just Hinch—had been bitten with the California bug, and as we trudged up the snow-covered steps to our freezing little hovel in Philly, I had to admit that the idea of sitting on a sun-drenched beach watching babes in bikinis sure beat the hell out of what we were returning to.

"I told you guys years ago that we should be moving to L.A.," Cody kept saying, for once aligned with Hinch. Even the normally stolid Trucker brothers seemed enthused at the idea. I guess the two southern boys had had their fill of northern winters.

The next day I got on the phone with Schiffman and told him of the band's desire to relocate. "I like it, Donnie," he said. "It'll make it a lot easier for me to keep my eye on the boys, plus all the big record labels are out here now, so it will be easier to take meetings."

Take meetings? That was a new one on me. Here in the real world, we *went* to meetings. I guess in L.A., meetings were commodities to be possessed, like everything else in the sleazy underbelly that lay beneath the glamorous exterior of the entertainment business. Prodded by Hinch, I foolishly asked Schiffman if the place we had stayed in might be available as a band house.

"That place?" he laughed. "Ten grand a week. Your boys aren't quite in that league yet. But tell you what, I'll start looking around for something that's more in your price range."

I started to ask about specific financial arrangements, but he cut me off. "Let me find the right place first, Donnie, then we'll talk turkey. In the meantime, tell the guys I'll catch them at a gig soon."

But he did neither. Over the next four weeks, with the band pestering me almost daily to see how Schiffman was getting on with the search for a house in L.A., he managed to avoid my calls, and he didn't turn up at any of our gigs either. Why the sudden change of heart? I had no idea. Once again, I turned to JJ for the answer, only this time she wasn't a lot of help.

"The guy's just incredibly busy," she told me. I could hear the irritation in her voice. "You're not his only client, you know."

"I know that, Janet. But he's clearly ducking me, and I want to know why."

"That's why: he's just busy. Look, these things take time. You'll hear from him soon enough, don't worry."

But I *was* worried. It seemed that was becoming a state of mind for me, and I was getting tired of it.

A few days later, Schiffman finally called. He sounded chipper and bright, as if nothing was wrong, as if he hadn't been incommunicado for more than a month. When I started to lodge a gentle complaint about his prolonged silence, he even apologized. Sort of.

"You're right, my man, I have been lax in returning your calls. But I have also been setting wheels in motion."

"Does that mean you've found us a place to stay? They're really itching to get out of Philly and into that California sun."

"I'm working on it," he tap-danced. "Trust me, I'll come up with something suitable before much longer." *Yeah, right.* "Listen, is Hinch there? I really called to talk with him."

I handed the phone to Hinch, who had been hovering nearby, desperate to hear any news Schiffman might be reporting.

"Hey, Alan," he said eagerly. "What's going on with the house? Uh-huh. Okay, I understand. Katie? She's fine. Yeah, that's right, we've got five days off in the middle of this next tour. You ought to know," he laughed, "you booked it."

Hinch's brow knitted as he listened intently to Schiffman. "Hmm, not sure. I'll ask her. Sure is nice of you to invite us, though. Yeah, I'll call you back. Tonight if I can, or maybe tomorrow. Uh-huh. Okay, bye."

I looked at him quizzically as he returned the phone to its cradle.

"You know that five-day gap we have in next month's tour?" he asked rhetorically. "Well, Alan's invited Katie and me to fly out to Vegas to hang with him then. Says he's got some important business to discuss."

"Business to discuss? Doesn't he realize I'm the manager of this band? What could he possibly want to discuss with you that he doesn't want to discuss with me?"

Hinch shrugged his shoulders. "Don't know, man. Anyway, lighten up. Of course he knows you're our manager. He probably just wants some company at the craps table."

We both knew that was total bullshit. I was concerned, of course, that Schiffman was extending the invitation to Hinch alone, as opposed to all of us, but that didn't altogether surprise me: divide and conquer, I'm sure, was his plan. But what was completely baffling to me was why he would want Katie there. She was the one person in Hinch's life who gave him a moral center; with Katie present, Hinch was incapable of doing the wrong thing. Which is what I was certain Schiffman wanted him to do.

I just didn't know exactly *what* wrong thing he wanted Hinch to do.

21

MONDAY FINDS the Amsterdam weather finally returning to normal, or at least what passes for normal in December: gray, dreary, cold and damp. In recognition of the wretchedness outside my window, I decide that it's the perfect day to stick my head under the covers, which is exactly what I do for the first part of the morning; even Hans's normally shrieking mobile phone is leaving me alone in tacit cooperation with my desire to remain *im*mobile.

But tourist hotels like this one are not built for lazy days of nothing, and before long the chattering maids are out in force, some solemnly pushing dysfunctional vacuum cleaners back and forth over the frayed carpeting in the hallway, others studiously maintaining a steady rhythm of toilet-flushing in a futile effort to eradicate the dubious stains of decades, all the while keeping a running conversation going throughout the whole pointless endeavor. Tempted as I am to yell "Shaddup!" as if I were still in the Bronx tenement of my youth, I restrain myself to simply reaching over to the night stand and throwing the clock radio against the wall, a gesture as ultimately ineffectual as the labors of the housekeepers themselves.

Fuck it. Might as well get up. Distractedly, I switch on the TV and marvel at how grainy the images are, even here at the dawn of a new millennium; haven't they heard of cable in this town? Probably so, Amsterdam being one of the most modern of the old European cities, but joints like this roach motel will likely be the last holdouts. It's my own fault for being so goddamn cheap, I realize somberly. All too often I seem to be the cause of my own misery. It's quite a revelation, especially this early in the day.

Out of habit as much as anything, I dial Hans's number. Turns out he has almost as little on his agenda today as I do. With a couple of concerts coming up in mid-January, there's a bit of paperwork to get done; other than that, not much. We make vague plans to perhaps meet up for an early dinner or something, though he's not sure if Rudie will be able to join us, as he is off running errands, after which he'll probably check in with his police buddies just in case there's any news about Schiffman. After all the ups and downs of the past couple of days, I'm beginning to think that locating the slimy manager is turning into a hopeless proposition, though I don't share this with Hans. In my mind, I'm starting to formulate a Plan B for locating Hinch which doesn't involve Schiffman, or Hans or Rudie, at all. But of course I'm not going to tell Hans that—not any sooner than I have to, anyway.

The plan is nebulous at this stage but it basically involves packing my bags and traveling to London, where Hinch is still scheduled to play at the end of the week. My thinking is that, if he's going to honor that commitment, that's where I'll find him, at which point I'll do my best to try to speak with him and find out what's been going on. Perhaps the fact that Hinch has fled from Schiffman's over-protective reach means that he'll be more willing to talk to me now. Or maybe not. Either way, all I really want to do at this point is make my way back to L.A. so I can get some kind of closure, not only to the book, but to my relationship with Britney, the dissolution of which I now view as inevitable. *You've known it was coming for a long time now, Bernie boy,* I keep telling myself. *Take it like a man.*

Taking it like a man; that was something I really admired about Donnie Boyle. I can't imagine facing up to a serious, and ultimately terminal, illness with anywhere near the grace and poise that he exhibited during the months I got to know him. Yes, he might have gotten a bit cranky at times, but I never got the sense that he was actually afraid of what he was facing, even though in his case it was going to mean losing everything: a life he loved, a woman he adored, and children he cherished. In her own way, Donnie's wife, Jen, had been every bit as accepting. She was careful to leave us plenty of space when her husband and I would get together in their modest Sherman Oaks home for those interview sessions every week or two, yet she was always warm and welcoming, even though I was appropriating some of their remaining moments together.

Fifteen hours after my last interview with Donnie Boyle, I recall sadly, he lapsed into a coma. Two days later he was dead.

The drone of the hotel TV set fades to a background blur as the memories of Donnie's funeral come flooding back. The chapel was packed—not only with his large family but also with the many friends he'd made throughout the years. Not so much from his touring days—though Cody attended, sobbing softly from a back pew—but the many young men and women he had mentored and counseled after he'd left the rock 'n' roll business for a quieter, but infinitely more fulfilling life. One by one they paid their final respects to the body lying silent in the coffin, murmuring soft expressions of sympathy to Donnie's widow and children as they filed past. It was sobering testimony as to how much this kind, gentle man—short in stature but a giant in so many other ways—had touched their lives.

I wondered if Hinch was going to turn up. He didn't, choosing instead to be represented by an ostentatiously large floral display that wouldn't have looked out of place at a strip mall opening. Was the man even capable of human feelings? Hard to say, considering the way he ultimately betrayed Donnie, and Cody, too. This was, I had come to realize, the one unanswered question, the one missing element in my book, yet it was an issue I probably would have never even considered were it not for Donnie. Without Donnie, my book might still be filled with verifiable facts, but it would be void of emotion. That epiphany—the idea that we human beings are nothing without the things that make us human—was perhaps the greatest gift Donnie could have given me, and it arrived at just the right time in my life.

Suddenly I find myself weeping. The tears rolling down my cheeks, I realize, are as much for me as they are for Donnie Boyle. Sobbing uncontrollably at all the sadness and injustice in the world, I fall back onto my bed, thankful at last for the intrusion of the housekeepers as their labors obliterate my self-pity in waves of rattle and hum.

BY MID-AFTERNOON I have pulled myself together sufficiently to begin making some phone calls. I start by dialing Landis Publishing. The receptionist sounds vaguely familiar, even though I have never visited their offices and had done my best to scrupulously avoid their calls for the past year. She informs me that the editor whose call I was returning was no longer assigned to my book; he had been replaced by the squeaky-voiced geek who used to be the guy's assistant back when I first started working on the project. Based upon his general air of ineptitude and frequent misusage of the word "like" (as in, "like, he's not here" and "okay, I'll, like, give him the message"), I had judged this newly promoted wordsmith to be no more than thirteen years old. That's the publishing game these days: Why pay a twenty-something to do a job when you can hire a teenager to do the same job just as poorly, and for half the salary? Fortunately, this new editor is, like, unavailable, so I am able to get away with simply leaving a message for him instead of having to pay obeisance directly. Upon being transferred to his voice mail, I tersely convey the information that I am in Europe completing the manuscript and that I hope to have it in his hands shortly. Being vague, I have found, always works better than being specific. More or less.

Then I dial the international operator and ask her to connect me to the *Rolling Stone* office in New York. To my surprise, Clive answers on the first ring.

"Hey, what's shaking, *compadre*?" I ask him in as sprightly a tone as I can muster. Sprightly tones, I have found, always work better than brooding ones. Sometimes, anyway.

"Who is this?" he asks, annoyed.

"It's Bernie," I reply. "Bernie Temkin. Returning your call."

"Hold on a second."

I hear the sounds of a stereo being turned down and a door slamming shut.

"Bernie? You still there?"

"Yes, I'm here."

"Listen to me, you motherfucker," he hisses angrily. "Pull a stunt like that again and I will sue your ass so fast and so hard that you won't know which end to crap out of."

I gulp. "What are you talking about?" I stammer. Playing dumb, I have found, always works better than playing smart. Except when it doesn't.

"Don't play dumb with me, you piece of shit," he snarls as if reading my mind. "You've been using my name to gain access to Hinch's people. That is so fucking unprofessional and unethical I can't begin to tell you. Not to mention uncool."

Uncool: the ultimate heresy in the world of the music journalist. I decide to abandon all pretence of innocence and instead throw myself on his mercy.

"Clive, I'm sorry. Really I am. I just kind of blurted it out. Hinch's people won't talk to me, on orders from his manager. I figured that maybe if they thought I worked for the *Stone*, they'd give me a little information. I'm just trying to get the damn book finished and get my life back...." I had to stop or I'd be blubbering in a minute.

"Totally uncool," he repeats, this time with a little less venom. There is a long pause while we both consider what to say. I sense his fury may be dissipating slightly in the face of my bald-faced groveling. And groveling, I have found, always works better than … oh, never mind.

"Who told you?" I ask in a tiny voice.

"Alan Schiffman's office called me, you asshole. That's who."

"Was it a Trudy Cox, by any chance?"

"Yeah, I think that was her name. Anyway, what difference does it make who called me? The point is that you violated my trust in you."

Tempted as I am to point out that Clive Swindon has never expressed any degree of trust in me whatsoever, I remain silent.

"She's a real bitch, don't you think?" I finally murmur.

"Who?"

"Trudy Cox. Bit of a lard-ass, too."

"I don't know, she sounded pretty hot to me," Clive says. "But don't try and change the subject. The point is that you really got me in deep shit here. Schiffman's people are threatening to cut off all access to their artists. Not just Hinch, but artists that people actually care about. You know, the ones who are actually selling records."

Hinch has sold more records than any five of Schiffman's other clients combined, I think, but once again I restrain my lips from forming the words. This is no time to be a smartass, I remind myself.

"Don't get too smug," Clive continues. "Your deception didn't work all that well, anyway. After I convinced this Trudy Cox that it wasn't me, she asked me if I thought it was *you* peddling that line of bullshit."

"What did you tell her?"

"I told her I thought it probably *was* you, of course. What did you expect me to say? I'm not here to cover your pathetic fat ass, you know."

"I know. You're right, of course." After what I hope is an appropriately long enough pause to convey my contrition, I add another sorry for good measure.

"Well, don't fucking do it again," Clive barks with finality. It seems as if my unqualified apology—something I almost never do—has rattled his brain cells sufficiently to dampen down his anger.

I'm curious as to who ratted me out, but I decide that the less I ask Clive about the phone call from Trudy Cox, the better. I'm pretty sure it was Silent Stu, but what about Miranda? No, my guess is that she hates Schiffman almost as much as she hates Hinch himself; in any event, the likelihood of her getting her act together enough to pick up the phone and call the office—hell, the likelihood of her even remembering my visit—is slim to none.

"So," Clive says, once he is satisfied that I have nothing more to add, "have you found out anything of interest? About Hinch, I mean."

"Actually, quite a bit. He's apparently strung out on smack these days, for one thing. I'm told he actually fell asleep onstage at the gig he played here in Holland two weeks ago, which resulted in a near-riot. He's gone underground since." Part of me wants to tell Clive the whole story, just to impress him, but I decide that discretion is the better part of valor. Besides, I want to keep all the juicy stuff for my own book; the last thing I need is for *Rolling Stone* to dispatch one of their investigative reporters and take the wind out of my sails.

"Sounds interesting," he says disinterestedly. "Mr. Clean nodding off in front of his fans. Would have made quite a headline … twenty years ago."

I ignore the subtle dig. "Well, anyway, I'm heading to London at the end of the week to see if he actually has the balls to turn up for the Millennium Dome gig."

"And if he does turn up, whether he can manage to do anything more than pass out onstage," Clive adds.

I force a laugh. "Good one," I say, trying to win a brownie point. "I can't imagine he'll be in any kind of shape to turn in a decent performance, anyway."

"Not unless he's been for a visit with Peggy McFarlane," Clive says.

"Who?" It's a name I'm unfamiliar with.

"Dr. Margaret McFarlane, the electro-shock pioneer," he explains. "She's cleaned up more famous musician junkies than you can shake a stick at. Clapton, Townshend, even Keith Richards—they've all been to her clinic. She's invented this little black box that they clip to their ears or something. It's supposed to be able to cure a heroin addiction in just days. If your guy wants to hit that London stage clean and sober, it's probably his only option."

"How is it that I've never heard of this person?" I ask rhetorically.

"Well, you would have if you actually did this for a living." That's Clive—never wastes any opportunity to twist the knife.

"You say this McFarlane has a clinic?" I ask, trying to keep him on track.

"Yeah, up in Scotland somewhere, in some big old gloomy castle, I'm guessing. But they say her treatment works. If I were you, that would be the first place I'd look for a missing junkie rock star."

I'm scribbling down notes frantically. Clive may be full of shit generally, but this is a world he knows a whole lot better than I do. "Um, thanks," I mumble. "Really appreciate it."

I'm about to hang up, but to my surprise Clive indicates that he wants to continue the conversation. "Okay, well, listen, there was actually another reason why I called you. Other than to ream you a new asshole, that is."

"What's that?"

"I think I may have a little assignment for you—something I suspect you may find of interest. Something that ties in nicely with your book, too."

"I'm all ears."

"Well, one of the editors here is a bit of a propeller-head—you know, into the techie stuff. We normally only cover artists, but he's managed to talk Jann into running a 'Where Are They Now?' kind of piece on some of the big name record producers from the '60s and '70s—guys like Phil Spector and George Martin, who have pretty much dropped out of sight in recent years."

"Where do I fit in?" I ask. "I wouldn't know one of those guys, or what they do, if they came up and bit me on the ass."

"Jesus, let me finish, willya?"

"Sorry."

"You fit in because there's one of them I think you *will* want to talk to, for your book if nothing else. Ever hear of a hit-making machine by the name of John Thomas Wallingford?"

The hairs on the back of my neck stand up. "John Thomas Wallingford?" I repeat stupidly. "As in JTW?"

"The very same. Back in the early '70s, he was the hot hand, you may recall. He even produced an album for your boy Hinch, I understand, though it was never released."

"Yes, I'm familiar with that story. But I thought he had disappeared."

"That's what we thought—disappeared, or dead. But one of our sources tells us that Wallingford is still alive, though very much a total loony these days."

"I get the impression he was a total loony even back then."

"Yes, but not certifiably so. Now he is, literally: a resident at a mental hospital just outside of London. But I hear he has moments of lucidity in-between bouts of raving madness, so it's possible you may get something usable out of him. He's got a young wife, too, who is interested in gaining him a little publicity, no doubt because it will help the state of their bank account."

"Yeah, there's always a young wife, isn't there?" Images of the Countess Miranda de Couqueville fill my head. Both of them, in fact. I can feel the blood racing to my nether regions as depraved fantasies reenter my consciousness.

"Bernie? You still there?"

"Yes, Clive. Just allowing myself a momentary lapse of reason."

"Anyway, if you want to do a brief interview with Wallingford and write a short piece on him for this article, I can arrange it and even get you a little bread for your troubles. I'll need it quickly, though. Interested?"

"I am. Very much so. And, Clive...."

"Yes?"

"Thank you."

IMMEDIATELY AFTER HANGING UP I pull out my laptop and connect to the Internet. Excited as I am to meet John Thomas Wallingford in the flesh, I'm even more stoked about the possibility of unearthing Hinch at Peggy McFarlane's rehab clinic. A few clicks of the mouse reveal a plethora of detail about the formidable Dr. McFarlane, who is apparently quite well-known in the rock world, as Clive had said. From what I can gather, she's no quack, anyway: She's got impeccable credentials and has developed a technique for addiction recovery that combines electroshock with psychotherapy, acupuncture and traditional Chinese herbal remedies. Though very expensive and therefore only the province of the monied class, it's a treatment which appears to work, and quite rapidly, too; in fact, McFarlane claims initial recovery inside of a week, though she is always careful in her interviews to add that continued treatment is necessary to prevent relapse. With a veritable parade of rock stars passing through her doors, she has achieved an exalted status in those circles, as much as for the positive results she achieves as for her sense of discretion—she's never once blabbed about her high-profile clients to the tabloids, despite being offered astronomical sums of money to do so.

So high is this level of discretion that I am unable to determine an exact address for the fabled clinic, other than verification that it is indeed located somewhere in the craggy hills of Scotland. I scribble down what little information I can gather and resolve to call Clive back to see if he can narrow it down for me. As I reach for the phone, however, I see the message light blinking. Could it be Britney, perhaps having second thoughts? My hopes are deflated when I call the operator and am informed in a thick Dutch accent that there are no messages waiting, only a fax from *Rolling Stone*. I trudge down the steps and retrieve the document from the bored desk clerk; it contains a phone number for Wallingford's wife and instructions as to word count, due date, and the address to send my invoice and travel expense reimbursement.

Images of Super Bernie rescuing a rock star in distress by the name of Hinch once more swimming in my head, I'm thoroughly distracted by the time I return to my room, only to be greeted by the shrill tones of Hans's cell phone yelping at me.

"Hello?"

"Bernie, it's Hans. Where are you?"

Again with the "where are you," another penny in royalties for whatever lucky bastard was smart enough to copyright the question.

"I'm in my hotel room, Hans. I've been here all day. What's up?"

"There's a little news: Rudie just got back from the police station, and they think they have located the hotel where Schiffman and the others were staying."

"*Were* staying? So they're no longer there?"

"No, they checked out this morning. It's one of those places out near the airport with the self-catering suites."

"You mean like an extended stay hotel?"

"Yah. One of those places with limited maid service, which is why they hadn't been in to clean it for quite a while. It seems that Schiffman left quite a mess behind—takeout food containers, dirty dishes ... and, this time, *two* envelopes stamped with the mark of the wolf."

"Let me guess: both white."

"No, actually this time one of the envelopes was blue. The police are not quite sure what to make of that."

I'm not either. Is it possible that Cody or Ryker or even Schiffman was using as well? It's too difficult a concept for me to wrap my head around right now. "Other than the envelopes," I ask, "what makes the cops so sure it was Schiffman staying there?"

"Oh, just the fact that the guy who checked in was wearing an expensive suit and fitted Schiffman's description. Plus they arrived late the evening of the Paradiso gig, and paid cash. Little things like that."

"Fair enough. But you say he's checked out. Do they have any idea where he's gone?"

"I'm afraid not. It was only Schiffman and one other man—presumably our friend Henry Ryker—who checked out, even though the desk clerk is certain that it was a party of four who checked in."

"So what's the plan now?" I ask.

"Frankly, I'm not sure. I suppose we can discuss it further over dinner. Any news at your end?"

You mean, other than the fact that I'm finally getting the fuck out of this place? "Actually, yes. I think I may have a lead as to where Hinch might be, at least if he's planning on cleaning up before his gig in London at the end of the week."

"Let me guess: the McFarlane clinic," Hans says smugly.

I'm dumbfounded. "You've heard of it?"

"Of course. Everyone has heard of it."

Not me, apparently, at least not up until now. I press on, determined to cover my ignorance. "Well, it seems as if it's the only place in the world where Hinch could get cleaned up in time to play the Millennium Dome gig straight."

"*If* he intends to play straight," Hans points out.

"Right. Well, anyway, I want to check it out, just in case. I'm thinking about grabbing a flight outta here first thing tomorrow morning."

"I think it will be a waste of your time."

"I know. But you said the same thing about me traveling up to Groningen, and that proved to be worthwhile."

"Ach, I'm glad you reminded me," Hans says. "I received word a little while ago from my friends at the immigrations department that Hinch's band and road crew have moved on. They took the noon ferry across the North Sea to Harwich; their paperwork indicated that they were going on to London from there. So maybe Hinch is planning on doing the show after all."

"They weren't stopped?"

"Why should they be stopped? They haven't committed any crime … not that we know of, anyway. No, we only asked that our friends keep an eye on their movements."

"So do you think Schiffman and Ryker will follow?"

"Hard to say. If they do try to leave the country, we'll know about it. Then Rudie will be able to have his fun at last."

"I have another reason for heading to England," I add. "I've received an assignment from *Rolling Stone* magazine to interview this record producer who once worked with Hinch."

"You write for *Rolling Stone*?" Hans says, surprised. "I'm impressed."

"Well, this will be my first piece for them," I confess. "But I do have a contact there. In fact, if you want to hear something funny, I actually pretended to be him when I was up in Groningen. I thought the band and crew would be more inclined to talk to me if they thought I was a music journalist."

Hans chuckles. "That's pretty good," he says. "So they think you are a reporter from the famous magazine."

"Well, they *did* think that. Apparently I got busted. My friend there got a call from Schiffman's office, and they were pretty angry about it. He told them he thought it was me pretending to be him."

There is a long, long pause, during which the temperature of the room seems to drop ten degrees.

"Hans?"

"Yes, Bernie, I'm here. Look, did you just tell me that Alan Schiffman's office knows that you are in Holland making inquiries about his whereabouts?"

"Well, they know that I'm here making inquiries about *Hinch's* whereabouts."

"Same difference. Bernie, listen to me carefully. I want you to hang up the phone and begin packing your bags immediately. I'm sending Rudie over to fetch you. We have to get you out of that hotel."

"Oh, come on, Hans, don't be so dramatic."

"Bernie, this is a serious game we're playing here," he snaps at me. "I'm not going to say it again: Pack your fucking bags *now*, and stay in your room with the door locked until Rudie gets there. He should be no more than twenty minutes. Don't answer the phone, don't move a fucking muscle until you see him. You understand?"

"I understand."

THOROUGHLY PISSED OFF, I begin stuffing clothing into my bags, thinking the whole time about what a goddamn worry-wart Hans is and what a pain in the ass he's become. *I just came here to finish my book*, I reflect as I fling dirty underwear into my suitcase, *not to get caught up in some international conspiracy that involves a sleazebag like Alan Schiffman.* I'm starting to get infuriated at the sheer inconvenience of it all. *What the hell have these guys actually done other than bop me over the head and buy me a couple of decent meals?* I think as I hurriedly shove my laptop into its carrying case, tangled wires fighting me every step of the way.

Moments later there is a knock on my door. I peer out and it is Rudie, looking grim-faced but a little sheepish, too.

"Come on, let's go," he mumbles as he picks up my bags and heads to the door. "I bet you won't be sorry to leave this shithole," he comments as he surveys the dismal surroundings.

"Well, to tell you the truth, it's not all that bad," I reply defensively. "At least not for the money. I was planning on checking out tomorrow, anyway, if you want to know. I'm not sure what the big deal is about getting me out of here tonight. If you ask me, Hans is being over-dramatic."

Rudie ignores me as he stomps down the steps in haste, banging my cases mercilessly against the grimy walls of the dimly lit stairwell as he does so. Puffing, I strain to keep up with him.

Finally, we emerge into the dingy lobby, where Rudie chucks my bags onto the floor haphazardly and instructs me to wait until he brings the car out front. Disheveled and sweating, I settle my bill with the desk clerk, who doesn't even take the trouble to ask me if everything was alright during my stay, fearful as he must be of an honest answer.

A moment later, Rudie reappears. Over his shoulder I can see his blue Renault idling noisily in the street below. After grabbing my bags and tossing them into the trunk, he races to the driver's side and flings himself into the front seat while I am busily fumbling with the passenger seat belt.

"You know, Rudie, I really don't understand what the grand rush is," I grumble, turning to face him as I do so.

A split second later there is a single crack of lightning as two small holes magically appear in the windshield. "What the fuck?..." I ask the hulking Dutchman seated beside me.

There is no reply, other than a disturbing gurgling emanating from deep within his lungs. Blood begins to pour out of the small wound in the precise center of Rudie's forehead as he slumps over, dead as the proverbial doornail.

22

Transcript: Interview with Donnie Boyle, May 22, 1998

By early '76 it had become obvious to me that Schiffman was playing Hinch against the rest of us, but I didn't have a whole lot of time to dwell on it, or to wonder what kind of "business" he wanted to discuss with our lead guitarist in Vegas. That's because I was preoccupied with getting the band ready for its next tour—a task that kept me busier than a one-legged man in an ass-kicking contest.

This tour was going to be considerably more important than any we'd done to date because, despite our still not having a record out, Schiffman had achieved the near-impossible in securing us headlining status everywhere we played. It was mostly at smaller venues, but he'd also booked us into a lot of pretty hip mid-size places—the Bottom Line in Manhattan, the Ratt in Boston, the Aragon Ballroom in Chicago—as well as scheduling a long swing through the Pacific Northwest, a part of the country we hadn't visited before. During the relatively quiet Christmas period, Hinch and Cody had written a bunch of new songs—mostly separately but occasionally with a degree of collaboration—and these all needed to be rehearsed. Plus we were breaking in a whole new bunch of roadies, courtesy of Schiffman Entertainment: Our booking agent had learned of the big blowup between JD and Muscle Beach Len and the resulting fallout, and he'd decided to do something about it. Shortly before we received his contract, Schiffman told me how he proposed to solve the problem.

He began by stating the obvious. "Donnie, we can't have you guys hitting the road with a crew that's at war with your drummer."

"I know, Alan, but I'm not sure what I can do about it," I said. "Word about Joe Dan seems to have spread around the circuit awful fast."

"That's because you're using amateurs," he replied. "I think it's time you started using professionals instead."

Until that moment, I had no idea there *were* such things as "professional" equipment humpers—frankly, it sounded like a contradiction in terms to me. Besides, even before we started paying commissions to Schiffman, we'd barely been able to afford the road crew we had. I assumed that the kind of guys he was talking about charged a whole lot more. But when I voiced my objections, Schiffman made me an offer I couldn't refuse.

"Yeah, I thought you might say that. Tell you what: I'll take care of the hiring, and I'll even split their salary with you—just deduct half the crew expenses from my monthly commission check."

"Really?"

"Absolutely. I'll put it in the agency contract. Deal?"

I was immediately suspicious because he was making what seemed like a generous offer—something that was completely contrary to the very nature of the booking agent. Nonetheless, he was presenting a potential way to fix a problem that so far had seemed unfixable, so despite my misgivings, I agreed. Sure enough, when the contract arrived a few days later, buried inside the pages of legal gobbledegook was a clause that stated, "In the interests of maintaining a professional performance from Artist, Agent assumes sole responsibility for hiring all necessary road crew and half the expense for said road crew shall be deducted from Agent's monthly commission."

A week later, I got a call from a rather gruff individual by the name of Hank—no last name, just Hank—who introduced himself as the head of our new clutch of roadies. The next day, he turned up at our rehearsal, accompanied by three other mugs, complete with the obligatory bulging muscles and tattoos. They also had matching crew-cuts, which was pretty unusual in those days of long hair. Despite the fact that they were all wearing the requisite black T-shirts, they looked more like Marines than roadies, and, as it turned out, that's exactly what they had been prior to being interviewed by Schiffman for the job. They comported themselves that way, too: total no-nonsense.

We were a bit intimidated by them, to tell you the truth, but they kept to themselves for the most part and they proved to be reasonably competent at getting our gear to and from gigs and keeping everything fairly well-maintained. Plus their thuggish demeanor ensured that we'd have no future difficulties with other bands' road crews or slimy club owners trying to hold back our wages. More important, they were no less standoffish with JD than they were with the rest of us. Over time, Hank and his crew would loosen up to the point where we actually started socializing with them a bit, even to the extent of including them in some of our partying.

That, as it transpired, was exactly what Alan Schiffman had in mind.

THE TOUR BEGAN smoothly enough. Following weeks of intensive rehearsal, Hinch and Cody's new songs had been integrated into our already powerhouse set, and they sounded good, damned good. Even to my untrained and obviously biased ears, a couple of them even sounded like hits, and the renewed spark of creativity got me refocused once again on the goal of landing that elusive record deal. The difficulty I faced this time was twofold: One, we'd been around for awhile so we were kind of yesterday's news, and, two, since our first album had vanished without a trace, the labels were a bit suspicious of us. Then there was the old and familiar problem of my simply not being connected enough, which meant that my phone calls were not getting returned. When I tried to recruit JJ as an ally to make another assault on the record companies, she politely but firmly refused, saying that all her time was taken up with running Schiffman's New York office and dealing with the other acts he had signed since setting up the new agency. I even tried broaching the subject with the great man himself, but he blew me off, claiming he was "working on it," same as he was working on finding us digs in L.A.—another promise I was by now convinced he wouldn't keep.

"You should cut the guy some slack" was Hinch's standard response when I would complain about Schiffman. "He's done a lot of positive things for us, you know. It's almost as if the more he does for us, the more you expect him to do."

I had no real comeback. Thanks to all the ego-stroking, Hinch was by now completely sold on Schiffman, and I knew that the more I disagreed with him, the more likely he was to remain entrenched in his thinking. I decided to do all my bitching to Cody instead, who I felt sure was seeing things the way I did.

Only he wasn't. "Yeah, I know you think the guy is a lowlife and I kind of agree," he said when I began popping off about Schiffman one day. "But I gotta give the slimeball credit, too: He *has* landed us a ton of gigs, and he's pretty much left us alone otherwise. At least he hasn't tried to tell us what to play, like that English scumbag did."

Cody was referring, of course, to our long-lost producer, who to his way of thinking had committed the cardinal sin of interfering with the band musically. That, to Cody, was the ultimate offense, and one that could not be forgiven.

"Plus," he pointed out, not unreasonably, "Schiffman has found us a road crew that isn't trying to cut Joe Dan's balls off every time he's passed out drunk. Sure, it's a drag that he hasn't been able to find us a house in L.A. yet, but I guess these things take time. You could be looking, too, you know."

Much as I wanted to take offense at Cody's parting shot, I had to admit he was right. Sleazy as our agent was, he was just that: our agent. I was the band's manager, and I needed to assume more responsibility. I resolved to start calling rental brokers out in La-La Land as soon as we got to the break in the tour. Perhaps while Hinch was away, doing God knows what with Schiffman, I could reassert control and start regaining the faith the band once had in me.

In the meantime, I had a tour to run, with a million details to look after: suitable food and accommodations, efficient itinerary planning that kept the costs under control yet got us to the gigs on time, bookkeeping, accounting, banking, nursemaiding, and the like. In addition to making sure the band took the stage punctually and vacated it before the promoter or venue manager pulled the plugs, I had to keep them amply supplied with booze, drugs, and groupies. Slowly but surely, though, Hank and his crew started taking over the latter chores in the time-honored manner of their profession. I didn't mind: all it meant to me was fewer things to deal with.

Still, the band was playing well, and the crowds were receptive, and the money and perks were good. Gradually my concerns about Alan Schiffman began to fade in the background. I even began enjoying myself a little.

"Donnie, what's wrong?" Vernon asked facetiously one night as we relaxed in the dressing room after an especially good gig. "You actually appear to be smiling."

The others gathered around and made a show of examining my face carefully.

"Yeah, he's right, that's definitely a smile I see," said Hinch, acting alarmed.

"Our resident prophet of doom?" asked Cody. "Can't be. Let me take a closer look." He motioned to Hank for a mag-light and shined it into my eyes. "No sign of a brain tumor. Must be something serious, then."

"Okay, guys, I get it," I said, blushing furiously despite myself. "But I'm your goddamned manager; I have a God-given right to be worried. Look at what it is I'm managing!"

"Managing a nervous breakdown, from the look of it," mumbled Joe Dan, his sole comment that night.

Actually, it wasn't far from the truth. But at least I was having a good time doing it.

ALL TOO SOON WE WERE at the halfway point in the tour, and Hinch and Katie Q were on a plane to Vegas, en route to their mystery meeting with Schiffman. A couple of days later, Hinch called and reported that no business had in fact yet been discussed.

"Alan's got his wife here with him," he explained, "and so we've barely had time to chat. In fact, all we've done so far is hang with them at the casinos shooting craps. He got us all tickets to see Elvis tomorrow night, too, man—I'm totally psyched."

Now I was completely puzzled. Was this all about setting up a foursome?

"No way, Donnie," Hinch protested when I put the question to him bluntly. "You know Katie would never go for that kind of thing. Look, we've just been, I don't know … it's like we're double dating. Honest, everything's straight out of Ozzie and Harriet. Katie and Cherisse have totally bonded—they're out shopping right now, in fact—and I have to tell you, I've been digging just grooving with Alan, watching him operate. He's actually a pretty cool guy when you get to know him."

I was still suspicious. "So he hasn't talked business with you at all?"

"Not a word, D. It's just basically been vacation all the way. Man, last night I was served the biggest steak I ever saw in my life—it was like eating a cow on a plate…." I listened to him going on and on about the glories of the Vegas buffets until his voice trailed off into a drone. After we hung up, I sat back and contemplated what was, or rather, was not, going on. *There's got to be more to it than that*, I thought.

As it turned out, I was right. Or perhaps not. The paranoid in me thinks that Schiffman had the whole thing planned out from the start. But maybe he didn't—maybe it was just fate working its mysterious ways. I guess I'll never know.

What I do know is that you could have knocked me over with a feather when Hinch and Katie came back home and announced that they had gotten married.

THE EVENTS OF THAT DAY are kind of a blur now, but I remember thinking that our fair-haired frontman looked like a proud Viking prince returned from a foreign conquest, and that Katie was as radiant and regal as you'd expect a Nordic princess to be. We all gathered around and admired her wedding ring, which sported a diamond the size of Rhode Island. I couldn't help but notice that she seemed to be a little embarrassed about it.

"Jeez, Hinch, you can't afford a rock that big," I hissed at him the moment we had a chance to talk alone.

"I know that, Donnie. It was a gift from Alan."

I was appalled. "Since when does someone give a wedding ring as a gift? Unless you're marrying them, that is."

Hinch laughed. "Calm down, D. It was just a nice gesture, that's all. He knew I didn't have the bread to buy Katie the kind of ring she deserves. I think it was very generous of him, actually." There was conviction in his words but I could also see him blushing slightly. Even Hinch had to know that a line had been crossed.

"What the hell made you decide to tie the knot anyway?" I asked him.

"I don't know, man, it's just that we were all having such a fantastic time together, and Alan and Cherisse kept telling us what a great couple we were and how cool marriage was and all that. It was just a spur of the moment thing—we were passing this chapel, a real tacky place just like you see in the movies, and, I don't know, it just seemed like a fun thing to do."

Lowering his voice to a whisper so that his new bride couldn't hear, Hinch confided, "Donnie, I got to tell you, the sex with Katie has been even more amazing than it was before we got hitched. I'm even starting to think about having kids with her. Like Alan tells me, I've got to keep that Hinch line going, you know."

Kids? Hinch was the last person on earth I ever thought would be interested in having kids. The guy was destined to be a rock star from the day he was born, not some average Joe putting up a swing set on a suburban lawn.

He must have seen the look of alarm on my face. "Down the road, Donnie, down the road. After I get rich and famous."

"Thank fuck for that," I mumbled as I walked away, feeling, what? Dismay? Disdain? Or just discarded? I don't know which. Certainly I felt confused.

But the difficulty I had in dealing with my feelings paled in comparison to what Cody was going through. 'Collateral damage,' I believe they call it in the military. He put on a big show for Hinch and Katie that day, congratulating them with this big phony grin plastered all over his face, but I could tell he was shaken to the core. He looked not just dazed but physically assaulted, as if he'd been punched in the solar plexus. Clearly in a state of shock, Cody spent most of the afternoon wandering around aimlessly, shaking his head and mumbling *I-don't-believe-its* to anyone who would listen. When the newlyweds finally retired to their bedroom for the evening, Cody sank into the living room sofa, where he sat motionless, remote and silent as a Sphinx, until dawn. I tried my best to comfort him, as did Vernon and JD, but he was inconsolable. The poor guy never looked more lost, or more alone.

I had long known that Cody was kind of sweet on Katie Q—hell, if I'm completely honest, I have to admit that I was, too—but I had also always assumed that Cody accepted the fact that she was Hinch's woman and therefore unattainable. Now he was acting as if he had lost the one thing he had been living for. It was pitiful to witness, let me tell you. But with the tour about to resume in just a couple of day's time, I could only offer so much sympathy.

The day before we were due to hit the road, we attempted a tune-up rehearsal which was completely ruined by Cody's continued moping. As his annoyed bandmates drifted out of the room and the roadies began packing up the gear, I took Cody aside and whispered in his ear, "Come on, man, you and I need to have a private chat."

We headed off to my office and closed the door. "Look, you've got to snap out of it," I said as forcefully as I dared. "I'm telling you this not just as your manager, but as your friend." Getting no response, I continued my lecture. "Dammit, Cody, as long as I've known you, you've always put the band first. Now you've got to find a way to do it again."

He slumped in his chair, head down, eyes staring vacantly at the floor. After a long pause, Cody finally looked up at me. I could see tears streaming down his face.

"I've been having these weird dreams, Donnie," he finally said, so softly I had to strain to hear him.

"We all have weird dreams," I started to say. "It's not that unusual."

"No, you don't understand," he interrupted, the words tumbling out in a rush. "Sometimes I dream that I'm onstage and the music is all wrong. Everything sounds completely messed up, yet the crowd is roaring, totally digging it. I'm looking around at the guys in the band and they're playing away like they can't hear how bad it all sounds—they're into it just as much as the crowd is. I'm the only one who can hear how *wrong* it all is, and when I try to explain, no one will listen to me, no one will believe me."

"It's only a dream, Cody," I tried to tell him.

"Then other times I dream exactly the opposite," he continued, ignoring me. "We're on an outdoor stage playing in the middle of a thunderstorm and I'm getting soaked to the skin. Finally I give up; I take my guitar off and lay it down on the stage. The rain is pelting the strings, playing notes randomly, sparks flying each time a raindrop hits. My amp is feeding back and the audience is booing and the guys in the band are yelling at me to get off the stage."

"Sounds pretty intense," I said, not quite sure what he was getting at.

"I guess. But the craziest thing is that those random notes sound to my ears like the most beautiful love song ever written. And there's only one person who hears it the way I do. You know who it is? It's Katie, man, sitting in the front row: the only person in the dream cheering me on. The only person who *understands*."

"Cody, this isn't helping."

All of a sudden he began wailing like a wounded animal. "She deserves better!," he screamed. "You know how much he disrespects her, how he's always cheating on her. She fucking deserves better!"

"You're right," I replied gently, trying to calm him down. "But none of that matters. This is what Katie wants. She's a grown woman, Cody. You've got to let go."

As the sun's last rays slowly melted away, the two of us sat together in an awkward silence broken only by the muted sounds of Cody's sobbing. It was clear that something deep inside the guy had been shattered. I could only hope that he had the inner strength to regroup and soldier on. When he was all cried out, Cody rose slowly and embraced me in a feeble hug before shuffling out of the room like a zombie.

As I watched him leave, I remember thinking, *Maybe that was the worst of it. Maybe the poor guy just needed to vent. Maybe he'll be okay after all.*

Yeah, and maybe someday they'll prove that the moon is made of green cheese.

LATER I HAD A CHANCE to reflect on Cody's dreams. I guess I hadn't realized just how angry he was at Hinch for, as he saw it, "selling out" to Wallingford, nor had I understood the depths of his feelings for Katie—the only person he viewed as being on his side—and how utterly alone he felt now that, in his eyes, he had lost both the musical integrity of the band *and* Katie.

Still, the world didn't stop turning and the tour continued, and we did the best we could, even with the heart and soul of the band crippled and nearly non-functional. Hinch insisted on bringing Katie with him on the last leg of the tour, too, which I at first thought was incredibly insensitive. But when I stopped and tried to see things from his perspective, I couldn't get mad: After all, this was likely to be the only honeymoon they'd ever have, what with our schedule getting busier and busier.

In true rock 'n' roll tradition, Cody killed the pain with drugs and alcohol. He began boozing regularly with the Trucker brothers—something he'd rarely done in the past—but I felt that as long as he restricted himself to getting high *after* gigs, I could turn a blind eye. *Anything to help the guy cope*, I thought. In the back of my mind perhaps I was even hoping the pain would lead to his writing a masterpiece, as Clapton had done with "Layla."

But it never happened. In fact, things went from bad to terrible. Cody began numbing himself before gigs as well as afterwards; once or twice I even caught him swigging from a bottle of Jack Daniels onstage, which he'd never have dreamed of doing—or tolerated from anyone else—before. He began missing cues, hitting bad notes, playing in the wrong key altogether: all the things he abhorred in other, less disciplined musicians. In short, he was losing pride in his craft, which in his case meant that he was losing himself altogether.

It was a sad state of affairs, but the one silver lining was that it forced the other guys to take up the slack. There were nights when, even though all four of them were onstage, the band played like they were a three-piece again—that's how useless Cody was. To their credit, they even kicked ass on those nights—Hinch hiding the holes in the music with his showmanship and everyone doing whatever they had to do to make up for the void left by Cody's empty presence. Mind you, there were other nights when Cody got his act together—kind of—but they were few and far between ... and they were growing more infrequent as the tour went on. Unfortunately, those gigs only served to remind us of how great the band could be when it was actually firing on all cylinders.

I was starting to think that things couldn't possibly get any worse when they did. One night, about twenty minutes before the band was due to take the stage, I saw Cody nodding off in the dressing room. Something about how utterly pathetic he looked suddenly caused all the resentment that had been building inside me to explode into rage, like a dam breaking. Before I could stop myself, I hauled off and smacked him in the face as hard as I could. It was something I would have never dared do before that night, because I knew better than anyone how dangerous Cody could be when riled. But I was fed up with his irresponsible behavior, and, besides, I doubted if even assault and battery could bring him back to life.

I was right. Cody just sat there, looking up at me with a dazed expression, grinning slightly, looking like a total doofus.

"Hey there, Donnie boy," he slurred.

"You motherfucker!" I shouted. "What the hell are you on?"

The answer came painfully slowly. "What do you mean? I'm high on life, man." He faded back to never-never land.

I slapped him across the face again, this time a bit harder. Out of the corner of my eye I could see Hinch and the Truckers watching in horror; they'd never seen me act this way.

Cody roused himself just a little. "Hey, quit hitting me," he whined like a five-year-old. "Oh, it's you, Donnie. Okay, fair enough. Hell, I guess if I'm on smack, I deserve to be smacked." He giggled as he started to drift off to sleep again.

Now, this band had ingested plenty of drugs over the years, don't get me wrong. But for all the coke and uppers that had been floating around, I had never seen any evidence of heroin. It wasn't that I was any kind of saint when it came to drugs, or anything else, for that matter. It was just that, besides being addictive and soul-sapping, it was impossible to play decent music on the stuff, as everyone in the business knew.

"Who the hell has been giving you smack?" I demanded of the now-unconscious Cody. Infuriated, I raised my hand to deliver another blow. This time it was stopped in mid-air.

"Leave him alone, Donnie. I was sent here to put an end to the fighting, and that's what I intend to do."

It was Hank, our new chief roadie. I whirled to face him.

"What the fuck do you know about this?"

"I know that your friend here is a grown man and perfectly capable of making his own decisions."

"And do you know who is supplying him with heroin?"

"I am," he admitted without a trace of contrition. "Same as I get drugs for everybody else in the band, same as every roadie does for every asshole in every band everywhere in the fucking world. You don't like it, take it up with my boss. But leave the guy alone or I'll have to start slapping *you* around."

I was livid. "Are you threatening me?" Too angry to be sensibly afraid, I got right in the face of the crewcutted prick who, I noticed, was now surrounded by the other members of his hand-picked road crew. All four of them were glaring threateningly at me.

"I'm just telling you to leave the guy alone," Hank repeated grimly.

That I was on the verge of having my ass handed to me somehow made me even more angry. "Who the fuck do you think you are?" I yelled. "And who the fuck are you to talk that way to me? I'm the guy who signs your paychecks. I *am* your boss."

"With all due respect, *Mr.* Boyle," Hank said sarcastically, "you are *not* my boss. I was hired by Alan Schiffman, and that's who I answer to."

"We'll see about that, motherfucker." I stormed off to find the nearest phone. As I slammed the door behind me, I heard Hinch say to the others. "Come on, guys, time to hit the stage. We're gonna have to do this as a three-piece tonight."

Schiffman, needless to say, was not in, and he managed to avoid my calls for several hours before I was able to track him down.

"Yeah, I heard there were some problems with Cody," he said offhandedly when I finally got him on the line. "But there's nothing I can do about Hank. He and the others have an airtight contract to finish out the tour; in fact, their contract runs all the way through the end of the year. So you're just going to have to grin and bear it."

"Grin and bear it? The bastards are feeding my guy drugs that are making it impossible for him to do his job."

"Look, Donnie," he said icily, "roadies get drugs for the band, same as they get pussy for them. That's part of the gig. Their job is to do whatever the band asks them to do. The drugs they provide to Vernon and Joe Dan could kill a horse, but you don't seem to mind that."

"What you're conveniently forgetting," I snarled down the mouthpiece, red-faced with rage, "is that Vernon and Joe Dan do coke and speed—stimulants that help their playing, not shit that incapacitates them."

Schiffman remained unruffled. "I guess that's why God made vanilla and chocolate," he said. "Look, the problem is not Hank; the problem is Cody. Cody is the one asking for smack. Hank's only doing what he's asked to do, which is his job. Take it up with Cody. But know this: If you can't get your band under control, there *will* be consequences."

With that, he hung up, neatly dumping the problem squarely in my lap.

For the remainder of the tour, I struck an uneasy truce with Cody and Hank. "I'll let Hank supply you with the drugs of your choice," I told Cody, "but in exchange you have to agree not to get fucked up for at least four hours before showtime." He nodded his head dully in agreement, and for the most part stuck to it, although there were still nights when he took the stage in a stupor, or not at all.

It was when the tour ended and we were back to sporadic gigging that things took a turn for the worse again, as Cody not only continued to mess with heroin but began popping downers of every variety—seconals, tuinals, percs, even quaaludes—with disastrous results. In the past, he had always spent our off-days writing new songs or practicing his guitar. Now he spent them staring mindlessly at the TV, or sleeping, or wandering the streets of Philadelphia aimlessly, unkempt, unbathed, and often still dressed in his pajamas. His hygiene was atrocious, his mind was wandering, his muse was gone. It was down to Hinch to call the rehearsals—something he'd always hated, and so they happened only infrequently. Sometimes Cody would attend, contributing little if anything; other times, he'd simply fail to turn up.

One afternoon I discovered Cody sound asleep in the backyard, sprawled out between the garbage cans. I remember thinking how ironic it was: he looked like nothing so much as a piece of refuse himself. Unable to rouse him, I frantically called out for help. Vernon was first on the scene, checking Cody's pulse with the efficiency of a trained paramedic. "He's okay, Donnie," he said. "His lips aren't blue and his breathing is pretty normal. He just needs to sleep it off."

"How do you know so much about it?" I asked angrily. I wasn't mad at Vernon, mind you, just frustrated with the whole sorry situation.

"Give me a break, man," Vernon protested. "You know that me and

Joe Dan have been around the block a few times. Cody's been asking us about smack for months now. Good thing he's just snorting it and not mainlining."

I must have looked confused.

He rolled up his sleeve and pointed to a series of faint red scars on his arm—the remnants of track marks. "Shit, I was using when you first found me playing with those good ol' boys down in Virginia. I thought you knew that. Cody sure as hell did."

"He did?"

"Hell, yes. Didn't you ever wonder why it took me so long to get into this here group of yours? It was Cody who told me I couldn't join the band until I cleaned up. I went cold turkey, brother. That's how much I wanted to hook up with your little crew here."

My jaw was hanging open. That manipulative little motherfucker!

"Come on, Donnie," Vernon said gently. "Let's carry your boy inside and tuck him into bed."

People don't understand what a serious matter it is when a performer misses a gig. It's the same for musicians as it is for actors: When you're expected to be on that stage, you damn well better be there. Every night there's another club, theater, or stadium, all full of paying customers who aren't interested in excuses. The audience has parted with their cold, hard cash and in exchange they expect to be entertained, and by the people they bought their tickets to see, not some stand-in. I've heard stories of audiences in Broadway theaters getting up *en masse* and demanding their money back when the announcement went out that an understudy would be appearing that night instead of the star of the show, and that's nothing compared to what would happen if you had an arena full of stoned and drunk rock 'n' roll fans denied the chance to see the musician they worship.

Beyond the risk of riot and physical assault, there's a whole lot of money at stake. No promoter in his right mind ever wants to shell out refunds, which is why a lot of them put severe penalties in their contract should the artist fail to appear for any reason short of a bona fide Act of God—and some of them even try to get away with removing that one little loophole too; damned if they're going to give any money back even if there *has* been an earthquake, flood, or recurrence of the Black Plague.

Which is why you see musicians of all stripes, and rock 'n' roll stars especially, taking the stage when it's clear they are utterly incapable of giving any kind of even vaguely worthy performance. They'll be slumped against their amplifiers if they can't see straight, seated in a chair if they've broken a leg, laid out flat on the floor if it's too painful to stand or even sit. They'll have been injected with painkillers if they've pulled a muscle, antipsychotics if they're on a bad trip, Benadryl if they've gone into anaphylactic shock. They'll have had a gallon of coffee poured down their throat if they're intoxicated, Gatorade if they've gotten cramps, Kaopectate if they've got diarrhea. There will be buckets nearby if they're suffering from food poisoning, towels soaked in ice if they're running a fever, dixie cups filled with vodka if they're going through the DTs. Backstage, they'll have been hypnotized if they've been hit with sudden stage fright, massaged if they got a crick in the neck, yelled at mercilessly if they're simply acting like a jerk.

But one way or another, they *will* take that stage. Either that, or face the wrath of a promoter who would much rather cut your genitals off and stuff them in your asshole sideways than give a penny of his money back.

That's why it was such a big deal when Cody started missing gigs, getting so far gone backstage we couldn't rouse him. Fortunately for us, he wasn't the star of the show, and fortunately for him, he had a manager and three band mates who were also his friends and were therefore relatively sympathetic. Anyone else, and his ass would have been fired long ago.

We all did what we could to help Cody through this crisis, but between the pain he was in and the downers and smack he was consuming it was damn near impossible to get through to him. Whenever we tried, the conversation invariably ended with the poor guy in tears, something we all found embarrassing to the extreme. At one point even Katie quietly took him aside to try to talk some sense into him. Cody did his best to be nonchalant with her, she later told me, but in the end just ran out of the room crying like a baby. An hour later, she found him nodding off in a corner.

JD was probably the closest to Cody in the band at that point, and even he seemed flummoxed. He clearly held the roadies responsible for Cody's condition, and he wasn't shy about voicing his opinion to anyone who would listen. One night I heard him arguing with Hank, who had proven himself to be a slimy, though apparently fearless, piece of shit.

"I catch you giving him any more smack, you're going to have to answer to me personally," Joe Dan was telling him.

"Fuck you, hillbilly," Hank snarled, getting right in JD's face. Although Joe Dan stood a good head taller than Hank, there was no question that the roadie was completely unintimidated. "Believe me, you don't want to be getting into a whupping contest with me," he warned. "Me and my crew will put a serious hurt on you, country boy."

Here we go again, I thought. We simply couldn't afford to have our drummer start another war with our roadies. Beyond the tensions that such infighting would bring, I was afraid that JD would be seriously hurt. As big as Muscle Beach Len had been, he was also, as Schiffman had pointed out, just an amateur. These guys were trained killers, courtesy of the United States Marine Corps.

I inserted myself between the two rutting males just as they launched into their primal chest-thumping. You could almost smell the testosterone in the room. "Okay now, guys, we don't want any trouble here," I said softly, trying to bring things down a notch. "We're all on the same team, let's not forget."

"If you don't want any trouble, just tell this asshole to keep out of my face," Hank replied, keeping his eyes fixed on Joe Dan the whole time.

"Come on, JD, let's just take a walk together, you and me," I improvised. "I want to go over tomorrow's set list with you."

Still pointing his finger threateningly at Hank, JD slowly backed off, to my relief. As soon as I got him alone I told him in no uncertain terms that I wanted him to no longer talk to the crew at all unless it pertained specifically to his equipment. "No good can come from this; trust me," I said.

"I know. I hear you, Donnie," Joe Dan sighed. "I just can't stand watching what those motherfuckers are doing to Cody." He wiped his nose with the back of his hand.

Our big, macho drummer crying? The sight of it nearly brought me to tears myself. "Me either, JD," I commiserated. "Me either."

I never felt so powerless in my entire life.

CODY'S INFATUATION with smack did more than affect our live performances: it essentially marked a dead end in the band's progress musically. Without anyone to prod them into new areas of exploration, Hinch, Vernon and JD began stagnating, coasting on auto-pilot. Audiences may not have noticed it, but I damn well did and when I tried to confront the guys in the band about it there was a long, embarrassed silence.

"Hell, Donnie, how much better could we get, anyway?" Hinch finally blurted out lamely before stalking out of the room. As long as he continued to receive the adulation he craved, he was content to stand pat. That's the way Hinch had always been, and it never changed, not in all the years I knew him. So he basically didn't give a shit, and Vernon was too laid back, and JD too unstable, to assume the mantel of leadership. The irony was that it had been Cody who had almost single-handedly pushed this monstrous boulder to the top of the mountain, but was now incapable of stopping its inevitable journey back down.

Alan Schiffman, however, was determined to put a halt to the backsliding. "Alright, Donnie, it's time for some drastic action," he announced after summoning me out to L.A. for what he had termed an urgent business meeting.

I tensed, fearing what he was about to suggest. But Schiffman, as usual, caught me off guard.

"I think we've gotten as much mileage as we can get out of the band's 'missing' first album," he said, referring to the Wallingford debacle and not, to my considerable relief, to Cody's recent problems. "It's time to put that particular dead horse to rest."

He peered at me, waiting to see my reaction. I gave him none.

"I'm listening, Alan," I said.

"Good. As you know, I've had my lawyers examine the contract you signed with Noteworthy, and they've come to the conclusion that, having failed to live up to their legal obligation to get your album in the charts, you're free and clear of any further commitment to them."

"I'm glad to hear that," I said, and I was: Finnerty's estate had been making noises lately about wanting to hold us to the contract. I thought they didn't have a leg to stand on, and that had also been Schiffman's opinion, but neither of us was certain of the legalities, so when he suggested I turn the contract over to his attorneys to take a look, I had jumped at the opportunity.

"So we have a green light to start shopping for a new record deal, but we're going to do things a little differently this time around," Schiffman told me.

There was something about the tone in his voice that I immediately took offense at. He must have seen me bristle because he jumped right back in before I had a chance to respond.

"Relax, Donnie, relax. I'm just going to make it easier for you and your boys to get back on top, and in the process we'll all make a lot more money. They'll get to exert a lot more creative control, too."

The "easy" and "money" parts of that sounded pretty good to me, but the last part sounded even better, especially after what we'd been through with John Thomas Wallingford. The need for creative control, I knew, had become Cody's mantra, at least before his descent into a drug-addled hell.

I sat forward in my chair. "What do you have in mind?" I asked.

"Here's what we're going to do, Donnie: we're going to make our own album first. *Then* we're going to sell it."

I studied Schiffman carefully, trying to read his mind. What he was proposing was in and of itself not a preposterous idea: established artists like Frank Sinatra had done deals like that for decades. The problem was the enormous expense involved in recording an album: The better studios—the ones that were capable of turning out a suitably professional product—charged hundreds of dollars an hour for their services.

"Who's going to pay for it, Alan?" I finally asked. "I mean, your tours have provided us with a good living wage, but we don't have that kind of money."

"Not to worry, Donnie. Schiffman Entertainment will foot the bill."

I was dumbfounded. Agencies didn't pay for record production: record companies did. "That's an incredibly generous offer, Alan," I said. "But what's in it for you?"

Leaning so far back in his overstuffed executive chair that he looked like he might topple over at any minute, Schiffman smiled a toothy smile, which led me to believe that they had been capped recently. "I admire your bluntness, Donnie," he began, "and, frankly, I'd have been disappointed if you hadn't asked me that question." He paused for a moment before continuing. "Look, we're both businessman. You know that I'm not in business to lose money, nor am I here to do anyone favors. I'm viewing this as a business opportunity, and I'm confident that your band will produce a commercial product that will yield an income stream that will reimburse me for my outlay, plus interest. What's more, I'm anticipating bigger bookings and therefore increased commissions after the record achieves a level of success. The bottom line is that I have faith in your boys to make money for me, and I'm prepared to gamble that they will do exactly that."

I pondered his response, which struck me as both direct and, dare I say it, truthful. Frankly, after the miserable experience we'd had with Noteworthy, it was hard to see a down side in what he was offering. *The guy's grown new pinky rings since I saw him last,* I remember thinking. *And somehow he's also managed to acquire a tan that would make George Hamilton jealous.*

"Will the band have complete creative control over the album?" I asked. "I know that Cody's going to want to produce it."

"From what I hear, Cody's having trouble producing a bowel movement at the moment."

That's right, kick the guy when he's down. "Tackling a project like this might just be enough to get him cleaned up and back in the saddle," I replied evenly.

Schiffman cocked his head sideways at me. "You think so? I'm not so sure."

"I am. And I know him a lot better than you do."

"Yes, you do, Donnie. That you do. I'll tell you what: If your boy gets his act together, I'll let him take the reins. *If.* But I'm going to want a co-producer in there with him—someone I can rely on—just in case he can't pull it off." I must have looked a little askance, because he continued, rapid-fire. "Come on, you can't begrudge me that: This is a lot of money we're talking about. Look, we're going to do this right. I'll book the band in one of the top studios here in L.A., and I'll make sure they put their chief engineer behind the board. Shit, it'll be costing me a hundred bucks every time one of your guys goes to the bathroom to take a pee."

I looked at Schiffman long and hard. I knew that I couldn't trust the guy any further than I could throw him—hell, less than that, convinced as I was that I could probably hurl him a good twenty feet if he pissed me off enough—but there was no denying that he was offering the band a way out of its downward spiral. In the process, he was also tossing a possible life preserver to a friend who was drowning.

"Okay, Alan, you've got yourself a deal," I found myself saying, though I made the sign of the cross as I walked out of his office. *It's in God's hands now*, I thought.

God's ... and Alan Schiffman's.

23

Someone somewhere is screaming. Off in the distance, lights are flashing. Shadowy figures come and go, appear and disappear, manifest and vaporize. Looks of concern, looks of fear, looks of pity. Where are they all coming from? Where are they all going to?

Hands unbuckling seat belt, hands lifting me out of the car, shards of glass, the warm, sticky spray of blood. Now I am outside, on the ground, the cool night air chilling me to the bone. The pavement is wet, my head is pounding, my chest is heaving. Without warning I begin shaking uncontrollably, sweat and vomit pouring out of me in a torrent. White coats, white faces, feet, arms, hands, fingers everywhere, shuffling, probing, pushing, prodding. When will it all end?

It slowly dawns on me that I am the center of all this hubbub, the eye in this storm of frantic activity. A stethoscope is being pressed against my chest, a blood pressure cuff wrapped around my arm, a thermometer inserted between my parched lips. I want nothing more than to make it all go away, yet I am powerless to make it stop.

"*Hij heeft in een shocktoestand, maar anders ongedeerd*," says one of the paramedics. "What? What does that mean?" I ask another in alarm. "Shhh, just lie still," he whispers gently. "He's saying you're okay, you're unharmed. You're just in shock. We're going to give you a shot of something to calm you now."

I'm okay. I let the words wrap around me like a warm embrace.

"What about my friend?" I ask the paramedic as he jabs me with a needle.

He looks me over carefully, trying to determine if I'm ready to hear the truth. "Not so lucky, I'm afraid," he finally murmurs. "I'm sorry."

I exhale slowly and close my eyes. *I knew I never should have come here* is my last thought before surrendering to unconsciousness.

Those lights again, blinding me, stabbing me, fiery lasers burning into the center of my brain. Make them stop! All I want to do is sleep, sleep this away, sleep my entire life away. But those fucking lights won't let me.

"I think he's coming to, Inspecteur."

The source of my misery reveals himself to be a young doctor shining a small flashlight in my eyes. "He seems to be alright," he finally pronounces after checking my pupils for dilation. "Just give him a little while to rest before you start your questioning. I'll prepare the discharge papers."

The doctor leaves the room and I am left alone with Inspecteur VandeVoort and a dejected-looking Hans.

"Rudie…?"

"Yes, Bernie. He's gone."

"Oh my god. I am so sorry."

"Yah. Me too." It feels like there is so much more to be said, but Hans seems to be in no mood for commiseration. "We will have plenty of time to grieve for him later," he intones softly. "Now … now we have work to do."

I look over at VandeVoort, who shakes his head sadly. "Do you feel well enough to answer a few questions?" he says.

"Yes, I think so. Do we know who did this?"

"No, we only know who did not do this," he replies enigmatically.

"Surely it was Schiffman and that other guy, Ryker, wasn't it?"

VandeVoort and Hans exchange doleful glances.

"It wasn't them," Hans says glumly.

I'm starting to get angry despite myself. "It *had* to have been them," I sputter. "Thanks to you, no one else in Amsterdam wants me dead except Alan Schiffman and this Ryker guy. That was *your* theory, a few hours ago, anyway."

"I know," sighs Hans. "But it wasn't them who shot at you."

"How the hell do you know that with such certainty?"

"Because, Bernie, at the exact moment you and Rudie were getting in that car, Schiffman and Ryker were halfway across the North Sea on a flight to London."

"What??" I turn to VandeVoort. "How did you let that happen?"

The detective stands up, clearly affronted, and addresses me formally. "Mr. Temkin, you are a guest in our country and you have been vouched for by my good friend Hans here. Clearly, you are upset after this unfortunate shooting, which, I would point out, has taken the life of a dear friend of mine. Nonetheless I would remind you that you are talking to a police officer and that you need to show the proper respect."

I deflate. "You're right. I'm sorry," I finally mumble.

"Look, Bernie, I know you are very emotional now," Hans says. "Imagine how I feel. My *vriend van kinds-afaan*—my childhood companion, my best friend in the whole world—is dead. But this is not the time for pointing fingers."

After a brief pause to dab his eyes with a handkerchief, VandeVoort takes a deep breath and continues. "As you may recall, Mr. Schiffman and Mr. Ryker have not been charged with any crime, due to the, shall we say, sensitive nature of the situation. So we had no legal grounds for detaining them here, or for preventing them from leaving the Netherlands. However, they are still deemed persons of interest, so rest assured that we have been in contact with Scotland Yard and with Interpol, and that we are keeping a close eye on their whereabouts and movements. And it is precisely this surveillance which has allowed us to ascertain, without any doubt whatsoever, that neither of those two gentlemen were responsible for this shooting, at least not directly."

"What about indirectly?" I ask.

"Well, if they hired some person or persons with the intent of causing grievous harm, then, of course, that would be viewed as a serious crime and they would be charged accordingly. Tell me, Mr. Temkin, is there anyone else here in Amsterdam who would want to see you killed?"

"No, of course not. I've never been here before in my life, and, other than Hans and Rudie, I don't even know anyone here."

"Then we will proceed on the assumption that Alan Schiffman and/or Henry Ryker are behind this incident, and will take all measures necessary to bring the guilty parties to justice."

For a moment all three of us sit there silently, taking in the scope and enormity of what has happened. Hans, I notice, is taking no pleasure whatsoever in the idea that his long-sought quarry may have just placed himself squarely behind the crosshairs of an international police net. That won't be sufficient revenge for him, I suspect.

During the next twelve hours, I discover just how right I am.

OUR FIRST STOP is the police station, where VandeVoort and his colleagues put me through a thorough grilling. Were it not for their unrelenting politeness and willingness to include Hans in the interrogation as a corroborating witness, I might have thought that I myself was a suspect. Their forensics team has been impressively efficient in the hours since the shooting took place and has located the weapons used in the assault on Rudie and me. Two high-powered rifles equipped with sophisticated night scopes were discovered on the roof of the building facing my hotel, confirming that there were two gunmen, not one, even though, judging from the single crack of gunfire I heard, they must have fired simultaneously. Though no fingerprints have been retrieved—indicating that these were indeed professional hitmen at work—both the shell casings and the bullets themselves have been found: one taken from the seat headrest behind Rudie, slightly flattened by its lethal travels through his brain tissue, and the other lodged firmly in the upper part of the passenger seat. It was only the last-minute turning of my head to face Rudie that saved my life, VandeVoort gravely informs me.

Faxes had already been sent out to every legitimate arms dealer in Holland with the ballistics specifications, and detectives dispatched to all the known illegitimate ones. The police were hoping one of them would be able to provide a lead as to the purchaser of those weapons and bullets, but that would probably take a few days at minimum, we are told. In the meantime, we were to remain watchful in our surroundings and careful in our dealings with strangers.

"Am I free to leave the country?" I ask VandeVoort.

"I suppose so," he replies. "Where are you planning on going?"

"To England. First thing tomorrow morning. I have an interview to do there."

"Well, I don't see why not," he says. "You might want to check in with the local police when you arrive, though, just so they know your whereabouts."

Finally, somewhere in the middle of the night, we are dismissed, and under police escort, we retire to Hans's modest apartment on the outskirts of town. With neither of us capable of sleep, we proceed to pull a good old-fashioned all-nighter, something I haven't done since I was in college. The long darkness is filled with remembrances of Rudie and a single toast to his memory—I notice that Hans offers one, and only one glass of genever. It is evident he wishes to remain clear-headed on this evening, for reasons that soon become apparent.

As the first glow of sunrise begins to fill the sky, phone calls are made and we receive visitors, Hans's brother Petrus, and his friend Aachie among them. Everyone is offering expressions of sympathy, of course, but slowly the tone of the conversation changes from personal to more business-like.

Ideas are being tossed around which eventually evolve into a plan. A dangerous, risky, almost crazy one, to be sure, but a plan nonetheless. And having a plan, I have found, is always better than having no plan.

By noon we all know what we have to do. Time is our enemy here: With the Dutch *Korps landelijke politiediensten,* Scotland Yard, and Interpol all after Schiffman, and with the gig at the Millennium Dome looming, we have only a very limited window of opportunity available to us.

"Even if this insane idea somehow works to perfection, won't the police take a dim view of it?" I ask Hans.

"Some of them, perhaps. But right now what they don't know won't hurt them. And we can count on VandeVoort to work with us, and to give us cover. He and Rudie were very close, you know."

Close how? I want to ask. But I realize it really doesn't matter. The main thing is that we have all lost a friend, and we have been galvanized into action as a result. Sooner, rather than later, this whole thing will be coming to a head and I will be able to finish the damn book and escape this nightmare, back to my own personal hell in L.A. One nightmare might be as good as the next, I ponder soberly as I yawn and stretch, weary to the bone.

But with the London concert just three days away, there is no time for sleep. A quick phone call to Wallingford's wife secures the promise of transportation from Heathrow to the insane asylum and an audience with the madman himself later this afternoon. There's just enough time for a quick shower before I get to gather up my bags and leave Holland, at long last.

"Good luck with all the arrangements, Hans," I say as I embrace him in the Schiphol departure lounge an hour later. "I'll see you in two days."

"Yah, Bernie, in two days. Good luck to you, too. If you find Hinch, tell him I said hello and that I bear him no grudge."

"I'll do that, Hans. I'll do just that."

BASED ON OUR BRIEF CONVERSATION, I had the impression that Mrs. Wallingford would simply arrange for a car service to pick me up at the airport, which is why I am so surprised when she herself is waiting for me at the baggage claim area, holding a small white sign with my name on it.

"Mr. Temkin? I'm Lilith Wallingford," she says by way of introduction. She's pretty in an English-rose kind of way, in her thirties, I would guess, with long black hair that falls in curls down the back of her graceful neck and a pallid, almost ghostly white complexion that bears witness to the appalling lack of sun in this part of the world. Clearly dressed for comfort and not fashion, she is wrapped in a puffy coat slung carelessly over a hippie-esque long skirt, hardly looking like the spouse of a flamboyant icon whose Svengali-like talents once dominated the music charts. But she has an agreeable smile and an open, almost radiant face, and I am charmed immediately by her refreshing lack of guile.

"You look like hell," Lilith observes after giving me the once-over.

"Sorry," I say. "It's been a long night and I didn't have a chance to visit the spa before getting on the plane." Damn, why can't I stop this sarcastic blabbering *before* it leaves my lips?

She lets out a laugh—actually more like an impossibly cute giggle. "No, *I'm* the one who should be sorry," she says with a grin. "I don't know why I blurt out these things. My husband is always telling me I'm honest to a fault."

A woman after my own heart, I think. Hmmm, I could really get to like this Mrs. Wallingford, I decide improbably. *Come on, Bernie, you're here to do some serious work. Stop screwing around for once, willya?*

We make pleasant chit-chat as we wait for my bags to arrive. "So, how long have you known JTW?" I ask.

"Nearly twenty years, since I was a teenager." She blushes. "We'll have been married ten years next month," she replies wistfully, "though it sometimes seems a lot longer than that."

"I can imagine," I say, although I really can't. "It's got to be difficult seeing him deteriorate to the point where he has to be in a, you know, facility." *Loony bin* is what I really want to say, though even *mental hospital* seems too harsh.

"It is. I wish he were at home, of course. But the truth of the matter is that JTW hasn't really changed all that much. He's always been a bit crazy. Maybe that's why I fell in love with him in the first place." She smiles that soft, delicate smile at me again, melting my heart.

My last bag arrives just as I run out of small talk. It's just as well; I have no idea what I'm saying, anyway. I just wish this journey were over already.

"You look like you could use some sleep, Mr. Temkin. Come on, Ian's waiting out front in the car. You can nap on the way."

Ian, I presume, is Lilith's chauffeur, but I am wrong. Instead, he turns out to be an earnest young man sitting patiently in the driver's seat of a modest Opel parked in front of the terminal. As he takes my bags and places them carefully in the trunk, Lilith introduces Ian to me as "John's production assistant."

"I didn't realize JTW was doing any production work these days," I comment as we shake hands.

"Well, no, not so much these days," he admits as he climbs back behind the steering wheel, Lilith beside him, me given the full width of the rear seat to stretch out. "But up until a year ago, he was still tinkering in his home studio most days, recording local bands and the like."

"He has a home studio?" I ask.

"Yes, it's become all the rage, what with computers and everything. I designed his studio myself," he says proudly.

"John doesn't really understand the new technologies," Lilith explains, beaming at Ian. "That's where our chappie here comes in; he's a total whiz at those things, a real boffin."

From my vantage point behind them I see the back of Ian's neck begin to turn bright red. "Come on now, don't embarrass me," he laughs, patting Lilith affectionately on the hand as he does so. *Boffin, huh? I'll bet there's a little more boffin' going on here than meets the eye.*

I return my attention to the scenery passing by. It turns out that the mental hospital that JTW currently calls home is not, as Clive said, somewhere on the outskirts of London, but a good seventy-five miles away, in an Oxfordshire town charmingly called Chipping Norton. Without traffic, Ian smilingly informs me, we could make the trip in an hour and a half. However, given that there is never no traffic within a fifty mile radius of Heathrow, it is likely to take us more than three hours—ample time for a refreshing nap, as Lilith points out encouragingly.

Much as I would like to remain awake and soak up the English countryside—or at least the congested morass of urban sprawl that surrounds London like a constricting snake—I eventually succumb to the rhythm of stop-and-go traffic and start to doze off. *Who is Norton? I wonder blearily as my eyes begin to close. And why exactly is he chipping?* These are questions I intend to find the answers to as soon as I wake up.

Which I hope is a long, long time from now.

24

Transcript: Interview with Donnie Boyle, May 29, 1998

NO, NOT REALLY. What the hell, Bernie—when you feel like crap all the time, I guess it kind of becomes a way of life.

I think we left off last time talking about Schiffman's offer to fund the recording of a new album, right? It seemed like a godsend at first, but, as usual, there was a lot more going on beneath the surface than any of us realized at the time. Still, the prospect of getting back into a studio—and this time in sunny L.A.—lifted all of our spirits, even Cody's, to some extent. Sure, the guy was still in a serious funk, and still doing way too many drugs for his own good, but for the first time in months I could see signs of life in his clouded eyes, even if only for brief periods of time. I remember wandering into the music room one day and finding him hunched over his guitar, like he used to do back when we were kids. He was working out some kind of complicated chord sequence, and he was so deep in concentration that he didn't notice me standing there at first. But when he finally became aware of my presence, he got all flustered and embarrassed. That was a first. I had never known Cody to be self-conscious about his music, but there was no missing the deep blush that came to his cheeks.

"Sorry, Donnie," he stammered. "I just kind of got this idea and thought I'd try to get it down before I forgot it."

"No need to apologize, bro," I reassured him. "It's great to see you working again."

Cody looked up at me with a hurt expression, as if I'd somehow insulted him. "It's not as if I'm not trying, man," he muttered as he put his guitar down and headed for the door. A couple of hours later I found him nodding off in the kitchen, fucked up into oblivion. That's the way it was with Cody at that point in time: one day he was almost like his old creative self, the next, he was as out of it as a human being could possibly be.

The roller-coaster ride continued over the next few weeks as the band began rehearsing for the album. One evening Schiffman called with good news: he'd found digs for everybody in L.A. "It's just a short-term rental," he cautioned, "but it'll cover you and the guys for the time it will take to record the album, and for a little beyond. After that, you're on your own." Then he asked for the phone to be passed to Hinch.

I couldn't glean much from Hinch's end of the conversation: Mostly, he just seemed to be mumbling *yesses* and *I understands*, but when he hung up he had a broad grin on his face that invited interrogation.

"I don't mean to pry, but what's the big news?" I asked him. "You look like you just won first prize in a shit-eating contest."

"Almost as good," he said. "Alan's found a place in L.A. for me and Katie."

"I know—he just told me the same thing."

Hinch looked down at his feet as he shuffled uncomfortably. "Well, actually, I think he was talking to you about the house he'd rented for you and the rest of the guys."

"What do you mean? He told me he'd found digs for all of us."

"That's true," he replied awkwardly. "But he's found a place for Katie and me as well."

The truth began to dawn on me. "Are you saying you and Katie won't be living in the same house as the rest of us?"

Hinch shrugged his shoulders like a guilty teenager. "Come on, Donnie—we're married now. Things are different."

I was starting to get seriously pissed. "Different? How are they different? It's just a goddamn piece of paper, for chrissake."

"That's my damn wife you're talking about," he snapped at me. "I suggest you remember that. And I suggest you remember your place."

"My place? What the hell are you talking about? I thought we were in this thing together."

Now he began to calm down. "Well, yeah. We are. Okay. But, you know, I've still got to do what's best for me and Katie. I'm just saying …" With that, Hinch stalked out of the room, saying nothing. Like I said, he always hated confrontation. His way of doing things was to go around you, or behind your back—any path other than directly head on.

Clearly, the subject was closed for discussion as far as Hinch was concerned, so I called Schiffman back and wormed the truth out of him. Yes, he had found a short-term rental for me and the band and crew, but, yes, he had also found a separate place for Hinch and Katie, citing their need for privacy as a married couple.

"You know that's bullshit, Alan," I challenged. "We've been listening to their nightly screwing through the thin walls in this house for years now. It's gotten so I can almost tell what position they're in by the quality of their moaning."

"Maybe they're sick of you listening in, Donnie. Did you ever consider that?"

Well, no, I hadn't, I had to admit. But considering how closely we'd all been living out of each other's pockets for what seemed like a lifetime—and especially considering the intimate moments we'd all shared in motel rooms filled with groupies—it still seemed like false modesty to me. Defeated on moral grounds, I retreated to the more familiar turf of dollars and cents.

"What about how much this is going to cost us?" I argued. "Why should the band pay the rent on two houses instead of one?"

"It won't cost the band one thin dime extra," he explained. "The band will only be paying rent on their own place. Tommy will be paying his own mortgage."

My jaw dropped. "Mortgage? Are you telling me Hinch is buying a house? With what money?"

"Yes, he's buying his own house—a very nice two-bedroom cottage in Topanga. And why shouldn't he? He's a married man; he and Katie are talking about starting a family one day, as you well know."

"He may be a married man," I said, "but he doesn't have a pot to piss in. No one knows that better than you, Alan."

"That's true, Donnie, and, frankly, as the band's manager I think you should take some responsibility for that. But Schiffman Entertainment has already advanced him the down payment and has paid the first year's mortgage up front, so he's set for the time being. A year from now I expect the new album will be bringing in sufficient income to allow Tommy to pay me back—with interest. After that, he should be able to carry his own load."

Something deep inside caused me to continue to protest, even though I knew that the argument was already lost. "What about a little something called band unity?" I asked, lamely.

I heard a snort on the other end of the phone as Schiffman suppressed a belly laugh. "Overrated. Anyway, they'll only be living an hour or so away. They can get together any time they want to. From what I hear, I think it will be good for your boy Cody to perhaps see a little less of Hinch and his new bride."

That may have been a shot below the belt, but there was also a lot of truth to what he was saying. I sighed.

"Okay, Alan, I give."

"That's the spirit, Donnie. Look, whatever makes Hinch happy should be making you happy. That's the way I see things, anyway. Take my advice: you'd be better off if you also started viewing things that way."

I didn't want his advice. In fact, by this point, I didn't want anything from the guy except to leave us the hell alone. But we were now in debt to him up to our eyeballs, with even bigger bills to come, so there wasn't a damn thing I could do about it. Which, of course, was just the way Alan Schiffman liked things.

AFTER WHAT SEEMED like an never-ending series of delays and hiccups with the arrangements, we finally made our move to L.A. shortly before the Christmas of '76; I remember that clearly because it was so weird seeing lights and decorations in the balmy heat of southern California. I have a distinct memory of driving down the Hollywood Freeway behind a line of convertibles with their tops down, Christmas trees strapped into the back seat of every one of them. For an East Coast guy like me, that was real culture shock.

My shock carried over to the house—more correctly, hovel—that Schiffman had found for us to live in. Not only was it tiny and run-down, it was also situated near the heart of the Valley, half a block off the scummiest end of Van Nuys Boulevard. The area was strictly no-class: our neighbors consisted mostly of down-on-their-luck winos and illegal Mexican immigrants who loudly drank away every hard-earned penny they scraped together by mowing the lawns and cleaning the toilets of the rich white folks in the better parts of town. We soon learned that everyone in L.A. proper looked down their noses at people who lived in the Valley, and it became a real source of embarrassment whenever we met girls and tried to get them to come home with us: more than a few of them simply laughed in our faces.

Now Hinch, on the other hand, got to enjoy several well-manicured acres in the decidedly more upscale Topanga Canyon, surrounded by lemon trees and gentle, rolling hills. His neighbors were mostly starlets, all of whom were quite interested in the new arrival—an interest that was lustily reciprocated whenever Katie's back was turned, I'm quite sure. As the weeks went by and the garbage piled higher and higher on our unkempt front yard—courtesy of our equally unkempt neighbors—we all became more than a little resentful of the fact that Hinch was living a lifestyle that was far different from our own. When I tried to broach the subject with Schiffman, he threw his hands up in the air to signal that he had no intention of even listening to my complaints. "You want a better house in a better neighborhood, you go find one," he told me. "It took me months of searching to find the place you're in; if you want to go ahead and break the lease and get sued for your trouble, be my guest. Just leave me out of it."

I would have done just that if it weren't for the fact that we'd spent every penny we had on the cross-country move, and with nothing but weeks of rehearsing and recording ahead of us, there was no opportunity to go back out on the road and replenish our bank account any time soon. So we were stuck in our pathetic shithole, at least for the moment, and we just had to accept the fact that Hinch was getting special treatment. It wasn't the first time, and it certainly wouldn't be the last.

I may have hated Schiffman's guts, but I have to give credit where it's due: the studio he booked us into was primo—a lot nicer even than the place Wallingford brought us to. It was so luxurious and well-equipped, in fact, that I began thinking Cody might snap out of it if only just to take advantage of all the fancy doohickeys they had there, but it wasn't long before he started nodding out in the control room when he should have been taking charge of shaping the record. It was a real shame, because this time around he wouldn't have met any real resistance; the producer Schiffman had hired was an absolute pussycat compared to JTW. In fact, he was such a nonentity I can't even remember his name—just basically some geeky guy who had been an engineer for years and still was more interested in the settings of the knobs and dials than he was in the music being laid down. But he was competent enough, and I have to admit that the tracks we were recording sounded damn good right from the start.

And the vibe was pretty good, too; so confident was this producer in his ability to make just about anything sound great, he was amenable to pretty much anything anyone suggested. Which would have been great for Cody if he had been the least bit interested, but he wasn't.

We kept waiting for Cody to take control, but other than the occasional moment of lucidity when he would rouse himself to offer a comment or play a simple part, he mostly sat around nodding off like the stone cold junkie he had become. It was tough to witness, but none of us could afford to spend any more time trying to bring him back to life. The truth of the matter is that he had become excess baggage. It sounds cold and heartless, I know, but especially given the bad experience we'd had making our first album, we all knew our careers were on the line. Don't get me wrong: Cody was a friend and we all had sympathy for his situation, but there's only so much energy you can expend on someone who doesn't want your help.

Inevitably, as the work progressed and we got more and more focused, we began seeing less and less of Cody. Almost as soon as he'd arrive, he'd disappear into the studio lounge with the roadies, who'd be sitting around watching TV or shooting pool, waiting until they were needed to change a string or run an errand. I guess he just started feeling more comfortable around the crew than he did the musicians; he must have realized on some level how much he was letting us down. This way, he didn't have to face our disapproving stares ... plus he didn't have to watch Hinch and Katie holding hands or snuggling up on the control room sofa.

Schiffman also pretty much stayed away from the sessions during the recording process, but he did start dropping by with regularity once the mixing began, listening intently as each track was played for him in its nearly completed state.

"Smells like a hit to me, Donnie boy," he whispered to me one evening as we listened to a series of thunderous chords pouring out of the mammoth speakers mounted in the walls.

"Yeah, Alan, I have to admit it sounds good," I agreed. "But don't you think it's a little bland?"

"Bland?" He blinked at me uncomprehendingly.

"You know, unadventurous. Musically, that is."

Schiffman laughed. "Who gives a shit about adventurous? And for that matter, who gives a shit how good the album sounds? There's a much, much more important sound to focus on."

"Oh yeah?" I asked innocently. "What's that?"

"The sound of cash registers ringing," he replied. "Now that's music to *my* ears."

And indeed it was. Artistic considerations mean nothing to the Alan

Schiffmans of the world, as he was quite happy to tell anyone who would listen. The only sound that matters to them is the clinking of coins changing hands.

ALRIGHT, STOP MAKING such a fuss. It's just a bump on the noggin. No, I don't need any help getting up: just get that fucking machine out of my goddamn way. Look, I said I'm alright. Just give me a goddamn minute, will you? And stop treating me like a sick old man. I can't stand that shit. Let's get on with this thing, because, trust me, the story only gets better.

Now, weird as it was to see Cody hanging out with our roadies, what was even weirder was the way Joe Dan actually began bonding with one of them—a guy who went by the name Robbie the Mechanic. Robbie was, like JD and Vernon, a good ol' boy from south of the Mason/Dixon line—Temple, Texas, I believe, was his home town—and he'd gotten his nickname because of his knack for fixing things. That's a particularly useful trait for a roadie to have, and so Robbie kind of became our go-to guy whenever a fuse blew or a piece of drum hardware went awry. Since drummers by their very nature are good with their hands, that provided the basis for JD and Robbie to form a friendship. They each seemed a bit wary of the other at first, but when they discovered the things they had in common—mainly their Southern background and a mutual love of the rock 'n' roll life—they slowly became bosom buddies, to my amazement. Even Vernon started to warm to Robbie after awhile, and the three of them soon became inseparable. I found the whole thing very odd, especially given JD's hatred for roadies in general, and I have to say there was something about Robbie that just plain made me uncomfortable. He wasn't exactly shifty-eyed, but I just had this instinctive distrust for the guy.

Robbie was also unusual among our road crew in that he didn't just look like a biker but actually *was* one. He was totally into motorcycles of every stripe, and he didn't just fix them up, he rode them competitively. It therefore came as no surprise when the bug bit JD and Vernon too, and it wasn't long before they acquired a couple of beat-up Japanese junkers and began roaring home on them at all hours, scaring the crap out of all the little old ladies from Pasadena they encountered and pissing off our lowlife neighbors—something which, frankly, was fine with me.

Robbie's pride and joy was a gleaming Harley, which he stored in the back of our cramped garage and worked on incessantly. Enthralled, Joe Dan and Vernon would watch him for hours on end as he adjusted camshafts and tinkered with gear ratios. Soon they began badgering me for Harleys of their own.

"Come on, man, you know we're going to be rich rock 'n' roll stars once this album is out," JD and Vernon would moan. "All we're asking is for you to advance us a few grand of the band's stash so we can ride in style with our bro here."

"Look, the band has no money to advance you," I would explain truthfully. "Anyway, you both already have bikes."

"This piece of shit?" JD would respond derisively, kicking his banged-up Kawasaki. "This ain't no *real* bike, son. It's a fucking lawnmower on pep pills."

"Well, it's just going to have to do until we start gigging again … or until Schiffman and I can sell this album."

"Fuck you, Donnie," Vernon would say with a grin as he playfully flipped me the bird. "You ain't no fun anymore, you know that?"

It was irritating, but shit like that just goes with the territory. Managing a rock 'n' roll band isn't actually all that different than trying to teach kindergarten. You're constantly besieged with complaints and demands, accompanied by the sounds of nonstop whining, and the more you do to fulfill the children's needs, the more is demanded of you. Moments of peace are few and far between, and it always seems as if someone's pooped in their pants and needs their diapers changed. Somebody's always bawling, somebody's always tattling, everybody is jealous of the toys and goodies the others have, and no one ever offers up any thanks.

You're laughing, Bernie, but I swear it's all true.

Anyway, let me finish telling you how this little saga played out. Once the album was completed to everyone's satisfaction—not that we'll ever know what Cody thought, zoned out as he was at the time—Schiffman decided to throw a celebration party at his Beverly Hills mansion, catered by Chasen's. To nobody's surprise, Cody failed to show, but while Hinch and the Truckers were busy guzzling the free champagne and wolfing down ridiculous amounts of Beluga caviar, Schiffman ushered me into his ostentatious library for what he termed a "spontaneous strategy meeting." It soon became clear that this was about as spontaneous as the landing on Normandy Beach.

"What we need to make this project succeed, Donnie," Schiffman lectured me from behind his palatial desk, "is coordination and teamwork. As a vital member of the team, I'm counting on you to cover my flank."

I nearly gagged at the military reference. Alan Schiffman was the last person on earth you'd want to have on your flank if bullets were flying.

"What do you have in mind, Alan?" My radar was scanning for warning signals, although in retrospect it wasn't operating very well that day.

"It's very simple. All the big record labels have offices both here in L.A. and in New York. We need to strike while the iron is hot—while the buzz is out there—but being in two places at once is a feat even I can't pull off." He grinned as if he'd just said something incredibly clever.

"Well, of course you can't," I replied evenly. He sat there looking at me as if he expected more of a response. I stared back at him blankly; damned if I was going to play his game.

"That's where you come in, Donnie," he continued. "Now's the time for you to shine in the eyes of your artiste"—yes, he actually said "artiste," complete with an exaggerated 'e' on the end. "Time to earn your fifteen percent."

I bristled. *I've earned every penny I've made with this band, you son of a bitch. In fact, I should get extra aggravation pay for dealing with pricks like you.*

He noticed the darkening expression on my face. "No need to take offense, Donnie—I'm only joking." He examined the cuticle of one carefully manicured finger, pretending to be nonchalant. "Here's what I propose: a simple sharing of the labor as we shop the new album. I'll take meetings with all the label heads here in L.A., you huddle with the A&R people and VPs back in New York."

It was true that Schiffman golfed regularly with most of the record company honchos in town, while I barely knew any of them. I had, however, established tenuous relationships with many of the second-tier guys in New York, if only because I'd been pestering them so much throughout the years.

Still, I was resistant to the idea, if only on financial grounds. "It could take quite a while to see everyone in New York there is to see," I countered, "and an extended trip is likely to run into lots of money—money we don't have."

"I don't think it will take all that long, actually. Look, I'll have Janet make all the necessary calls, and if you're worried about finances, you can stay in the apartment Schiffman Entertainment maintains in Manhattan."

Up until that time, I didn't know that they kept an apartment there, but it made sense, given the lecherous agent's proclivity for hosting orgies. And I have to admit that my loins tingled a bit at the possibility of perhaps reviving my friends-with-benefits status with JJ in what I imagined was an opulent love-nest.

Still, I wasn't sure about the wisdom of my making the trip, especially while the band was in a state of limbo, and particularly with Cody in such bad shape. Of course, when I expressed my misgivings, Schiffman had an answer at the ready.

"Donnie, this band is at a critical juncture; what happens in the next month or two could well make or break their career. It's your duty as their manager to do whatever's necessary, and I think you can do them a lot more good in New York than you can by staying here. And don't forget, it's me who's out all this money. You owe it to me—and to them—to do everything you can to sell this album."

As usual, I couldn't argue with his logic. Why then was my heart so full of doubt? Once again, I let my brain overrule my gut. *Maybe he's right*, I thought. *The guy has put his money where his mouth is, to the tune of tens of thousands of dollars; maybe he's just anxious to get a return on his investment.* Splitting the labor between the two coasts made sense, and it was clearly the most efficient way to canvass the record companies and try to spark a bidding war. This was, after all, a once in a lifetime opportunity—our second chance in an industry that was renowned for giving no second chances. If the strategy worked, we'd be set for the rest of our lives. If it failed, we'd be no worse off than we were now.

Or so it seemed.

I would soon find out how completely and utterly wrong I was.

25

Charlbury Manor Hospital is a pretty inviting place, for an insane asylum. From its majestic iron gates to the leafy country lane that winds its way to the main complex, the prevailing feeling is: *Welcome. Glad you're here. Pull up a seat and stay awhile.*

Which most patients do, apparently. According to Lilith, who turns out to be a walking encyclopedia of information about the stately institution, the average length of stay here is a tantalizing 8.6 years. Whether that means the staff and administration are especially good or especially bad at what they do, I can't decide. But I suppose if you've got to be in a loony bin, this is probably as good as it gets.

Substance-Induced Persisting Dementia brought on by decades of drug abuse, Lilith had informed me as we neared the facility, was the official diagnosis. There was no clinical sign of Alzheimer's yet, but the symptoms were similar and the doctors believed it was only a matter of time before Wallingford descended behind that impenetrable wall. Like most mental patients, he had good days and bad; up until about a year ago, the good days predominated and Lilith and Ian had been able to keep JTW on a relatively even keel at home, with the help of powerful psychotropic medications. But Wallingford had taken a distinct turn for the worse in recent months and had begun experiencing megalomaniacal episodes in which he not only believed he had super-powers but no need of basic human functions such as eating and toileting. Exacerbating matters was his deep-seated alcoholism, which had evolved into periods of frightful binge drinking—fifths of vodka, chased down by carafes of brandy. Ultimately, Lilith had been forced to make the painful decision to commit her husband to Charlbury, where, based upon the medical staff's gloomy prognosis, she fully expected he would spend the rest of his life.

"Still, having said all that," she informed me with a brave smile, "I think you'll be in luck in terms of your interview. I phoned ahead while you were snoozing in the car, and the nurse on duty said JTW is actually having a pretty good day today."

I'm not entirely sure what that means, but I uncharacteristically decide to make the best of the situation, whatever the situation might be. Frankly, I've got more important things on my mind; this pit stop is more by way of thanking Clive for his forbearance than anything. Based on everything Lilith's telling me, I don't have much hope that the once formidable producer will be able to shed any new light on Hinch, anyway.

As the three of us wait in the reception area for clearance to enter, I notice long, meaningful gazes being exchanged between Lilith and her husband's erstwhile assistant. There is little doubt in my mind that they are lovers, but there seems to be a deeper connection between them than sex alone would account for. I am somewhere between profound contemplation and fatigue-induced catatonia when a buzzer goes off, rudely snapping me back to reality.

Startled, I turn to Lilith.

"Don't mind that; it's just their way of issuing a general alert when a patient is running amok and needs to be caught in the butterfly net," she informs me, poker-faced.

"Really?" I ask, wide-eyed and now thoroughly awake.

"No, I'm having you on; they're just buzzing us through to the ward. God, you Americans are so gullible." Laughingly, she hooks her arm through mine and escorts me through the swinging doors and down a long corridor, Ian padding silently behind us.

Determined as I am to keep my eyes straight ahead, I can't help but notice some of the human misery occupying my peripheral vision. To our right, a group of elderly women in wheelchairs, moaning like Macbeth's witches in a rising and falling chorus of inharmonious discord. To our left, a bald-headed man with thick glasses babbling nonsense to himself as he shuffles from one foot to the next, back and forth, going nowhere, a study in perpetual motion. Ahead, a disheveled middle-aged lady skipping along as if she were a schoolgirl in a meadow, a trail of urine following in her wake as it streams from beneath her soaked nightdress. Everywhere, clamor: Nurses and aides hustling from one crisis to the next, doors flying open and slamming shut, shrieks of pain followed by whoops of glee, all intermingled into a cacophony of the deranged and the demented.

And there, at the end of the hallway, an oasis of serenity: John Thomas Wallingford himself.

IT'S HARD AT FIRST to reconcile the slightly stooped gentleman standing before me with the photographs of JTW I've seen before. Of course, they were all taken in the full flowering of his youth a quarter of a century previously, when he was at the height of his fame and creative abilities. Now all I see is a baffled—no, thoroughly confused—wispy-haired old codger who looks as though he's spent his entire life as an accountant, hunched over a desk entering numbers in a ledger.

"JTW! How are you, darling?" cries Lilith.

JTW looks bewildered—his normal facial expression, I soon discover.

"Pardon me?" he asks politely. "Do I know you?"

Lilith lets out one of her huge guffaws. "Know me?" she repeats gleefully. "I'm your wife, sweetie. You see me practically every day, remember?"

A look of recognition begins to wash over his face. "Oh, yes, of course, of course. Lilith, right? How could I be so daft?"

They hug perfunctorily. "And who are these chappies?" he asks, turning to Ian and me.

Lilith laughs again. "Come on, JTW—I'm sure you remember Ian, your assistant. This other fellow is Bernie Temkin, the American reporter from *Rolling Stone* I told you about."

For the first time Wallingford's features come to life. Now thoroughly animated, he begins to pump my hand vigorously. "So nice to meet you, so good to know you," he chants over and over again as he does his best to dislocate my shoulder. Finally he breaks the spell with a quizzical, "To what do I owe this pleasure?"

"The pleasure is all mine, sir," I reply with forced politeness. "I'm here to do an interview with you. About the old days."

"The old days, of course, of course," he fairly booms. "Come on into my private office and let's have a drink."

I look over at Lilith, who winks at me approvingly. "Good idea, darling," she tells JTW. "You and Bernie go have a drink and a nice chat. We'll leave you to it. Just let the staff know when you're done and we'll come and fetch Mr. Temkin."

"Jolly good," he says. "See you later. By-ee." As Lilith and Ian retreat back down the corridor, he waves like a five-year old saying goodbye to his mother on the first day of kindergarten. *What the hell have I gotten myself into?* I ask myself silently as they disappear through the ward door.

"Now then, my good man," JTW says, returning his attention to me. "What did you say your name was again?"

"Bernie. Bernie Temkin."

"I'll call you Bootsie if you don't mind. Like Bootsie Collins, my old friend from Supertramp. Alright?"

"Sure," I reply, having made the decision that informing him that Bootsie Collins was never in Supertramp is probably a very bad idea.

"Excellent! Now then, Bootsie, let's go have that drink." With a courtly bow, he ushers me into his 'office'—actually a small dormitory-like room furnished with a narrow bed, a chest of drawers, a small writing desk, and a single plastic chair. The desktop is cluttered with CDs, records, tapes and all manner of music-related ephemera. A dozen gold records are hanging on the wall, surrounded by twenty or so framed photographs showing JTW mingling with the rock elite of the '60s and '70s.

"Here I am with John Lennon," he says proudly, pointing to a picture of himself with his arm slung around an unsmiling Eric Clapton. "I discovered the Beatles, you know. Produced their first three records before handing them off to Brian Epstein."

I nod dumbly, wondering what George Martin might have to say about that. I am careful, however, to keep from correcting him: A dose of reality, I suspect, is the last thing this guy needs.

He continues his guided tour. "This is me and Mick Jagger, hanging out backstage at a Stones gig," he says, indicating a faded Polaroid of a hungover Stevie Nicks lounging on a poolside chaise. "And here I am with Bowie." Amazingly, he is absolutely correct about that one. Next, he points to a photo of himself with Elton John. "This is a great shot of me and Reg, taken a few months before he was assassinated, poor bugger." *Well, at least he got the name right*, I think, recalling from my limited repository of rock trivia that the still very much alive star's real name is Reginald Dwight. The deluded producer wraps things up by pointing to a picture of the real Bootsie Collins and identifying the black bass player as Marianne Faithfull "in her younger days." I feel as if I am Alice fallen down a hole, in the presence of the Mad Hatter.

Then the jackpot: a snapshot of Wallingford intently manipulating the controls of a mixing console as a youthful Hinch stands off to one side, watching bemusedly. I think I can spot an out-of-focus Donnie Boyle hovering in the background.

"This one I know," I say brightly. "That's you with Hinch, right?"

"Hinch?" Wallingford looks at me blankly. It's as if a switch has been thrown and the lights have gone completely out.

"You know, Tommy Hinchton, the rock star. I'm writing a book about him."

A long pause while JTW continues to search my face for a clue. "Sorry, old chap," he finally says. "I have no idea who you're talking about. Who are you again?"

"I'm Bernie ... no, Bootsie. The reporter from *Rolling Stone*, remember?"

The switch is thrown once more. "Bootsie! How the hell have you been, you old reprobate?" he booms. "Come on, let's have that drink."

The "drink," as it turns out, is white grape juice poured from a brandy bottle—a time-tested strategy for keeping alcoholic patients calm, I am later to learn. "Delicious!" I exclaim as I drain the proffered glass. "A vintage, I presume?"

"Of course, dear boy, of course." He examines the bottle closely. "1962, I believe. The year I had my first hit with Madonna."

Yes, when she was four. "You sure did make some great records with her back in the '60s," I declare with every ounce of enthusiasm I can muster. " 'Like A Virgin,' wasn't that your first big hit with her?"

"A virgin? My good man, the girl was wife to Jesus. Virgin, indeed." He harrumphs softly to himself several times as he helps himself to a second tumbler of grape juice.

Will this interview never end? I think. *In fact, will it ever start?*

"So, um, JTW," I say, clearing my throat. "Do you mind if we begin?"

"Certainly, dear boy, certainly. Ask away. Any questions you like." He sits down on the edge of his unmade bed and beams up at me expectantly.

"Well, let's start with what you've been doing the last ten years or so," I say uncertainly.

"Why, I've been going mad," he replies nonchalantly. "I would have thought that much was obvious."

I'm taken aback by his candor, and it shows on my face. Suddenly he bursts out into laughter.

"My god, for a moment there I really had you!" he cackles, slapping his thigh for emphasis. Almost instantaneously his mood changes and he confides in a conspiratorial tone, "They said the same about Syd, you know. Poor boy."

"Syd Barrett?" Having been a Pink Floyd fan in my youth, I'm familiar with the tale of the schizophrenic guitarist who snapped from one dose of LSD too many.

"One and the same. I produced his last eight solo albums, you know."

I nod gravely, choosing to ignore the fact that Barrett only ever recorded two solo albums, neither of them with Wallingford at the helm. "I understand you have a home studio, equipped with the very latest in computer equipment," I say, trying my best to steer him into an area in which he might be at least slightly coherent.

"I do, indeed," he crows, puffing his chest out proudly. "Marvelous what you can do these days with computers. Of course, I don't know a thing about them. I leave all that up to my assistant—Ian, I believe his name is. He's responsible for the technicalities; I provide the inspiration."

At last, something sensible. "And what sort of projects have you and Ian done in your studio?" I ask naively.

"All sorts, old chap, all sorts. The new Jimi Hendrix album, for one thing. Otis Redding. Sam Cooke. Janis Joplin. You name it, we've done it."

But they're all dead, I want to scream. *Kind of like you from the neck up.*

"So tell me, my dear American friend, what is it that brings you to England?" he suddenly blurts out, changing the subject for what seems like the tenth time in the last three minutes.

I sigh. The truth will obviously make as little sense to his confused brain as any cover story, so I decide to level with him. "Actually, apart from the interview I'm meant to be doing with you, I'm here to attend a gig Hinch is supposed to be playing in London at the end of the week. Only he's gone missing. I'm hoping to find him up in Scotland, which is where I'm headed this evening."

"What, up at Peggy McFarlane's place?"

I am dumbfounded. For all of the madness I've witnessed this afternoon, this is the craziest thing yet.

"You know Peggy McFarlane?"

"Of course I do, dear boy. Doesn't everyone?"

It's really starting to piss me off that apparently the entire known universe is familiar with this person, outside of me. "Are we talking about Peggy McFarlane, the addiction therapist?" I ask tentatively.

"Why, certainly. How many other Peggy McFarlanes are there? She's a great friend of mine."

Like Madonna? I wonder. Still, I plow on.

"Seriously, are we talking about the same person?"

"Look, Bernie, or Bootsie, or whatever it is you want me to call you, I don't know who you might be referring to, but I am talking about Dr. Margaret McFarlane of the famed McFarlane Clinic. She's treated me for heroin addiction several times. Wonderful woman, salt of the earth."

Several times? Tempted as I am to pose the question, "Did it work?" I restrain the impulse. Instead, I simply say, "Would you happen to remember where her clinic is located? I've had a bit of trouble finding out exactly where it is."

"No problem, dear boy. She's about an hour west of Edinburgh—off the causeway in Torryburn, as I recall. Hand me a piece of paper and I'll write down the address and phone number for you."

"You know the phone number too?"

"Of course. Know it better than my own, in fact."

He scribbles something down on a scrap of paper and hands it to me. I'm half expecting an autograph of Mickey Mouse, but sure enough it looks like a legitimate address and phone number. I thank him profusely and place the folded paper carefully in my pocket.

"Now, then, is there anything else I can do for you?" he asks cheerfully, looking very pleased with himself.

I decide there and then to abandon the interview: Lilith can provide me with all the background information I need to write the *Rolling Stone* piece anyway. We appear to be in one of those brief windows of lucidity that I have been told Wallingford slips in and out of, and I am determined to take advantage of that.

"Can you share with me any memories of working with Tommy Hinchton?" I ask hopefully.

He looks thoughtful. "Hinch. Hmmm. His band was named, let's see, Hinch Reload, was it?"

"Yes, that's right."

"Noteworthy Records, 1974. I was hired by Joe Finnerty, God rest his soul."

"Exactly."

"The studio was, let me see, Hit Factory in New York."

I'm getting a tingly feeling all over. "Precisely."

"Sixteen tracks, Dolby A. The engineer was Jim Mulcahy. Blond hair, short, rather dumpy chap with a bit of a speech impediment. Pleasant enough fellow, but couldn't dial in a drum sound worth a damn."

"This is great!" I exclaim, about to burst with excitement. "But tell me, what do you remember about Hinch himself? About his band? About the music?"

Leaning back onto his bed, John Thomas Wallingford scratches his chin, then his forehead, then his left elbow, before turning his attention to a spot of lint on the blanket which he carefully removes before making his final pronouncement.

"Sorry," he finally says. "Can't remember a thing."

Can this really be happening to me? I feel like Bud Abbott to Lou Costello, Zeppo to Groucho, Moe to Curly. I stare at the producer wide-eyed. Is this madman simply toying with me?

"Honestly, I don't recall anything at all about those sessions," he repeats, reacting, I suppose, to the look of chagrin spreading over my face. "But if you like, I can tell you how I introduced Bono to Yoko."

The window is apparently closing rapidly. I decide to roll the dice one last time.

"Can you at least tell me where the tapes are? I'd love to hear them sometime."

"Tapes?"

"Of the Hinch recordings. You took them away to complete them, but the album was never released."

"Oh, *those* tapes. Well, yes, I was working on them for quite some time. But they've disappeared, I'm afraid."

"Disappeared?"

"Yes, dear boy. There was a break-in. At my studio. A couple of months ago, I believe. Lilith and Ian can tell you all about it. Personally, I'd prefer to discuss the album I made with Dylan and his musicians up in Woodstock. To keep the sessions running smoothly, the engineer and I snuck laxatives into everyone's coffee. We came up with a great title for it, too: *Band on the Run.*"

The window has slammed shut. Behind its pane of opacity the madman explodes in torrents of unbridled laughter. As gracefully as I can, I extricate myself from the web of confusion spun around me. *All in all, just another brick in the wall,* I think as I ring the bedside bell to summon a hulking psychiatric aide. Time to return to reality.

Or what passes for it these days.

"Was there really a break-in?" I ask Lilith as we drive back. The sun went down hours ago—jeez, I can't believe how early it gets dark in England this time of year—and Ian's already searched the World Wide

Web on his ever-present laptop and discovered that there's no chance of my making the last flight out of Heathrow to Edinburgh, hence Lilith's kind offer to put me up for the evening.

"Yes, there was, and it came as quite a surprise to us. Chipping Norton's not exactly a hotbed of crime."

"Not much to rob around here except the sheep and pigs," adds Ian.

From what I can see as we thread our way along the narrow country roads, he's right: nothing but farmland stretching in every direction.

"What was stolen?"

"Just some of John's old tapes," Lilith replies. "Although I have no idea what anyone would want with those things. They've just been sitting on a shelf gathering dust for the last twenty years."

"Do you know which tapes, specifically?"

Ian pipes up. "That's the thing that's really baffling, because JTW's got all sorts of valuable master tapes lying around, of albums that sold millions of copies. But these were just from some obscure sessions he did back in the '70s—a project that never even got released."

"Let me guess," I say. "They were for a band named Hinch Reload."

"Yeah, I think you're right. Sounds vaguely familiar, anyway. I'll check the logs when we get back to the house."

Given the zillions of record sales Wallingford has been at least partially responsible for over the years, I'm expecting a mansion on the order of Hinch's palace in St. Moritz, but we instead pull up to a modest farmhouse in what appears to be the middle of nowhere. Leave it to the ever-observant Lilith to spot the look of disappointment passing over my face.

"We're quite comfortable here, you know," she says softly as we exit the car.

"Of course," I mumble. "I'm sorry if I appear impolite. I guess I just was expecting something, er, larger."

"John is a brilliant producer," she explains, "but he always was a lousy businessman."

So it's not just the musicians who fall prey to the sharks. I'd always assumed that producers were part of the predatory class—like managers, agents, and record company executives—but gazing around my ramshackle surroundings, I can see how wrong I was, at least in this particular case.

Lilith disappears into the kitchen to get dinner started while Ian offers to give me a tour of the house. He turns out to be quite an affable young man who is clearly devoted to both his employer and employer's wife.

"They're pretty amazing people," he tells me as he slides open the glass door leading to Wallingford's home studio. "I can't believe how lucky I was to land this job. JTW is—or at least was—one of the most brilliant record producers in the world, and Lilith is ... well, just an incredible woman." Through the dim light I can see him blushing slightly.

"How did you meet them?" I ask.

"JTW did a talk at the recording school I was attending in London a couple of years ago, and we just kind of hit it off. When he asked me if I might be interested in working as his assistant, I jumped at the chance."

Like a true propeller-head, he begins pointing out the studio's many high-tech features. Most of it goes completely over my head, though I am impressed by the mountain of equipment arrayed around us. Dominating the center of the room is a large mixing console, atop which sits a massive computer monitor. "We've got the very latest Pro Tools recording system," Ian is babbling, "which gives us almost unlimited tracking capabilities, plus full mix automation." I nod my head sagely, though I barely understand a word he is saying.

When he pauses to take a breath, I remind him that he was going to check the tape log, whatever that is. "Sorry," he says. "I tend to get carried away. It's here, in JTW's tape library."

I follow him through another doorway and we enter a large connecting room. Metal shelving up to the ceiling surrounds us on all sides, filled with hundreds of tape boxes. Every one of them, Ian points out proudly, has been carefully labeled with the name of the artist, the date of the session, and other relevant technical information—clear testimony to his organizational skills. I notice with some amazement that they have been painstakingly arranged in alphabetical order, too.

"What the hell do you do with all these things?"

"Well, for the past year or so I've been digitizing them—transferring them to computer—before they deteriorate to the point where they become unplayable. Some of these tapes arrived here in pretty bad shape; JTW wasn't especially good about storing them properly before I came along." He reaches up to a shelf and pulls down a thick black looseleaf. "This is the log I was telling you about," Ian explains. "It contains information about all these tapes." He begins turning pages, studying each one as intently as if it contained the secret to life.

"Okay, here it is," he says after a moment or two. "Hinch Reload. Twenty-six tapes: nineteen multitrack masters, seven mix reels. Recorded back in 1974...."

"... Hit Factory, New York, engineer Jim Mulcahy," I finish.

Ian looks at me. "JTW remembered that?"

"He did."

"Amazing, isn't it, how the human mind still functions, even when it's...." Ian lets the words trail off. "Anyway, yes, those are the tapes that are missing. The only ones, too, which is really weird."

"Any idea who might have taken them?"

"None whatsoever. The police came up completely empty-handed: the lock to the house was picked cleanly, and there were no fingerprints, no evidence of any kind. The only conclusion they could come to was that it was professionals."

"Professionals?"

"Yes, either professional burglars ... or MI5. That's JTW's theory, anyway."

He's smiling broadly, though after all I've been through this past few days, I wouldn't doubt it. But before I have a chance to fully digest the information, Lilith announces that dinner is ready, giving me an opportunity to instead digest the first home-cooked meal I've had in weeks.

THE THREE OF US eat mostly in silence. Lilith has dimmed the lights and lit candles, and every now and then she and Ian exchange looks amidst the flickering shadows, similar to the ones I noticed in the reception area at Charlbury. After we finish, Ian gallantly offers to clear up, leaving Lilith and me to chat by the fireplace in the tiny front room.

I begin by showing her the piece of paper Wallingford had given me.

"Yes, that's Peggy McFarlane's address and phone number," Lilith confirms. "You don't strike me as someone who is in need of her professional services," she adds with a gleam in her eye, "but if you like, I'll be glad to call ahead and vouch for you. I don't think she takes new patients without referrals."

"Much as I appreciate the offer," I tell her, "I think I'd prefer to drop by unannounced. And the purpose of the visit is not professional, if you must know; I'm just hoping to get information about someone who I think may be a client of hers."

"Good luck with that. I think discretion is very much her byword."

"I've heard the same. But I think I need to give it a shot anyway."

She looks at me with slight concern, but is careful not to pry. Every moment I spend with her, I like this woman more and more.

"So, did you get everything you needed today?" she asks politely. "The interview, I mean."

"Well, John—JTW—was certainly welcoming. Though perhaps his memory isn't all it could be."

Lilith laughs heartily at my understatement. "JTW's memory wasn't all that good the day I met him, to be honest. It's not one of his strong points."

"What are his strong points?" I ask, perhaps a little too directly.

She pauses and considers the question. "He's a brilliant man who is generous to a fault," she finally says. "He's also capable of being enormously kind and caring. Yes, he's also a womanizer and an alcoholic and a drug abuser, but, what the hell, you can't have everything, can you? I mean, where would you put it all?"

We both giggle like schoolchildren sharing a secret. God, I love this woman's sense of humor. For the next hour, she regales me with stories about JTW's upbringing and childhood, followed by uproarious tales of his entanglements, musical and otherwise, with the rich and the fabulous. So vivid is her storytelling that it never once occurs to me to pull out my tape recorder and treat this as a formal interview. There isn't a single doubt in my mind that I will remember every word she is telling me—indeed, every glorious moment of this glorious night—long after the final embers of the fire before us glow into nothingness.

At the stroke of midnight we drain our wineglasses and clink them together in a silent toast. She bids me good night and begins to make her way upstairs to the master bedroom, where Ian awaits. Just before reaching the door she turns to me with infinite sadness in her eyes and says, simply, "I love him, you know."

In that moment, I do know. Who I am to judge, after all? We're all entitled to love in this world, I decide.

Wherever we can find it.

26

Transcript: Interview with Donnie Boyle, May 30, 1998

IN THE TWINKLING of an eye, everything changed. Taking that trip to New York was the biggest mistake of my goddamned life. It's the one regret I'll carry to my grave. And I have no hope of atoning for it, no excuse other than goddam fucking stupidity.

You see, once Schiffman had me out of the way, he was able to make all the final moves in his sick chess game, unchallenged. Bishop to king's rook four, check. Knight to queen six, check. Rook to king three, checkmate.

Schiffman never had any intention of sharing the workload, or anything else with me. The whole trip was a ploy. I wasn't able to get a single meeting with the New York record company executives, other than a couple of pointless lunches with low-level A&R guys who didn't have the power to wipe their own asses, much less make a deal. JJ—who I'm convinced never knew that she was being used, any more than I did—would dutifully get on the phone every morning and talk to every perky secretary of every honcho in town, only to be told that so-and-so was on another call, or had just stepped out, or was on a foraging trip to Antarctica. Anything to avoid actually doing their job. Frankly, the results were no better than I would have gotten if I'd stayed behind in L.A. to look after the guys and made the calls long-distance.

She and I didn't even end up in bed. I discovered that our little nymphomaniac had developed a proclivity for genuine rock stars with oversized genitalia, and let's just say that I didn't qualify on either count. Worse yet, she insisted on confiding in me, telling me in graphic detail about her latest conquests and inability to walk straight for days afterwards, to my genuine embarrassment. Sweet girl, but a total perv. Maybe that's what I liked so much about her.

I was doubly frustrated at the lack of news I was getting from L.A. Schiffman, of course, rarely if ever returned my calls, but that was par for the course—I was used to that. The bigger problem was that, with the album completed, the guys in the band had scattered to the four winds and were largely unreachable. Hinch and Katie had headed south to Cancun to enjoy a belated honeymoon. The Trucker brothers, accompanied by Robbie The Mechanic, were off at some motocross in the desert. Only Cody stayed behind at the house, minded by Hank and the other roadies, none of whom I trusted worth a damn. Most of the time there was no answer when I called; on occasion Hank would pick up and report that Cody was either sleeping or "unavailable." On the few times he put Cody on the phone, our conversation was brief and pointless:

Me (to Cody): "What's shaking, bro?"

Cody (sleepily): "Nothing, man, just hanging."

Long pause.

Me: "Are you looking after yourself? Writing any new songs? Getting enough exercise?"

Cody (sleepier): "Nothing, man. Just hanging. Just going with the flow."

Longer pause.

It was a total exercise in futility, and I was getting pretty antsy about what was going on in my absence. After some three weeks in limbo, I'd had enough. I was just about to pack my bags and book a flight back to L.A. when Schiffman called.

"Donnie? Great news. We've got a deal. Major label, multi-year, five albums with an option for a sixth." Despite the big news he was trumpeting, his voice sounded cold, the sentences oddly clipped.

"Nice to hear from you, too, Alan," I said sarcastically.

"Yeah, well, I've been kind of busy at this end. JJ tells me your appointments didn't go so well," he added in a smarmy tone that made me want to smash his face in.

"You heard right. Anyway, I'm on my way home."

"Good. We have a lot to talk about." I was about to agree, but he hung up so abruptly I found myself talking to a dial tone.

I couldn't shake a sense of dread about what awaited me upon my return. As it turned out, I was wrong. Things were actually way worse than I imagined.

THE NEXT MORNING, I jumped on the first flight back to L.A. I was fed up with all the manipulative games and lack of communication, and had decided to head to Schiffman's office straight from the airport. *Time to have it out once and for all*, I thought as I fidgeted in the cab. *Either this prick understands his role or he's fired.*

True to form, the bastard kept me cooling my heels in the reception area for more than an hour—the oldest trick in the book, invented by insecure assholes trying to assert their authority. I was determined not to let it faze me, though. This time I was planning on letting Alan Schiffman know exactly what I thought of him.

Finally, I was ushered into his office. He had company with him. Bad company.

"Donnie," Schiffman said from behind his fortress of a desk, "before we begin, I'd like you to meet two of my business associates, Luigi and Salvatore Antucci." He gestured to the two behemoths flanking him on either side—Frick and Frack in identical sunglasses and pinky rings. Both wore matching outfits, too: hand-tailored jackets draped over cashmere polo-neck sweaters, slacks pressed to a knife-edge, shoes so shined you could see your scared face in them. Neither of them said a word, nor did they offer so much as a nod in my direction. They were clearly there to intimidate, and I got the message loud and clear.

"Why the muscle, Alan? You don't seriously think I'm going to take a swing at you, do you?"

Schiffman laughed nervously. "No, of course not. Though I'm guessing you won't be altogether pleased about what I have to tell you, either. Louie and Sal are just here to keep the peace. Things have to be done in an orderly fashion, you know."

"Things?" I said. "What things?"

He cleared his throat. "Well, Donnie, I told you some time ago that we were going to do things differently. I've decided that incremental changes are simply not going to be sufficient to move Hinch's career forward. As a result, I've made some rather significant changes. Vital changes, you might say. After all, we are all here to serve Hinch's best interests."

"I thought we were here to serve the *band's* best interests," I replied. "Of which Hinch is just a single member."

For a moment he looked confused. "Band? Oh, you're talking about Hinch Reload. Stupid name, don't you think? One of Cody's ideas no doubt."

I glared at him, lips pursed.

"No matter," he continued. "Because there is no band any more."

"What the fuck are you talking about?" I yelled, starting to rise from my seat, fists at the ready. Frick and Frack each took a step toward me, hands simultaneously reaching for their breast pockets.

"Sit down, Donnie, and shut up." There it was—that same icy edge I'd heard in Schiffman's voice during the previous night's phone call. "You're here to listen, not talk. When I'm done telling you what I have to tell you, you can get up and leave. Not before."

What the fuck is this? I remember thinking. *Am I an extra in a* Godfather *movie?* I slowly sank back down into my chair, fists still clenched tightly.

"Now, as I started to say, everything I'm doing is because it's in Tommy's best interest, not because I have a grudge against you or anyone else in his circle of friends. As a matter of fact, both he and I are extremely grateful for everything you have done to advance his career thus far."

This was typical of Schiffman's brand of bullshit. Who the fuck did he think he was, patronizing me like that? And who the fuck gave him the right to speak for Hinch? I made up my mind there and then that no matter what he had to say to me, Schiffman was out, record deal or no record deal. I knew Cody would back me on that, and the Truckers too, none of whom liked Schiffman any more than I did. And I still felt that when all was said and done, Hinch would stand with us as well.

Stupid me.

But for the moment I bided my time, saying nothing. Schiffman stared at me curiously. "You don't believe me; I can see that," he said. "No matter. You and I are well past the point of blowing smoke up each other's asses, anyway. So here's the story in a nutshell. There is no more band. Hinch is now a solo act, signed to Warner Brothers Records as their exclusive artist."

"Bullshit," I blurted out. "He couldn't have signed any goddamned contract without his manager's approval."

"Oh, but he *did* have his manager's approval," Schiffman assured me with the faintest hint of a smile. "That's because you are no longer his manager. I am."

I was stunned, but more than that I was furious at myself for not seeing this coming. "No way," I protested. "There's no way Hinch would walk away from me, or Cody, or the rest of the band. He may be an egotistical asshole, but he wouldn't fuck us over that way...." As the words tailed off, I found even myself not believing them.

"Is that so?" Schiffman replied calmly. "I don't think you realize what a pragmatist your boy is. In fact, I don't think you know him nearly as well as you think you do."

For a moment we both sat there in silence.

"I'll fight you on this, Alan."

He snorted derisively. "Fight me? With your limited resources? Don't make me laugh. Are you prepared to fund long-term litigation against the army of lawyers Schiffman Entertainment and Warner Brothers Records have on retainer? Are you prepared to show a judge a legally binding contract naming yourself as Tommy Hinchton's manager? We both know that no such document exists."

He was right. The band and I had been operating on a handshake agreement for years. I trusted them to do the right thing. *Trust*: the one word that has no meaning in the entertainment business.

"I think you should take a deep breath and calm down," Schiffman continued. "This is a done deal, and there's nothing you, or anyone else, can do about it." He spread out a hefty sheaf of papers on the desk and pushed them in my direction. "Here, take a look for yourself. I think you'll find everything quite legal and above board."

I didn't have to see his goddamn papers: With all the expensive shysters he had in his back pocket, there was no way they would have been anything less than airtight. But there had to be a reason why all this was happening. I sat there helplessly for a moment or two, trying to decide what to say.

"Look, Donnie," Schiffman said, interrupting my train of thought, "even though you're out as Tommy's manager, that doesn't mean you're out altogether. Hinch wants me to make sure his friends are taken care of, even though, quite frankly, I urged him to make a clean break. We'd like you to continue in a new role, as road manager, organizing the day-to-day logistics while Hinch is on tour, collecting the box office receipts, things like that. It's something you're good at and something you've got a lot of experience doing. Hinch and I are prepared to offer you a good salary and a yearly contract, so you'll have job security and be well compensated. Frankly, I think you'll serve Tommy much better in that capacity."

Road manager? I was being demoted to road manager and being put on salary instead of commission? It was almost too much to take in.

Schiffman looked at me expectantly, awaiting my response.

"I want to talk to Hinch," I finally told him.

"Ah, yes, I thought you might say that, so I've arranged for a call to be placed to Cancun, and I'll put you on the line shortly. But first we have a little more business to discuss."

There's more? I thought. *Now I know what a punching bag feels like.*

"It's regarding Hinch's bandmates," Schiffman continued. "Or, should I say, his former bandmates."

"What about them?" I muttered.

"Well, overall the Trucker brothers have comported themselves in a professional manner, in my opinion. Don't you agree?"

"Comported themselves? What the hell are you talking about?"

He cleared his throat and glanced around the room, looking slightly embarrassed. Even Schiffman knew what an asshole he sounded like when he tried to talk down to people.

"I mean to say, Donnie, that they complement Hinch well, both on-stage and off. That's why they're being retained within the organization, on a salary basis, of course."

I glowered at him. "They're part of the band, Alan. They get an equal share. That's been our agreement since day one."

"That may have been *your* agreement," he replied, "but it's not mine. And, as I just explained, there is no more band. Don't worry: I think you'll find that both Vernon and Joe Dan are quite satisfied with the legal and financial arrangement I've made with them."

I was still trying to digest it all. Was Hinch complicit in this? I always knew he had a ruthless streak, but was he really capable of stabbing all his friends in the back this way?

"Then, of course, there's the matter of Cody," Schiffman added.

I looked up. Cody? What the fuck did he want with poor, drugged-out Cody?

The slimeball smoothed back his greasy hair as if preparing for an important announcement. "This, I'm afraid, is a more difficult situation. Quite frankly, Hinch and I don't exactly see eye to eye on this one, but he's the client, so I defer to his better judgment."

"What is it you're trying to say?" I asked, bracing myself for the worst.

"Well, what with the unfortunate heroin addiction he's developed, it's obvious that Cody is no longer useful to the organization. Personally, my inclination is to just cut him loose, but Tommy has a sentimental loyalty to his friends that sometimes precludes business sense." He paused for a moment, looking me straight in the eye. "As a result," he continued, "we've decided to keep him around for the time being, though obviously his role will have to change."

"Alan, get to the fucking point already." God, I was so fed up with listening to this dirtbag.

Shooting Sal and Luigi a sideways grin, Schiffman dropped his final bombshell of the day.

"Effective immediately, Cody has been reassigned to the road crew."

For a moment, you could hear a pin drop. I felt the blood rush to my head as I leapt to my feet. Sal and Luigi instantly lunged forward and grabbed my arms, holding me firmly in place.

"Are you out of your mind?" I exploded. "Cody *started* this fucking band!"

Schiffman sat impassively, clearly pleased that he'd achieved the intended result. "Donnie, calm yourself," he said. "As I keep telling you, there *is* no more band. We're just doing what's expedient. As I said, if it were up to me, we'd make a clean break with Cody altogether. It's Hinch who wants to keep him around, not me."

The muscle boys shoved me back into my seat, then planted a beefy hand on each of my shoulders to keep me pinned down.

"Look, even you have to admit that your friend Cody has become dead weight," Schiffman continued, still trying to persuade me.

"Alan, you don't get it," I protested weakly. "Cody is the musical heart and soul of this band. He's the whole reason Hinch took up guitar in the first place."

"No, Donnie, it's you who doesn't get it. Nobody out there gives a shit about the 'musical heart and soul' of your band, or any other band. In fact, nobody really gives a shit about the music itself. *Image* is everything. What the fans want is a rock star. Hinch is a rock star. The Trucker brothers, they might be rock stars. But your boy Cody is no goddamn rock star. So he's out. If you feel you owe him something, you can have him on your road crew … *if* he can carry his weight. Literally." He snickered at his sick joke. "Or you can just fire his ass. Either way, I don't care. But he's out." With a sneer, he added, "Fucking red hair. Who ever heard of a rock star with curly red hair?"

"Are you telling me this is about the color of his fucking hair?"

I felt the goons' grip on my shoulders tighten as Schiffman pounded his desk in fury. "Grow up, Donnie; you're in the big leagues now. That's why you failed so miserably: you're a minor leaguer trying to keep up with the big boys. This may be the music business, but it's a *business* first and foremost. So, yeah, it's the color of his fucking hair. Or maybe it's that he's a pathetic junkie. Maybe it's just that I don't like the little creep. Makes no difference. He's out."

"What about the songs, Alan?" I said defiantly. "What's Hinch going to play if Cody's not in the band? Cody writes most of the songs."

A sudden wave of calmness washed over Schiffman as he leaned back in his chair, smiling contentedly like the cat that swallowed the proverbial canary. "I think you're mistaken, Donnie," he said quietly. "Tommy Hinchton writes all his own songs."

"Bullshit. I was there when the songs were written."

"Is that so? And do you have copyright forms indicating song ownership? That's one of the duties of a manager, you know."

My heart sank. Fucking paperwork never was my strong suit.

Schiffman pulled out a stack of papers from his top desk drawer and waved them at me. "I think you'll find these, like all the other documents, legally binding." I squirmed as the goons on either side of me pressed down even harder on my shoulders, as if they were about to screw me into the ground.

"No need, boys, no need," Schiffman instructed them with a laugh. "Donnie, I think you misunderstand. It's not just these copyright forms and publishing agreements which assert Hinch's ownership of the songs."

I stared at him stupidly.

From another desk drawer he pulled out another legal document. "I believe you'll find this makes for interesting reading, too. It's Cody's relinquishment of all rights to said songs, in perpetuity, to Hinch, Incorporated—the entity Hinch and I have set up to administer his business interests."

My jaw dropped.

"Don't you get it, Donnie? Hinch, Incorporated owns all of Cody's songs. Excuse me, I meant *Hinch's* songs."

Rook to king three, checkmate.

THE PHONE CONVERSATION with Hinch went pretty much as expected. Clearly uncomfortable, he simply stammered, "Look, man, it's nothing personal; it's business," in answer to pretty much every question I put to him. When I challenged him on the decision to fire me as manager, he got slightly defensive ("changes had to be made; what more do you want me to say?"); when I brought up the moral implications of what he and Schiffman had done to the Truckers, he answered in legalities ("the lawyers tell me it's all above board."). It was only when I brought up the issue of Cody being thrown out of the band that a trace of humanity surfaced. "Look, man, I feel for the guy, really I do," he said. "But I gotta think of my career, I gotta think of my future. Like I told you, Katie and I are thinking about having kids."

"Is that what this is all about?" I asked him. "Is Katie pregnant?"

"No, but she will be one of these days. I mean, I want her to be. I mean, *we* want her to be." He was clutching at straws. "Look, I'm willing to do what I can for Cody—that's why I told Schiffman to give him a job within the organization, and believe me, he gave me a lot of shit about that—but even you have to admit the guy has become a total drag."

"He needs a lot more than a job, Hinch," I said. "He needs help. And more than anything, he needs his friends to stand behind him, not abandon him."

"You're starting to sound pretty ungrateful, you know?" was his reply. I could hear a trace of annoyance in his voice. "Try to see things from my perspective. I'm offering you and Cody well-paying jobs. That's not what I call abandoning my friends."

Ungrateful? After all we'd done to get Hinch to this point? I was shocked and angry and I told him so.

"Look, Donnie, I gotta go. I'll talk with you some more when I get back. Until then, whatever Alan says goes. Okay?"

I knew there was no point in arguing any further. After an awkward moment of silence, he hung up, and with that, my last chances of holding the band together were gone forever.

WHEN I GOT BACK to the house, more surprises awaited. The place was even more disheveled than usual, with beer bottles strewn all over the living room. It looked more like a college frat house than our relatively tidy crash pad. Vernon and I were the two neat freaks in the house, and with both of us away, the modicum of order we had established had been eradicated. Worse yet was the smell of puke, which, combined with the pungent odor of stale beer and unwashed bodies, made my stomach turn. Desperate for fresh air, I was in the middle of prying open one of the living room windows when Hank sauntered in, rubbing his eyes as if he was just waking up. It was three in the afternoon.

"Where is everybody?" I asked him.

He yawned and scratched his head. "Everybody? Well, let's see. Robbie and JD and Vernon aren't due back from the motocross until later tonight, and Cody's up in his room. Anyone else you're interested in?" He was referring to the other members of the road crew we shared the house with, and, no, I had no particular interest in knowing where they were.

I opened the door to Cody's bedroom and peeked inside with some trepidation, but instead of finding him passed out in some ghastly shade of blue, he was sitting in a corner, gently rocking back and forth with a beatific smile on his face. I coughed gently until he noticed me.

"Donnie? Is that you? Hey, man, where have you been?"

"Of course it's me. Don't you remember? I've been in New York. Can I come in?"

"Sure, man, sure. Take a seat. Wherever you can find one, that is." He chuckled to himself and began scratching his arms. For the first time I noticed that he was wearing a long-sleeve flannel shirt despite the Southern California heat; it had to have been eighty-five degrees in there.

"Cody, roll up your sleeves."

"Wha'?" He looked like a deer caught in the headlights.

"Roll up your sleeves."

"No, man. I mean, why should I?"

I took a step toward him. "Roll up your fucking sleeves!"

He cringed. But he rolled them up.

My heart sank: track marks.

"Jesus, Cody. How could you?"

My voice trailed off as I saw tears well up in his eyes.

"I don't know. I just thought...." His mouth moved but no words came out. Instead, a flood of sadness poured from his reddened eyes.

I enveloped him in a hug. "Cody, man, what am I going to do with you? I can't believe how you've screwed up your life."

"I know," he sobbed. Then, without warning, he suddenly brightened. "But it's okay, you know?" he said incongruously. "I mean, I've got money of my own now, so I can afford my own shit. That's good, isn't it? Having my own money is good, right?"

He was babbling, but his nonsense words snapped me back to reality.

"Cody, what the hell did you sign?"

He looked at me wide-eyed. "Sign? I didn't sign anything."

"Come on, Cody, stop trying to bullshit me. This is Donnie you're talking to. Show me the goddamn papers."

Suddenly contrite, he slowly opened a dresser drawer and produced a thick stack of documents. From the look of them, it appeared they'd been stuffed in-between his clean socks and his dirty underwear.

I took a few minutes to read them through while Cody sat on the edge of the bed, rocking back and forth and murmuring to himself in sing-song fashion. By the time I finished the last mind-numbing clause, my eyes were glazed over and the bile was rising in my throat.

"Cody, you signed away your rights to every song you've ever written, forever, for fifty thousand lousy dollars."

There was a long pause while he continued rocking.

"Do you hear what I said? Did you even understand what you were signing?"

"Yeah, I understood," he mumbled. "I'm not stupid. Fifty thousand dollars—that's a lot of money, right? I mean, I did a good thing, right, Donnie?"

"Cody, you didn't even get all fifty. Schiffman took back half of it as a credit against prior expenses—I guess for the dope you've been doing all these months. And the rest is just being doled out to you over the next twenty-five weeks. That's just a thousand bucks a week for six months, in exchange for a lifetime of work."

He started rocking even faster and began chanting, "A thousand bucks a week, a thousand bucks a week, a thousand bucks a week." He was like some kind of deranged toddler. As I stared at him, half of me wanted to cry, half of me wanted to slap him silly.

Then, without warning, his mood swung wildly. He abruptly stopped the rocking and chanting and leapt up to face me, planting his nose inches from mine. For the first time in months I saw fire in his eyes.

"Why don't you just mind your own business, Donnie?" he raged. "Why can't you just mind your own business for once? You don't understand. I *need* that thousand bucks a week. I need it!"

"You need it to feed your habit," I replied quietly.

"So what if I do?" he snarled. "I'm tired of being a drain on this band, Donnie. That's what Schiffman said I was: a drain. And you know what? He's right. But he and his lawyers gave me a way to not be a drain any more. They gave me fifty thousand dollars, which is more than anyone ever gave me in my entire life, and they gave me a good job so I can earn money instead of being a drain, so I can afford the pills I need to take and the shit I need to shoot up so I can be in a happy place instead of being a miserable fucking piece of shit drain on this band. And I can't stand being a miserable fucking piece of shit drain on this band any longer. Don't you understand that, Donnie?

Don't you understand? Goddamn it, I thought you were my friend!"

He was shaking with anger and bitterness, as was I, at the injustice of it all. Then the tears washed over us both and for a small eternity we held each other and wept.

It was a moment of epiphany. For the first time I understood the magnitude of what we had undertaken. And, for the first time, I understood that rock 'n' roll had broken us both.

LATER THAT EVENING, with Cody tucked up and fast asleep under the watchful eye of his worst enemy, Hank, I went out for a drink with Joe Dan and Vernon.

"Shit, we didn't know we was doing nothing wrong," drawled JD. "Schiffman just said he was doing some kind of re-or-gan-eye-zay-shun." He took a long time to get that last word out, as if it were too lengthy to wrap around his southern tongue.

"Hell, it's a pretty good paycheck he's giving us, you got to admit," added Vernon.

"Plus we got those Harleys we wanted," pointed out Joe Dan unhelpfully. They had indeed gotten the Harleys of their dreams—a pair of huge, noisy 1200 cc Low Riders—as a bonus, the carrot on a stick.

"I know, guys, I know," I sighed. "I just wish you'd talked to me before you'd signed those papers."

"Well, I don't know what you want us to say, Donnie," Vernon said as he twisted the cap off another high-neck. "You was in New York and we had no way of reaching you. We just assumed you knew all about it, so when Hinch said to sign, we signed."

We all took a slug of our beers and stared off into space wordlessly.

"So what are you gonna do, Donnie?" Vernon finally asked. "You gonna stick around as our road manager?"

"I don't know. I haven't made up my mind yet. It depends." I had no idea what it depended on; it just seemed like something to say. A whole lot better than, "I have no fucking clue," anyway.

We lapsed into another silence.

"Sure sucks about Cody, though," JD finally said. I'd never known him to be so talkative.

"Well, he doesn't seem too upset about it," I replied. "Much to my surprise. Me, I'd be pissed off beyond belief."

"It's the drugs, Donnie," counseled Vernon. "Smack and downers dull your mind."

"He oughta know," JD added with a grin.

"Fuck you, brother"—this last retort accompanied by a playful jab to the ribs. *They really are like a couple of eight year-olds*, I remember thinking.

"Well, anyway, it's hard to imagine Cody humping equipment instead of being up on that stage playing with the band," I said. "It seems like such a waste."

Vernon wiped a dribble of beer off his long beard. "I'll tell you what—after everything that boy's been through, a spell as a roadie might be exactly what he needs. It might give him a chance to clean up, for one thing. A whole lot less pressure, you know?"

I turned to Joe Dan, who was staring intently at his bottle of beer as if he were waiting for it to impart some pearls of wisdom. "What do you think, JD?" I asked.

"Well, I got to say I agree with Vern here," he replied after a long pause. "I reckon a spell as a roadie might do the boy some good. But not as a roadie with *this* band. If he sticks with us, he'll be dead within a year. Hank will see to that."

There was a lot of truth to what he was saying, we all agreed.

"I got me a drinking buddy—this English guy who crews with some of the top bands on the circuit," JD told us. "Let me make a phone call and see what I can do."

A few days later the doorbell rang and in walks the biggest, fattest roadie I ever saw in my life, clad in the obligatory black T-shirt and shorts, mag-lite hanging from his belt as if he was onstage at a gig. He also had the longest gray beard I'd ever seen—so long it nearly covered his huge belly—and an outsized personality to match.

"I'm looking for Joe Dan Trucker," he boomed in an accent that I found nearly indecipherable.

"Sounds like my no-good sonovabitch good buddy LB," shouted JD from the next room. An instant later the two man-mountains were belly to belly, locked in a bone-shattering hug, their roars of laughter rattling the windows.

"How's that scrawny little brother of yours?" Bob asked as they continued slapping one another on the back.

"Good, man, good. Getting too goddamned skinny; I can hardly see the little bastard when he turns sideways." As the two men finally disengaged, Joe Dan turned to me. "Donnie, this here's the fellow I was telling you about. Limey Bob, meet Donnie Boyle."

"A pleasure, old chap," said Bob, extending a meaty hand. I was grateful that he didn't offer to wrap me in a hug as well.

Without further ado, Joe Dan and Limey Bob disappeared into Cody's room. An hour later, the three of them emerged, carrying a couple of suitcases. Then, with a wave of his hand, Limey Bob disappeared into the night, Cody in tow.

It was the second time Cody told Hinch to fuck off, and the last time I would see my friend for more than a year.

And, now, Bernie, you're gonna have to excuse me while I go puke my guts out.

27

The predawn light filtering through the curtains of Lilith Wallingford's guest bedroom finds me sleepless and hunched over my laptop. Ian had made the mistake of telling me, with his customary pride in techno-related accomplishments, that he had hardwired the entire house with computer cabling so that the Internet could be accessed from any room. When my eyes opened involuntarily after just a few hours of tossing and turning, it was, for some reason, the first thing that popped into my mind.

Good thing, too. Ever since getting that last message from Britney, I haven't been able to shake this feeling that I somehow *do* know this Katherine Sommerville, the woman who had twice called, asking to speak with me. It took only a couple of mouse clicks inside a search engine to prove me right.

Katherine Sommerville, nee Quinn, is, I learned, the widow of Arthur Sommerville, a big-time Democratic party donor who was appointed by the Clinton White House to serve as deputy director of the Securities and Exchange Commission. Ms. Sommerville is a corporate attorney who was born in York, Pennsylvania. Her marriage to the late Arthur was her second: previously, she was wedded to a famous rock star who happens to go by the name of Tommy Hinchton.

Katie Quinn. Of course. How could I have been so dumb? If only I'd been there to take the call myself instead of airhead Britney.

But I wasn't. And now that the mystery of Ms. Sommerville's identity was solved, I was faced with an even bigger mystery: Why was Hinch's childhood sweetheart trying to reach me? *She must know Hinch is in some kind of trouble*, was all I could think of. My gut was telling me it was imperative I speak with her, yet she had left no call-back number, saying merely that she'd try again, and no amount of clicking around the Web could locate a phone number for her other than "unlisted." I had a strong feeling that, wherever she was, I would find Hinch, too.

One riddle solved, another one revealed. Frustrated, I turned my attention to a second research project, one that Hans had urged me to complete before the events of the next twenty-four hours were to unfold.

Among the many calls Hans had made early yesterday morning was to a Keith LeBron, head of Modern Style Events, the promoter who was putting on the New Year's Eve concert at the Millennium Dome. LeBron had confirmed to Hans that all the artists scheduled to perform, as well as their management and entourages, were being provided accommodation at the same place: a newly constructed hotel called The Gig. I'd read a couple of newspaper articles about the joint when it first opened a few months ago, but didn't know much more than the basics. Since so much of our cockeyed plan relied upon the unique design and layout of the hotel, I needed to find out as much as I could about it beforehand. Now I finally had the time to do so.

The Gig, I discovered, was the brainchild of international hotelier Adrian Bermondson, who began his unlikely career as lead singer for the '80s power-pop band Dubious Intentions. After reaping the benefit of a number of shrewd investments, Bermondson had turned his attention—and considerable bankroll—to real estate development, where his millions quickly multiplied into an obscene fortune. Latching onto the relatively new concept of the "boutique" hotel—where one went to be seen as much as to have a roof over one's head—Bermondson had constructed a number of them in places as far-flung as Dubai and Rio. Now he had returned to the city of his birth—London—to unveil what he considered his crowning achievement: a hotel constructed specially to meet the unconventional requirements of the professional touring musician, a life Bermondson once lived firsthand and therefore knows better than most.

The first decision Bermondson made was to situate The Gig within hailing distance of the Millennium Dome, which had been envisioned from the start as a music venue. Tony Blair's recently elected "New Labour" government had poured millions of pounds into the Dome's erection over the past two years, viewing it as a high-profile way to showcase their vision for the Docklands of the 21st century. The ambitious project had served as a catalyst for the rebirth of the once derelict neighborhood, spurring all sorts of new construction: shopping centers, office buildings, even a modernized tube station. And, of course, numerous hotels, including The Gig.

To call the upcoming New Year's Eve event—the official opening of the Dome—important would be a colossal understatement. Though the concert would only be performed in front of a relatively small, invited crowd, the audience would include every major celebrity and dignitary in the country, including Blair himself, and would thus receive blanket coverage from major media outlets the world over. Twenty years ago, Hinch would have been the headliner; now, he was relegated to a support slot way down on the bill, but for him to be part of such a high-profile event at all was huge, even potentially career-changing ... assuming he made an appearance. It was, I realized, quite a gamble for him, because if he delivered anything like the doped-out non-performance he'd given at the Paradiso Club a couple of weeks previously, he was probably finished for good. On the other hand, if he somehow managed to get his act together and dominate the stage like the Hinch of old, he could potentially ride the huge wave of nostalgia for '70s acts that was currently bringing a return of fame and fortune to so many of his contemporaries.

One thing was for sure: None of the musicians appearing that night could blame a bad performance on lack of comfort. The Gig was not just a luxury hotel but a meticulously appointed fifteen-story facility designed to cater to their every need. It offered 24-hour room service and concierge facilities, as well as several bars and restaurants—some fancy, some featuring basic pub fare. There were also a number of ballrooms which could easily be converted into rehearsal rooms, the largest of which could accommodate a full arena-sized stage. In addition to a gift shop that featured elaborate stage costumes alongside black "Gig" T-shirts—a favorite with the roadies—there was a well-equipped music store, where instruments, amplifiers, replacement strings, drum skins, and assorted accoutrements of the trade could be obtained at all hours of the day and night. In the depths of the basement was secreted a state-of-the-art recording studio and repair workshop—even an equipment rental house.

The rooms on the lower floors were intended for use by road crews and budget-conscious opening acts and offered only basic amenities, but the housekeeping hours didn't begin until noon, in deference to the often lopsided hours kept by those in the trade. The upper floors were where the stars stayed. They housed a series of monstrously large multi-bedroom soundproofed suites where the wildest of parties could be held with full discretion, with plenty of room for management, friends, wives, nannies, hangers-on, and, of course, groupies galore. Each suite had a balcony overlooking the Thames and was outfitted with the very latest in audio equipment, a fully stocked wet bar, and a palatial bathroom complete with jacuzzi.

Well aware of the feuds that can fester between, or within bands, Bermondson had specified that each of the upper floors be divided into separate quadrants, allowing the occupants of each to have no extraneous contact with one another. Each quadrant had its own recreation lounge equipped with a pool table, big-screen TV, and the very latest in video games, as well as a kitchen area in which tour chefs could fulfill any specialized food requirements. In order to assure absolute privacy, each quadrant also had its own security desk, posted right in front of a special key-access elevator, complete with elaborate video monitoring; guests could choose to man the desk with their own personnel, or, for an extra fee, could hire the hotel's own security guards.

It was on the fourteenth floor, LeBron had informed Hans, that Alan Schiffman and Henry Ryker were currently ensconced, sharing one of those luxury suites. Another suite, down the hall, was reserved in Hinch's name, though there had been no sign of him yet. Hinch's backing musicians and road crew were settled into various rooms throughout the lower floors, and, according to LeBron, had already run up a sizable bill at the hotel bar. Without going into any detail about the reasons for his inquiries, Hans had traded on their long-standing friendship and had asked LeBron to use his influence with the hotel manager to pass along any information he could obtain from the staff about Schiffman's and Ryker's comings and goings, and, in particular, about their early morning habits: Had they been requesting wake-up calls? Had they been ordering breakfast from room service, and, if so, at what time? Any information, Hans assured LeBron, would be handsomely rewarded.

NEXT, I SHIFTED MY ATTENTION to the Donnie Boyle transcripts. With all the whirlwind events of the past few days, I'd had little chance to continue reviewing them, despite my conviction that they would reveal important clues about Hinch's disappearance.

And so they had. There, before my very eyes, was the likely identity of Rudie's assassin and my near-murderer.

I reach for Hans's cell phone and shakily dial his home number, hoping the damn thing will work. Wonder of wonders, the call goes through. With his usual Dutch efficiency he picks up on just the second ring.

"Bernie?" He sounds sleepy.

"Yes, it's me. I hope I didn't wake you."

"No, it's okay, I was just getting up anyway. Where are you?"

For once, I forgive him the lapse into cliché. "In England, at Lilith Wallingford's home."

"You *are* a dirty dog," he chuckles. I detect a slight sense of admiration in his voice.

"No, it's nothing like that. It's just that the interview with her husband went so late, I missed the last flight up to Edinburgh. She and her assistant are going to drive me to the airport in an hour's time. I should be at McFarlane's place by late morning."

"So you still don't know if Hinch is alive?"

"No, but I'm starting to get a strong feeling he is, based mostly on the fact that his ex-wife's been trying to get in touch with me."

"Hmm, interesting," Hans says. He's thinking so hard I can almost smell the wood burning.

"So, tell me, how are the arrangements going?" I ask when it is clear he's got nothing to add.

"Fine, but there's been a complication."

"Oh?"

Hans pauses for a moment as if trying to decide how to break the news to me. "LeBron tells me that Schiffman's security people have checked in. Two guys, intimidating-looking pricks, he tells me. Presumably armed; definitely dangerous. We're going to have to think of a way to deal with them."

"Well, that ties in with the news I have for you," I say. "I know their names: Luigi and Salvatore Antucci. I'm pretty sure they're the same two guys who murdered Rudie and very nearly me, too."

Hans reacts with a sharp intake of breath. "How did you get that information?" he asks.

"Donnie Boyle told me. From beyond the grave."

"Don't play fucking games with me, Bernie. This isn't the time," he snaps.

"I'm not playing games, honest. I've just been going through the interviews I did with Donnie last year, and in one of them I realized that he had given me the names of Schiffman's bodyguards. It makes perfect sense that Schiffman would have them do his dirty work just when he and Ryker had a foolproof alibi."

I hear what sounds like a low whistle. "Okay, I'll pass the names along to VandeVoort and we'll see what we can dig up on them."

"That makes four of them at the hotel," I point out. "What the hell are we going to do? The last thing I want is to get caught in the middle of some damn gunfight."

"Believe me, that was the last thing Rudie wanted either," says Hans with a trace of irritation in his voice. "But VandeVoort will think of something. Don't forget, he also has a personal stake in this."

"Well, I just hope he comes up with something that precludes us getting our asses shot off."

"Me too, Bernie. Talk to you later."

LILITH, WHO IS WAY too chipper for this hour, greets me with a cup of steaming hot coffee and a hug. I need both, desperately, and am touched at the gesture. As we make our way out to the car, I catch the first glimmer of a spectacular sunrise over the rolling Costwold Hills off in the distance. Even the dreary English rain and fog has a positive side, I note, in the lush greenery that surrounds us even on this cold winter day.

As the steadily intensifying rays of the sun continue to add color to what moments ago was a world composed merely of shades of gray, the Wallingford estate is revealed in all its dingy glory: a farmhouse desperately in need of re-roofing and a coat of paint; a small chicken coop off to one side; a bedraggled pasture occupied by two bored-looking cows and a swayback horse on the other. Everything seems to be falling apart in a gentle state of decrepitude that reminds me of the lord of the manor himself.

"It may not be much, but to me it's a lovely home," Lilith says as if reading my mind once again. As I gaze at her, small and trembling in the breeze that sets the tree branches swaying overhead, I wonder if anyone but she could discern the beauty in such bleakness, and whether she really does have powers of telepathy. I hope so, because then she will know how I really see her. It's less than twenty-four hours since I first laid eyes on this extraordinary woman and she's already turned my life upside down. Not with lust, not even with love, as I might have expected. No, with respect.

As Ian backs the Opel down the narrow driveway, I have the curious sense that I will meet these people again. It's the first time in weeks I've allowed myself to consider a life post-Hinch, post-Hans, post-Schiffman—a life free of all the intrigues that are weighing me down like shackles of iron. I realize then and there that, come what may, these images of Lilith and Ian and this magical little farm out in the middle of nowhere will long be a part of me.

The small talk during the ride to the airport is, thankfully, kept to a minimum. At one point, Ian brings up the *Rolling Stone* interview. "Hopefully it will revive interest in JTW's legacy," he declares, as if the man were already dead and buried.

"It will just be nice to see John get some recognition after all these years," Lilith says, downplaying Ian's ill-advised proclamation, prompted, I am sure, more by youthful enthusiasm than any genuine ill-will toward his benefactor.

"It's just that he's made so many important contributions," Ian continues, unabated. "So many of his techniques have become standard operating procedure, even with today's computer recording, but people don't realize that they originated with him."

"And, frankly, darling, few people care," Lilith points out. "It's really only you and your mates that pay any attention at all to the technical aspects of making records. All most people care about is the music."

Words that could have come straight from Donnie Boyle's lips, I think as I bounce along wearily in the back seat, preoccupied with what I face in the hours ahead.

"It's just too bad that most people assume it's only the artist making the records they listen to," replies Ian. "It never occurs to them that there might be a producer behind it, and the artists rarely give credit where it's due."

"Yet those same artists are never the least bit reluctant to pin all the blame on the producer if the record fails to chart," Lilith adds with a chuckle.

"Which is why it's such a thankless job," Ian grumbles. "No matter; I still hope to make my mark one day in the recording world. If I can make just one record half as good as JTW's worst work, I'll die satisfied."

"Darling, you have no idea what you're saying," retorts Lilith. "John's worst work was total crap!"

Red-faced with embarrassment, Ian grips the steering wheel a little tighter. "Okay, then, well, maybe not half as good as his worst work. How about a half as good as his not-quite-worst-but-still-not-best work?"

Anyone watching us as we zoomed down the motorway would have thought our car contained three laughing hyenas. Still, it felt good to let some of the tension go. Hours of watching *Monty Python* reruns in the States had convinced me that the English are far better at deflating pomposity with silliness than we Americans. This ride to Heathrow had only served to strengthen that conviction.

As we pull to the curb, I suddenly realize that I have forgotten to ask Ian an important question, one that has been bugging me all night.

"Do you remember telling me that you were in the process of digitizing JTW's tape collection?" I say.

"Sure, why?"

"Well, I was wondering if you'd gotten around to doing that with the Hinch tapes before they were stolen."

Ian screws up his face in concentration. "Good question. Actually, I'm not sure. But I can check for you."

"How can you not be sure? Don't you listen to the tapes as you're transferring them into the computer?"

"Not necessarily. In fact, most of the time I don't, because the quality of so many of the raw tapes is pretty awful. Usually I just spool them up and let them run while I'm off doing other things. But I do keep a log of my progress"—of course— "and so I can check for you when I get back."

I hand him my business card and scribble Hans's cell number on the back. "Do that, will you?"

"Of course."

And with that, and a final warm hug from my hosts, I bid a fond farewell to rural England and make my way into the airport terminal. God only knows what awaits me at the end of this flight. And maybe even He isn't all that sure.

IAN'S SKILLFUL DRIVING has left me just enough time to nip into the Heathrow Burberry's and buy an off-the-rack suit—charcoal gray pinstripe—before heading to the departure lounge. The flight itself is uneventful, even boring, leaving me plenty of opportunity for contemplation. *You can do this, Bernie*, I keep telling myself. By this time tomorrow, things will be resolved, one way or the other. And then I will finally be able to get on with my life. Perhaps even change it.

I had made the decision not to call ahead to the McFarlane clinic, despite Lilith's suggestion that I do so. Maybe it's just my growing paranoia, but I had a gut feeling that I'd be better off not giving them advance notice of my arrival.

The taxi ride from Edinburgh Airport to the address Wallingford had given me takes only half an hour. We pass a couple of scenic castles on the way, each cheerfully pointed out by the driver in his thick Scottish accent, but the McFarlane Clinic is disappointingly located in a small, unobtrusive cottage perched on a small hill overlooking the Firth of Forth as it empties into the choppy North Sea. "Are you sure this is the right address?" I ask the driver as I hand over my fare, plus, dare I say it, a healthy tip.

"Aye, lad. Number 16 Logan Road in the village of Torryburn. It's Dr. McFarlane's place you're wanting, right?"

"Right."

"Well, this is it. They say she cooks a mean haggis. Good luck to you, son."

With that he roars back down the hill before I can take offense at being mistaken for a drug addict. A cold winter wind is whipping around me as I stand alone before a small iron gate. Tentatively, I press the buzzer. I have, I realize, no cover story this time, nor do I have any intention of pretending to be Clive Swindon or anyone else, for that matter. I'm just Bernie Temkin, writer, in search of Tommy Hinchton, rock star.

"Yes?" says the tiny voice emanating from the squawkbox.

"Uh, hello. I'm here to see Dr. McFarlane."

"Do you have an appointment?"

"No, I'm afraid not. But…."

"Well, I'm sorry, but the doctor only sees patients by appointment."

"Actually, I'm not a patient. I'm a writer."

A pause. "Sorry, sir, all media inquiries have to be made ahead of time."

"I know. But I need to speak with Dr. McFarlane on a matter of great urgency, and I've come a very long way to see her." I'm starting to stammer, but I'll be damned if I'm going to leave here without getting some answers.

"What's your name, sir?"

"Temkin. Bernie Temkin." I start to add more information, but to my amazement, I'm interrupted by the sound of a buzzer.

"Come on in, sir. You're expected."

Expected? Expected by who? Am I walking into a trap? Is Alan Schiffman, or one of his thugs, waiting for me at the end of the walkway with another high-powered rifle?

It is with the greatest of trepidation that I slowly make my way to the front door of the cottage ahead, but somehow I force myself to keep going, one foot after the next. Whatever happens, happens, I decide. To my amazement, my hands are steady as a rock as I rap on the door, tentatively at first, then a little more forcefully.

The door opens a crack, then a bit wider. "Mr. Temkin?" asks the attractive forty-something brunette standing before me. "We were wondering what took you so long."

I stare at her, mystified.

"I'm Katie Somerville," the woman says. "Come on in. I believe there are a couple of people here you've been wanting to meet."

28

Transcript: Interview with Donnie Boyle, June 22, 1998

SHIT, BERNIE, IT SUCKS, you seeing me like this. Fucking hospitals—I hate them, hate them all. Watched my father die in a goddamned white room just like this one. Poor bastard never had a chance. Once they wheeled him in on that damned gurney, I knew he was gone. And I don't have even half the sense he had; shoulda given up those fucking cigarettes years ago. My wife always told me they'd end up killing me. She was right, too.

Sorry, man, I hate getting all emotional. But if it weren't for Jennifer and the kids, jeez, I just don't know how I could face this.

You're right: life *is* a bitch. But at least then you die.

Yeah, I know; I sound like Cody now. No, he doesn't know I'm here. We lost touch years ago—in fact, it's been ages since I even saw Hinch last. I dunno, maybe Jen called them. I hope not. I really don't want them seeing me lying here like this. Not now, not like this.

Anyway, Bernie boy, I've still got some unfinished business to take care of, some things I got to get off my chest before I'm done. I told you before, all this conversation about the old days has been doing me a world of good, though you'd never know it to look at me now. Shit, Bernie, you may be the one goddamned thing keeping me alive.

No, I take it back. It's actually the ass on that nurse over there.

Stop making me laugh, you bastard. Set that goddamn machine off one more time and they'll throw the *both* of us out of here.

Okay, so ... tape rolling? Good. After Schiffman's little coup and Cody's departure, you might have thought it was a no-brainer for me to tell Schiffman and Hinch to go fuck themselves, but it wasn't that easy a decision for me to make, for a number of reasons. First of all, I had to face up to the fact that I had no training or qualifications in anything other than rock 'n' roll: If I were to quit, what would I do? I always had this practical streak in me, maybe to my detriment, but there was this nagging voice inside my head that said, *Come on, Donnie, swallow your pride and take the goddamned job*. I was pretty sure that Hinch was destined for big things, especially now that he had the backing of a major label, and he and Schiffman were offering a good salary, plus the security of a contract. If I turned them down, I'd be stuck in L.A. with no job prospects, and the one thing I was definitely *not* going to do was to turn tail and run back to York, Pa.

There had been a tearful phone call from JJ too, in which she disavowed all knowledge of Schiffman's manipulations—which I believed then, and still do—and said she hoped I'd stay. She assured me that the next tour was going to be a big leap upward—mostly stadiums and large arenas, with the band traveling in style, in a custom tour bus, as opposed to our cramped van. And even though Hinch would just be the opening act, he'd be playing to thousands—sometimes even tens of thousands—of people at a time, with a good chance that he'd be able to start headlining if the album, scheduled for release at about the midway point in the planned tour, was the success everyone expected it to be. And judging from the megabucks Warners was putting into hyping it ahead of time—full-page ads in the *Stone* and other trade magazines announcing in large type that "Hinch Is Coming," superimposed over a bare-chested photo of him looking every inch the rock god—there was a pretty good chance that just might happen.

But the final decisive factor was a long heart-to-heart I had with Hinch shortly after he got back from his honeymoon in Mexico. He'd invited me over for a home-cooked dinner, and after we'd eaten and Katie was clearing the dishes, we headed to his music room to talk things over. He wanted to explain why things had gone down the way they had, he said. I'd known Hinch pretty much all my life, and certainly well enough to know when he was full of shit, and I really felt he was being sincere that day. And what I discovered during the course of our conversation was that, for all his outward confidence, Hinch was scared. Scared to death, in fact. He was every bit as scared of failure, it turned out, as Cody had been of success. Scared to let his fans down, scared to let Katie down, scared to let himself down. Every morning when he looked at himself in the mirror, he confessed, he would find himself thinking, *You're not nearly as good as they think you are ... and one of these days you're going to be found out*.

Hinch insecure? This was a revelation to me, but it explained a lot. It explained how he was so easily able to get sucked into Schiffman's world of lies and deception, how he had so easily misconstrued the constant ego-stroking as confidence in his abilities. Yes, the challenges Cody had issued throughout the years had made him a better musician, Hinch acknowledged, but they had also filled him with self-doubt: *This guy can do it so much better than me; it comes so much more easily to him.*

The more we talked, the more convinced I became that Hinch did indeed love Cody every bit as much as I did. The difference was that he saw him as a threat as well as an ally. Maybe that's why he hadn't been able to lift a finger to help when the poor guy began self-destructing.

I didn't feel ready to let Hinch off the hook, but then I didn't think he was asking me to, either. And maybe that's what impressed me most about our conversation that evening. Later, when we had a moment alone, Katie Q begged me to stay. "Hinch needs you," she said. "Without Cody, he'll fall apart; you know that as well as I do."

"I'm still not sure what I'm going to do," I told her as we embraced warmly. "But I promise you I'll think about it."

Over the next few days, I did think about it, long and hard. Cody and Hinch and I had once been the Three Musketeers, a true band of brothers who had each other's backs, united in a single cause. One of us had fallen from grace but had landed in good hands, as Joe Dan assured me daily. There was nothing more I could do for Cody. But Hinch, that was another matter. Katie was right: He needed me, just as much as I needed him. So I decided to stay.

But I had conditions.

With a major tour about to begin, I understood the need for retaining an experienced road crew, but, I told Schiffman, I wanted an assurance that Hank and his fellow Marine buddies would have their asses fired the day their contracts expired, which I figured would be just after the tour ended. Second, I wanted autonomy in hiring and training a replacement crew. Third, I wanted a strict ban on smack—issued by Hinch, in writing—with any employee caught taking or distributing it fired immediately. And fourth, I wanted Schiffman and his goons to stay the hell away during the course of the tour.

Schiffman listened politely enough while I made those demands, although I caught him chuckling softly to himself a couple of times as I read the list out to him. "I'll discuss this with Tommy and get back to you," he said noncommittally when I finished.

A few days later, he called to let me know that he and Hinch would agree to the first three conditions, but not the fourth. That was not negotiable, he said icily, explaining in a barely subdued voice that no road manager anywhere in the fucking world would ever be granted the power to infringe on an artist's right to meet freely with his manager at the time and place of his choosing. If I didn't understand that, he added, I could take the job offer and shove it up my ass. Well, truth be told, I never did expect them to agree to that—I was really just trying it on to see how they reacted—and, anyway, the first three demands were far more important to me, so, taking a deep breath, I accepted the offer.

And so began a new chapter of my life. I was now Hinch's full-time road manager. The tidal wave that had drowned Cody and nearly submerged the rest of us was about to break.

ONCE SCHIFFMAN AND I entered into that shaky agreement, my life went into overdrive. The logistics of that first tour were so much more complex than anything I'd handled before, and I was essentially learning on the job, which made things even tougher.

I felt like I was up to the task, though. Hell, nobody knew these guys better than I did, that's for sure, and even though Hinch had stood by and watched silently while Schiffman stabbed his best friends in the back, I still felt a connection to the guy. Was it out of sheer loyalty? Perhaps. But maybe it was more curiosity: Did Hinch actually have what it took to become genuine rock royalty, as we all had believed for so many years? Or was he going to fall by the wayside, as most pretenders to the throne ultimately do? Either way, I was going along for the ride, and I have to confess that there was a certain excitement in knowing that I would be a first-hand witness to whatever transpired.

I have to admit also that, after years of traveling in that cramped van, I was looking forward to hitting the road in a proper tour bus. In addition to having comfortable seating and a decent sound system, there were four tiny but well-appointed bunks for Hinch, the Truckers and me, so it actually afforded a bit of privacy. There was even a small kitchen and a primitive bathroom of sorts, although you could really only pee in there—anything else and the stench would be unbearable.

Now this may sound like it was a generous gesture on the part of Schiffman, but it was actually a cost-saving measure in that we'd no longer be staying in hotels; instead, we'd take off for the next city immediately after leaving the stage, then sleep on the bus as our amphetamine-fueled driver put the pedal to the metal through the night. The next day, we'd roll up to the new venue, grab a quick shower in the dressing room, and meet up with the roadies, who'd have driven ahead of us in the small semi that held our equipment and the Harleys that Robbie and the Truckers insisted on bringing with them. It was hardly luxury, but the tour bus made us feel as if we'd finally arrived, and that boost of self-confidence in the wake of Cody's departure did a lot to get us through that difficult time.

Vernon and Joe Dan went out of their way to let me know how glad they were that I was staying on, which I appreciated. They chipped in and bought me a gift, too: a Zero Halliburton—the expensive, flashy aluminum briefcase which is the totem of the road manager. It may look ostentatious, even pretentious, but it's pretty much the only kind of briefcase built for the rigors of the road. That Zero held all the paperwork necessary to haul a dozen or so people around the country: vouchers, receipts, itineraries, and the cash payments that every promoter was expected to cough up before the band hit the stage. It served a practical purpose, too, in that it served as a fearsome weapon when aimed at a shady promoter's head. The morning after every gig, the excess cash would be messengered back to Schiffman's office, the rest used to provide the daily float for the band and crew per diems ... as well as bribes, where necessary. But probably the most important item I carried around in that briefcase was the Tour Bible—this huge book that contained every important phone number of everyone we might need to reach out to in every town we'd be visiting, including dope dealers, vetted groupies, music stores, equipment rental houses, lawyers, and all the local cops and judges known to be on the take. It's a nasty business we were in, and my role was to be the one guy who holds it all together in case the worst—or the best—occurs.

The itinerary had us tour-hopping throughout the summer, supporting different headlining bands: a few weeks with Foghat, a couple of dates with Savoy Brown, a month with Bachman-Turner Overdrive, one-offs with Cheap Trick, Wishbone Ash, and the Doobie Brothers. For the first half of the tour, Schiffman and JJ had carefully selected smaller cities where we already had a following, thus guaranteeing a receptive audience; for the second half, which would occur after the album release, they'd picked the big, important ones we had yet to crack: L.A., Chicago, New York. Hinch was doing three, four interviews a day, making the rounds of all the major radio stations, meeting all the top deejays and music journalists, and he was doing a great job of building a buzz for the upcoming album release. The final date of the tour itinerary had us taking the stage at Madison Square Garden, where we were scheduled to open for none other than Bruce Springsteen. Trying to top the Boss on his own home turf was a tall order, and an audacious one. I couldn't wait to see how Hinch would handle it.

But, as anyone with a reasonably long memory now knows, fate intervened, and our best-laid plans—like that of so many mice and men—fell asunder. We hit the big time, alright, but it didn't happen the way any of us thought it would. After all, this is no fairy tale I'm talking about. It's real life, where there are no happy endings.

Huh? Sorry, I guess I drifted off to sleep. Must be the goddamned pills or something. Damn doctors. And, no, I don't want you to leave. In fact, I've decided to tell you something I've never shared with anyone else, not even my wife. Tape rolling? Okay, let's hit it.

Now, to all outward appearances, the first half of that tour back in '77 went pretty smoothly. Punk was just starting to happen, but mostly overseas, so there was still a pretty strong market for traditional rock bands like us. And despite all the upheaval we'd just gone through, Hinch and the boys were playing up a storm; for some reason, the bigger the venue, the harder they rocked, and night after night they would win the crowds over, which is no easy task when you're opening for a major act that has its own following. In their eyes, the function of the support band is simply to provide a live soundtrack for an audience that's arriving and still in the early stages of getting properly drunk and stoned. And you're only supposed to be just good enough to divert the crowd's attention from the fact that things are running late—which they always are—but definitely *not* good enough to steal any of the headline act's thunder. We were actually threatened with being dropped from the tour more than once, which was a real badge of honor. It was only the clout of our record company that kept Hinch from being summarily dismissed.

There was one big problem, though, and that was Joe Dan Trucker. He was still fuming over the way Cody had been screwed over, and he was taking all his rage out on Hank, who he saw as the root of the problem. Hank was a total piece of shit, but, frankly, I thought that an equal share of the blame had to go to Schiffman for making the conditions ripe for Cody's downfall, and to Cody himself, for succumbing. But Joe Dan didn't see it that way. In his eyes, Hank was the sole villain, and Hank had to pay the price.

It started as needling—not the good-natured ribbing bands always engage in, but nasty, personal sniping—and soon escalated to fists being thrown. I warned Joe Dan repeatedly that he was in a battle he was destined to lose, and when he was sober he assured me that he'd cool it. But when he'd start drinking—which was pretty much every night—all bets were off.

One night after a gig, I was up in the venue's production office, going over the box-office receipts with the promoter, when one of the stagehands came barreling in. "You'd better get down to the backstage area on the double, Mr. Boyle," he said breathlessly. "We've already called the cops, but they're still going at it."

I raced through the stadium's labyrinth of stairwells and catwalks and arrived to find total fucking carnage. Joe Dan was sitting on top of Hank's chest, pummeling him in the face mercilessly despite Robbie's frantic efforts to pull the drummer off. The two men were covered in blood but were strangely silent, their low, guttural grunting interrupted every few seconds by the dull thud of flesh cracking bone. A few feet away, our other two roadies had Vernon in a death grip to keep him from aiding his big brother, who, from the look of things, didn't seem to need much help anyway. The stagehands and various members of the headlining act's crew were watching with a mixture of horror and amusement. Hinch, as usual, was nowhere to be found.

I jumped into the fray and, with the help of Robbie and the others, finally managed to pull Joe Dan off. A snarling Hank, bleeding profusely from the face, immediately leapt on him, brandishing a broken beer bottle he had grabbed from the floor.

"Put that fucking beer bottle down or I will shoot you dead! NOW!!"

I have never been so glad in my entire life to see a police officer. Instantly freezing at the voice of authority—this was, after all, a well-trained Marine used to following orders—Hank dropped the bottle and slowly slumped to the ground. A team of cops immediately swarmed in and ordered everyone, including me, face down on the floor.

"Okay, who's in charge here?" barked a sergeant.

"That would be me, sir," I answered in a muffled voice as I lay face down in a pool of beer, puke, and blood.

Within a short while, order was restored and Hank and JD were carted off to the hospital. This time Joe Dan had gotten the better of Hank, who had a broken cheekbone and needed more than fifty stitches to close the gaping wounds in his face and scalp; JD escaped with nothing more than bruised knuckles and a minor contusion or two. The cops threatened to arrest them both, but an on-the-spot offer of a large cash contribution to the local PBA, along with free tickets for the next night's show, proved sufficient to head off any legal action.

But it did nothing to stop the hostilities between Hank and Joe Dan. "The audience out there may see a musician, but I just see me a dead hillbilly," a scar-faced Hank began warning JD every night through pursed lips just before the drummer took the stage, to which the reply was most often, "Any time, any place, motherfucker." A bout of macho pushing and shoving between the Truckers and the roadies—all except for Robbie the Mechanic, who somehow managed to remain neutral in all this—became a nightly event. Revenge being a core value of road crews everywhere, I knew it was only a matter of time before the posturing erupted into violence again, and I began to seriously fear for the safety of our rhythm section.

A few nights later, Schiffman suddenly appeared backstage, flanked, as usual, by Louie and Sal—ever since he'd taken over, it seemed as if he never went anywhere without the two goons by his side. Dressed in matching cashmere polo-neck sweaters and oversized gold chains, they looked preposterous, but nobody was laughing. Schiffman's visit was obviously precipitated by the war in our ranks, but you'd never know it to hear him talk. All he wanted to chat about, apparently, was the size of the crowds and the enthusiastic reception Hinch had been getting.

"Aren't you concerned about the situation between Joe Dan and Hank?" I finally asked him when he'd finished polishing Hinch's ego to a fine luster.

"Not really," he said. "You're the road manager; it's your problem."

I was stunned. Normally Schiffman prided himself on taking control of *every*thing; the guy had never been one for delegating. Why then was he doing it now?

"Anyway," he said offhandedly as he walked away, "problems have a way of solving themselves. Right, Donnie?"

With a wink and a cheerful wave, he departed into the night, leaving me perplexed ... and more than a little alarmed.

WELL, AS EVERY HINCH FAN knows, that particular problem did solve itself, and in the most spectacular, and tragic, way possible.

Ten days before the album was due to be released, we found ourselves with an off-day in Vegas, having played the Motor Speedway the night before. That morning, Joe Dan and Robbie decided to head out to the desert to do a some riding. Vernon was supposed to join them, but was too hung over, so they left him behind to sleep it off.

Sometime around noon, as the news later reported, Joe Dan Trucker's Harley skidded out of control, then flipped over. Seven hundred pounds of chrome and steel rolled over on top of him and crushed his skull, killing him instantly. They were miles away from the nearest town, and Robbie had to ride, alone, for nearly half an hour before he could find a pay phone and call for help. When the paramedics finally arrived on the scene they pronounced Joe Dan DOA.

Did I mention that JD always refused to wear a helmet? It would mess up his hair, he claimed. What if he were to encounter some pretty little thing along the way? It wouldn't do for a rock star to have messed-up hair.

Stubborn fucking jackass.

Sorry, Bernie, I don't mean to get all teary-eyed. But, you know, I loved the big ox. When he wasn't drinking, he was one of the kindest souls I ever knew. And a helluva drummer. But he was also one stubborn fucking jackass.

Vernon, of course, was completely shattered. I'll never forget standing beside him as he called their mother with the awful news. Despite their shared grief, he seemed to draw strength from that sweet little old lady, and after they hung up I was amazed at the graceful way he accepted everyone's sympathy while working his way through his own pain.

I couldn't believe the turnout at the funeral. The Trucker family was huge—there had to have been a couple of hundred people jammed into their small-town church, and just about every one of them claimed to be a relation. I was there, of course, along with Hinch and Katie, and a visibly shaken JJ showed up also. But not one of the road crew attended, not even Robbie, which I found kind of surprising at the time. I'd managed to reach Limey Bob the morning after the accident, tracking him down in some bed-and-breakfast in England, where he and Cody were roadying for Uriah Heep. "Well, at least the motherfucker went out with his boots on," was his flip comment when I told him what had happened, but I could hear the shock and sadness in his voice. After a few moments of deliberation, Bob decided not to fly out for the funeral, saying he thought the best tribute he could pay to JD was to stay on the road. I asked about Cody, of course, and Bob offered to break the news to him gently. He said that Cody was doing well and was in fact starting to straighten up, but he also added that he was going to advise Cody not to fly back for the funeral either because he didn't think he could handle all the additional stress. So Cody wasn't there, though Vernon later showed me a long, heartfelt letter he received from our former bandmate, which I know he found comforting.

About the only unwelcome presence at the funeral was that of Alan Schiffman and his asshole bodyguards, along with the throngs of press he brought with him. Always eager to exploit our misfortune for gain, Schiffman and his PR people turned poor Joe Dan's funeral into what they would today call a media event, and I don't mind telling you that I was pretty pissed off about it. Vernon and Hinch seemed too shell-shocked to even notice, so as usual it fell to me to confront Schiffman, which I did, just as an unsteady Vernon, supported by an equally shaky Hinch, walked slowly up to the front of the chapel to pay final respects to his fallen brother, accompanied by a crush of cameramen and the glare of flashbulbs going off.

"Alan, what the fuck is this all about?" I hissed at him through clenched teeth.

He looked at me unperturbed as Sal and Louie instinctively reached for their breast pockets. "Freedom of the press is one of the privileges of living in this great country of ours," he smirked.

"What about guarding Vernon's privacy? Or that of his family? Isn't that supposed to be your job as manager?"

"I don't manage Vernon Trucker," he sniffed as he distractedly examined the sleeve of his hand-tailored suit. "Vernon is simply a loyal employee of my client, and that's why I'm here. I trust you won't forget that you're an employee as well—a loyal one, too, I hope. Our policy is that if the press deem this a newsworthy event, that's their business. I presume you will do nothing to go counter to that policy."

Then he turned his back on me, indicating that the conversation was over.

Fucking cocksucker.

From a business point of view, the timing of Joe Dan's accident couldn't have been more perfect. The wave of publicity that followed in its wake was unbelievable: One minute, Hinch was this up-and-coming opening act; the next, he was practically front page news. All three networks showed footage of Hinch somberly attending JD's funeral, gracefully supporting his bass player in his hour of grief. *Rolling Stone* ran a cover story featuring, I noticed with some disgust, a picture of Hinch and not Joe Dan. Suddenly my old friend from York, Pa., was a household name, and within hours of his drummer being planted in the green earth of Dalton Forks, Mississippi, Hinch's album was rush-released by Warner Brothers.

Keeping It Real, as the album had been named, immediately entered the Billboard charts at number eight with a bullet; no debut album by a new artist had ever done that before. By the next week, we were back on the road, with Vernon gamely returning to the stage and various high-profile guest stars recruited by Schiffman's office filling the drum seat, which in turn yielded even more publicity and propelled the album all the way up to number one, where it remained for most of the rest of the year. By late fall, the title track—one of Cody's songs, by the way—had been sitting on top of the singles chart for months, and Hinch was headlining at the largest stadiums in the country. *Keeping It Real* would spawn three more hit singles and would earn Hinch his first Grammy. It ended up selling more than twenty million copies worldwide, making a shitload of money for Hinch and even more for Schiffman.

You got a copy, Bernie? I thought so—most people who were into music in the '70s do. Some time when you get a minute, take a close look at the back cover. You'll find that the credits read: "All songs written by Hinch. Produced by Hinch. Executive Producer: Alan Schiffman." The Trucker brothers received a small musician's credit, and the real producer—whatever the hell his name was—was just listed as engineer, so he got screwed, too. And that was it. No mention of Cody, not even in the personal thank-yous. It was as if he never existed.

Keeping It Real kick-started Hinch's career into overdrive, and for many years afterwards he breathed the rarified air of the rock elite—wealthy, famous, and idolized by millions. Would the album have enjoyed such massive success if Joe Dan Trucker hadn't conveniently died so publicly days before its release?

Maybe.

But I doubt it.

Now you might say that it was stubbornness, or stupidity, that got Joe Dan Trucker killed, and you might be right.

Or you might be wrong.

Me, personally, I got reason to believe it wasn't the simple verdict of operator error that the coroner delivered. After years of thinking about this, I've come to the conclusion that it was that miserable no-good bastard Alan Schiffman that got Joe Dan Trucker killed. I've never shared this with a single person before, Bernie boy, and I'd never be able to prove it in a court of law, but I will be going to my grave believing that.

For one thing, Schiffman had plenty of motivation; that's obvious. JD's death made Hinch a superstar and generated millions of dollars in record sales. Then there was Schiffman's little problem of having his star act's drummer at war with his personally appointed chief roadie, a problem that was instantly solved. But did that make Schiffman a murderer?

Not necessarily... until you consider three facts I know firsthand, none of which ever appeared in the official records. One, Joe Dan was a pretty fair rider, and neither I nor Vernon nor anyone else ever saw him skid out or even come close to losing control of his beloved Harley, not even when he was blind drunk—and let's not forget that the coroner's report showed only traces of alcohol in his system. You see where I'm going with this, Bernie?

Which leads me to fact number two, which is that JD never let anybody—and I mean *any*body—work on his motorcycle except Robbie The Mechanic, who was constantly tinkering with it. So if the brakes failed, or there was some other mechanical malfunction that caused the bike to roll over on poor JD, there was only one person who could have made that happen.

Now before I tell you fact number three, let me share an interesting story, and then you tell me what *you* think. It goes back to the night Joe Dan and Hank got into their brawl. After their ambulances sped off to the hospital, I decided to follow along and see how bad the injuries were. As I called for a cab, a clearly worried Robbie asked if he could ride with me. I said sure, and we headed off into the night. As we were sitting in the emergency room waiting to get word, a nurse came over and noticed that Robbie was bleeding; apparently a flying shard from the broken beer bottle Hank had been brandishing had lodged in his arm. "We'd better take a look at that," the nurse said. "You don't want to be walking around with glass in your arm, and you might need some stitches to close it up."

Robbie turned ghost white as he shrank away from her. "No, ma'am," he said in this scared little voice. "No thanks. No way are you using a needle on me."

"Don't be silly," she laughed. "A big boy like you afraid of a few stitches?"

"Get away from me," he began shrieking like a madman. "Get the fuck away from me!"

As she stalked off, I said to him. "What the hell is wrong with you?"

"No needles, man. I don't do needles. I took some shrapnel back in 'Nam and the medic hit me with some morphine, but he was a damn rookie and he shoved the needle all the way into the bone. The pain was unbelievable, a hundred times worse than the shrapnel itself. So I ain't never doing that again, not ever. That's all there is to it. No fucking needles, period."

Those were his exact words, Bernie. Verbatim.

Which is why it was so surprising to me when Robbie The Mechanic was found dead of a heroin overdose six weeks after he and JD took that fateful trek into the desert, needle hanging off of his arm. It didn't seem to surprise anyone else, though: people just assumed that's because he was nothing more than a scruffy roadie—and all roadies are dopers, aren't they?—and maybe because he was distraught about what had happened to Joe Dan.

But he never appeared especially distraught to me; in fact, from the way he carried himself during those six weeks, laughing and joking as usual, you'd have never thought that he and JD had ever been friends. Plus the little sonofabitch was also as straight a shooter—and I use that word advisedly—as you'd ever find in our little world. He didn't pop pills, he didn't smoke dope, and he definitely never used smack. It was all you could do to get the guy to drink a couple of beers after a show—all he ever wanted to do was get home and tinker with his motorcycles.

In short, Robbie the Mechanic was the *last* guy on earth you'd ever expect to find dead of an overdose. I just don't think he had it in him to experiment with smack, much less mainline it. But what he *did* have was a crew chief with lots of experience with both smack and needles. Did I ever mention that when Hank left our crew at the end of that tour, he was given a job in Schiffman's New York office?

Like I said, I could never prove any of this in a court of law, especially since the only guy who was actually there ended up conveniently dead.

But what I do know is that if it looks like shit and smells like shit, you probably don't need to taste it to know that it *is* shit. So even if everyone else chalked it up to fate, I took Robbie's death, and JD's, as a warning. A warning that we had indeed, as Schiffman had said, graduated to the big leagues.

And in the big leagues, as everyone knows, the only game ever played is hardball.

29

There's something very odd about meeting people for the first time when you've already gotten to know them intimately through the eyes of a third party. Such is the case with Tommy Hinchton and Cody Jeffries, both of whom are alive, well, and quite happily wandering around the McFarlane Clinic with mysterious black boxes clipped to their belts. You'd think they were simply listening to Sony Walkmans if it weren't for the fact that the boxes are connected to their ears with small electrodes, as opposed to a pair of headphones.

Hinch, I decide, is very much as Donnie described him. Tall and lanky, he still looks every inch the rock star, though his long blond hair is thinning slightly, with just a touch of gray at the temples. Outwardly, he's calm, confident, and self-possessed, though unguarded moments reveal a trace of the "scared of his own shadow" persona that Miranda so scathingly depicted. Cody, on the other hand, is very different: quiet, almost pathologically shy, with an occasional facial twitch that betrays the trauma he has undergone and the inner conflict churning inside him. Short and pudgy, his cherubic face is spoiled by unfashionably nerdy glasses through which he squints at the world around him. To look at the guy, you'd never know he was the behind-the-scenes musical genius who had relentlessly propelled Hinch's career forward relentlessly, just up to the brink of stardom. Both men are dressed casually, Hinch in faded denim work shirt and designer jeans, Cody in the all-black costume of the roadie.

And then there's Katie, who is far more beautiful than Donnie ever let on. It's easy to see how both Hinch and Cody fell in love with this woman: her classic good looks have held up so well through the years that one can only imagine what a stunner she was as a teenager. There is also no question that she is very, very smart. It quickly becomes apparent that she is in complete control of this particular situation.

Rounding out the cast of characters is a tall, muscular, strikingly handsome gentleman by the name of Mike Testa—the band's first-ever roadie, back in the days when they were a three-piece with Cody on drums and

Donnie on bass. As Katie explains while making introductions, Mike had returned to the fold shortly after Donnie quit, back in the '80s; up until a few months ago, he had been Hinch's full-time road manager.

And then there are the McFarlanes: Peggy and Jimmy, both of whom I take an instant liking to. Peggy McFarlane is beyond petite—she can't possibly top four foot ten even in heels, and she looks as if the slightest breeze would blow her clear to Kansas. She's got a thick Scottish brogue and a twinkle in her eye, and she reminds me of my grandmother, were my grandmother to be a wee bonnie lass from the Highlands, as opposed to a large-boned peasant woman from the Ukraine. Jimmy McFarlane is also a doctor, as it turns out, though his specialty is cardiology, not addiction treatment. Still, he takes a completely subordinate role, acting more like Peggy's assistant than her husband, though it is clear he worships the very ground she walks on.

This being the holiday season, Hinch and Cody are currently the only two clients receiving treatment at the McFarlane Clinic. ("We've got someone very, *very* famous coming in week after next," Peggy informs me, before adding, with a wink, "I could tell ye who it is, but then I'd have to shoot ye.") Which leaves just the five of us to gather around the roaring fireplace, where I am regaled with a tale of intrigue, deception, and criminal intent so heinous I can hardly believe what it is I am hearing.

"I presume you know I've been trying to reach you," Katie begins. "I spoke with your lady friend several times but she wasn't very forthcoming about your whereabouts."

"Yes, I'm sorry about that," I reply. "My, um, lady friend is sometimes irrationally jealous." To my embarrassment, this prompts a fit of giggles from Hinch and Cody, halted only when Katie shoots them a dirty look. "Anyway, she did pass along a couple of messages, though she said you didn't leave a number."

"Is that what she said? Interesting. I did actually leave my cell number when I last spoke with her, but she seemed a little preoccupied at the time. I imagine you've been wondering why I was calling."

"I assumed it had something to do with the book I'm writing," I say.

"Indirectly, yes. But the main reason was that my two boys here"—she gestures toward Hinch and Cody, both of whom are indeed squirming in their seats like misbehaving schoolchildren—"were in trouble. And Donnie Boyle had told me to contact you if trouble arose. He's the one who vouched for you."

"I'm flattered," I say, and I am. "Donnie was a very special person."

"Yes, he was," she agrees softly. It occurs to me that I *have* seen her before, at Donnie's funeral, sitting next to Cody as they both grieved for their lost friend.

There's a moment of uncomfortable silence while she composes herself. "Quite a lot has been going on these past few weeks," she finally tells me, "and we're hoping that you'll consider including these events in your writing. I think it may well provide you with a pretty good ending, for your book."

"Of course. But what exactly is it that happened back in Amsterdam?" I ask.

"I think the boys will probably want to tell you themselves."

"Then they're willing to talk to me?" I look over at Hinch, who is still fidgeting awkwardly.

"More than willing," says Katie. "Isn't that right, everyone?"

"I guess so," says Hinch unconvincingly.

Then for the first time Cody speaks. His voice is so soft I have to lean forward to hear it. "Look, after all we've been through, we need to trust *some*one. Donnie said this guy is all right. That's good enough for me."

HINCH TAKES A DEEP BREATH. "Well," he says, clearing his throat, "I guess I should start at the beginning. Of the tour, anyway. I knew something was up when Hank showed up at my door instead of Mike here."

"Hank?"

"Henry Ryker. Back in the old days, we used to call him Hank. I would've thought Donnie would have told you all about him."

Hank. Of course. Hank the Marine, the vicious thug that Schiffman hired as chief roadie back when he was plotting to take over Hinch's management and break up the band. Hank the scumbag, who so carefully shot Cody full of dope and laid him out flat just when he was at his most vulnerable.

"You're right, he did tell me about Hank," I admit. "Somehow I never realized that he and Ryker were the same person."

I can see that Hinch is not impressed with my powers of deduction. "The guy was a complete prick back in the '70s," he says. "If anything, he's an even bigger prick now."

I study Cody's face for any sign of reaction. There is none.

"Fortunately, we haven't had much contact with him for the past twenty years," Hinch continues. "He was working in Schiffman's New York office most of that time, booking other bands. Anyway, there he is, telling me Alan has hired him to do this tour because Mike was unavailable."

"Total bullshit," Testa exclaims. "The fucker never even tried to get in touch with me."

"Look, I wasn't happy about the change, but there was nothing I could do about it," Hinch says petulantly. I notice Katie rolling her eyes, though she is careful not to interrupt. "But I did have the presence of mind to take one little precaution before I headed out," he adds. "And as it turned out, that little precaution saved the life of this ungrateful douchebag here." With a grin, Hinch pokes his elbow into Cody's ribs.

"Asshole. You couldn't save my life if *your* life depended on it," Cody shoots back, throwing a mock punch in Hinch's direction. I'm beginning to see a glimpse of that special camaraderie that only exists between childhood friends and foxhole buddies. It seems as if there's a little of both here.

Ignoring the insult, Hinch continues his narrative. "Anyway, things went pretty smoothly for the first couple of weeks of the tour, even though we had a new roadie and a new bass player—friend of my wife's—to break in. Still, after a few rough gigs, things were beginning to click. Then Hank started getting in my ear."

He pauses and sighs, clearly uncomfortable about what he has to say next.

"Go ahead, Tommy, it's okay," says Katie soothingly.

"Well, I've been having some problems in my marriage," he begins. "I don't know if you've heard the rumors."

"Actually, I've met your wife," I confess.

Hinch looks at me wide-eyed. "You have?"

"Just last week, in fact. And, yes, she did tell me that things were a bit rocky between you two."

"Rocky? The bitch is going to divorce his sorry ass and take him to the fucking cleaners, same as his last three ex-wives." This from Cody. I'm a little surprised at the glee with which he delivers the pronouncement, then even more surprised to see Hinch begin laughing, too. Clearly this is a joke they have been sharing for some time now.

"I guess I just don't have much luck with the women I choose to marry," says Hinch between chuckles, carefully avoiding Katie's gaze.

"I don't know; I think you've actually picked some fine women to marry," she retorts. "One of them, anyway."

Hinch looks over at Katie with some sadness in his eyes. "You're right," he says. "What can I tell you? I blew it."

"Okay, enough groveling," Katie finally declares—but only after taking a moment's delight in Hinch's discomfiture. "No need to air our dirty laundry in front of our new friend here. Let's focus on the events of the past few weeks, not dig up ancient history."

All five of us study one another's faces for a long moment. Taking stock? Taking measure? Hard to say. Then Hinch picks up the thread once again.

"Hank is a drug pusher, pure and simple," he says. "Always was, always will be. He buys from the local dealers, then jacks up the price. It's his way of making a little extra on the road. And he knows just how to get you reeled in: He probes for your weakness, then he tells you that, whatever it is, the problem can be easily solved with the help of a certain white powder. He did the same thing to Cody years ago, but I was too fucking lame to stop it. I should have learned my lesson then, but I didn't. And so he was able to pull the same damned stunt on me, all these years later."

I glance over at Cody's face, which remains impassive.

"Hank kept talking to me about Miranda, over and over again," continues Hinch, a look of hurt spreading over his face. "Kept talking about how it was common knowledge that she was screwing everyone in sight, how everyone knew she would end up divorcing me and taking all my money. He got me so goddamned worked up over it that the fifth or sixth time he offered some smack to help calm me down, I took him up on it. I thought to myself, what do I have to lose?"

"Been there, done that," Cody mutters sourly.

"It didn't take long before I was shooting every day," Hinch says softly. "Like a fish on a line, the bastard had gotten me hooked."

"Put me in a room with that cocksucker for five minutes and I'll hook him with a fucking tire iron," growls Testa.

"By the time we got to Paris," Hinch continues, ignoring the offer, "I was a stone cold junkie. Hank was shooting me up three or four times a day."

I turn to Cody. "What did you guys think about what was going on?"

"You mean the crew?" he asks. "We don't comment on what the

musicians are doing. Whatever they want to do, they do. Whatever they ask us to do for them, we do for them. That's what the gig is all about."

"But Hinch is your friend," I protest, realizing that I may be crossing a line. "How could you let something like this happen?"

"Listen," replies Cody with a trace of annoyance. "Hinch is a musician. In fact, he's the star of the show. I am a roadie. The crew is the crew. And never the twain shall meet. I won't say we weren't a little concerned about what was going on. But drugs are everywhere when you're on the road, and it wasn't our business to interfere."

I must look horrified, because Hinch is quick to jump back in before the celebrated Cody temper erupts. "He's right," he says evenly. "That's just the way things are on the road. We don't expect you to understand."

I don't, though I realize there is nothing to be gained by continuing this line of discussion. "Sorry," I mumble. "I don't mean any disrespect."

"Forget about it," Cody says.

"Okay," Katie interjects. "Let's get on with the story. We don't have a lot of time to spare."

Neither do I, I realize. I'm supposed to be meeting Hans and VandeVoort back in London in just nine hours' time. "Sorry again," I apologize. "Please, continue."

Hinch leans back with a big sigh and fixes his gaze on the ceiling. "Then something really weird happened in Amsterdam," he says. "Hank gave me my fix right before the show, as usual, but the shit was unusually strong. So strong, in fact, I could barely haul my ass onstage."

Cody begins giggling. "It was all you could do to stagger to the drum riser and pass out," he says.

Redfaced, Hinch begins grinning sheepishly, looking for all the world like a kid caught with his hand in the cookie jar.

"Yeah, you pass out and the rest of us have to deal with a riot." This last comment from Cody prompts an even louder gale of laughter. Mike Testa is joining in now, and even Katie is betraying the trace of a smile.

When everyone calms down, I point out that perhaps the riot wasn't quite so amusing to the promoter, who, I inform them, has become a close friend of mine.

"Hans?" Hinch says. "Hans is a good guy. I'm sure he saw the funny side of it."

"Well, he might have," I reply, "if it wasn't for the fact that Schiffman ripped him off for your full fee."

Hinch is clearly taken aback. "Alan did that?"

"He did. And Hans has been hunting him down like a dog ever since."

"Good for Hans; I'd do exactly the same thing. Look, if you're in touch with him, tell him I will personally pay him back every cent."

"Actually, there's more," I say.

"More?"

"Hans's friend Rudie was killed. In fact, they also tried to murder me."

"Rudie? Shit. I *liked* Rudie," Hinch says. "Big, goofy-looking guy, right?"

"That's right. He's dead now, probably courtesy of your manager."

"*Former* manager. His ass is so fired. I mean it, too."

"About time," Katie says quietly.

"Really, I mean it," Hinch repeats. Then, turning to me, "It wasn't Schiffman himself who offed Rudie, was it? That doesn't sound like him."

"No," I reply. "Turns out that he and Henry—Hank—had an airtight alibi at the moment the trigger was pulled. We suspect it was Schiffman's bodyguards."

"Sal and Luigi?" Hinch says. "Those two clowns? They always struck me as a couple of Hollywood extras hired to play the role of hit men."

"Bullshit," snaps Mike Testa. "They're a couple of lowlifes, same as their boss. Schiffman once sent them to strong-arm a promoter in Singapore who was giving us a hard time, and they pistol-whipped the poor bastard until he was puking blood, then left him to die. Which he did, the very next day."

"Really?" asks Hinch meekly. "I never heard that story."

"You never heard it because you never needed to hear it," Mike tells him. "The point is that your manager's bodyguards are murdering scumbags. Same as him."

"Ex-manager," Hinch mumbles. "Ex."

At that moment we are interrupted by a smiling Peggy McFarlane, who informs Hinch and Cody that it is time for their therapy session.

"Can't it wait until later?" Hinch complains. "We're in the middle of something important here."

"There's nothing more important than you getting well, laddie," McFarlane says sternly. "You and your friend are here to get treated, and you *will* be treated. My way or the highway, remember?"

The two supplicants turn to Katie for support, but find none. "Go on, do what the doctor says," she tells them. "I'm sure Bernie here can wait until you're done."

I nod in agreement. Truth is, wild horses couldn't keep me from waiting, so anxious am I to hear the rest of the story.

"We'll only be an hour," says the good doctor. "In the meantime, my Jimmy will make you a cup of tea and a bite to eat. Does anyone here like haggis?"

I USE THE BREAK to call Hans.

"Big news here," I tell him excitedly. "Hinch is alive, Cody too. You wouldn't believe the story they're telling me."

"At this point I think I'd believe almost anything," he says. "Do you know if they're planning on doing the gig in London?"

"I presume so, though I haven't actually asked yet."

"Is Hinch cleaned up?"

"Yes, he's pretty clear-headed. And thoroughly pissed off with Schiffman, who he's already referring to as his *ex*-manager. He also wanted me to tell you that he will personally pay you back all the money you lost at the Paradiso gig."

There's a pause while Hans considers the gesture. "That's good of him. Thank him for me, will you?"

"Of course. Any news to report on your end?"

"Not really. But I'm sure that VandeVoort will be pleased to hear that Hinch and Cody are alive and well and accounted for. Perhaps he'll find a way for them to help us in the task that lies ahead."

"Is there really any need for going ahead with this?" I ask. "I mean, now that you know you'll be getting your money back?"

"Will I be getting Rudie back?" Hans snaps angrily. "This isn't just about the money, Bernie. I thought you knew that. Don't forget, these are the same cocksuckers that tried to blow your head off as well."

He's right. In fact, the more I think about it, and the more I learn, the more I realize that neither Alan Schiffman nor any of his goons deserve any mercy. *We have become the avenging angels.*

"Okay," Hans finally says in response to my silence. "I'll call VandeVoort now and will let you know how he wants to proceed."

"Fine. And, listen, Hans...."

"Yes?"

"I want you to know that I'm in this with you. All the way."

Just like that. Just that easy.

"Thank you," he says softly. "I knew I could count on you." The phone clicks off.

HAGGIS IS, I DECIDE, totally disgusting. And totally wonderful. Or perhaps totally disgustingly wonderful. It reminds me of the stuffed derma of my youth, only much, much weirder. It takes many, many bites before I realize that I am completely unable to make up my mind about it.

"So," I ask Mike and Katie between mouthfuls, "are you still planning on doing the Millennium Dome gig?"

"Well," Testa replies, "it *is* looking like both Hinch and Cody are making a pretty spectacular recovery."

"Cody?" I've been meaning to ask why he's also wearing the little black box. Up until now I guess I assumed it was just in sympathy or something.

"I'll let him tell you the story," Mike says. "I think you'll find it very interesting. And, yes, we're planning on making the gig ... if we can overcome just one small problem."

"What problem is that?"

"The fact that Hinch's manager is trying to kill him."

"Are you certain of that?" I don't know why I'm shocked.

"Is the Pope Catholic?" he replies, before realizing his faux pas and turning beet red. "Sorry, Katie."

"No offense taken, Michael," she says with a wave of her hand. Her gentle laugh reminds me of Lilith. *How on earth could Hinch have gone from a woman like her to one like Miranda?* I wonder.

"Anyway, yes," Testa continues, "we are hoping Dr. McFarlane will agree to releasing our wayward children, at which point I plan on making it my business to get Hinch onto that stage. In one piece."

"It would help, presumably, if Schiffman and Hank and the two bodyguards were indisposed beforehand," I muse out loud.

"That would be a *huge* help. Do you have something in mind?"

"No, but I think Hans does."

"Something tells me this is a conversation I shouldn't be hearing," says Katie, excusing herself.

"She's Hinch's lawyer now," Testa explains after she leaves. "We don't want her getting mixed up in anything that might come back to bite her. Now me, on the other hand, I don't give a shit. And, like anyone who ever worked for the cocksucker, I hate Alan Schiffman's guts. So whatever it is you guys are cooking up, I'm in. Especially if it means giving that prick what he deserves."

"Thanks, Mike. I'll pass that along."

He winks at me. *Another ally in the cause.*

Just then Dr. McFarlane returns with her two patients in tow. "Okay, lads, I'll give them back to you now. Just be gentle; I think their psyches might be a little bruised from our session." She gives Cody a playful pinch on the cheek. I'm convinced she'd do the same to Hinch if she were tall enough to reach him.

Katie returns, teapot in hand, and we all gather in front of the fireplace once again. Outside, I can hear the wind whipping through the trees.

"I hope there isn't a storm brewing," I say by way of making casual conversation. "I've got to head back down to London in a couple of hours' time."

"*We've* got to head back to London," corrects Mike.

Katie gives both of us a quizzical look, then turns to Hinch. "Why don't you pick up where you left off?" she says to him.

Hinch studies Testa and me for a long moment before settling back onto the sofa. "Okay, well, I guess the next thing I remember after passing out on-stage at the Paradiso is being hustled into a limo by Alan and Hank."

"Yeah, that's when I decided to jump in," Cody interjects. "Literally."

"Good thing you did, too, bro," Hinch answers soberly. "Maybe you should take it from here; I was so fucked up at the time, I really don't remember much."

Cody closes his eyes for a moment as if carefully weighing what he is about to say. "There was no way I was going to leave Hinch in the clutches of those two," he begins, "so I jumped into the limo before they could stop me. I was pretty much convinced by that point that Hinch's OD had been no accident; Hank had been around junk long enough to not make a dumb mistake like that.

"Man, that was one wild limo ride! Schiffman and Hank were coked up to the gills; they couldn't stop laughing hysterically. They were actually celebrating as if we'd done the gig of our lives, even though it had been an absolute fucking disaster. I couldn't understand it at the time, but if you're saying that they ripped off the promoter for the money even though Hinch never played a note, then I guess I can see why they were finding the whole thing so amusing. Anyway, Schiffman tells the driver to take us to the airport, but then Hank points out that the Dutch cops were probably already waiting at the gate to put cuffs on him. While Schiffman is digesting that, Hank starts bitching that they're gonna have to get Hinch another fix before the night is out. That's when I started getting an idea in my head."

"First time in your fucking life," interrupts Hinch with a grin.

Ignoring the dig, Cody keeps plowing straight ahead. "It was clear that there was some major shit going down, only I didn't know what it was. I just figured that the best way to find out was to pretend to be stoned. So I started complaining loudly, saying that if they were going to get Hinch high, I wanted to get high too. At first they were telling me to shut up, but then Hank changed his mind. 'You know, why not?' he suddenly said to Schiffman. 'It'll help get the little prick out of our hair.' "

"I kept trying to tell you something in the limo, but I couldn't get you to understand," Hinch interrupts.

"Yeah, you kept saying 'spray,' but I had no idea what you meant," Cody says. "I thought you were trying to say 'let's pray,' which I found pretty funny since I've never seen you within a hundred yards of a church."

Hinch shakes his head like an exasperated schoolteacher. "You're such a fucking dumb-ass. Can't even understand plain simple English."

Cody continues, unabashed, "By the time we get to the airport, Hank and Schiffman have decided that the best thing to do is to lay low for awhile, but, see, they don't want the limo driver to know where we're heading. So we pile out and as soon as the guy has turned the corner, Hank hails a cab and tells the driver to take us to some airport hotel, just a few minutes away. It was one of those suite-type places with a couple of bedrooms and a kitchen and a living room, you know? We didn't have any luggage or anything, but I guess I was just assuming he'd have the crew bring the bags and meet us later.

"Once we got up to the room, Hank and Schiffman took off to score the dope, saying they'd only be a few minutes. I deposited Hinch on one of the beds and left him to sleep it off, then I made a pot of coffee. He was still pretty wasted, but he was breathing okay and I didn't see any signs of him turning blue, so I thought he'd probably be all right in an hour or two.

"Why didn't you leave at that point, or call the cops?" I blurt out, surprising myself at my own audacity.

Cody looks incredulous. "Leave? And leave drool-boy here on his own?" He gestures at Hinch, who seems more amused than insulted. "Besides, I think I had maybe six bucks in my wallet: Hank was holding my passport, and Hinch's too. So where would I go? I didn't know a soul in Holland, and I damn well wasn't about to bring the cops into this; for all I knew, the only thing they'd do is toss Mr. Rock Star here behind bars and throw away the key. No, I thought the best course of action was to stay put and try to find out what the hell was going on."

"Sorry," I mumble. "Guess I was getting ahead of myself. Please, go on."

"Anyway," he says after a moment's hesitation, "when they got back, Hank and Schiffman seemed good and pissed off at each other, but whatever was going on between them, it was obvious they weren't about to say anything in front of me."

Eyes brightening, Cody leans forward in his seat, his voice still modulated but the words starting to come out rapid-fire. "Like I said, I figured the best way to find out what it was they were trying to pull was to pretend to be out of it. So I pulled my bottle of Secs—Seconals—out of my pocket and threw a dozen of the capsules down my throat, right there in front of them. A few minutes later, I was passed out in one of the living room chairs … or so they thought."

He sits there grinning from ear to ear, waiting for me to coax the rest of the story from him.

"I don't understand," I finally say, rising to the bait. "If you took a dozen Seconals, you would have been passed out for real."

Hinch and Cody exchange knowing glances.

"True," Cody agrees. "But I never said I took a dozen Seconals. I said I took a dozen *capsules*. I'd taken great care to empty them out into the pot of coffee beforehand."

Now this is the Cody that Donnie had told me about, I think, totally impressed. The conniver who maneuvered Hinch into writing songs, the perpetrator of the Great Mono Swindle, the wizard who single-handedly replaced all the instruments on their first demo tape. He's doing his best to ignore the looks of awe on all our faces, but based on the blush of red in his cheeks, he's only partially succeeding.

"So now I'm snoring my ass off, pretending to be fast asleep," Cody continues, grinning despite himself. "And here's where my practice in the art of taking downers really paid off, because they were totally sold. After a few minutes of checking my pupils and asking each other, 'Are you sure he's really out of it?' they finally decided it was okay to talk in front of me. And talk they did.

"Basically, they were arguing like an old couple that have been married way too long. Schiffman was cursing Hank out, saying, 'I can't even trust you to do a simple job like this,' and Hank is saying, 'It's not my fault, it's that fucking dealer.' I thought at first that Schiffman was mad that Hinch had overdosed, but it turned out just the opposite: he was mad that Hinch *wasn't* dead."

I feel a chill in the room, and it's not coming from the howling wind outside. "Are you sure?" I ask, dumbfounded.

Cody shoots me a withering look. "Of course I'm sure. I know what I heard. 'I trusted you to take him out,' Schiffman kept screaming at Hank, 'and you couldn't even manage that!' Hank kept blaming the dealer, swearing that he'd been ripped off by the guy. 'He told me it was pure, off the boat,' he kept insisting.

"Finally, Schiffman started to calm down. 'Okay, so let's try to figure this out,' he said to Hank. 'We can't do the rest of the gigs in Holland, because Uhlemeyer will be gunning for me. So if we want to stick with the plan and take Hinch out in public, maybe the best thing is to do it in London.'

"But Hank didn't like that idea. 'That would mean keeping him alive for nearly three weeks,' he said, 'which will cost us a fortune. Not to mention his pain in the ass little buddy here. What the fuck are we supposed to do about him?'"

There's a pause while Cody glances over at Katie expectantly. "Go ahead," she urges. "Tell Bernie what Schiffman's answer was. It's important that he know."

Cody looks directly at me. "He said, 'You should have killed the redheaded prick years ago when you had the chance.'"

My eyes widen.

"Don't worry; I didn't take it personally," Cody says with a laugh. "I just kept pretending to be asleep. Then all of sudden Hank says, 'I got an idea.' 'Okay, I'm listening,' Schiffman says. Of course, he would have shit himself if he knew *I* was listening too. But Hank's plan was actually a pretty good one, even I have to admit."

In a low, gruff voice that I presume to be an impersonation of Ryker speaking, Cody re-creates the conversation. "'Let's take care of things here and now, but put the murder weapon in the hands of his best friend,'" he growls. "'One junkie shooting up another: One OD's, the other goes to jail for it. Simple. Done.'"

Then, back to his normal voice: "Schiffman thinks it over for a minute, then says, 'I like it. Go wake them up, and let's get it over with.' The next thing I know Hank is slapping me across the face. 'Go get Hinch,' he tells me. 'It's time for his fix.'

"I pretended to wake up, all groggy, and then I asked him, 'You got some for me too, right?' 'Sure, pal, sure,' he answers. 'Go get your friend and I'll get the shit together.' The bastards still hadn't drunk any of that coffee, though, and I was running out of time. I knew they both had guns, and I figured even if I could take one of them out, the other one would waste me *and* Hinch.

"So I say, 'Hey man, I need some java first to help wake me up. You want some?' Just to kind of plant the idea, you know? They both say yes, so I pour out three cups. Then I head off to Hinch's bedroom, making a quick pit stop in the bathroom first, where I pour the contents of my cup down the drain. I get Hinch to his feet and help him into the living room; by now he was coming around a little bit.

"I can see Hank busy getting the needles ready, and I notice he's real careful to prepare each one individually, which tells me he's planning to give us very different doses. Schiffman's got the TV on, tuned to the news; he's not paying us a whole lot of attention. But neither of them has touched their coffee yet. 'You want me to reheat this?' I ask, pointing to their cups. 'Nah, it's okay, we'll get to it,' Hank tells me.

"Then he takes the two needles and hands them to me, one at a time after carefully wiping each with a paper towel, making sure the only fingerprints on them will be mine, I guess. 'This one is for Hinch, and this one is for you,' he tells me. 'What, he gets the good shit?' I ask. 'Naturally,' says Hank. 'After all, he's the star. Don't worry, your fix will get you off.'

"Well, I have to admit by this point I'm starting to piss my pants. Just then, the news guy on TV says something about Bill Clinton. 'Who's been blowing Bubba now?' I ask, looking over at the television kind of wide-eyed, which causes both of them to glance over there too, for a split-second. It's just enough of a diversion to allow me to switch needles before quickly shooting Hinch up. Then, with Hank watching my every move, I have no choice but to stick the other needle in my own arm."

He pauses and takes a sip of tea.

"And?..." I ask.

"That's it, bro. The next thing I know I'm dying in a fucking bathtub."

SUDDENLY AND INCONGRUOUSLY, a burst of sunshine fills the gloom outside and sends a shaft of pure yellow into the dim room where we are seated.

"And the Lord saw that Cody was dying, and the Lord saw that it was good," intones Mike Testa, instantly breaking the tension. We all burst out in laughter and return our attention to Hinch, who has resumed the story.

"After Cody shot me full of dope," he says, "I started nodding off again, but even through the haze I could tell that the shit was a lot less strong than what I'd been getting the last few days. I remember Cody getting up from the chair after fixing himself, swaying a little in the wind, and announcing that he was going to take a bath. Why the hell he decided to do that, I have no idea."

"I guess it seemed as good a place as any to die," says Cody softly. We are all stunned by his answer, but he merely shrugs his shoulders as if to say, *Hey, whatever.*

After a long pause, Hinch continues. "After awhile I was able to rouse myself. To my surprise, both Schiffman and Hank were passed out, sawing wood like a couple of lumberjacks. I wandered into the bathroom to take a pee and found Cody lying in the bathtub, turning blue.

That's when my precaution came in handy. I raced into the bedroom and grabbed my jacket where Cody had left it, draped on the bed. Thank God it was still there, in the pocket."

He shakes his head, shivering at the memory of it.

"Thank God *what* was still there?" I ask.

"My nasal spray. The spray I tried to get dickweed here to dose me with in the limo, only he was too lame to understand what I was saying."

"Fuck you," says Cody with a grin.

"I don't understand," I say, totally baffled. "Why was nasal spray so important? It's not like you were having an attack of hay fever."

"Bernie, Bernie, Bernie," Hinch tsks. "And Donnie said you were smart."

"Go ahead, Tommy," Katie implores. "Stop teasing him."

Hinch turns to me, a serious look replacing the smirk. "This was no Sudafed we were talking about, big boy. It was Narcan."

Having no idea what that means, I stare at him blankly.

"I can tell you've never been a junkie," Hinch says. "Narcan is a nasal spray that blocks the effects of heroin, at least for an hour or so. It's strong shit, only available by prescription and very expensive ... but I happen to know some pretty hip doctors, and fortunately I'm able to scrape together a buck or two when I need it. As soon as Hank turned up at my door, I thought, uh-oh, I better pack a couple bottles of the stuff, just in case, and I'd better be sure to keep one handy, so I shoved one in my jacket pocket. I hit my buddy here with a couple of blasts of it, and in a few minutes his color started coming back and his breathing returned to normal. As quick as I could, I got him out of the tub, toweled him down, and threw some clothes on him.

"When I get back to the living room, Schiffman and Hank are still fast asleep, and now Cody's starting to tell me a little bit about what he overheard, so I decide the best thing we can do is to split. But not before I have one last brainstorm." Once again Hinch pauses for dramatic effect.

"And that brainstorm was...?" I ask.

"The Zero Halliburton." He holds up the small aluminum briefcase which Donnie had once described as the 'totem of the road manager' and exchanges high fives with Cody and Mike.

"It had *every*thing, man," Hinch explains. "Tons of cash, from both the Amsterdam and Paris gigs, plus not only our passports, but *their* passports.

"Hank had left it right by the door when he got back from scoring the dope, so I grabbed it, along with his and Schiffman's wallets, before we headed out. I figured the fact that we had their passports, plus all their cash and credit cards, would keep those two assholes detained in Holland for awhile. If you're saying they only made it to London a few days ago, I'm guessing it took that long for Schiffman's office to arrange for new passports and credit cards to be issued back in the States and to have his bodyguards bring them over to him."

"After which they no doubt made a stop at my hotel, where they took a shot at me and murdered Rudie," I say, the whole picture finally dawning on me. "So where did you guys end up staying?"

"Just another funky airport hotel," Hinch replies. "I figured that when Schiffman and Hank came to, they'd probably assume we had taken off as far away as possible; I thought the last place they'd look for us was at another airport hotel just down the street. And the first thing I did after we checked in was to call my little Katie here"—at this, I can see her frowning slightly—"and the next thing I know the cavalry has arrived. Me and Cody just hunkered down until her flight landed, ordering in room service and watching cartoons on TV.

My man here was still a bit shaky, but I could see that he was going to be okay; no need to take him to a hospital and risk having Schiffman find us."

"And then?"

Katie turns to me. "Tommy was pretty incoherent when he called, to tell you the truth," she says, "but I was able to get enough out of him to realize that he and Cody were in big trouble, and I'd seen enough of Alan Schiffman back when I was Mrs. Hinchton to know what kind of person we were dealing with. So the first thing I did after hanging up was to call Michael here. I knew we'd need brawn as well as brains to get Tommy out of this mess." I study Hinch's face for any trace of jealousy, but see only sheer admiration.

"I always told Katie to call me if she ever needed anything," Testa explains. "I'm glad she did."

"I'm glad, too." She pats his arm affectionately. Were they once lovers? I suppose it's possible. In the end, though, what does it matter? "Anyway," she continues, "Michael grabbed the first flight out of Atlanta and met me at Dulles airport, where we jumped on a plane to Amsterdam. We landed eight hours later and found our boys here having a party in their hotel room."

"Yeah, big party," Hinch complains. "Room service swill and 24-hour Scoobee-Doo cartoons."

"The 'cartoons' you had on when we walked in the door were hardly G-rated," Katie points out.

"Okay, so we were watching a little porn, too. But that was the extent of our partying, I swear. Right, Cody?"

Cody merely winks and mimes zipping his lip.

"What was your next move?" I ask. I'm enjoying the repartee but the clock above the mantelpiece reminds me that time is evaporating away.

"Well, Michael here knew of Dr. McFarlane, and, as Tommy said, we had adequate reserves of cash, so a few phone calls were made to friends in the business"—Testa is mouthing the words "Keith and Pete" off in the distance—"and we made arrangements to hire a private boat to discreetly take us from Hook of Holland across to Newcastle, where another friend of Mike's was waiting to drive us up here. And here we have been, patiently anticipating your arrival. Based on what Donnie had told me before he passed away, I felt sure that you'd connect the dots eventually. Though I have to say I didn't think you'd cut it quite so fine."

———

When I call him a little while later, Hans takes it all in without a word of comment. I'm not sure if his silence means that he's enthralled or somehow disappointed. Maybe he's let down by the fact that Hinch and Cody had found a way to slip out of the Netherlands without him knowing about it. Makes no difference. We now have only seven hours until our meeting in London.

"Okay, listen," he says when I'm done, "If you're still certain that Mike Testa will join us, VandeVoort has come up with a modified plan."

"I'm certain."

"Good. But there is a catch: we'll need Hinch too."

"I'm not sure that's possible," I tell Hans. "I don't know if the doctor will discharge him early, and even if she does, I'm not sure Katie will allow him to be put in harm's way."

"Let me tell you what VandeVoort has in mind. Then you can decide."

When our conversation is done, I take Testa aside and explain VandeVoort's idea. "Let's do it," he says excitedly. "Big Vic and the others will want in, too—I'm sure of it. Vic was good friends with Cody's buddy Limey Bob, you know."

"But what about Hinch?" I ask.

He scratches his head. "Well, I agree that Katie might not go for it, but Hinch is a grown boy. Let's see what he has to say about it."

"Maybe it's best not to say anything to Katie at all," I reason. "Maybe we should just talk to the guys."

Once again, we ask Katie to excuse herself. Without a word of protest, she heads off to help the McFarlanes with preparations for dinner. Mike and I sit down with Hinch and Cody and explain what Hans and VandeVoort have in mind.

"No problem," says Hinch. "I'm in."

"Wait a minute: there *is* a problem," interjects Cody. "The problem is that you're the star, and you have a show to do on Friday—the most important show of your fucking life. There's no way you're going down to London with these guys tonight. If I have to stop you by blocking the goddamn door, that's what I'll do."

"The hell you will," says Hinch glumly. It's as empty a threat as I've ever heard.

"Try me," Cody challenges. "Let me repeat: There is no fucking way you're doing this."

Hinch looks over at us with a helpless shrug of his shoulders. I'm amazed at the little guy's forcefulness, and doubly amazed at Hinch's readiness to bend to Cody's will.

The next words that come from Cody's lips leave me triply amazed.

"Hinch is staying here," he reiterates one last time. "*I'm* the one going with you tonight."

A HALF HOUR LATER Cody, Mike Testa and I are heading out the door to catch a late afternoon flight down to London, over Dr. McFarlane's vehement objections. "Both men need as much treatment as possible, not just one of them," she points out.

"I know," Katie tells her with a sigh, "but there's nothing anyone can do once Cody makes up his mind."

Hugs are exchanged all around. I notice the longest and warmest one is between Cody and Katie. As she leans over to give me a peck on the cheek, I whisper in her ear, "If you can, date the papers firing Schiffman today. I mean, literally, today."

Katie smiles at me and whispers back, "It's already been taken care of, Bernie. And don't worry—I'll make sure Hinch gets to the gig."

A stoic Cody spends most of the journey back to Heathrow staring out the airplane window contemplatively, a storm of conflicting emotions clearly raging beneath the surface. Much as I want to talk with him, I decide it is prudent to leave him to his thoughts. Instead, I occupy the time by engaging in conversation with Mike, who is every bit as outgoing and gregarious as Cody is taut and introspective.

"Tell me, why do you think Schiffman wants Hinch dead?" I ask him at one point.

"Two words: Jimi Hendrix."

I look confused.

"Okay, then, I'll give you six more: Jim Croce. Janis Joplin. Harry Chapin. The answer is simple, Bernie: Hinch is worth more to Schiffman dead than alive. Think about it: his records haven't been selling, his tours have been shorter and shorter, his fan base has been shrinking. Don't get me wrong, I love the guy to death, but he's yesterday's story. Having him offed brings him back into the public eye. Which means big bucks. That's the only thing that pricks like Schiffman care about."

"But why this need to kill Hinch in public?"

"Schiffman's always been a major publicity hound. If Hinch drops dead at home, or in some stinking hotel room somewhere, it's back page news. If he does it in front of a thousand screaming fans, it's front page news. The bigger the headlines, the more money Schiffman stands to make. And now that he's failed to take Hinch out with a needle, I'm guessing he's going to try to get it done with high-powered rifles, probably courtesy of those two goons of his, and probably while our boy is onstage at the Millennium Dome. Think of what kind of headlines that would yield."

I do, and it's pretty sobering. "I would have thought that a dead client means smaller commissions," I finally say.

"If Schiffman were merely Hinch's manager or booking agent, that might be true. But Katie's been looking into his affairs, and she's discovered that Schiffman has wormed his way into much, much more. For one thing, he owns the exclusive rights to Hinch's name and likeness, and that's big bucks once the memorial T-shirts start rolling off the factory floor. For another, he owns the rights to any unreleased Hinch recordings which may surface—and, believe me, they *will* surface if the guy is dead."

"Sounds illegal," I say, a chill running down my spine as I think of those missing tapes from Wallingford's library.

"It probably is," Mike replies. "But as long as Schiffman is alive, he'll be paying a team of high-powered lawyers to fight any litigation that may come his way. And I believe Katie's planning a heap of lawsuits. I feel sorry for her having to face that kind of frustration in the courts; it'll probably be tied up in the system for years."

"Maybe we can do something about that."

He grins at me. "Maybe we can."

A little after eight, we arrive at the modest East End hotel where Hans has booked rooms for the three of us, and by nine o'clock we are seated in a small conference room on the second floor, sitting across from VandeVoort, Hans, and Hans's brother Petrus.

The grim-faced detective quickly takes charge of the meeting. The staff at The Gig have taken to their spying duties with great enthusiasm, he reports, partly in reflection of their greed, partly because Schiffman has proven himself to be a bad tipper and a royal pain in the ass. The information is solid, and the plan is proceeding smoothly. Because Schiffman and Ryker have shown themselves to be creatures of habit, no major problems are anticipated, VandeVoort assures us, although he is quick to add that the only predictable thing about situations like this one is their unpredictability.

"Are you sure we can count on the full discretion of everyone you plan on approaching?" VandeVoort asks Testa.

Cody answers for him. "Don't worry; they'll come through," he says tersely.

VandeVoort concludes the meeting with a word of warning. "Remember, every single person we will be dealing with tomorrow will be armed and extremely dangerous," he cautions us. "Ryker may have left his weapon behind at Wolter's place, but you can be sure that he has bought another gun since then. As far as he and the bodyguards are concerned, you can assume their weapons will be on their person. Schiffman, probably not: My guess is that he will be keeping his gun hidden, most likely in a place where it is easily accessible. Whatever happens, keep that in mind. Got it?" He looks around the room to make sure we all understand. "Good. See you gentlemen first thing tomorrow morning: 5 a.m. sharp."

With that, we all go off into the night. There is work to be done, and no time to dwell on the consequences of whatever lies ahead.

30

Transcript: Interview with Donnie Boyle, June 25, 1998

Hey, Bern, good to see ya. Yeah, I'm still hanging in there, but I got news. Bad news. The doctors have finally leveled with me. It's the big C, same as my old man had, and it's spread all over my damn body. There's nothing more they can do, and nothing more I can do now except wait it out. The good news is that I won't have long to wait, or so they tell me.

I appreciate your sympathy, but you know what? It's just as well, because I really am pretty weary of fighting this thing. And I've come to realize that I've actually got a lot to be thankful for. Thankful for my family, thankful that I was able to quit the rock 'n' roll game before it chewed me up and spat me out like it did so many others. You know, as rich and famous as Hinch has become, I wouldn't trade one day of my life for one day of his. He's got all the fame and fortune he ever hoped for, but it hasn't brought the miserable bastard one ounce of happiness. Me, at least I can die with a clear conscience. At least I never had to trample on anyone to get where I am … even if the only place I ended up was this damned hospital bed.

I'm thankful I met you, too, Bernie. All this talking about the old days has been good for my soul. After years of trying to bury my past, you forced me to face it, warts and all. I know I did a lot of dumb things back in those days, and a few things I'm even ashamed of, but at least you gave me the opportunity to come clean about it all.

So now, whatever happens, happens. If the dude with the scepter pays me a visit and brings me upstairs, I'll get to see my folks again. Even if he ends up dragging me downstairs, at least I'll have the pleasure of seeing Alan Schiffman there some day.

Goddamn it Bernie, if I told you once I told you a hundred times—stop making me laugh, you bastard.

Alright, well, let's get on with it. To be honest, I'm not sure what more there is to say, or how long I can do this before the bells start going off and the nurses come in to kick you out, but, what the hell, let's give it a shot.

I guess you heard the news about Vernon a few years back. He always was a game little guy, and I give him a lot of credit for sticking it out with us after the accident, but by the end of Hinch's second tour as a headliner, it was obvious that Joe Dan's death had taken a huge toll on old Vern. The spark was gone from his eyes, and even without Hank and Schiffman's other toadies hanging around, he soon succumbed to smack, same as Cody had. I guess it was the only drug strong enough to blunt the pain, but with our "no heroin" edict firmly in place, I had no choice but to fire him. It happened shortly after the one-year anniversary of JD's passing, and, strangely enough, he was grateful to me for doing so.

"You've freed me up, Donnie," was the tearful way he put it when I told him, as gently as I could, that we'd be letting him go at the conclusion of the tour. "Now I can go back home and take care of momma, the way Joe Dan would want me to."

This time around, though, I made sure Hinch did the right thing and paid for Vernon's rehab; I even chipped in a few bucks myself, just to get the ball rolling. Ol' Vern got himself cleaned up, all right, then spent the rest of his life working his family farm, supporting all his poor relations for many years until he finally drank himself to death. I only heard about it some months after the fact, so I never did get to visit Mississippi again, but when I got the news I immediately got in touch with Hinch and prevailed upon him to set up a scholarship in their honor: The Joe Dan and Vernon Dean Trucker College Fund. Maybe it'll help some kid down in the boonies escape a lifetime of drudgery. Hopefully it'll save that same kid from the rock 'n' roll meat factory, too.

And that's what it is, Bernie, make no mistake about it: a goddamn meat factory. As long as it's inhabited by monsters like Schiffman and willing dupes like we were, that's all it will ever be. Tastes may change, and music may evolve in ways we can't even imagine, but there are three things you can always count on: death, taxes, and Madonna changing her image every few years. It's not just her, of course—it's every rock star and pop diva and teen idol everywhere, driven by monstrous egos and fed by lackies willing to stroke those egos at every opportunity. That's the worst part of the music business: the lack of importance that the music itself plays. It took me years to figure that out, but it's the goddamn truth. Take it from me: I spent too much of my life in what seemed like the eye of the storm, only to find that it was a storm of bullshit covered in glitter, fake as a Disney E-ticket ride.

So anyway, yeah, with the help of a few good people and one scumbag named Alan Schiffman, Hinch finally grabbed the brass ring. I was to ride the carousel with him for the next four years, touring the world over as he and a variety of anonymous pickup musicians performed before millions of screaming fans, all completely oblivious to the web of lies and deceit that had gotten him there. Backstage and on off-days, I used to get a perverse pleasure out of watching so-called celebrities of every stripe fawning over Hinch, practically tripping over themselves to get next to him and bask in his glory. Talk about your idols made of clay! But Hinch took to the trappings of high office as if he had been born to them, and there wasn't an ounce of gratitude in the preening bastard, either. The more adulation he received, the larger his ego swelled; he actually felt *entitled* to the throne and all the goodies that went with it. As I said, I stuck with him more out of curiosity than loyalty, but as the years went on we grew more and more estranged, not least because of the way I saw him treating his fellow musicians … not to mention the way he was treating Katie.

One of the first things Hinch did when that first big royalty check came in was to buy himself a luxury tour bus so that he could travel separately from the rest of us. He claimed that the reason was to give Katie more privacy, but really what it did was alienate him from the musicians and make them feel like the hired hands they were. What's more, he soon began inventing all kinds of excuses not to take Katie on the road with him. Before long, we began referring to his bus as The Rolling Orgy. Given the level of press coverage he was receiving, it was more than disrespectful to Katie—it was disgraceful. I mean, if he wanted to screw around, that was his business, but the least he could have done was try to be discreet about it.

Katie eventually left him, you know. Hinch had planted her in this huge Beverly Hills mansion where she had cooks, maids, gardeners, chauffeurs, and every material thing anyone could ever ask for, but what the poor bastard didn't realize was that all she wanted was *him*. With no kids in the picture—I heard that she couldn't have any, which strikes me as the likely reason, judging from the number of paternity suits filed against Hinch—she simply wanted to devote herself to her childhood sweetheart. But Tommy could never be satisfied with one woman, and in any event, love to him was always a one-way street, so Katie finally walked out on him and moved back East. I guess she wanted to get as far away from the rock 'n' roll life as she could, because she went back to college, got her degree, and then went on to law school, where I hear she got remarried.

Hinch's reaction to Katie's leaving was to immediately move in with a fifteen year-old Lolita and her forty year-old mom. Actually, the mom was the better looking of the two, and the cover story was that she was Hinch's paramour. But we all knew from his backstage bragging that he was fucking them both—often at the same time, in the same bed, in acrobatic displays that left the mind boggled. Hinch's living arrangements made for lurid gossip—publicity that Schiffman loved, of course—but somehow the scandal didn't tarnish Hinch's image with his fans, because his records kept selling and his tours kept selling out. A few years later, when the girl turned eighteen, he publicly proclaimed his love for her and not the mother, which, as everyone knows, caused the whole thing to collapse in as messy and ugly a fashion as you could imagine, with lawsuits flying everywhere. That time around, many of his fans *were* outraged, at least the American ones. His somewhat more sophisticated European and Japanese fans didn't give a shit who he was screwing, though, and they remained loyal, and still do, to this very day. That's why the guy can barely get arrested in the States but still sells out 3,000-seat arenas in Stuttgart and Tokyo. Moving to Switzerland back in the mid '80s was probably the smartest thing Hinch ever did; there's no question that it prolonged his career well past the point that anyone expected.

Still, I have to admit that Hinch blossomed in those first years of rock stardom, both as a performer and a guitarist. His songwriting also improved, even though Schiffman often brought in one of the many song doctors floating around L.A. Ever hear the term? It's one of the music industry's dirty little secrets, but everyone in the biz knows about them: talented yet undiscovered songwriters who come in and rewrite the work of established stars for a modest fee. There's always a Schiffman hanging around, of course, to ensure they sign paperwork that assigns all rights to said star in perpetuity—much the same kind of document that Cody signed in exchange for a measly fifty grand—and also promise to keep their mouths shut about it, on pain of both legal retribution and getting their kneecaps broken. I couldn't tell you exactly how many of Hinch's supposed songs underwent that kind of surgery, but, based on what I saw, I would say it was more than half of them, including a few that went on to become huge hits and earn him monstrous royalties.

So the money kept pouring in by the bucketload, and the tours kept getting bigger and bigger, despite the fact that JJ disappeared from the scene soon after Hank started working in Schiffman's New York office; she couldn't stand the SOB any more than I could, and she didn't trust him any more than I did, either. She called me shortly before she split to tell me that she was leaving to join some commune in Oregon, I think it was. She confessed with a charming lack of embarrassment that all the commune members except her were male, and that one of them had, and I quote, "the biggest dick I've ever seen." Bless her heart. JJ was by far the sweetest little slut I ever knew.

And Cody? Well, one bright morning, not long after Katie left, Cody returned. He wasn't the same guy, though. He'd cleaned up—the strongest thing in his repertoire was now a long-neck or the occasional joint—but his stint with Limey Bob and the rigors of the road had hardened him, toughened him to where he was almost unrecognizable. Gone was the soft-spoken dreamer who'd fall in love with every groupie he encountered and then spend hours composing beautiful ballads to her limpid eyes and virtuous soul. Gone too was the master manipulator, the consummate musician who fiercely pursued his craft and challenged everyone around him to greater heights of perfection.

In their place was a roadie. Cody the roadie.

I never again saw Cody pick up a guitar, unless it was in a flight case, and I never again saw him dress in anything other than black: black T-shirt, black shorts, black socks, black sneakers … and a mag-lite hanging from his belt. Cody had been indoctrinated. He'd joined the brotherhood of the road. And when Limey Bob gently returned him to my care, Cody firmly declined any role in the Hinch organization other than that of anonymous equipment-humper. He and Hinch had no great reconciliation, no coming together of two old souls who had grown up closer than brothers and passed through all the rituals of manhood side by side. Instead, their relationship was now merely one of employee and employer, protector and protectee. Hinch treated him exactly the same as any of the other roadies, no better, no worse, and that's exactly the way Cody wanted it. And whenever I'd try to explain to any of the constantly changing cast of supporting musicians that Cody had been the founding member of our little band of brothers, and that he had not only been its musical heart and soul but the catalyst for all of Hinch's success, Cody would silence me with a withering look. He simply wanted no reminders of the past. He was determined, it seemed, to live his life in the present tense only. Which, you know, really doesn't seem like such a bad idea.

I was thrilled to have Cody back, yet at the same time saddened at how little of him remained. All my attempts at renewing our bond were gently rebuffed by him; it's not that he was ever unpleasant about it, but his body language spoke volumes. It said, *I don't want to be anything more to you than one of the roadies. No more, no less.*

In the end, I gave up and honored his request, giving him all the distance he craved. It was a tough note on which to end a lifelong friendship, but after all the pain he'd been through, I thought it was the least I owed him.

Me, I hung on for as long as I could. The final straw was Hinch's unbearably stupid decision to align himself with Nancy Reagan and her Just Say No campaign. Just say no, my ass. I happen to know for a fact that Hinch was coked up out of his mind the day he visited the White House and posed for those pictures you see of him grinning like an idiot, arms wrapped around Ronnie and Nancy. It was not only a bad career move, it was a hypocrisy I couldn't stomach. Just like that, I quit. And, you know, saying goodbye to Hinch was actually one of the easiest things I've ever done. It was like waving farewell to a ship pulling out of harbor, a vessel you understand is destined to sail the seas without you. I haven't heard from Hinch, or Schiffman, to this very day. No great loss, as I see it.

You know that old saying about how one door opens whenever another door closes? Well, in my case, it proved to be absolutely true. Within weeks of walking away from rock 'n' roll forever, I met Jen right here in L.A. We fell in love and instantly a whole new world opened up for me: a world of love and commitment and marriage and family. I'd socked away enough money to fulfill a dream and go back to school to get my degree in American Literature, and so for the past fourteen years I've been living a great life, surrounded by my beloved books, being a husband and a dad, doing a little teaching at the local community college, and, in my spare time, counseling young musicians about the perils and pitfalls of the industry. And until I met you, Bernie boy, I haven't wasted one moment looking back.

So that's my story, and Hinch's, or at least as much as I know about it. All I can say is that I consider myself incredibly lucky. That may sound strange coming from a dying man, but it's the goddamned truth.

And now, my friend, I need to get some rest. Catch you on the flip side.

BT note: This was the final interview conducted with Donnie Boyle.

31

"Gentlemen, I hope you appreciate the, ah, delicacy of the situation. As U.S. citizens you would of course normally be entitled to the full protection of the law under American jurisprudence. But given the sensitive nature of this particular dilemma, I'm afraid there simply is not much your government can do. You may be aware of the strategic importance of Turkey to certain national security interests in the Middle East?" Here the Vice-Consul of the United States Embassy to the Netherlands pauses to let his words sink in, carefully tracing the crease of the trousers of his charcoal gray pinstripe Burberry suit as he does so.

Alan Schiffman is not having a good day. Bad enough to be paid a visit by this diplomatic dweeb from the State Department, but now he's starting to get the feeling that he's being shaken down. And Alan Schiffman does not like being shaken down, especially since he's usually the one doing the shaking. Twitching slightly, he turns to his tormentor.

"I read the newspapers," he growls. "Get to the fucking point already."

"The point, Mr. Schiffman," says the Vice-Consul politely, "is that both the United States and Turkey are signatories to mutual extradition treaties. Which means that we cannot legally prevent the deportation of a citizen who has been found guilty of a capital offense. And murdering a credentialed diplomat—a full Ambassador, no less—is most certainly a capital offense. What I am trying to say, Mr. Schiffman, is that there are overriding international concerns of a very sensitive nature which render us powerless to protect you, or your colleague Mr. Ryker, from serving the full sentence rendered by a Turkish court for a crime for which you have been convicted under due process of law."

"What he's saying, boss," says Henry Ryker snarkily, "is that you're going to be spending the next twenty years getting butt-fucked in a Turkish prison. Ever see *Midnight Express*?"

"That is not necessarily what we are saying," interjects the fourth member of this little chit-chat, Interpol Chief Inspecteur Andreas VandeVoort. "Even though the ballistics tests indicate that the weapon causing the fatality was a gun similar to the one registered by Mr. Schiffman, the warrant issued by the Turkish government does not name him specifically. Pending the results of our final investigation, it currently is what we call a 'Johannus Doew'—John Doe, I believe you would call it—document."

"And," adds the Vice-Consul, "we have managed to make a certain, shall we say, arrangement with the Turkish government that obligates us only to surrender into their custody a single individual, even if there are indications of complicity by third parties. Thus, assuming your complete cooperation, one of you may end up retaining your freedom, courtesy of these delicate diplomatic negotiations. It is, I am afraid, the best we can do."

"Well, since it was his gun that shot the motherfucker, I don't see why I should be going down for this," says Ryker, calmly examining his fingernails.

Alan Schiffman jumps to his feet. "You bald-headed prick! I could tell them things that would land you in the fucking electric chair."

"Gentlemen, please!" VandeVoort implores. "As I said when we first arrived, we are here to have a civilized discussion." He turns to Schiffman. "Please, sit down. There is no reason why this cannot be resolved amicably. The problem is not an especially difficult one. True, one of you must, unfortunately, be turned over to the Turkish authorities so that justice can be meted out. However, the other party will be allowed to return to America, thanks to the efforts of my colleague here, and granted immunity from prosecution, provided that he is willing to fully cooperate with federal law enforcement officials in their investigations of criminal activities, past and present. We are here merely to determine which of you will be flying west … and which of you will be flying east."

The two combatants glare at one another from across the room, weighing their options.

THINGS HAVE BEEN difficult for Alan Schiffman almost since he woke up. As it had done for the past two days, his bedside phone began ringing promptly at 6:30 AM, at the behest of the wake-up call he had ordered when he first checked into The Gig. At 6:40, he arose, peed, brushed his teeth, and then pounded on Henry Ryker's bedroom door to wake him, same as he had done yesterday, and the day before. At 6:45, the same surly waiter who had been bringing him coffee and the morning newspaper for the past two days knocked gently on the door of Suite 1423 and, upon gaining admittance, deposited two large pots of strong coffee, one on the desk which dominated the center of the living room, the other on a side table off to the left of the elegant beige leather sofa. As had happened for the past two days, the waiter was followed into the room by Salvatore and Luigi Antucci, both already dressed immaculately in matching cashmere sweaters and double-knit slacks. Wordlessly, they crossed the room and poured themselves steaming hot cups of coffee.

Schiffman pulled his bathrobe tight and addressed the two men with annoyance. "Listen, you dumb wops, how many times do I have to tell you, come in here one at a time! I always want at least one of you out there."

Salvatore—or was it Luigi?—mumbled something under his breath. It was hard to make out but it sounded vaguely like "spring naughty hell." With that, he and Luigi (or was it Salvatore?) turned and left the room, coffee cups in hand.

Alan Schiffman had always been a cautious man—some might say even paranoid—and on this particular morning, his caution was not misplaced, for while he and his two bodyguards were engaged in this little bit of repartee, a number of grim-faced men had filed out from the elevator across the hall and, using passkeys issued by the hotel manager (now the proud possessor of two crisp new fifty-pound notes, carefully folded in his wallet), silently opened the doors to two of the darkened rooms on the fourteenth floor, slipping inside before the bodyguards emerged to resume their place at the security desk.

Meanwhile, back in Suite 1423, the waiter unfolded that morning's edition of the *International Herald Tribune* and placed it on the desk next to the coffee. With a perfunctory "Will that be all, sir?" he extracted the room service bill from his jacket pocket and handed it to Alan Schiffman for his signature. Schiffman, he noticed, left him the same crappy tip he had left yesterday, and the day before. Task completed, the waiter bowed and left the room. "Never mind," he said to himself reassuringly as he got into the elevator, smirking at the thought of the twenty-pound note burning a hole in his pocket.

At 6:50 AM, Alan Schiffman poured himself the first cup of coffee of the day, then glanced at the newspaper. The headline caught his eye immediately.

TOP TURKISH AMBASSADOR SLAIN
IN AMSTERDAM CHRISTMAS DAY SHOOTING.
TWO AMERICANS SUSPECTED

Frantically, he whipped the newspaper off the desk. The story, four columns wide, took up nearly half the front page. In its impassive journalistic style, it told of a major diplomatic incident brewing between Turkey, the Netherlands, and the United States, the latter of which, it was believed, was the native country of the two gunmen suspected in the shooting. The corpse causing all the ruckus was the Turkish ambassador to Holland, who had apparently been making a Christmas Day visit to an orphanage in Amsterdam when a stray bullet from a drug deal gone awry found its way into his brain, which then exploded messily, traumatizing several nearby toddlers in the process. The incident, the article further went on to report, had been kept secret for almost a week owing to the fact that said ambassador was also the brother-in-law of the extremely popular Turkish prime minister, who was eager to guard his family's privacy. Now that word had leaked out, there had been rioting in the streets of Ankara and much public outcry for justice. In anticipation of such outrage, the country's antiquated legal system had already gone ahead and tried and convicted the shooter—to be named later—for murder in the second degree. The putative sentence for such a crime was twenty years in prison, although in practice, the article's author pointed out, no one ever survived anywhere close to that in the famously brutal Turkish penal institutions.

"Hank! Get the fuck in here!"

Shuddering with fear, Schiffman turned on the TV to see what they were saying about the shooting on the cable news channels. Girding himself for the worst, he was almost relieved when all he got was static. But his relief quickly turned to frustration, then anger, as he dialed the front desk and castigated the unfortunate recipient of his call with a diatribe about "this fucking country" and "you'd think the least a so-called luxury hotel could provide was fucking TV service," and "if this were L.A., I'd sue your ass so fast your head would spin."

"Terribly sorry, sir," came the response from the desk clerk, who actually wasn't the least bit sorry since this minor disruption of service had netted him a brand new ten-pound note which he was already planning on spending in the pub that evening. "We're working on it, I promise you. Hope to have it fixed in a jif."

Schiffman slammed the phone down and turned to Henry Ryker, who was busily reading the article, his mouth moving as he came to the big words. "This is trouble, serious trouble," Schiffman said angrily. "I told you we shouldn't have gone back to that fucking dealer."

"Fuck you," said Henry Ryker in response. "I told *you* not to pack heat. Who do you think you are, Roy fucking Rogers?"

For the next ten minutes, the two men fumed and argued and Fuck You'd until the air was blue with profanity and they were fairly spitting at one another. Deprived of any real news from the outside world, they were unaware that the cause of their quarrel was in fact a very special edition of the *International Herald Tribune*, with a front page prepared with great care the night before by Hans and Petrus Uhlemeyer at an East End print shop owned by a friend of theirs.

"I'm taking a shower," announced Schiffman to Ryker when he was all argued out. "Let me know when the fucking TV comes back on."

AN HOUR LATER, the television was still not working, and Alan Schiffman was starting to get seriously pissed off. He tried placing a transatlantic call to his thousand-dollar-an-hour attorney in L.A. to instruct him to begin proceedings against The Gig, only to be informed by the hotel operator that the phones were temporarily out of service. Midway through his expletive-filled diatribe against her and her as-yet-unborn children, there was a knock on the door.

It was Luigi.

"Hey, boss, I think Hinch is here. I hear guitar coming from his room down the hall."

"Are you sure?" said Schiffman.

"It sure sounds like him playing," said Luigi. "He's doing that song of his—what's it called? 'Keeping It Real'? I like that song."

Finally, some satisfaction. "About fucking time," Schiffman said, hanging up on the operator (who didn't care, since the five-pound note she had been handed moments before meant that she'd be able to splurge on fish and chips that night instead of having to cook dinner). "You and Sal go get him and bring him here. Tell him I want a word." This was the way Alan Schiffman did things: he never went to people, he had people come to him. If they wouldn't come to him, he had Louie or Sal bring them to him. It was all part of the psychology of respect, or more correctly, subjugation, as he saw it. And there was no way he was going to stand for any of his artists disrespecting him. He knew Hinch would come crawling back—the lure of the Millennium Dome gig would be too much for him to resist—and he was looking forward to making Hinch grovel before allowing him to do the concert. Hinch had to pay for all the aggravation he'd caused, after all. In fact, as Schiffman saw it, Hinch was responsible for the pickle he and Ryker were in, for if Hinch hadn't survived the overdose they'd given him, they never would have been in Wolter's apartment in the first place.

So it was with some degree of pleasure that he anticipated the knock on the door that followed, just five minutes later. Imagine his surprise when he found himself face to face with two strangers in itchy suits instead of a couple of muscle-headed bodyguards and a repentant rock star.

"Who the fuck are you?" was Schiffman's not at all pleasant greeting. He glanced to his left and saw the vacant security desk next to the door. "Sal! Louie!" he shouted. "Get your asses out here."

"I'm afraid that won't be possible, sir," said the courtly gentleman standing directly in front of him, tall, mustached, distinguished. "Please allow me to introduce myself," he continued, flashing an ID that had been carefully crafted by Aachie Tjingerman the day before. "Andreas VandeVoort, Chief Inspecteur with Interpol. This is J. Winthrop Endicott, Vice-Consul of the United States Embassy to the Netherlands." A similarly pedigreed ID is produced. "My colleague and I would like a quiet word with you, if you don't mind."

"And if I do mind?"

VandeVoort laughed. "I'm afraid that's not an option, sir."

And so it has come to this: Alan Schiffman and Henry Ryker, sitting in the living room of Suite 1423 at a London hotel named The Gig, sharing coffee and conversation with a Dutch flatfoot and a chubby, balding diplomat from the U.S. State Department. In a room down the hall, Salvatore and Luigi Antucci are being handcuffed by four off-duty Amsterdam detectives and formally charged with the murder of Rudie Haanraats and the attempted murder of American citizen Bernard Temkin, who is currently otherwise engaged in his charcoal gray pin-striped Burberry suit. A few minutes previously, Sal and Louie had burst into the room expecting to interrupt and intimidate Tommy Hinchton as he blasted out his signature licks on a cherry-red Stratocaster, plugged into a vintage Fender practice amp. Instead, they found themselves face to face with a Zen-like Cody Jeffries, smoothly running through the guitar part he had originated so many years ago, using an instrument and amplifier purchased at The Gig's in-house music store several hours previously. More to the point, they found four guns pointing at their temples and jugular veins, courtesy of

Amsterdam's finest. A few moments from now, they will be driven to a chartered plane waiting on the runway of nearby City Airport. The short flight back to Holland will take less than an hour. This evening, and for many, many evenings afterward, they will be dining on stale *kroketten* and reconstituted *bami goreng* prepared in a prison kitchen instead of sausage and peppers in some fancy Los Angeles restaurant. It is an image that will long bring comfort to Hans Uhlemeyer.

Back in Suite 1423, the tense conversation continues. Like two piranha in a goldfish bowl, Alan Schiffman and Henry Ryker are in the process of shredding one another to the bone, prodded by the careful questioning of Andreas VandeVoort. Enthralled, I sit back and watch and listen as the litany of viciousness continues. I become so wrapped up that I have to remind myself that Ryker, and probably Schiffman too, is armed and still incredibly dangerous.

"It's Hank here who has been supplying Hinch and his band with drugs for years now," snarls Schiffman in hopes of saving his slimy skin. "He got Hinch's guitarist Cody hooked, then he got Hinch himself hooked."

"And it was *you* who hired me with specific instructions to supply them with drugs," Ryker counters. I am fascinated by the long, ugly scar on his face, which seems to throb and move with his every grimace.

"He's the one who ripped off that promoter in Amsterdam," Schiffman says.

"And he's the one who told me to do it."

Back and forth, back and forth they go, tearing, ripping, shredding.

Then Schiffman decides to up the ante. "Do you remember Joe Dan Trucker, the original drummer in Hinch's band?" he asks VandeVoort, who looks at him blankly. "Come on, you can't be that out of it. It was in all the papers back in the '70s. The guy died in a motorcycle accident."

"I'm afraid I'm not much of a pop music fan, sir," says VandeVoort blandly. "But if you think it is a story of interest, please go on."

The scar. That's where it came from. Courtesy of Joe Dan Trucker.

"Well, it was this scumbag here who offed him," Schiffman continues, pointing at Ryker. "Or at least he arranged to have the drummer offed. Got one of his buddies to rig the brakes on the guy's motorcycle so they'd fail. Then, so he wouldn't talk, he murdered his own friend by shooting him up with pure smack."

Another thing Donnie got right.

Enraged, Hank jumps to his feet. "You cocksucking prick!" he cries.

"I did all that on your instructions, you son of a bitch! You masterminded the whole thing!" Out of the corner of my eye I see him start to reach inside his pocket, but almost immediately VandeVoort gets directly in Ryker's face. "Don't even think about it," he warns the heavily sweating thug in a low, even tone. "There are dozens of armed police in the hallway outside, and a SWAT team watching you from the window. Pull out that gun and I promise you will be shot dead instantly. Talk sensibly and you'll walk out of here alive."

After a moment's hesitation, Hank seems to calm down. "I'm not going to take the fall for that motherfucker," he growls, gesturing towards his erstwhile employer.

"You know," Schiffman suddenly announces, shifting tactics, "I think you're right; maybe we can work this out reasonably. Perhaps what we need to do is to try to come to some kind of arrangement that would be beneficial to us all. I am, after all, a fairly wealthy man."

An uncomfortable silence settles over the room. I can see VandeVoort thinking about what the next move should be, as if this is some kind of chess game.

"Mr. Endicott, is it?" Schiffman says, pointing to me. "Can I have a private word with you?"

I look to VandeVoort, who nods almost imperceptibly. Tentatively, I move over to where Schiffman is standing, next to the coffeepot on the desk.

"We're all practical men here, aren't we?" he says softly, pulling me close to his face.

"I suppose so, sir. Within the bounds of protocol, of course." *Where the hell do I come up with these things?*

"Tell me, Winthrop—or should I call you Winnie?—how is the Ambassador these days? We used to summer together on Martha's Vineyard."

This, I know, is a trick question. "She's fine," I reply. Thank God for the World Wide Web.

"And her two lovely daughters?"

This one I don't know. "Fine, fine," I improvise.

"Glad to hear that." The perspiring manager puts his arm around me, then leans in so close I can smell the acrid sourness of fear on his breath.

"You're a lying motherfucker," he whispers in my ear. "She has two sons."

Then, full force, to Ryker: "SHOOT THEM! NOW!"

Like the trained soldier he is, Henry Ryker reaches beneath his jacket and unholsters a fearsome looking pistol, which he proceeds to stick directly in the center of VandeVoort's forehead. *Shit! No! It can't end like this.*

"MANDELA!!"

There is a crash at the door accompanied by that one strange word, bellowed at the top of someone's lungs. The next thing I know, wood is splintering everywhere as Hans barrels into the room headfirst. The distraction is literally momentary but it is sufficient to allow a surprisingly nimble VandeVoort just enough time to knock the gun out of Ryker's hand and bodyslam him to the floor. At the same time, I do exactly what VandeVoort had carefully instructed me to do in case of emergency and knee Alan Schiffman in the groin as hard and as viciously as I can. To my great delight, he instantly collapses in a heap on the floor, holding his nuts and groaning loudly, giving me the opportunity to reach into the desk drawer and extract his gun, which I then proceed to point shakily at his testicles. Meanwhile, Ryker has been subdued by the collective weight of Hans and VandeVoort sitting on top of him, battering him mercilessly. Seconds later, VandeVoort has both Ryker and a doubled-over Schiffman in handcuffs.

At which point Chief Inspecteur Andreas VandeVoort, Vice-Consul J. Winthrop Endicott and promoter Hans Uhlemeyer bid a fond farewell to Alan Schiffman and Henry Ryker. As we turn to leave, Ryker says, simply, "What the fuck?"

"Ah, my dear Mr. Ryker," says VandeVoort. "It seems as if the Ambassador from Turkey has made a miraculous recovery. I wish you and Mr. Schiffman a good day, or what remains of it; I don't believe we'll have the pleasure of meeting again."

As the three of us depart, our places in the room are taken by Mike Testa and several dozen other large gentlemen in black T-shirts and shorts—Hinch's entire road crew, plus the crews of several of the other Millennium Dome acts, all recruited by Mike the night before. They have all spent a most interesting morning listening in to every single word of our conversation over the portable PA system set up in the recreation lounge down at the end of the hall, courtesy of the tiny wireless microphones that Silent Stu had so skillfully secreted in the rims of the two coffee pots delivered earlier by a surly waiter with a brand new twenty-pound note carefully folded in his wallet. And each of the black-shirted gentlemen, I observe, is carrying a large flashlight and/or the pool cue he was using earlier—for much more pleasant reasons—in said recreation room. Stu's bearded face, grim and foreboding, is among those I see entering the room as we leave. "Nice work," VandeVoort says as he places the handcuff keys in Stu's meaty palm. We get the briefest of nods in acknowledgement.

Just as I am about to step out of Suite 1423 forever, I hear Big Vic's booming voice, commanding everyone's attention the way I imagine his friend Limey Bob might have done all those years ago.

"What you did to Hinch, what you did to Joe Dan, that's bad enough," Vic says to the handcuffed duo quaking in the center of the room. "But when you mess with Cody, you mess with all of us."

The door slams shut behind me.

AN HOUR LATER, VandeVoort is landing at the Amsterdam Schilpol with his fellow police officers and the two suspects in the murder of Rudie Haanraats, both of whom are shackled and in safe custody. Last night, he had lectured us all on the importance of alibi; hence, Cody has spent the past sixty minutes purchasing guitar strings and drumsticks in the lobby music store while Hans and I have been having a not-so-quiet drink in the hotel bar, being careful to engage the bartender in frequent and memorable banter.

"Okay, I have a few questions," I say to Hans when we've removed ourselves to a quiet table in the corner.

"Go ahead, shoot," he says, before adding, with a laugh, "Sorry, poor choice of words."

"Well, for one thing you can tell me where the fuck you came up with the name J. Winthrop Endicott," I ask with a grin. "I nearly shit myself when I saw that on the ID."

"I don't know. It was Aachie's idea. I guess that's what he thought an American diplomat might be called."

"And why did you shout 'Mandela,' of all things, when you broke down the door?"

"Good question. Well, as you know, VandeVoort and I have been quite busy the last few days gathering information. One of the Interpol reports he received turned up a rather interesting fact about our friend Henry Ryker. It turns out that, yes, he is an ex-Marine, as you seemed to think...."

"Actually, it was Donnie Boyle who thought that," I say, interrupting.

"All right, as Donnie Boyle thought. But Ryker actually only did a very short tour of duty in Vietnam. Most of his military training came as a mercenary—a soldier of fortune—working for the Vorster government down in Johannesburg in the mid-'70s. And that administration, if you don't know your South African history, was one of the most virulent practitioners of apartheid ever to disgrace the dark continent. According to those reports, Henry Ryker killed many more innocent black Africans than he ever did Viet Cong. It occurred to me that, in the light of recent political developments, he might find that particular word extremely distracting."

Damn, this guy is good. "Okay, one last question: How were you able to break down the door so quickly when you realized that Schiffman had figured out I wasn't the real Vice-Consul?"

"Simple precaution," he tells me. "Last night, I asked Silent Stu if he could wire the mics into the video monitors at the security desk outside the room as well as the PA system in the lounge. I was sitting there the whole time, listening in. I just wanted to be nearby if something bad went down."

"I'm grateful," I say, and I am.

"You're a friend," he replies. "That's what friends do."

Indeed: That *is* what friends do. And if I remember nothing else from this whole, long, impossible journey, it is that which will remain.

FROM TIMBUKTU TO KALAMAZOO, from Marrakesh to Memphis, from the tallest skyscrapers of Manhattan to the deepest canyons of Los Angeles, it is a story which will elicit a round of drinks and the heartiest of laughs wherever and whenever roadies gather. The official report filed by the London Metropolitan Police on December 30, 1999, includes sworn statements from members of the Hinch road crew that, upon arriving in the hotel suite shared by Mr. Schiffman and Mr. Ryker for a scheduled morning meeting to discuss the concert planned for the following evening, they discovered the door ajar and the two occupants engaged in what they described as a "vigorous act of sodomy" whilst perched on the railing of their bedroom balcony. Their surprise upon being discovered in this display of passion apparently caused the two gentlemen to lose their balance and plummet to their death on the concrete court fourteen stories below. The coroner later found that, due to the "ruinous damage" done to the corpses from the impact of the fall, it was impossible to make a definitive determination as to the cause of death; hence, the case was ruled death by misadventure, a finding corroborated by sophisticated DNA tests conducted on the widely scattered remains that indicated high levels of cocaine in both bodies.

Famed rock star Tommy Hinchton stated in a press release that while he was "dismayed to hear of the passing of his ex-manager and former tour manager," he would not comment on their alleged sexual orientation or drug use, adding that he considered it to be a "private matter between two consenting adults."

It was, I had to conclude, a fitting way for Alan Schiffman and Henry Ryker to leave this world. The very same black humor that bonds together those who spend their lives on the road had served to usher out these two thieves and pimps in a way that both besmirched their reputation and held them up as lasting objects of derision. Cruel but fair, a musician might say. Somewhere up in heaven, I am sure Donnie Boyle is smiling.

The concert itself was a triumph. True to her word, Katie had indeed gotten Hinch to the gig on time, where he joyfully reunited with his band and road crew, including one Cody Jeffries. In the absence of Henry Ryker, Hinch drafted Mike Testa to resume the role of tour manager, and he did a spectacular job at the Dome, taking full charge of all the arrangements. In his capable hands, the show ran smooth as clockwork. Part of it may have been the festive atmosphere as a crowd of partygoers welcomed in a new century; part of it may have been the swirling laser lights and the smoke of the dry ice; part of it may have been the open bar at the back of the hall. But mostly it was down to a rejuvenated Hinch, fully clean and sober, who dominated the stage like a true champion, singing full throttle yet pure and soulful, churning out ferocious lick after lick on his signature cherry red Strat, shaking his long locks at girls in the audience who weren't even born when his first record hit the charts. No matter: He whipped them into an orgasmic frenzy, same as their moms ... and probably more than a few of their dads, for that matter. There were a dozen artists on the bill who were far bigger than Hinch in today's music market, but none of them had as enthusiastic a response nor earned as many encores.

It was on his fourth and final encore that Hinch made a gesture of redemption that caused Katie, standing next to me in the offstage wings, to burst into tears. Perspiration pouring off his face after the exertions of the previous hour, Tommy Hinchton stepped up to the microphone and asked for a moment's silence. "I want to dedicate this next song," he said, "to someone who's been with me from the beginning, someone who has been my comrade in arms for more years than I care to remember. There used to be three of us; now there are only two. But I want you all to know that this is the man to whom I owe my life, the man who put me on this stage."

At that moment, Big Vic Farrell strode out, holding a cherry red Stratocaster aloft. Waving his arms, he began urging the crowd to their feet.

"Ladies and gentlemen," said Tommy Hinchton to the cheering audience, risen as one, "please give a warm welcome to my brother, Cody Jeffries."

A few feet from where we stood, I could see Cody the Roadie blushing with embarrassment, shaking off his fellow crew members, who had him locked in a bear hug, literally trying to drag him on the stage. Finally Katie walked over and gave him a kiss. "Do it for Donnie," was all she said.

Tears streaming from his eyes, Cody marched to the center of the stage, strapped on his guitar, and played the sweetest, most perfect solo anyone on this planet has ever heard.

32

THEN, JUST LIKE THAT, we headed our separate ways. Energized by the triumph of his London concert, Hinch was eager to get back on the road, but Katie advised him to first return to Switzerland and get himself legally disentangled from the Countess Miranda de Couqueville before weighing the offers which had begun flooding in. With the planned tour suspended indefinitely, Cody returned to York, Pa., to begin a lengthy recuperation at the home of his sister Amy, where he became reacquainted with his niece and nephew and, to his surprise, slipped easily into the role of doting uncle. Katie decamped to her fashionable Georgetown terraced home and began the long process of litigating with Schiffman Entertainment International and the byzantine web of difficult-to-trace holding companies which controlled the mega-corporation in the absence of the deceased manager. Mike Testa, Hinch's new permanent road manager, returned to his wife and children in Atlanta.

And me, I eventually made my way back westward to La-La Land, but not before first making a brief stopover in Amsterdam, where I witnessed the mortal remains of Rudie Haanraats laid to rest with the full honors normally accorded slain Dutch policemen, courtesy of some judicious string-pulling by Inspecteur Andreas VandeVoort. Before we left the cemetery, Hans joined me in a little ritual ceremony of my own, cheering me on as I removed my toupee for the final time before carefully setting it on fire and stomping the ashes into the ground.

When I finally hauled my tired ass back to Malibu, it was to an empty condo, as I expected. Britney had packed her things and gone, leaving me only with several maxed out credit cards and a note which read, "Bernie, I think it is for the best that we say goodbye. I'm staying with friends in Westwood, hope you had a nice time in Europe, bye, xox Britney." Brief, simple, and no words wasted. Just like our relationship.

In her absence I found that I grew to enjoy solitude. With no distractions around, I was able to focus on completing the manuscript and healing myself. Routine began taking hold: I'd wake up early in the morning—something I'd never done before—and write for a couple of hours before driving down to Topanga Canyon to walk along some of the very same winding paths that Hinch and Katie might have hiked all those many years ago. It cleared my head and gave me an opportunity to think, unencumbered by the realities of modern life. The sole concession I did make to the new millennium was to go out and buy myself one of those damned cell phones, but not before insisting that the salesman show me how to turn it off—and off it remained most of the time, unless I had specific reason to turn it on. Nonetheless, from that day forward, I swore never to ask the question, "Where are you?" of a fellow mobile phone sufferer. I think I've pretty much been able to stick to it, too ... so far.

But there was something bothering me, and it had nothing to do with Britney. Though the demise of Alan Schiffman at the hands of the brotherhood of the road had a poetic justice to it, there were just a few too many loose ends to satisfy me. I couldn't quite put my finger on it, but somehow it seemed as if I'd only uncovered part of the Hinch story.

Leave it to Donnie Boyle to confirm my misgivings, and to point me in the right direction once again. One day, late in February, Katie called and announced she was making a brief visit to L.A. in order to file some paperwork with the local courts in her monumental quest to untangle Hinch from the many-tentacled corporate beast.

"Would you have time to meet me for dinner?" she asked. "I have something I'd like to show you."

As we sat across from one another at the most fashionably unhip restaurant in town I could find, she reached into her purse.

"Do you remember me telling you that Donnie had vouched for you? I thought you might like to see the actual letter he wrote me."

She unfolded the paper carefully and handed it to me. As she watched me read it, I could see her eyes starting to mist up.

```
Dear Katie,
    It seems as if I may be coming to the end of
the line and I wanted to be sure and say goodbye
to you. Please, don't waste any tears on me,
because the truth is that I am happier now than
I've ever been in my entire life.
    With the help of Bernie Temkin, that writer I
told you about, I've been spending a lot of time
reliving the old days, back when you and Hinch
and Cody and I thought that anything was possible
```

and that the world was just there for us to conquer. It seems as if we got a lot of things wrong, but I've come to realize that we also got a lot of things right.

There's something else I wanted to say. I know that I've been convinced all these years that Alan Schiffman was the cause of all our problems, but now that I've had a chance to really think about it I'm not so sure. I will go to my grave convinced that he's an evil bastard, but somehow he never quite struck me as smart enough to have masterminded everything that happened after he got us in his clutches. I wish I had the answer, but I don't. Perhaps it's a matter of tracing the money. JJ might be able to help with that--she always was one smart cookie

One last thing: if anything bad goes down after I am gone, get in touch with Bernie. He's a good man, and you can trust him. Maybe he can help you get to the bottom of things.

Love,
Donnie

"When did he write this?" I ask.

"Two days before he died," she replies, "just hours before he slipped into his coma."

"I did my last interview with him that morning," I recall with a shudder.

"I know. He dictated the letter to Jen shortly after you left and had her mail it to me that same afternoon. By the time I received it, he was gone."

A WEEK OR SO LATER, a package arrived. It contained a cassette tape and a note from a Stuart Martinson, a name completely unfamiliar to me. "Dear Bernie," it read, "I thought you might enjoy listening to this."

Perplexed, I popped the tape into my Walkman and started to listen. It was a recording of the tension-filled morning I had spent in Alan Schiffman's hotel room in my itchy Burberry suit. Then it all made perfect sense. Any sound man worth his salt—and Stuart Martinson, better known as Silent Stu, certainly was that—would have recorded the conversation at the same time it was being broadcast to Hans and the group of roadies that Mike Testa had assembled in the recreation lounge. I listened to the tape all the way through filled with trepidation: The last thing I wanted to hear was sonic evidence of Alan Schiffman and Henry Ryker being beaten to death. To my great relief, the recording ended shortly before the roadies arrived to take justice into their own hands; presumably Silent Stu turned it off just before he and the others departed the lounge and began heading down the hall.

Later that day, I dubbed a copy and air-mailed it to Hans. A week later, he called to thank me. "Very entertaining," he said. "If your book fails to sell, I think you have a bright future ahead of you as a diplomat."

"No thanks—once was enough," I replied with a laugh. "But there was another reason why I sent the tape to you, other than for your amusement."

"Okay, why?"

"There's something bothering me about the whole Schiffman thing. I can't quite put my finger on it, but I'm sure there's more here than meets the eye. Do you remember the part when Schiffman yelled at his bodyguards for abandoning the security desk and coming in to the room together to help themselves to coffee?"

"Vaguely."

"Well, for one thing, he called them a couple of 'dumb wops.' You'd have thought they would have taken offense at that. They didn't strike me as the kind of guys who take shit from anyone, even someone who's paying them a lot of money."

"Good point," he replied. "But I don't see what that proves."

"It doesn't prove anything. But then there's something else that's bugging me about that exchange. Do you remember what it is that Sal, or Luigi, *does* say to Schiffman after he bitches at them about the coffee? He kind of mumbles it, so it's hard to make out, but it sounds something like 'spring naughty hell.'"

"Tell you what," Hans said. "I'll go have another listen and call you back."

About an hour later, my phone rang.

"Okay, I listened to the tape again," Hans reported, "and I also played it to my brother Petrus, who's more familiar with dialects than I am. The last two syllables of the phrase you're talking about sound to my ears like 'de hel,' which means 'to hell' in Dutch."

"So maybe he's telling Schiffman to go to hell?" I asked. "But why would a mafioso hit man be talking to him in Dutch?"

"Well, that's just it," Hans said. "Here in the Netherlands the way you say 'go to hell' is *ga naar de hel*, and the first part of what he says definitely doesn't sound anything like that. But then Petrus pointed out that someone speaking in the Dutch dialect used in South Africa—the Afrikaans language, I think they call it—would say 'go to hell' as *spring na die hel*. Which I think is exactly what we are hearing."

"So Sal and Luigi were friends of Ryker's, from South Africa?"

"I have no idea. But I can ask VandeVoort to pose that question to his contacts at Interpol."

The plot, as I would say if I were writing a mystery novel, noticeably thickens.

By mid-summer I had the manuscript finished and ready for delivery. Though both Hinch and Cody had left me their contact information, along with a sincere offer to help in any way they could, I decided not to take them up on it. I felt that Donnie had already given me the best, and probably most objective look at their early years, and that I had gotten a good sense of the two grown men from my first-hand encounter with them in Edinburgh and London. Better to leave them their personal space, I thought. It was a gamble that paid off when Katie returned the pre-publication draft I had sent her with a note saying that both Hinch and Cody were happy with it. Hinch was even willing to provide an enthusiastic quote for the front cover, which I knew would boost sales tremendously. It was, I suppose, his way of thanking me for getting the true story out there.

So now here I am in the sweltering August heat waiting in Jack Landis's outer office for an audience with the great man himself. It's a meeting that was not easy to set up, but it was one I insisted upon. Through Sol, the message was conveyed that I was only willing to turn over the manuscript to Jack Landis personally, not one of his flunkies, and it was only the hint of the publicity opportunity afforded by such a ceremony that eventually persuaded him to agree. Armed with the strong sense that I had him over a barrel, I further specified that the press could be admitted only *after* I had a few minutes of quality alone time with Landis. He made it abundantly clear to Sol that he did not appreciate having terms dictated to him, but finally acceded, mumbling ominous threats as he did so.

"Mr. Temkin?" says the fashionably chic executive secretary from behind her ultra-modern designer desk. "Mr. Landis will see you now."

I glance at my watch: The summons has come nearly two full hours after our scheduled meeting time—exactly what I was expecting. After taking a moment to straighten my tie, I pick up my bundled manuscript and march into Jack Landis's cavernous lair on the top floor of the World Trade Center. Every available inch of wall space, I notice, is filled with pictures of the billionaire posing with presidents, kings, prime ministers, and Popes, not to mention assorted captains of industry, professional athletes, movie stars, talk show hosts and other n'er-do-wells.

"Bernie! So nice to meet you at last," the beetle-browed tycoon booms, rising from behind his desk and offering a meaty hand. "You don't mind if I call you Bernie, do you?"

"No, not at all," I reply. "And I'll call you Jack, if that's okay."

The dark cloud that passes momentarily over his face indicates that it's most definitely *not* okay, but he presses on nonetheless.

"I understand you've got something for me," he says, looking pointedly at the bulky package under my arm. "Worth the wait, I presume?"

"I certainly hope so," I reply as I hand it over.

He gently places the five-hundred page manuscript on his desk and studies the title page. "Hinch: It's Only Rock and Roll, by Bernie Temkin" is all it reads, but he examines it intently anyway.

"Hmm," he finally says. "I'm not sure about the subtitle, but I'm sure our editors can punch it up a little. Give it some more more pizzazz, know what I mean?"

I nod at him noncommittally while he begins to turn the pages slowly.

"What is this, some kind of fucking joke?" he growls after a moment or two.

"Joke?" I reply. "Jack, it's no joke." Tempted as I am to slip into Groucho schtick ("That can't be right: isn't it 'Joke, it's no jack?'"), I restrain the impulse.

"Then perhaps you'd like to tell me why all these pages are blank."

I stare at him. Blankly, I hope.

"They're not all blank, Jack. Page 242, for example, has something I think you'll very much enjoy seeing."

He glares at me, torn between a desire to have me eviscerated and curiosity at what lies on page 242. Finally the latter wins out, and he begins ruffling through the manuscript. Taped to the center of page 242 is a cashier's check in the amount of one million dollars, made out to Landis

Publishing. On the back, as per Katie's careful instructions, are the words "Endorsement signifies unconditional release from all contractual terms without legal recourse."

Carefully removing the check, he holds it up to the light as if trying to gauge its opacity.

"Is this real?" he finally demands.

"Absolutely," I tell him, and it is. It's actually quite easy to get a certified check for one million dollars when you have two million dollars in the bank, courtesy of Random House, who signed the rights to the Hinch book ten days previously.

Landis studies the back of the check and my hand-written inscription. "You don't think I'm actually going to accept this, do you? I have a legally binding contract that says I own your book. And if you don't hand over the real manuscript in the next sixty seconds, I will sue your ass, and that of your thieving agent, so fast you will wish you had never been born."

"Actually, Jack," I say with as much nonchalance as I can manage, "our contract automatically terminated ninety days after I failed to meet the delivery deadline. The only thing you can do to me at this point is to sue for the return of my million dollar advance, which I am hereby forthwith delivering." Katie, who had studied the contract and discovered the loophole, would have been proud of that last flourish.

I can see from the look on his face that Landis is now thoroughly pissed. He begins to reach for the button on his desk that I know will summon security, so I decide to play my ace in the hole.

"I wouldn't do that just yet, Mr. Launspach," I tell him.

He pauses, hand poised above the button. "What did you just call me?"

"Come on, Jack. It's your name. Your *real* name. Joop Launspach. President, CEO, and sole stockholder in the corporation known as Diamond In The Rough, Inc."

He glares at me. If looks could kill, I would be dead by now. "Go on," he snarls. "You have exactly one minute to say whatever it is you want to say before I have you arrested. Or worse."

"I know the whole story, Jack. It took me quite a while to unravel, but I think I've got it all figured out. Maybe you'll be kind enough to correct me if I'm mistaken about anything."

He pulls out a cigar and lights it, studying me the whole time. "Forty-five seconds," he warns.

"Okay, I'll talk as fast as I can. Diamond In The Rough, Inc. is a holding company which owns a controlling interest in several other corporations, most of which are engaged in highly questionable activities. One of the few that is actually above-board and vaguely legit is Schiffman Entertainment International. Alan Schiffman, in other words, was your employee. You were his backer, the money man that got him set up in the first place. How else would a second-string booking agent have the dough to establish a fancy Beverly Hills office overnight?"

"You'll never be able to prove that," he says, continuing to stare me down like some deranged wrestler.

"Oh, I think I will ... if it comes to it. A certain former employee of Mr. Schiffman's—someone who was with him at the very start of his career—recalls a whole series of wire transfers to and from a bank in Johannesburg during the course of her time in his employ. Money laundering, I believe they call it." With a smile, I recall the visit Katie and I paid to Janet Jaworsky some weeks previously; now a middle-aged woman leading yoga classes in the upstate New York hippie paradise known as Woodstock, she was quite happy to provide us with tons of incriminating evidence against her hated former employer.

"You fucking cocksucker," he bellows, slamming his desk for emphasis. "Do you have any idea who you're talking to? You have just signed your own death warrant."

"I don't think that's a good idea, Jack," I reply calmly. "You may be powerful and rich, and you may be used to threatening and intimidating people, but killing me will only make things worse for you. You must know that or you would have thrown me out of here ten minutes ago."

Landis sits down, fixing me with a withering look. "Go on," is all he says. It's certainly not surrender, but I can see that he wants to know what I know, and who else I may have shared that information with.

"I'll start from the beginning, if you don't mind. Back in the summer of 1974, shortly after you first emigrated here from South Africa, you were trying to establish yourself as a legitimate businessman. On the surface, you were in the diamond trade, but you also knew that you needed to find ways of hiding the mountains of cash that came from smuggling and other illegal operations, so you were looking to diversify. You were also a bit of a music fan, am I right?"

He gives no answer, no hint of a response, just continues to glare.

"Fine, I'll do the talking for both of us," I say breezily. "That's how you came to be hanging out with a bunch of goofy socialites at a club on

Long Island, which is where you first heard Hinch play. Donnie Boyle remembered you being there, though he had no idea who you were at the time—he simply described you as a rather annoying geek, I'm afraid. But Hinch apparently made quite an impression on you, as both a potential cash cow and a babe in the wood, and I'm guessing that you began hatching your little schemes then and there.

"It must have been frustrating for you to see Hinch appear to slip through your fingers at first. But with the untimely death of Joe Finnerty—and especially after John Thomas Wallingford absconded with the band's first album—you saw your chance, and you grabbed it … courtesy of a sleazy booking agent by the name of Alan Schiffman.

"I'm guessing that you saw in Schiffman the same kind of evil and greed that is in you. He must have been an easy mark: ambitious, grasping, and in need of cash to further his career. Together you conspired to get Hinch, and Hinch alone, in your clutches—much easier to control a single individual, especially one as stupid about money as Hinch was—than a full band. That's when you brought in your old buddy Hank Ryker—a drug-fueled mercenary whose specialty was murder by the needle—to poison the atmosphere and force Hinch's two childhood friends out of the picture. They were the only two people whose advice Hinch might have heeded, so they had to be gotten out of the way.

"Then, through Schiffman, you proceeded to finance the recording of *Keeping It Real*—an album you knew would yield huge profits because of the planned high-profile fatal 'accident' of Hinch's drummer, again at the hands of Ryker and his people. I'll give you credit: it was certainly a master stroke. Tell me, Jack, old buddy, was that your idea, or Schiffman's?"

Tight-lipped, Landis continues his silent barrage. He is, I observe, starting to turn noticeably red in the face.

"Alright, don't tell me. Doesn't matter. The fact remains that you both have blood on your hands. Afterward, life was good for you and Schiffman, for many years. Courtesy of Hinch, the money was rolling in, giving you plenty of opportunity to pursue your other business activities, both legitimate and illegitimate—and to launder the money coming in from those that were of a more dubious nature.

"Then you guys hit a brick wall, at least where Hinch was concerned. Thanks to his dumb decision to associate himself with Nancy Reagan, of all people, he became persona non grata in the music world almost overnight. Suddenly he was an object of derision instead of a rock star—an expatriate whose records weren't selling, and a money drain to you and Schiffman. Eventually you decided that he was worth more to you dead than alive.

"I'm curious, Jack. Was it you or Schiffman who came up with the angle of not just offing Hinch, but doing it in public?" Still no response. "I'm thinking you probably cooked that up at around the time that you first met my literary agent, who unwittingly presented you with the perfect opportunity to maximize the publicity that would result. What could be better than having a major book come out about the very celebrity who'd just died of an overdose in front of thousands of his adoring fans? Plus, as head of the publishing company, you'd stand to profit not only from the increased posthumous sale of Hinch's recordings, but from the book itself. 'Double-dipping,' I believe they call it in the corporate world.

"However, that is where your plan ran a little afoul, and I'm afraid I have to take credit for that. You assumed that the combination of the huge advance you'd given me and the cat-and-mouse game being played in terms of access would serve as sufficient incentive for me to give the book my all, but unfortunately Sol had sold you a bill of goods. He'd somehow convinced you that you'd signed a professional author, but the truth of the matter is that, at that point in my life, I was really just playing at being a writer. I was actually so wrapped up in the phony existence I'd constructed for myself that the opposite happened: I was on the verge of giving up altogether.

"That's why, after Hinch managed to somehow survive the overdose that Ryker had given him in Amsterdam and escape from Schiffman's clutches, you came up with what you must have thought was an even better plan: Croak Hinch at the Millennium Dome in front of the British Prime Minister and half his cabinet—an event that would ensure maximum media exposure the world over. And to make sure I was lured in, you had Schiffman issue a mysterious press release intended not for the actual press—who, after all, barely gave a shit about Hinch any more—but primarily for my eyes. Which is why you planted that cute little receptionist in Schiffman's office: to make sure that I would get a copy and then race to Europe in search of the missing star … where I could serve as eyewitness to the assassination of Tommy Hinchton on a London stage." I smile at the memory of Chloe and at my sudden realization a few months ago that the familiar voice I had heard when calling the offices of Landis Publishing from my hotel room in Amsterdam was in fact hers.

"You know, this is all very interesting," says Landis—the first words he has spoken for quite some time. "You may be a lousy biographer but you could make a name for yourself as an author of fiction."

"Thank you," I reply politely, resisting the temptation to take a bow. "But you may not feel that way when you hear the ending to this particular story, which I fear may not be quite as happy as you might like. Shall I go on?"

With the slightest movement of his head, he nods in the affirmative.

"Okay, well as I figure it, when I accidentally crossed paths with Hans Uhlemeyer in Amsterdam, that presented you with a problem."

"And why would that present me with a problem?" Landis asks, though I am sure he knows the answer.

"Because now you not only had an angry promoter and his dumb but extremely violent assistant hunting down your increasingly paranoid employee, but you also had me tagging along. Schiffman was bitching that you needed to get them off his ass, yet you needed me in London in time to witness Hinch's demise, so I could write about the shocking scene first-hand in my book. I imagine you thought that would make it an instant best-seller."

I glance over at Landis for a reaction, but he's back to stony-faced silence once again.

"That's where Sal and Louie Antucci come in," I continue. "Old friends of yours, I presume?"

"I have no idea what you're talking about."

"Oh, come on, Joop. Sal and Louie Antucci: you remember. Maybe it'll come back to you if I use their real names too: Sebastianne and Ludo de Vos. Does that ring a bell?"

Landis's face is beginning to turn beet red. I'm starting to think he's in real danger of apoplexy, so I decide to wrap things up as quickly as possible.

"It's amazing what kind of information Interpol can turn up when you ask them to," I say. "Did I mention that Interpol has been consulted in this matter? Sorry, but a good writer doesn't reveal all his sources. Anyway, yes, Sebastianne and Ludo de Vos. Sharpshooters in the South African army, trained by the SAS, rabid white supremacists and fierce defenders of the vile way of life known as apartheid. Probably served alongside of Ryker, though I have to admit we have no direct proof of that. But all three of them were past acquaintances of yours, of that there is no doubt.

"They were the ones who took out Rudie Haanraats—Hans's Uhlemeyer's assistant—but the fact that they missed me by inches was no accident, was it, Jack? After all, I was still needed. It was meant to serve as a warning, though, and I have to tell you it worked. Got me so pissed off, in fact, that at that point I was doubly determined to find Hinch, wherever he was. And find him I did, and here we are, Jack, at the conclusion of what I have to tell you has been quite an adventure."

"Are you finished now, Mr. Temkin?" Landis says to me, somewhat wearily. "It's a fascinating tale, but you'll never be able to prove a word of it in court. I have a legal team on retainer that will make your life a living hell from this day forward: I guarantee it."

"Oh, there's no need to prove any of this in court," I assure him. "I have no intention of making any of these charges public. In fact, I don't even plan on writing about most of this in my book. As long as you sign this document, that is." I reach into my bag and remove the four-page Assignment of Rights that Katie had prepared for Landis's signature.

He scans it peremptorily. "Are you mad?" he says. "I'd never sign this in a million years."

"Oh, I think you'll sign it a lot sooner than that," I say nonchalantly. "For one simple reason: Complete documentation of all of the illegal money laundering conducted by Schiffman Entertainment International during the first year of its existence—when I believe quite a lot of Diamond In The Rough, Inc. funds passed between New York and Johannesburg—is already in a sealed envelope in the office of the chairman of the Securities and Exchange Commission. Did I mention that my attorney used to be married to the deputy director, a good friend of the chairman? Well, if she does not receive this document, signed by you, within forty-eight hours, or in the event of something unfortunate happening to her, or to me, at any time in the future, that envelope—or one of the duplicate envelopes we have secreted in various safe deposit boxes around the country—will be opened."

He stares at me open-mouthed, like a guppy in a goldfish bowl.

"Look, I'm not rich enough or dumb enough to think that I can put you behind bars, Mr. Landis," I say. "But if that envelope is opened, I am quite certain that it is *your* life which will be a living hell from now on."

I pause before delivering what I believe will be the knockout blow. "At the very least, your ability to earn a living in this country will be severely curtailed." *Hit him where it hurts the most: in the wallet.*

"But this piece of paper," he reads out loud, "it says that I permanently relinquish all rights to any income from the activities or works of Tommy Hinchton and his associates, in all forms of media."

"I know, Jack. Including the rights to the master tapes of the first album Hinch ever recorded, missing for decades and now, I believe, in your possession, courtesy of a burglary committed and confessed to by two convicted felons languishing in the Dutch prison system."

TWENTY-FOUR HOURS LATER a signed copy of the release agreement appears on Katie's desk and a call is placed to Cody Jeffries in York, Pa.

"Cody?" says Katie. "Exciting news. I hope you're ready to fly to England to start work on those tapes, because we're good to go."

Cody is reluctant, but a week later he is ensconced in the Chipping Norton home studio of John Thomas Wallingford, remixing the digitized transfers of the first Hinch Reload album with the expert assistance of Ian and endless cups of tea provided by a smiling Lilith.

"Go ahead, good buddy," Hinch had told Cody in a telephone conversation five days earlier. "I don't need to be there; there's nobody I trust more than you."

"But it's your album," Cody had protested.

"No, it was *our* album. You just go and do your thing; I'm sure it will end up sounding amazing. I hope it sells a ton of copies, too, because you're going to be getting the bread from it. Katie's already seen to that."

"I don't understand. Why are you doing this?" Cody asked.

From his lonely mansion in St. Moritz, Hinch pondered the question. A warm late-summer breeze wafted in from the open window. Down below he could see activity in the village as the citizens of Celerina went through their daily rituals, scurrying in and out of shops and homes and sidewalk cafes, on their way to wherever it was they were going.

"I'm not exactly sure," he finally said. "Maybe it's just what friends do."

Previously authored by Howard Massey

The Great British Recording Studios (Hal Leonard Books)

Here, There, and Everywhere: My Life Recording the Music of the Beatles (co-authored with Geoff Emerick) (Gotham Books)

When I'm 64: Planning for the Best of Your Life (Tributary Press)

Behind the Glass and *Behind the Glass Volume II* (Backbeat Books)

The MIDI Home Studio (AMSCO Books)

The Complete DX7 and *The Complete DX7II* (AMSCO Books)

A Synthesist's Guide to Acoustic Instruments (AMSCO Books)

Howard Massey's short stories have also appeared in the Hudson Valley Writers Workshop anthologies *Renderings* (CreateSpace) and *Ramblings* (CreateSpace). *Roadie* is his first novel.